ECHO OF EIGHTS

ELIZABETH COLEMAN

VOID BUNNY

ECHO OF EIGHTS
Copyright © 2025 by Elizabeth Coleman
All rights reserved.

Cover artwork by Augusto Silva @_.augustosilva._

ISBN: 979-8-9873902-3-8 (paperback)
ISBN: 979-8-9873902-2-1 (ebook)

Library of Congress Control Number: 2025910145

Published by Void Bunny
San Francisco, California

Printed in the United States of America
First edition

Also by Elizabeth Coleman

City of Sevens

For my twenty-three-year-old self

CHAPTER 1

Arcane magic swirled around Nadia.

She sat at a long wooden table at the back of Myst's subterranean library, her soft movements echoing in the cavernous stone chamber. Open in front of her was a leather-bound book—an old and powerful one, by the magic spiraling out from it—illuminating her face and dark hair with a golden glow. Although she longed to linger on the faded ink and the palimpsest spells woven through its parchment—penned in secret by a Benedictine monk, as it turned out—she had to keep on schedule, or she'd never get through the cataloging backlog. Her boss Rune, the CEO of the Numinal startup Myst, wanted all the uncatalogued mystical artifacts in the database "yesterday." To accomplish this, Nadia had given herself exactly four minutes per artifact. Four minutes to magically float one at random from the small shipping crates and boxes that lined the back wall, photograph and catalog it, and verify the entry's accuracy and completeness. Thank the gods for QuillFill: one of Myst's smartcharms that Nadia had loaded on the grimoire in her Psionic smartwatch. The smartcharm blended AI and genie magic to help her fill out the forms.

Data entry. This is what her life had come to.

But Nadia didn't mind. She liked cleaning up her little corner of the universe. Every marble in the right bucket, inbox zero.

With the QuillFill charm, Nadia reduced the time it took to complete the work to fifteen seconds. That gave her three minutes and forty-five seconds to study, admire, and appreciate each item. And study, admire, and appreciate them she did. New to the Numinal world and her own magical powers as a Septer, Nadia spent most of her free time in the library studying as she tried to get up to speed.

Only a couple of months ago, Nadia was an ordinary twenty-two-year-old, newly graduated from college and trying to make it in the real world. She had no idea that magic was real, that Numinals—the magical people and creatures from folklore and myth—ran the tech industry in San Francisco and Silicon Valley. But then on her twenty-third birthday, she had learned of the magic hidden in plain sight, learned of her own powers as a witch, and her world had cracked open.

Nadia knew she was damn lucky. While others toiled in boring offices or had to do manual labor, she got to work in Myst's library every day. Modeled after the Klementinum in Prague, where the CEO had studied for many years, the space was practically a museum. Rows and rows of leather-bound tomes lined the stacks along one side. Antique airships and flying machines hung from the ceiling beneath Roman frescoes that depicted mythological scenes of Numinals. Spinning globes, sundials, and telescopes stood on pedestals. Nadia liked to think of it as a magical Leonardo da Vinci workshop, her own personal study room and curio cabinet, that she only occasionally had to share with others.

Even though she could have spent hours cataloging, Nadia had other responsibilities at the startup. She evaluated her never-ending to-do list scribbled on a legal pad and mentally tried to prioritize her day. *But the artifacts!* Just yesterday, she had cataloged these totally amazing green earrings that were from a

High Fae queen's personal collection. And before that, a scimitar rumored to be used in the Genie War of 1654! She didn't even know what the Genie War of 1654 was all about, but the more she learned about Numinal history and culture, the more she wanted to know. She devoured knowledge, soaked it up like a light-starved plant finally seeing daylight. One more box. She could do one more box.

Nadia floated a large book-filled crate toward herself. It wobbled and threatened to crash to the ground. She was still working on controlling her magic, and heavy objects that defied gravity tended to rub up against the part of her brain that didn't believe any of it was real. Inside the crate, the books vibrated and pulsed with magic. Nadia picked up a thin leather-bound one sitting on top and turned it over.

"*The Mysteries of the Order of the Sacred Flame: Initiate's Workbook*," she murmured. "I wonder..." The symbol on the front seemed familiar. A triangle with a smaller one inside.

As she leafed through the booklet, she realized it was Rune's. Various exercises and lessons were annotated with his precise, slightly slanted handwriting. She flipped back to the cover. The symbol on the front was the same as he had inked on his wrist—a tattoo that either she hadn't noticed until this week, or that he had kept glamoured before then.

She paged through the book and stopped at a section Rune had clearly read many times, the worn page dog-eared and starred with ink.

SOULWISHES

Upon initiation into the Order, each initiate is granted one Soulwish. A Soulwish is a plea to the Numinous for one's deepest desire. Upon successful casting, the Numinous will grant the initiate's Soulwish. But a word of warning—impure casting of one's Soulwish can result in unforeseen consequences and unfortunate surprises. Therefore, it is recommended that the initiate be absolute—

Nadia's cell phone beeped. She fished it out of her back pocket and checked Slack.

> #veilteam
> Piero 10:03 AM
> Where r u @Nadia??
> Veil meeting NOW.

"Shit," mumbled Nadia. She was missing a team meeting for the startup's launch of their new mobile gaming app. She packed up her laptop and slipped the booklet into her bag to read later.

Piero ambushed Nadia as she stepped out from the elevator to the main coworking floor.

"There you are!" said the waify harlequin, a born schmoozer who was the head of talent and recruitment. Always a snappy dresser, he wore that day a blush-pink suit decorated with enamel pins. "Thank the Light. I did not want to go down to that musty old vault to find you. We're all in the Artemis Room. Carson ate all the pastries—*again!*—so I need to tell the Keebler Elves to send more." He turned on his crystal-studded spats and set off toward the giant tree in the center of the building.

Nadia jogged after him. "I didn't see a meeting on my calendar earlier."

"Maybe it's email gremlins." Piero shrugged. "By the way"—he motioned in a circle with his palm at Nadia's thigh-high black skirt, white blouse, punk necktie, and knee socks—"this is definitely working for me."

Nadia graciously accepted the compliment; she was trying to ditch false modesty. Determined to optimize and hack her life, Nadia had scoured both the charms and spells on her Psionic smartwatch and the library for anything useful. One of the better ones she had found cataloged wardrobe and picked outfits based on work and social calendars. The goth-punk, prep school outfit had been hovering outside her closet that morning when she woke up after she had told it to give her something "a little witchy, but not too much" the night before.

They moved quickly through the bustling main room. At Myst, the main coworking space was a colorful frenzy of productivity, innovation, and magic. Vega, the Fae head of HR, hovered several feet off the ground, her translucent wings fluttering in annoyance. She was overseeing the rollout of a new inter-office delivery system to deal with the recent influx of Amazon packages, testing the potential airpaths the boxes and envelopes could take as they flew overhead. Rows of boxes collided with airborne Numinals as Vega identified pinch points and logistics issues, ducking as a rogue cardboard box came whizzing close to her head.

Nadia waved to a woman who sat on a nearby desk, throwing pink rose petals into the air and watching them disappear as she took a call on a Bluetooth headset. The woman—Nadia could never remember her name for the life of her—was an Anjana, a Cantabrian fairy-like creature, delicate and winged, with rainbow-colored ribbons tied through her braids. The woman waved back and mimed that they should have a coffee date later.

A giant bird's foot nearly came down on their heads.

"Watch it!" Piero yelled as they ducked to the side. Baba Yaga, wearing a house like a barrel, was picking through the open coworking floor on tall stilt-like chicken legs, and had almost stepped on them.

They stopped by the goblin snack tree, a leafy mammoth in the center of the warehouse ringed with tiny goblin structures that acted as their work/live space.

"Grudax!" Piero trilled out as he waved his arm in the air.

The Ewok-looking head of catering and hospitality glared at

him as he jumped up and down with the other goblins on a large pile of dough, flour puffing up into the air.

Piero pursed his lips. "We need another pastry cart in the Artemis Room, thanks."

"Each meeting get one cart," Grudax grumbled.

"We're out of creamer as well," Sophie called out as she strolled up to Piero and Nadia. "I'm getting so sick of them forgetting to restock the human things around here."

"There's like five of you," said Piero. "Chill. I'm sure they're not trying to forget the humans on purpose."

Sophie Lu was one of the few other humans besides Nadia who worked at the Numinal-run startup. She was kind of a train wreck, though Nadia was trying not to beef down on Sophie. She was only a Sixer, after all. No magic powers for her. That morning, Sophie was cosplaying an anime girl in a sailor outfit, complete with knee socks topped with bows and a Dixie Cup hat.

Order in with the goblins, Nadia, Piero, and Sophie made their way over to one of the conference rooms that lined the perimeter. The others were assembled around the boardroom table as they entered. Maya, Nadia's best friend at work, slid a chair over to make room for her, her neon-painted nails drumming on the table in an idle rhythm. An up-and-coming electronic artist with a love of dark beats and glitter eyeliner, Maya was an elf who doubled as both a developer and Myst's resident DJ.

She held out her wrist. "Check it out. Just got it done." A magically enhanced tattoo of a runic symbol shimmered and undulated under her dark skin. "It's a protection charm. It'll repel demons and other bad energy away from me."

"Carson's still here," said Piero, turning to look at the lanky wolf-shifter over his shoulder as he poured himself a cup of something steaming and green. "Must not work on *his* bad energy."

"Har, har." Carson, the head of engineering, leaned back and yawned, his eyes bloodshot and tired. He wore the same flannel he'd had on yesterday, and that could only mean one thing: he'd pulled another all-nighter working on the upcoming Veil launch.

"I have two," said Sophie, holding up her wrists to show them the shimmering symbols. "I figured as a human, I need extra precautions."

Recently, there had been a string of inexplicable deaths around San Francisco. Victims were either found mysteriously dead in back alleys or ripped apart by what appeared to be rabid animals. The Numinal community suspected that demon attacks had caused the deaths, but the human authorities and community had come up with all sorts of theories, now focused primarily on the city's fentanyl problem. Two to three people a day were being found dead from "overdoses," though many of those were actually caused by demons draining humans. The Numinal community had been thrown into a state of panic, trying to deal with the fallout and hide the truth from the human media.

"They need to bring in a whistler," said Piero.

"A what?" asked Nadia.

"A whistler," repeated Piero. "You know, one of those guys who whistles to lure the demons away? Like a Pied Piper . . . sort of."

Rune's deep, silky voice interrupted their chatting. "Now that we're all here, let's get started, shall we?"

As the CEO of Myst, Rune Christiansen was a law unto himself. Tall, intimidating, and powerful, with his dark hair cut in a classic gentleman's style and piercing sapphire-blue eyes, he balanced ruthless efficiency with carefully curated philanthropy, using Myst as a platform to drive social change. Nadia had never quite figured out what kind of Numinal Rune was, but she suspected High Fae, with his chiseled features, strong chin, and dazzling smile. He carried himself with the distinctly regal air of a Fae who was comfortable with his place in the world and knew how to bend it to his will.

"Kami was robbed last night," said Rune as he took a seat at the head of the table. "The thieves took a copy of their source code that had been made for outside counsel." Kami was a Numinal startup out of Japan that implanted *yōkai* spirits into domestic aid robots. Humans thought the robots were advanced AI, and with the explosion of the AI industry in San Francisco, Kami was one of the most promising companies to push the bounds of integrating magic and technology.

"Do you think it's linked to the break-in here?" asked Carson.

"Possibly," said Rune. "The rumor is that the same oni mercenaries were used."

Nadia nearly choked on her coffee. Maya shot her a worried look and thumped her back.

Rune glanced at Nadia quizzically. *Are you okay?* he mind-spoke to her. Nadia and her boss were entangled and could telepathically communicate. She didn't know exactly why or how this had happened, but she figured it had to do with their morning workout and training sessions where Rune had been trying to teach her to control her magic. The best Nadia could come up with was that two people became entangled when they shared some psychic importance to each other.

The coffee was hot, Nadia thought. *Surprised me, that's all.* She would not—could not—tell Rune that she had been the one responsible for letting the oni mercenaries gain access to Myst.

Rune narrowed his eyes at her. *I missed you at the gym this morning.*

Slept in, sorry, Nadia lied. The truth was, she was trying to take a step back and unblur the lines of her relationship with her boss. Things had become a little too tangled for her liking.

Rune turned back to the group. "You know the drill. Don't let people you don't recognize follow you after swiping in, clean up your workstations so no confidential information is left out on the floor, and for the love of Light, don't post Myst business on social media."

Piero looked up from his cell phone. "Everyone is talking about the Kami break-in. It's all over Threads, X, and Woven."

Nadia nudged Maya and leaned over. "Woven?"

"Numinal social media and dating site," Maya whispered. "I'll make you a profile."

Nadia smiled and nodded, mouthing, "Thanks."

"Interestingly enough," said Rune, "Pact has not been hit. Yet."

Carson scowled, his fangs out. "You think they're behind it?"

"It wouldn't surprise me," said Rune. "We all know they 'borrow' others' ideas. That takes me to the next situation." He aimed a clicker at a projection screen. "You might have seen the news today." Results for a Google alert compiled headlines from various news sources. Splashed all over websites like Wired and TechCrunch were articles and pictures about Myst's biggest competitor, Pact, and the new features in their Lovecraftian mobile app game The Call. This normally wouldn't have been a big deal, except for one little problem: the new features in The Call were augmented reality, just like in Veil. The interface was nearly identical. And they were planning on releasing it on Halloween. The same day Myst was launching Veil.

The team glanced at each other. It was well known that Rune despised Pact and its tech, finding its ideas weak and derivative. But it made a killing in the Numinal startup world—managing to rival Myst in some ways—much to Rune's constant annoyance.

Carson clenched and unclenched his fists, breathing heavily as he fought the urge to shift.

Maya put a steadying hand on his arm. "Rune, what can we do?" she asked. "Should we push back the launch?"

Piero nodded. "We can't both launch on Halloween. We'll look like we're copying them."

"But we've already announced that we're launching on Halloween," Sophie countered. She was in charge of Myst's social media. "We've released screenshots of the game. People will know they copied us."

Carson growled, "People are stupid."

Rune took off his glasses and wearily rubbed the bridge of his nose.

Nadia's heart ached for him. Rune cared deeply about Myst and the success of each of his company's divisions. Veil wasn't just a game. It was a creative endeavor that took years to build. It was a work of art, on par with titles from AAA game makers. And it carried out Myst's mission of employing Numinals in meaningful work, both as developers and as the talent used in the live role-playing component of the game. Reviews of the game by Numinals even said they felt closer to the Numinous while playing.

Pact's game, on the other hand, did not exhibit the level of care and creativity that Myst put into its work. It stole ideas from others and executed them in a sloppy, albeit flashy, manner. But like many things in life, the copycat was more successful than the original. Once again, Pact would benefit from Myst's hard work.

"Piero's right," said Rune. "We need to push back the launch date. But it will give us time to get it perfect. No more glitches, no more bugs. I want everyone focused on this."

Sophie pouted. "Stupid Mercury retrograde."

"You can't blame everything on that!" Piero rolled his eyes. "If you want to blame something, blame Pact. You know they have their eyes on us."

Carson sat back, looking at the Pact headlines. "They're going to be at Numinox . . . And I bet they will make some big, splashy announcement."

Nadia leaned over to Maya. "Numinox?"

"Big Numinal rave," she whispered. "I'll tell you about it later."

Nadia nodded, grateful that Maya was so patient with her ignorance of Numinal culture.

Rune's eyes gleamed. "You thinking what I'm thinking?" he asked Carson.

Carson grinned. "Blow 'em out of the water."

Piero held up a hand. "Um, hello? Can someone please translate out of Bromance and into plain English?"

"We're going to hold an ideathon," said Rune and Carson at the same time. "Jinx!" they both shouted. Two frosty mugs of beer popped into existence in their hands.

"What on earth?" said Nadia. "So, if I jinx with someone, we each get a beer?"

Maya nodded. "Vega is testing out some new HR benefits software. Part of the system upgrades. Killer, huh?"

"Next item on the agenda," called out Rune, "is the battery issue. Carson?" He took a sip of his beer.

"Almost done," said Carson. "I've isolated the mechanism and created a temporary patch so that the player's energy isn't drained too fast. I have the whole thing ready to push, but I need to model the permanent one on something self-sustaining. I'll work out the details."

"Good," said Rune. He glanced over at the meeting's note-taker, a large quill pen and spelled piece of parchment hovering in the corner. "Redact that last part. If Pact is somehow getting our information, I don't want any trade secrets in meeting notes."

The pen nodded.

Piero hid behind his hand, whispering loudly to Nadia, "What's up with the Society for Creative Anachronism pen? What, we couldn't splurge for a typewriter?" He laughed at his own joke.

"Like, why did someone not spell a computer to capture notes?" Nadia asked. "I don't get it."

"It's not funny if I have to explain it," Piero huffed.

Sophie examined the quill. "It's kind of retro," she said. "I dig it."

"All right," said Rune as he stood up. "That's all for today. Go forth and conquer."

As Nadia packed up to go home for the evening, the Godspeaker blasted an announcement throughout the building. The receptionist and greeter, Anya, spoke in her lilting nymph voice over the speakers. "Calling all Mystics! All Mystics, please listen! Please report to the common area for a special announcement."

Mystics rose from their habitats and drifted over, forming a loose collective in the center of foosball tables and bean bag chairs. Nadia spied her friends and headed their way.

"What's going on?" Nadia asked as she joined them.

Carson gazed up to the ceiling and whistled loudly.

Sophie jumped in front of him, pigtails flying. "Tell me now!"

She gave him a playful punch to the stomach. "Is this about the ideathon? Please tell me we are all going to Numinox!"

"You're going to find out in, like, half a minute." Carson deftly sidestepped her attack. He grinned and pretended to launch a counterattack.

Sophie squealed. Nadia glanced at Maya to gauge her reaction to their flirting, but Maya was absorbed with something on her phone.

Rune strode over. "All right, everyone. As you are aware, we have our annual employee retreat in the spring. After recent events, I've decided to move it up to coincide with Numinox."

The crowd broke out in shouts and cheers, fists pumping into the air. A centaur next to Nadia reared up, front hooves kicking, while a troupe of purple-and-pink pixies flew about excitedly in circles. Only Grudax seemed unimpressed, grumbling to himself from his tree.

Rune shushed everyone before continuing, "Myst will be hosting an event on Sunday to have the public test Veil and to crowdsource ideas for a new module via an ideathon. Mystics and non-employees are both allowed to participate. The goal is to come up with the best idea to expand on the current game offerings, and we will take the winning pitch and incorporate it. I know this is last minute, but I hope everyone can make it. We will be staying at the Temenos Retreat Center, so no need to bring your own camping gear. Transportation will leave on Friday from Myst, eight a.m. sharp."

"Yes!" Piero shot his fist in the air. "I knew it!" He rushed up to Rune. "I have ideas about our booth. We're going to have a booth, right?"

Nadia and Maya headed back to their habitats. "What's up with this Numinox thing?" Nadia asked.

"It's, like, the biggest Numinal party in the world," Maya

replied. "Like Burning Man, but on steroids. Dancing, camping, rituals, music . . . I'm DJing a couple of sets. I'll have to bring my music gear, but at least now I don't have to camp." They reached Nadia's desk. Maya jutted her chin at Nadia's laptop. "May I?"

"Go for it," said Nadia.

Maya hunched over her desk, her ring-heavy fingers clicking quickly over the keyboard, and pulled up YouScry, the search engine for Numinals. She typed in Numinox and hit enter.

The search results were flooded with beautiful images: a sparkling blue lake set among the redwoods, steam rising from natural mineral pools under a starry night sky, huge art installations with giant domes and LED lights in front of grape-and-tangerine sunsets, and Numinals in their full glory—ears, tails, and neon magic on naked display—busting loose on packed dance floors as DJs played on stages with strobing light shows behind them.

"Whoa," said Nadia.

"I know. It's going to be mental."

"And we're staying at some retreat center?"

Maya nodded. "Temenos. It's this gorgeous Numinal glamping spot on a lake and hot springs near Tahoe, right next to where they hold Numinox. It's a little pocket reality, away from the rest of the area. I'm sure Rune had to pull some strings to get us last-minute rooms this weekend."

Nadia leaned back on her desk. "But we still are having an employee retreat, right? Like, team-building exercises?" She pictured something lame, like trust games where people had to catch each other before falling.

Maya shrugged. "Last year it was a cooking thing with this Indian deity. We made some pretty good curry." Maya glanced over to Carson, who sat across the room at his habitat, headphones on, typing furiously as he stared at his screens.

"What was that?" Nadia wagged her eyes provocatively. "Something happen with the curry?"

"Shut up." Maya had a sly smile on her lips. "Nothing happened. Nothing real, anyway."

"But seriously—" Nadia tipped her head in Carson's direction. "You think you and . . ."

Maya shrugged. "I don't know, maybe. I'm not going to overthink it."

Must be nice, thought Nadia. All she did was overthink things.

Chapter 2

That evening when she got home from work, Nadia pushed open the red front door to her grandmother's aged Victorian with a cheery, "I'm home!"

"We're in here!" her grandmother called out from the living room.

Nadia's grandmother, Marina, sat on the floor, a mess of herbs spread out in front of her, packing boxes and shipping material scattered over the coffee table. Marina's dark hair, generously sprinkled with gray, was tied up in a floral bandana, and she wore a bright-orange tracksuit. Next to her, their Fae roommate, Avery, matching floral bandana around his dirty-blond man-bun, sat cross-legged, putting stickers on vials. He was shirtless in gray sweatpants, and his translucent wings were folded demurely down his lean back. Their black cat, Monday, was perched on top of an old grandfather clock, flicking her tail back and forth.

Nadia flopped down on the velvet couch. "How's business?"

The bohemian-styled room with its patterned throw pillows, candles, and eclectic art was normally cluttered, but it had become almost uninhabitable as central command for Marina's newest endeavor: The Tambourine Lady's Shoppe, which made small-batch herbal remedies and tonics for the Sixer and Septer community of psychics, witches, and other humans with extrasensory perception and powers. The living room was littered with little vials and bottles, logo stickers, and various herbs and oils. The shop's motto was "Put a little jingle in your jangle," which Marina would shout each time she made a sale, pumping her fist into the air and clanging her silvery bangles together in some sort of compounding abundance and success spell she had concocted. Each sale led to at least one more, often two or three.

"It's been nuts," said Marina with a dramatic sigh. "I can't keep supply up with demand. We decided to go to Numinox this weekend, and I'm trying to get everything ready before the festival." She eyed Nadia, a cunning expression on her face. "You wouldn't be able to come with us to Numinox to woman the booth, would you?"

"Yes, please do," said Avery without looking up.

Nadia narrowed her eyes at him. He probably just wanted another person to cover the booth so he and her grandmother could go party together.

Avery and Marina were best buddies. Two peas in a pod. The Harold to her Maude, without the sex. Or at least Nadia hoped so. She tried not to think about her grandmother's sex life, although that was exactly the sort of thing about which Marina would undoubtedly overshare, not being a big fan of boundaries and social norms.

"Myst is holding its annual retreat at Numinox," said Nadia. "Sorry, I'd love to help, but I think we will be doing a lot of team-building exercises and goal planning."

"Oh, fine," said Marina. "Abandon me in my hour of need. But I know how you can make it up to me. Come harvest with us tonight."

Avery shot her a worried look, and Marina waved him off. Marina and Avery were entangled like she and Rune and often shared wordless conversations.

"I'll show you how to harvest ingredients under moondogs," Marina pressed. "Every witch needs to know about moondogs."

Nadia groaned inwardly, but her interest was piqued. Her grandmother knew exactly what carrot to dangle to get her way. Nadia would do anything to up her game, even if it cut into her sleep.

"Sure, I'll help out."

"Great!" said Marina. "We'll go after dinner."

Dark clouds obscured the waxing moon as Avery pulled Marina's teal Eldorado over in a squeal of tires and smoke and parked on the side of the road next to the cemetery. Nadia shivered as she stepped out of the car, wrapping Marina's heavy, spell-laden cloak that she had borrowed around herself and bracing herself against the icy gusts of wind. The drop in temperature had not been in the weather forecast.

Nadia scanned the scene. Beyond a brass fence covered with ivy, mausoleums and gravestones cast spectral shadows. A few cypress trees peppered the area, their flattened tops rustling as they swayed back and forth. Something moaned, but when Nadia turned to the sound, the wind swallowed it up.

"I'll look near those mausoleums," said Marina as they hopped the fence. "Nadia, you take that hill over there, and Avery—" Marina cut off with a curt nod from him.

"What am I looking for?" asked Nadia, ignoring their mind-speak.

"Wolfsbane," said Marina. "Big stalks with purple flowers. You can't miss 'em."

Nadia cast a night-vision-enhancing charm from her Psionic. The spell lit up the night with an eerie green glow, and she headed over to the hill with her basket and got to work, walking back and forth in a tight pattern as she scanned the plot of earth looking for the flowers. Her footsteps crunched dry twigs and leaves on the grass, the twigs reaching up like dead fingers.

On the next hill over, Marina was dancing as she searched, a ghostly sight with her robe flaring out as she spun in circles. Avery stood watch, perched on top of a small stone mausoleum like a gargoyle in a hoodie, his lit cigarette glowing orange against the inky night. Nadia glanced up at the stars, with the sudden feeling that someone—or something—was watching.

She shivered but got back to work. The quicker she found the wolfsbane and learned about moondogs, the quicker she could get home and try to get a decent night's sleep. She wanted to be fresh and on her A-game for work tomorrow.

Off to the side, Marina and Avery motioned to each other in another wordless conversation. They both glanced around furtively. When Marina thought no one was watching, she disappeared behind the mausoleum on which Avery sat. A few minutes later, she emerged without her basket and resumed her search around the cemetery for the wolfsbane as if nothing unusual had happened.

They were definitely up to no good, but Nadia barely had time to think about it before Marina dropped to her knees with a cry. Nadia rushed over, sure that her grandmother had twisted her ankle stepping in a gopher hole, but instead found her clearing the earth around a clump of wolfsbane. The stalks of the plant jutted up about three feet from the ground, bearing deep-purple hooded flowers. Nadia pulled out a harvesting knife from her basket and dropped to her knees.

"Wait!" Marina cried out. "The conditions aren't quite right." Nadia rocked back on her heels as she sheathed the knife. Her grandmother dug around in Nadia's basket, pulled out thermoses, and poured them whiskey-laced coffee. Avery unfurled his wings and gently glided down through the chilly night air to join them.

"What happened to your basket?" Nadia asked.

Marina took a big sip of her drink and settled into a comfortable sitting position. "Don't ask questions you don't want the answers to."

Nadia let it drop. She had learned it was best not to ask too many questions when it came to her grandmother.

Marina glanced up at the clouded moon. "Any moment now." She had explained to Nadia that they could only harvest the herb under moondogs, optical illusions of faint orbs of light on either side of the moon caused by ice crystals in the clouds. Wolfsbane harvested under moondogs during a waxing moon in a cemetery was supposed to be the best for making potent elixirs. Magic was very particular like that.

So, they waited. Nadia yawned. Scratched an itch. Traced the sigils on her cloak with a finger. Inspected the robe she was wearing, noting the stash of Dandelion Chocolate hidden in a secret pocket in the lining. Tried not to wonder what Rune was doing. Finally, the clouds cleared. Above them, the moon shone bright. And then the moondogs appeared, faint on either side, circled by a halo of light.

"Wunderbar!" Marina happily got to work, snipping and bottling. Nadia tried to feign her grandmother's enthusiasm, but really, she just wasn't that much into herbs. In theory, she was, because she was going all-in on being a witch. But in practice, she found herbs kind of boring and tedious. It wasn't her kind of magic. It took too long. Some herbal concoctions took days or weeks to prepare properly. Nadia preferred the instantaneousness of magic based on visualization and energy. But Marina loved them.

"Why are you so into herbs?" asked Nadia as she clipped stems and pulled petals.

Marina tilted her head to the side, pondering the question. She held up a purple wolfsbane flower to the moon. "This little flower looks so beautiful but is highly toxic. It can be incredibly deadly if not prepared properly. People used to use it on the tip of spears when hunting and even as a method of execution during Roman times."

"Shouldn't we be wearing gloves or something?" asked Nadia as she pulled petals off the stem and stuffed them into a glass vial. She glanced at Avery, who shrugged.

"Well, don't eat it." Marina laughed. "It would kill you in seconds. I just think there is something wonderful about how potent these plants are. The mature plants are the deadliest. People underestimate them because they look innocuous, starting to wither. They have no idea what they are capable of and how much harm they can inflict. I like herbal magic because there's such a fine line between medicine and poison." Her eyes sparkled in the moonlight. "Makes you feel alive, playing with that fire."

Nadia was pretty sure that Marina was telling her she was adept at poisoning people, and she wasn't sure exactly how she felt about that if it were true.

They continued quietly snipping and bottling, an occasional glass clink interrupting the faint rustle of plant material being torn and fabric brushing against the ground as they moved to a new patch of wolfsbane. A wolf howled in the distance.

Avery sniffed the air from the shadows. "The shifters are out tonight," he murmured.

Carson probably was out and about as well. He tried to keep his wolf-shifter tendencies under wraps and didn't talk much about what he did in his free time, apart from gaming and working. Maya had mentioned before that she was one of the only people from work who had seen Carson in his wolf form.

"With Samhain coming up in a few weeks," said Marina, "Numinals are starting their preparations."

"Samhain is the Celtic New Year," said Avery in a bored voice. "In case your limited human understanding of the universe is unable to comprehend one of our great sabbats."

"I know what Samhain is," huffed Nadia. Avery was always trying to one-up her, jealous of her growing relationship with Marina. He used to be the only one she doted on, and now he had to share.

"It is the best time to cast any sort of difficult magic," Marina added. "Traditionally, the veil is the thinnest then. If you have anything big you want to do, Samhain is a good day to do it." Nadia knew this was because there was more wild magic in the air. It was riskier to cast on the sabbats. The magic was unpredictable, but the payoffs could be great.

"Are you going to do anything special?" Nadia asked Avery. "I mean, to celebrate or whatever. Do you have family plans?"

An invisible wall went up, and Avery sat back. "Why are you asking?"

Marina glanced at him and then forced a laugh to lighten the mood. "Oh! I'm sure we will do the usual. Carve gourds, leave offerings, make soul cakes. It's fun to get all into it, especially with the Halloween celebrations around."

Nadia narrowed her eyes at Avery. He was hiding something.

"I'm trying to get Avery to dress up like Thor so I can go as Loki," added Marina.

Avery snorted like that would happen over his dead body.

"I haven't even thought about Halloween, with everything that's been going on," said Nadia. She had been so preoccupied with work and trying to manage her powers that she barely knew what time of year it was, let alone be able to plan for a holiday or festivity.

"You should dress up," said Marina.

"Yeah, maybe I will," said Nadia. "Hey, we could all go as Loki variants."

Marina grinned. "Now we're talking."

Chapter 3

A little after midnight, they returned home.

Marina stowed the bottled wolfsbane in her kitchen pantry and kissed Nadia on the cheek. "Good night, hon. Thanks for helping tonight."

"It was fun." Nadia eyed Avery, who was poking around in the fridge. "G'night." She ran up the stairs to beat him to the bathroom they shared.

Nadia quickly got ready for bed by brushing her teeth, washing her face, and tying up her hair. She slathered some of Marina's herbal night cream under her eyes and picked at her pores.

When Nadia unlocked and opened the bathroom door, Avery was leaning on the hallway wall, arms crossed.

"All done." Nadia brushed past him. Avery grunted loudly and slammed the door behind him.

In her bedroom, she changed into PJs, turned off the light, and snuggled under her duvet, her white-noise maker playing soothing sounds of waves breaking on the shore.

As she lay there, she tried to quiet her mind and practice meditating. It helped her magic to have a clear mind. But thoughts of work and what she had to do the next day infiltrated her mental defenses—there was some new mandatory HR training about recognizing demons hitchhiking past the wards that was due tomorrow—and she let them roam for a while until she tired.

Nadia was drifting off when something startled her awake. Her eyes darted around her bedroom, searching for the source of the sound.

There it was again: *tink*. A pebble or other small object hit her windowpane.

She scrambled to the window and peered through the curtains. Her demon handler, Thomas Drake, paced outside the boundaries of the translucent wards that surrounded the house. Hunched in a black trench coat, he held a small slingshot.

"Oh, hell no," muttered Nadia, annoyed he had figured out a way to lob objects through the wards. Ever since he had tricked her into stealing from Myst—using those oni mercenaries as a distraction while he tried to break into Rune's computer— Thomas had officially been at the top of Nadia's shit list, and she had been avoiding him.

Nadia grabbed her cell phone. She had several missed calls and texts from him, unnoticed while her phone was on silent.

Nadia dear, we need to talk.

Please answer my calls.

Hello???

ANSWER THE PHONE DAMMIT.

This isn't funny, Mercurio will have both our heads if you don't respond. I promise I'm not lying. Pinkie swear.

The last one got her attention. She knew she had to keep her vampire overlord happy if she was to survive her servitude to him.

Nadia shrugged on a hoodie over her pajamas and slipped on her bunny slippers. Minimizing the squeak of the bedroom door with a quick silencing charm, she snuck down the wooden staircase to the ground floor and slipped out the front door.

Thomas had worked himself into a frenzy. Sweat trickled

down his long sideburns, his eyes wild. "Thank God. You need to come with me. Now."

"Now? It's the middle of the night!"

"Mercurio requested you. He heard that you leveled up your powers, and now he finds you more interesting."

Nadia crossed her arms. "And he learned I leveled up my powers how?"

Thomas looked up to the sky and huffed loudly. "Fine. I told him. Be mad at me later. Right now, his wishes need to be appeased. A Blood Muse Septer is rare. He wants a taste."

"I will *never* let him feed from me again," she snapped. Mercurio had attacked her and bit her neck the last time she had seen him. She was still dealing with the PTSD, and she wasn't too keen on a repeat experience.

"Never say never, my dear. That's a valuable card to hold up your sleeve. No, he has an extraction apparatus. Very scientific and sterile. It will just feel like a little pinch."

A pinch? What the hell did that mean?

Nadia started back toward the house. "I'm not going."

"Don't make me invoke the vow," Thomas warned.

Nadia paled. She had unknowingly made a vow that if she disobeyed Mercurio, he could seize her firstborn. Even if she hemmed and hawed to Thomas, she always ended up saying yes to whatever Mercurio wanted. She hadn't wanted to test the boundaries of what disobeying meant.

"Can I at least go change?" Nadia gestured to her pajama pants and bunny slippers.

"No time. The show starts soon." Thomas grabbed her arm, and with a small *pop!*, teleported her across the Bay to Mercurio's Ambrosia distillery in Alameda, a steel-sided warehouse on the water.

Thomas practically dragged Nadia into the building. She

tried to shrug him off—she wasn't keen on just rolling over dead—but he held on to her upper arm and frog-marched her over to where Mercurio was holding court. Alexander Mercurio was a rich and powerful Numinal crime lord and business mogul who ran San Francisco's seedy, magical underbelly. And he just happened to be Nadia's overlord and master, the vampire who owned the Blood Oath that bound the women in her family to him in exchange for their powers as witches.

It was something that Nadia was learning to deal with. Part of her held out hope for some unpredictable solution, a *deus ex machina* to save her, but the other part of her was trying to be realistic about her chances of success. Marina currently served him, but once she died, the Oath would pass to her, and Mercurio would have the ability to compel her to do anything that he so desired. Nadia was trying to figure out a solution, but with her limited understanding of magic and Numinals, she didn't even know where to start.

Mercurio commanded from his baroque throne chair, legs draped over the arms like an insolent king. He wore a deep-purple velvet coat with tails, his dark hair slicked back. His face was beautiful and cold, with high cheekbones and a look of boredom reserved for the disgustingly rich forced to mingle with their inferiors.

The other guests clustered around the parlor at little tables, a bar with a line of seating tucked in the corner of the room. Most were Dark Numinals, some wraiths, demons, and sirens. Several had cloaking spells shrouding them so that their identities were concealed.

Thomas deposited Nadia in front of Mercurio. She fell to her knees, scowling, but bowed to Mercurio, her forehead touching the floor in supplication.

"I've brought the witch, as you asked, my lord," said Thomas.

Nadia peeked up to see if she should rise to her feet yet.

Mercurio flicked his wrist, shooing Thomas away. "You may go." Her demon handler slunk away into the shadows.

Nadia got to her feet and faced the vampire. She squared her shoulders, ignoring his frown at her bunny slippers.

"You requested to see me?" she asked with what she hoped was a chipper tone.

"I am about to start the show, and my main attraction has gone missing," he said, his voice smooth. He gestured to a ring of patrons hanging out around a bar. "These are some very important people, Council people, and I promised them"—he flicked his wrist, and a poof of glitter and magic flew into the air—"a *spectacle*."

"I-I'm not sure I understand," Nadia stammered.

Mercurio directed her gaze to a giant structure off to the side. Nadia wasn't sure exactly what she was looking at, maybe some sort of carnival ride. Eight clear boxes with chairs inside circled an elevated platform like the eight spokes of a wheel. A mess of wiring and tubes was attached to each box, jutting up and out to giant vats.

"Now you are aware that if you disobey me, you break your vow of allegiance and your firstborn is mine," Mercurio said. "But for the taste to be pure, I need you to be willing to offer your . . . essence. So, I will remove the vow if you agree to participate in tonight's dinner theater."

Nadia's eyes darted around the room. The contraption was an Ambrosia still, the elixir a delicacy among Dark Numinals. Instead of directly draining energy from humans—a no-no in the more cultivated Numinal circles—Mercurio captured and bottled the energy to sell. His nightclub was a favorite harvesting ground; he skimmed human energy straight out of the air. Human emotions had distinct flavors to Numinals, and

Mercurio often bragged he was a master chef when it came to mixing the perfect balance of essences for the discerning palate. While Nadia didn't agree with demons taking *any* energy from humans, she did like the idea that this was a sort of harm reduction mechanism. Humans didn't have to die or be fed from directly, and Mercurio still got his energy to make Ambrosia. It was a win-win.

Dark Numinals licked their lips, eyeing her. The machine didn't look too scary. She was pretty sure she could handle it. And this was a way out of that vow she had unknowingly made back when she was a n00b and didn't know how to navigate the Numinal world. She could finally undo that mess—and all it would take was a little bit of her energy.

"I agree to your terms," said Nadia. The pact snapped into place, and the vow dissolved. She considered bolting, but she didn't want to risk pissing the crime lord off. He was notorious for unscrupulous methods of doing business, a mafia kingpin who reigned supreme in the wild west of San Francisco. The best way forward was to do this quickly, escape, and hopefully stay off his radar.

"Thank you for your compliance. It makes everything so much easier. Now, if you will." Mercurio gestured to a technician in a white lab coat and face mask who stood to the side.

The technician led Nadia over to one of the plexiglass boxes and sat her down inside. The room itself was about the size of an elevator, with screens in front of her.

"What are these—" Nadia started.

The technician cut her off with a startled look. "Shh! We're not supposed to talk." He pulled leather straps around and buckled Nadia into the chair, the straps crossing her chest and stomach, pinning her arms to the armrests. He then took a bunch of sensors and hooked her up to them, placing little nodes on her temples and chest. She felt like a lab rat in some sick, fucked-up test. She gazed at the other plexiglass boxes. The other humans were being similarly strapped in by their technicians.

"Please tell me what's going to happen," Nadia whispered. "I-I need to be ready. How does the still work?" If she knew how it worked, she would know her part in it and how to mentally prepare.

The technician glanced around furtively and leaned in. "You're lucky," he whispered. "You got admiration. Each person is going to be primed to feel a certain emotion: terror, amazement, grief, loathing, rage, vigilance, ecstasy, and admiration. Lord Mercurio always lets the guest of honor have admiration. Apparently, it makes you taste good." The man shuddered.

The screens in front of Nadia blinked on, and a series of images and videos started cycling: athletes overcoming adversity, musicians performing at the peak of their careers, Gandhi.

"I will be up there"—the technician jerked his head up behind them—"monitoring your emotional output and brain waves on the console."

Nadia sneaked a glimpse behind her at what looked like a DJ's soundboard, with little knobs and dials.

"The emotional energy that you expel will go through here." He pointed to the neighboring experiment boxes where tubes ran from the top of each box up to the warehouse ceiling in a jumble of wiring and copper. "The energy flows into those vats and then is distilled with Resonance Stones to filter impurities. Then each flavor is ready for tasting." He nodded to the Dark Numinals who sat along the perimeter holding hookah hoses attached to the wall like a tap. "Good luck," he whispered. "Hopefully, everyone makes it."

Suddenly, a sharp pinprick pierced her aura at the top of her head. "Ouch!" Nadia cried, trying to pull her arms up from the straps. "What the f—" She cut off as the other glass canisters activated one by one, psychic lightning crackling.

Nadia took a deep breath. Images cycled in front of her on the screen, but her mind was elsewhere. She couldn't help worrying over what the man had said. As a Blood Muse—a Septer who was historically kept as a pet and feeding source by a dark master—Nadia could pull energy from the environment and wouldn't die from the harvesting. But the other humans . . . she worried she was about to witness a mass execution. Mercurio was going to press each human like grapes for winemaking, squeezing the energy out of them. The vampire often boasted about his skills in harvesting energy from humans, extracting just as much as he could without killing them, taking them to the edge, but accidents could happen. The tech could malfunction. Someone could have a preexisting condition.

A blonde siren dressed in a skimpy latex bikini sauntered across the floor carrying a tray with a glowing red bottle and a small cordial glass. She stopped in front of Mercurio and curtsied. He took the small glass from the siren and drank a little, rolling it around his mouth and smacking his lips. "Needs more grief." He motioned to the technician monitoring that octant. The woman fiddled with some dials, and a sharp, painful wail erupted from the human. The Dark Numinals tittered and made clicking noises of approval.

The sounds of moaning and sexual pleasure filled the air. Ecstasy was to Nadia's right. She recognized a well-known kink queen, an Amazonian woman who went by the name Athena. Her little glass box was filled with writhing, sweat-slicked limbs and pornographic images. To Nadia's left was terror. He screamed, eyes clamped open à la *A Clockwork Orange* to torture videos. Loathing was the octant directly across from her, and the man in there was wailing and self-flagellating with a barbed wire whip. The other humans in the room were similarly exhibiting strong reactions to the images on their screens, much to the delight of the mythical onlookers. Nadia tried to find the silver lining, glad she didn't have to watch torture scenes or porn in public.

To her great annoyance, amid the panic threatening to choke her, Nadia started having admirable thoughts about how impressive Mercurio and the whole setup were. So innovative. Bleeding-edge. Her gaze lingered on the sharp lines of her dark master's gothy, villainous face as he watched her, rubbing the tip of his fang with his tongue in a decidedly sexual manner. Nadia's thoughts became clouded and dark and sensual as she sat mesmerized by her vampire overlord's glittering gaze.

A slow, wicked smile crept up Mercurio's face, and he looked away, breaking the spell. Nadia jolted back and tried to clear the lingering wisps of the vampire from her mind, afraid he had somehow imprinted on her.

Mercurio jumped to his feet and clapped his hands. Showtime.

A lone drumbeat sounded out from a live band tucked in a corner. The musicians all played Medieval-looking instruments—sitars and duduks and castanets and tabor drums. A haunting, reedy melody filled the room as Mercurio climbed to the podium in the center of the wheel like a maestro. The lights dimmed, and Nadia was bathed in emerald green. The other humans were each backlit with a specific rainbow color that Nadia assumed corresponded to their assigned emotion—red, orange, yellow, and so on. The technicians stood above each of the test subjects, looking like DJs at color-block soundboards.

The music intensified, turning into a dark Saracen song. Snapping his fingers to the beat, Mercurio started to dance, lifting his knees up and making little kicks and hops, performing some sort of ridiculous folk dance. He spun around in a circle, his arms outstretched, his coattails fanned out behind him. And then he started waving his hands toward specific emotions, like a conductor orchestrating a symphony. At each hand wave, the scientist in charge of each emotion turned the dials, releasing the pressure valve to the tubes and channeling some of the built-up energy from the transparent boxes. As each one was released, the corresponding color backlight and tubes lit up, and a different note played. Blue, then purple, then green . . . it was like the *Fantasmic!* light show at Disney World, a multicolored spectacle of lights and sound, a remix of the dark beats from the live band. Mercurio was really getting into it, dancing about, sweating up a storm, flinging his arms in all directions. Nadia stifled a nervous giggle. Last time she laughed at him, he had bitten her.

The finale was nearing, the music coming to a crescendo. Mercurio flipped a hand and took a deep, theatrical bow in her direction, handing the stage over to her: the main attraction. All eyes locked on her octant. The Dark Numinals sitting at the perimeter bar licked their lips, fangs extended in anticipation of what she alone would taste like. Nadia vibrated in fear. Her energy rose up from the soles of her feet, through her knees, thighs, womb, and abdomen, up through her stomach and chest, through her heart, throat, and face to the top of her head. It was a strange feeling, slightly tingly and unnatural. She was highly aware of her body, of the blood coursing through it.

Nadia took deep breaths and tried to still her rabbit-fast heartbeat. The Myst Psionic smartwatch beeped at her wrist as her mood swung from admiration to fear to panic. Above her, the technician struggled to keep her energy locked in admiration and failed. Mercurio shouted something, but she barely heard it. Her survival instincts kicked in, and she sucked all her

Blood Muse energy back into herself, reversing the flow. The energy disappeared in a vacuum.

Shock waves exploded from her like she had detonated a bomb. It must have been mere seconds, but it felt like an eternity, the energy rolling out from her ragdoll body, sound slowing. She flew backward and hit the plexiglass hard, glass shattering in a rain of crystal. Nadia fell to the ground in a mangled heap. When she opened her eyes, it was to destruction and chaos: humans and Numinals shouting and crying out as they emerged from broken glass, overturned tables, and melted equipment. Mercurio glowered at her as he stood up from behind his toppled throne chair.

And then, in the blink of an eye, he was in front of her. He seized her throat and pulled her up by the neck. Nadia grabbed onto his arms, her legs kicking at empty air, her breath shallow gasps as he brought her face-to-face with him, the stench of blood and Ambrosia rolling off his tongue.

You test my patience, witch, he mindspoke to her. He squeezed her throat, cutting off all air, and Nadia's vision went black at the edges.

The pupils of his eyes flared; her pain was exciting him. A lecherous hand wrapped around her midriff, and he caressed and dragged his claws against her skin.

"Master!" Thomas called out as he appeared at their side.

Mercurio's head snapped to him. "What?" he snarled, a black forked tongue snaking out.

"She is worth more alive than dead," said Thomas, supplicating himself. "Think of the possibilities. A virgin Blood Muse. It's a delicacy. So extremely rare. You can't put a price on that. People would pay anything to have a taste."

Mercurio's gaze swiveled back to her face. Nadia struggled to breathe.

"Well, well, well, Drake does make a good point." His lips curled into an evil smile. "Be prepared. When the Oath passes to you, you will be mine. My own personal Blood Muse. Oh, what fun we are going to have. What a *treat*." He gave her one last squeeze, as if he might snap her neck, and threw her to the ground. "Get her out of my sight."

Nadia stood behind Marina's house, shaking uncontrollably, unable to stop. The night was still, porch lights in the neighborhood all dark. A dog barked in the distance.

Thomas paced back and forth. "This is not good," he muttered to himself. "Not good at all. I told him you hadn't mastered your Blood Muse powers yet, but he insisted . . ." He seemed to remember she was there and turned to her with concern on his face. "Are you hurt?" His eyes raked over the blood and the grime covering her.

Nadia crumpled to the ground, tears streaming down her face. "What am I going to do?" The question echoed around her mind as she stared off into the distance, not really seeing anything. "I need to break the Blood Oath. Get away from all this. As soon as it passes to me, he's going to keep me locked away in some cage and just . . . *feed* from me all day." She covered her face with her dirt-streaked hands, incredulous that this was her life. "I can't. I just . . . can't. I wish this wasn't happening."

"Wishes won't get you very far, I'm afraid," said Thomas, looking down at her. "But a contrite apology may. Lord Mercurio does like groveling . . ."

Nadia scrambled to her feet and grabbed his hand. "You must know of a way. You must know how to break the Blood Oath. Please. I'm begging you."

Thomas took both of her hands in his and kissed her bone-white knuckles, a look of pity on his face. "If I knew, I would tell you. I'm so sorry, my dear."

In her bedroom, Nadia got back in bed and turned off the light. She stared at the darkness, duvet cover pulled up to her chin. Her mind churned as she tried to find a solution. How would she break the Blood Oath? How could she keep her powers in the process? How could she escape her fate as Mercurio's personal juice box?

Recently, Nadia had learned that "anything is possible" from Rune's lessons. He had helped her rewire her brain and bypass limiting beliefs. She had been able to open Rune's grimoire loaded on her Psionic. She held up the smartwatch on her wrist and scrolled through spell lists. There had to be something on there to help her. One was called "Order of the Sacred Flame." She clicked through, but there wasn't anything that seemed like it would help her situation. It was mostly protective spells, a few energy transference spells. Something called Flame of Prometheus.

But Nadia was no quitter. She sat up and turned on the light with a snap of her fingers. Grabbing her work bag, she hauled it to her lap and began digging through it. From its depths came the Order of the Sacred Flame chapbook that she had found earlier in the library. She paged through it, looking for something. She wasn't sure what. "Anything is possible," she murmured to herself as she scanned the pages. There would be a solution in there. She focused on that thought until she found the section on Soulwishes.

"'Upon initiation into the Order,'" Nadia read out loud, "'each initiate is granted one Soulwish. A Soulwish is a plea to the Numinous for one's deepest desire. Upon successful casting, the Numinous will grant the initiate's Soulwish.'"

That was it! She would cast a Soulwish to remove the Blood

Oath from herself, Marina, and any future daughters down the line. And to keep her powers in the process. She didn't want a repeat experience of what her mother had gone through, losing a piece of herself when she gave her powers back to Mercurio. It had destroyed her, made her a hollow, empty shell of the person she was supposed to be, and had destroyed Nadia's childhood.

Nadia was tired. She was tired of being a commodity. Her body, her blood, her energy . . . Mercurio just wanted to taste it. Bottle it up. She wasn't a person to him. She was a slave. A witch. His own personal Blood Muse. As a vampire, he thought of her as nothing more than something he could consume. Something he could use.

She was tired of being used.

Nadia paced back and forth in her tiny bedroom, thinking. All she had to do was become an initiate in the Order. And certainly, Rune would help her, wouldn't he? Despite all the potential awkwardness and boundary-blurring, Rune was a good guy and would keep it professional like she would. And Samhain was just a few weeks away. The time when the veil was the thinnest and magic went farther with the Numinous. She should cast the Soulwish then. It would help overcome any obstacles standing in her way and give her the best chance of success. But how on earth would she become an initiate in such a short amount of time? It could take months, or even years! She had no idea, really, of the scope of what she was thinking about.

She imagined Rune's voice echoing around her. *Anything is possible.*

Chapter 4

Nadia slammed the Order's chapbook down on Rune's desk in front of him. "I want to be your apprentice."

They were in his office on the second-floor perimeter of the headquarters. Rune had been working on something or another when Nadia had barged in unannounced. He put his papers to the side upon seeing Nadia's frazzled appearance, the result of staying up half the night scouring YouScry for any information on the Order. He pushed a button under his desk, and the glass walls of the office went opaque with a privacy screen.

Rune sat back in his leather chair and stared at the booklet. His dark sapphire eyes flicked up to meet hers. "You found my old workbook."

Nadia pulled a chair out and took a seat, paging to a section. "It says here that a master is required to take on an apprentice, and I know you haven't done so yet."

Rune glanced at the tattoo on his inner wrist, a triangle engulfed in a flame: the symbol of the Order, as Nadia now knew. It was incomplete, with only one side of the triangle inked on, a smaller triangle inside the larger unfinished one. A fractal image within itself. In her research on the Order, she had discovered that an apprentice receives the smaller triangle tattoo upon initiation, and one side of the larger triangle when they become a master. The second and third sides of the larger triangle are later inked when the master takes an apprentice, and when that apprentice becomes a master themselves—completing the triad and their duty to perpetuate the Order. Assumably, for whatever reason, Rune had previously glamoured the tattoo to be invisible.

"I see you've done your homework," he said.

"I'll work hard. Like you've never seen me work before."

Rune sat back in his chair and stared at her. She couldn't read the expression on his face. He tilted his head to the side, one elbow up on the armrest, and idly rubbed his bottom lip with his knuckle, lost in thought.

Nadia gave him a small smile. "Okay, say something. Anything."

He gave a small chuckle and sat up. "I thought you hated our trainings."

"No, not at all," she said quickly. "I am grateful for everything you've done for me. And the quickest way for me to master my powers is going to be by learning. From you."

Rune shook his head. "This isn't a good idea. If you choose to apprentice yourself to a master in the Order, there are . . . consequences. It can be very . . . *intimate* and personal. It is not something to be taken lightly. We are already entangled. Our magic would be bonded. Mine would shape yours. We would get to know each other on a whole new level. I know you've been concerned with us crossing professional boundaries, and with what almost happened last week. This would be an entirely . . . different kind of relationship."

Nadia knew he was talking about how they had almost kissed.

In her mind's eye, she saw that moment. The shocked expression on Rune's face after she cast a major battle spell. How they had leaned in toward each other, their lips close. She had closed her eyes in anticipation, the electricity between them sizzling, his breath on hers. And then . . . nothing. Her eyes had fluttered open to see the regret and shock and anger on his face. He had backed away from her, horrified, an invisible wall up between them. She was certain that he thought her schoolgirl crush on him had gotten out of hand, and he deeply regretted ever hiring her.

Nadia needed to seize the narrative. "Let's just clear the air here. In the heat of the moment last week, I might have gotten a little carried away and crossed a line. I don't want to give you the wrong impression of me and my professionalism. I ... admire you and your work here at Myst, and in my eagerness to learn, I might have come across as too familiar or crossed a healthy workplace boundary."

The corner of Rune's lip curled up slightly. "I don't have that impression of you at all, but I appreciate your candor and willingness to get ahead of a ... delicate situation."

They lapsed into silence. Rune picked up the Order's chapbook and paged through it. Nadia glanced about the room. She had always liked Rune's office. The decor reflected his minimalist tastes, Scandinavian furniture mixed in with his own personal effects: pictures of him on a yacht with Obama, the Clooneys, and Lady Gaga, signed baseballs, and ancient weapons on display racks on the walls. She noticed he had a new computer: a brand-new MacBook Pro sat on the desk. She had fried his last one to prevent Thomas from breaking into it during the attack. Nadia stilled her leg. She had been kicking it back and forth impatiently.

Rune closed the chapbook and put it down. "Why do you want to be an initiate in the Order?"

She had prepared this answer. "I want to be stronger. I need to be stronger. I don't want to be a target or a victim, and right now, I feel like both."

Rune's expression softened. Nadia knew he was thinking

about how she had been attacked by demons in her short time in San Francisco. Rune's guilt for failing to protect her was displayed all over his face.

"You said it yourself," Nadia pressed, "there are nightmares out there. Demons. Dark Numinals who prey on humans. I need to learn to protect myself. I know I'm weak and powerless right now. But I don't want to be. I want to be hard and strong and be able to take care of myself. Surely, you understand that."

He stared at her. She stared at him. Finally, he shook his head slightly, resigned. "All right. I will take you on if you pass the initiation tests. There are three of them."

Relief flooded Nadia's body.

He tossed the chapbook over to her. "Give me a few days to think about where and how to conduct the first one."

"So . . . I have a bit of a time crunch with this. Do you think we can do all three tests before Samhain?"

"No." Rune stared at her.

"Really?" Nadia scrunched up her nose. "I was really hoping that was possible. No chance, huh?"

"Why do you need to become an initiate before Samhain?"

Nadia decided to be truthful. "I read that upon initiation, you get a Soulwish. I want to cast a Soulwish on Samhain."

Rune sat back and regarded her thoughtfully. Finally, he said, "I won't ask what it is you desire, as that is a personal matter. But I don't think it's possible to pass all three tests in such a short amount of time. Samhain is a mere six weeks away. It can take people months, years even, to master their skills enough to even attempt the tests. And you lack basic, foundational magical training."

"You've been working on getting me up to speed," Nadia countered.

"Yes, but even I have limits."

"I have full faith in your abilities. You were the one who told me that 'Anything is possible.'"

Rune took off his glasses and cleaned them with a cloth. The seconds ticked by. "All right," he said at last. "We'll do the first test at Numinox. But after the ideathon. That takes priority, and I need to focus."

A smile broke out over Nadia's face.

"Make sure you practice all the drills and exercises in the first section," he continued. "It will be critical that you know those inside and out to be able to pass the first test. I don't have time to help you train until after Numinox, so you're on your own for the first test."

"Understood." Nadia got to her feet. "You won't regret this." She turned to leave.

She couldn't be sure, but Nadia thought Rune murmured, "I hope not."

After Nadia had left, Rune sat back in his office chair, staring out the window at the Bay. Along the industrial metal warehouse of the headquarters was an old pier, dinghies and weathered floats bobbing in the choppy water. Fishing boats struggled against the wind, water frothing and splashing around their hulls. Seagulls surfed on air currents, cawing and looking for crabs and other little marine life that could be their next meal. Rune was fully aware of both the seen and unseen forces at play, his life a link in a cosmic chain that he couldn't even begin to comprehend. Over the years, he had learned to listen to the subtle clues from the universe urging him to action. He figured it was his higher self, an ideal he sought to become. This higher self had told him to plant his old workbook in a box of books in the vault for Nadia to find. He knew she would connect it to the Order's tattoo on his wrist—he had left unglamoured, just so she would see it. He knew she was to be his apprentice; he just didn't think it would happen so fast.

Nadia's proclamation that they had crossed a healthy workplace boundary didn't surprise him. They had been toeing the line for far too long: flirting, training in the mornings, and the almost-kiss. Now that she wanted to be his apprentice, he could put himself squarely in the position of being her master. There would be no confusion about where they stood, even if the relationship was a personal and intimate one. He was good friends with his master and always would be. And now he could be good friends with her too. Rune tried to tell himself this was fated, that he was fulfilling some cosmic role. He was duty-bound to take on an apprentice at some point in time, and Nadia was meant to be that—and only that—to him.

Last week, Rune had retreated into the wilderness. He did that often, losing himself in the sights and sounds and smells of dark canyons and dense forests, places of his childhood where he had learned of the old gods. Sacred places of magic where he felt closer to the Numinous. But instead of going where he thought he would, places of redemption and renewal, he had found himself—with almost an unrelenting urge that defied logic and reason—seeking his sifu, his master from the Order of the Sacred Flame.

In Nepal, Rune stared up at the base of a familiar mountain, its snow-capped ridges sharp against the sky. He free-climbed the vertical cliff face, bits of rock tumbling thousands of feet down as he went. Himalayan tahrs, the wild mountain goats of the region, watched him from their perches on crags as he climbed, shirtless, the sun harsh on his tanned skin, the patches of icy snow on the rocky outcrops magnifying the glare. Muscles straining, he finally reached the top of the cliff and pulled himself over the edge.

His master was meditating in a shrine, legs crossed in a lotus pose, as he hovered above a colorful mat. Brass prayer wheels turned slowly beneath fluttering prayer flags.

The monk opened his eyes as Rune approached and smiled. "Rune. My dear friend. You always must do things the hard way." He gestured toward the stone staircase that wound around the backside of the mountain.

Rune took a seat beside the floating monk. "Sifu, I seek your counsel and wisdom." The monk dipped his head in acknowledgment. Rune continued, "There is a woman."

The monk gave a knowing smile and gently lowered himself to the ground. "Matters of the heart are never to be taken lightly."

"She knows my Soul Signature," said Rune, referring to a being's unique karmic fingerprint.

"I know your Soul Signature," the monk countered.

"But you are my master."

"Ah, yes." The monk looked pleased with himself. "Tell me about this woman. Is she fierce and loyal? Does she fight for what's good and pure on this earth? Does she believe in using the Numinous and the powers it bestows to raise up the collective vibration of humanity and Numinals together as one?"

Rune narrowed his eyes. "She embodies everything the Order stands for."

The monk smiled. "You already know the answer you seek. You are meant to take her on as an apprentice."

"How would she know my Soul Signature already if I haven't taken her on yet?"

The monk manifested a lapsi fruit and threw it at Rune. The yellow plum bounced off his forehead. "Time works differently with the Numinous." The monk tsked. "You know this. There is no cause and effect. There just is. This woman already knows your soul, as I do, through the training you will undergo with her. Your magic, your soul, already thrums on the same frequency."

Rune couldn't tell if he was relieved or not. "Could she be both . . . apprentice and soulmate?"

There was a sparkle in the monk's eye. "Do I detect regret? Are you hoping for more than what the Numinous is giving?"

"Of course not," said Rune quickly.

The monk chuckled.

They sat in silence. Fluffy white clouds passed below them. A hawk soared by. The prayer wheels turned.

"I made a Soulwish for a soulmate," Rune finally confessed. "Long ago. So long, I had given up hope. I never told you."

"You didn't need to," replied the monk. He regarded Rune thoughtfully. "She could be both. Only time will tell."

"How will I know?" asked Rune. He held his breath, waiting for the answer.

"A soulmate makes a Soulwish for you too."

Rune sat, looking out at the vistas, the echo of those eight words sounding in his mind as he tried to clear it and meditate.

Nadia sat at her computer, trying to study the Order's chapbook. She had her AirPods in, an attempt to shield herself from the noises of the workplace, but her attention kept drifting to everything around her. A troupe of Yumboes—West African Numinals with a short stature and long silvery hair—was leading a dance class and drumming circle in the lounge area. At one of the coworking tables, a shaman was teaching a bunch of newbie consultants how to make power talismans. And it was "take-your-house-spirit-to-work-day," adding to the general chaos of the place, with brownies, kobolds, and Lares holding Segway races around the perimeter of the room. It was nearly impossible to focus when so much was going on.

Nadia pulled her AirPods out, turned around, and yelled, "Can you please keep it down? I'm trying to work!"

Snickers and laughter erupted from the floor. A few Mystics gave her pitying looks, but she was largely ignored.

Maya, a few habitats over in the loose cluster they called Andromeda—the habitats were loosely grouped and named like galaxies in the night sky—swiveled around in her chair and pulled down her headphones. "Hey, Winters. Why don't you use the new focus rooms?" she called out.

"What are focus rooms?" Nadia called back across the way.

Maya gestured to the back. "There's a door near the elevators marked with a picture of Bodhidharma!"

"Who?" Nadia yelled.

"Buddhist deity of focus and determination! You can't miss it!"

Nadia gave her a thumbs-up and then gathered up her things and headed toward the back. Sure enough, an easily overlooked door had a picture of an ancient Chinese man sitting under a tree, a red cloak covering his head and body. She swiped her employee badge to enter.

Glass-walled circular pod rooms lined both sides of a hallway. A few were occupied, their opaque privacy shrouds lowered, blurring the occupants inside. Nadia took one of the unoccupied pods, shivering as she entered. It was as cold as an icebox. Her breath came in little puffs. A winter Numinal must have used the room last and turned down the heat. The pod was maybe ten feet across, mostly empty, save for a first aid kit and magical supply cabinets scattered around in corners. In the center of the pod was a futuristic-looking recliner covered in soft fur. Nadia sat down in it, settling comfortably into the reclined position and locking her computer into the console. She hit the "On" button, a glowing purple triangle with Myst's symbol.

The room went dark, and the pod walls turned into computer screens so that Nadia had a 360-degree workstation extending from her laptop. The temperature in the room rose as it adjusted to her body, the air turning crisp and refreshing to keep her alert. The chair could rotate around, and Nadia spent longer than she should have figuring out how the joystick worked before she discovered that she could change the settings with magic and intention. With a quick incantation, she could rotate the chair and move the computer screens around with her mind. She linked her phone to the console so music could play through the pod's speakers.

Nadia pulled out the chapbook and got to work. The drills for the first test were familiar. She had practiced similar ones with Rune before. They were rudimentary: manipulating objects to move them, drawing energy from various power sources like light sockets or cell phones, calibrating the body to work with certain conditions and environments. Electronic funk music came on, and she chair-danced as she did the drills until she decided that she was having way too much fun. She put on classical music instead to help her focus. After a while, Nadia's stomach growled. She pinged Grudax with a lunch order for a salad and a sparkling water, and he sent a goblin to deliver it, the foot-tall creature stumbling under the weight of the bag in his arms as he carried it over to her.

"Thanks." Nadia relieved the creature of the bag.

"No problem, Ms. Nadia," the goblin replied.

Nadia cringed. She had no idea what the goblin's name was. She promised herself she would try to learn more about her co-workers.

Nadia ate lunch as she continued to page through the chapbook, reading Rune's annotations and notes that clarified the lessons. She stopped again on the page about Soulwishes.

But a word of warning—impure casting of one's Soulwish can result in unforeseen consequences and unfortunate surprises. Therefore, it is recommended that the initiate be absolutely certain in their desire.

Nadia closed her eyes and visualized what it would be like to cast a Soulwish. The feeling of being absolutely, dead certain about wanting to break the Blood Oath. That was what she wanted, wasn't it? The end goal of the arduous journey that she had undertaken. The memory of Mercurio's mesmerizing gaze filled her mind. She wanted to free herself of him, didn't she? She didn't want to be his Blood Muse slave. She thought about his sharp fangs sliding slowly into her neck and gasped slightly, clenching her thighs together. *Oh gods!* The thought was turning her on.

With a start, Nadia snatched her hands away from her pants. She had almost touched herself, thinking of Mercurio. She whipped her head about, but no one else was there to witness her shame, thank the gods.

Her cell phone dinged, and Nadia almost had a heart attack. She fumbled for it, nearly dropping it, and pulled up the text. It was Marina.

Will you be home for dinner? Lasagna tonight.

Nadia shot off a text back: Sorry, working late. Sounds delicious though.

More for us then :-P

With a sigh, Nadia put down her cell phone and got back to the drills.

Chapter 5

On Friday, Nadia stepped off the Muni bus in front of Myst, a weekend bag slung over her shoulder. A crowd of Mystics milled around in front of the headquarters. Nadia crossed through the shimmering wards protecting the building and made her way over to where Carson and Maya were sitting on a concrete bench.

Maya wore stunner shades and was listening to music playing from a Bluetooth speaker clipped to her bag. Her tank top had an image of a flying saucer and the words "Get in loser, we're doing butt stuff" printed across it. "I hope you packed your swimsuit," she said. "Weather is going to be excellent." She passed Nadia a flask.

Nadia took a sip. Whiskey. She scanned the other Mystics. Everyone wore sequins and tie-dye like they were off to a day-rave, their glamours lowered to reveal horns and wings and tails.

Carson stood up and stretched. As he did so, the bottom of his T-shirt rode up, revealing a ripped stomach with a happy trail reaching up to his navel. Maya snuck a glance. She saw Nadia watching and winked, grinning. They were for sure going to hook up.

"Move aside, move aside," Piero's distinctive voice trilled out. He and Sophie came barreling through the crowd, bumping people out of their way. With oversized sunglasses, floppy hats, and bright-white vacation wear, they could have been on their way to Mallorca. Piero snapped his fingers, and a gnome intern in a blue cap ran up with their bags and placed them at his side.

"Thank you, Felix," said Piero crisply. "You may go."

Felix nodded and backed away.

"I can't believe we have to ride with gen pop." Sophie turned up her nose in disgust at the crowd.

"We can hear you, you know," Maya called out.

Rune strode over, carrying a black duffel bag. He wore a vintage patterned button-down with a black kilt, the shirt open to reveal his broad, hard chest and defined abs. Light shone on his aviator sunglasses and metal wrist cuffs. Piero pulled his sunglasses low down his nose and peered at Rune. "Well, well, well, what have we here?" He nudged Sophie and murmured something inaudible to her. She giggled, and he shushed her, laughing himself.

Nadia glanced down at her dress, glad Marina had intercepted her in the kitchen when she had been planning to wear all black with purple lipstick, insisting she go back upstairs and change. Her grandmother had suggested something more "fun and flouncy" with a "bohemian earth-witch look" for Numinox. Nadia had taken that advice and programmed it into the outfit-picking smartcharm. She had on a long, strappy green-and-brown tribal-patterned dress that showed a good amount of thigh when she walked, wedge sandals, gold dangly earrings, and wooden bangles. *Do you think he notices?* She immediately squashed that thought. Pull it together, Winters, she told herself.

Carson and Rune clasped hands and slapped each other on their backs.

"Hey man, you ready for this?" Rune grinned.

"Born ready," said Carson. "We are going to come up with

something so amazing, it will blow Pact and their lame-ass game out of the water. I was up all last night finishing the sequences we're going to demo." He scanned the area. "Where's Kevin? I need him to do a quick once-over on the ride up." Kevin was a game tester and the only non-Sixer human that Myst employed. Rumor was that he only got the job because his father was a well-known politician who had pulled some strings. It was easier for Myst to hire him and wipe his mind each night than call attention to itself by refusing to employ him. HR assured Nadia that there were no long-term ill effects, though she wasn't sure she believed that.

"Kevin's driving up separately with the booth and equipment," said Piero, sidling over.

Carson growled.

"What?" asked Piero. "I didn't see you volunteering, and the Light knows I have better things to do than man a booth all weekend."

As Piero and Carson squabbled about the booth and Kevin's job priorities, Rune went off to talk to others. Nadia glanced at her Psionic, noting it was just past eight a.m. And then a speck in the sky appeared. A hush fell over them as several people pointed up. Nadia shielded her eyes from the sun and tried to make out what it was.

Rows of glowing train cars trailed one after the other like a diamond tennis bracelet. Nadia, at first, thought it was Starlink, SpaceX's satellite system that orbited Earth. But as it came closer, circling above them before the front descended, it revealed itself to be a series of linked cargo containers. The silver boxes slowly rotated, shining in the sunlight.

"You have got to be kidding me. What is this thing?" asked Nadia. This was definitely rubbing up against her ideas of "normal."

"Isn't it cool?" Maya grabbed her duffel, and they queued up with the other Mystics. "Rune usually makes us take human buses to the retreat—"

"Boring!" Piero interjected.

"But this year, we get to take the Wild Hunt Express. One benefit, I guess, to all the demon attacks around."

Nadia frowned. "I didn't realize that was happening outside the city."

Maya nodded. "There are even more demons and Dark Numinals in the forests, out in the wild. The Beacon radio—it's a Numinal and Septer-focused pirate radio station," she added when she saw Nadia's confused expression, "is reporting that there've been ambushes on the highways, whole hordes of demons working together and attacking cars stuck in traffic jams going in and out of Tahoe. Humans are saying it's wild animals. Rabid wolves and bears. Rune doesn't want to take chances."

Nadia had seen a news headline that mentioned animal attacks in another part of California, but hadn't paid much attention to it, preoccupied with her own situation and life. She made a mental note to start checking headlines. "Wow, I had no idea."

Piero leaned in conspiratorially. "I don't think Rune's worried about demon attacks. That dumb bus we took last year had enough defensive shellacking to withstand an army. I personally think that after Pact's announcement, Rune's trying to show off Myst to the people at Numinox. Show what a great place it is to work, the amazing perks, blah blah. Peacocking, if you ask me. But don't tell him I said that."

The linked containers came to a stop, the one in front of them hovering about ten feet off the ground. A door slid open, and a Valkyrie poked her head out. "All aboard!" Her eagle-like wings spread out as she jumped from the pod, pulling a staircase out and down with her as she glided to the ground.

Mystics lined up and entered. As each pod filled, it rose

back up again, and the next took its place, so that the linked chain spiraled into the sky like a double helix. Nadia tried to peer through the crowd into the pods. Each was ornately decorated with organic patterns and fractal elements from nature. Seashell spirals, coral motifs, and tidepools in one. Smoothed rocks, a waterfall and pool, and giant tropical leaves in another. Piero and Sophie pulled the Valkyrie aside to ask which pod had the most amenities and opted for one where a Numinal with octopus tentacles was giving massages.

Finally, Maya and Nadia were at the front. Wisps of clouds billowed out of the pod's entrance, obscuring the decor inside.

"Ready for this?" Maya glanced back, grinning at Nadia as they climbed up the staircase.

Nadia's eyes went wide as they stepped inside.

The pod's walls were entirely glass, giving Nadia the impression that she was walking on air. The glass ceiling was peppered with real clouds, dry lighting zinging between them, a low rumble of thunder echoing around. A pixie flew over, barely able to carry a glass in her arms, and handed a drink to Nadia, explaining it was called a Karl. The beverage was milky white with fog rolling off the top. She took a sip. It tasted sweet and slightly salty, like a hot cocoa spiked with caramel liquor and dashed with salt. Nadia and Maya sank into a puffy white bean-bag chair. The chair activated, and magic fingers started massaging their backs.

"Can you be in love with a chair?" Maya wiggled down into the cushion. "Because I am definitely in love with this one."

Nadia closed her eyes, enjoying the sensations. Bits of relaxation magic seeped into her skin.

And then they were off. The ride was surprisingly smooth as they soared east over treetops and mountains toward the Lake Tahoe region. Glamoured to be invisible, they alternated between low altitudes, barely skimming the tops of eighteen-wheelers on the freeway, over fields and orchards, between valleys and along streams, and then to the sky, high up alongside formations of geese, passenger airplanes, and hot air balloons in Napa.

"I could get used to this," said Maya as she plucked another fruit kebab from a passing tray.

"Are Myst's employee retreats always this . . ."

"Luxurious? Nope. But I'm going to enjoy it while it lasts." Maya signaled to the waiter for another cloud cocktail.

Nadia peered through the glass. Something outside shimmered: two cables of gold magic, twining around each other like binary stars, two trains on a rotating track. "What's that?" she asked Maya, pointing to the two cables.

Maya sat up and glanced out of the window. "Oh, that's the Helix. They're like Muni tracks . . . sort of. They power the Express. Out here, the air isn't saturated with magic like it is in San Francisco. Harder to cast. Not as much power to draw from. You need to run lines from power sources."

"I think Carson was talking about a potential partnership with Tesla?"

"We're consulting on a system overhaul. It's super outdated. Rune was thinking we could use the existing network of electric car chargers to power magic, instead of having to put in our own or fix this dinosaur. But with all the political stuff . . ." She shrugged. "Who knows what's going to happen now."

Too soon, they started their descent. Numinox came into view: a cluster of tents and stages nestled in a redwood forest clearing beside a glassy lake. They made a leisurely flyby of the festival, making a giant figure eight so they could scope the scene. Fireworks erupted from the pods and sprinkled magic over the festival in a fine mist. Piero was right, Nadia thought.

They were showing off. From the ground, festivalgoers pointed up as they soaked up the magic.

After the flyby, the Express came to a stop next to a big wooden sign indicating they were at Temenos Retreat Center. The doors to the pod opened. Nadia stepped off onto the dirt and stretched, looking around. They were in a clearing next to the blue lake. Across the water were the tents of Numinox, the low thump of the bass echoing through the woods.

A young woman with long black hair and tiny antlers joined them from the reception area. She walked up in a plain muslin dress, her deer hooves barefoot.

"Welcome, Myst!" said the woman. "I'm Winona, the Preserve's warden."

While Winona outlined the ground rules for the weekend, Vega passed out cabin assignments and a schedule of activities. She flitted through the group, her translucent wings vibrating behind her. She handed Nadia her packet.

"Where are you?" asked Maya. She glanced at Nadia's packet. "Sweet! We're sharing a yurt."

Dozens of geometric yurts stood in a neat formation next to the lake, their muslin-covered domes draped with twinkle lights that hadn't yet turned on in the daylight. Inside Maya and Nadia's yurt, it was sparse but cozy: two cots, a low table, and a scatter of pillows around a modest tea service. They quickly set up and changed into their bathing suits while sipping on cups of rejuvenating ginger tea.

"What's first on the itinerary?" asked Maya.

Nadia glanced down at the paper. "Looks like we have free time until dinner, then a group dinner and team-building exercises, and then an optional movie night." After her week of cramming for the initiation test and trying not to think of Mercurio, the festival was a welcome distraction.

Maya put on her stunner shades. "All right, let's do this thing."

Set next to the sparkling blue lake, the festival was laid out like a fractal blossom, the symbol for the Numinous. In the center was the main stage, surrounded by vendors, food trucks, and art installations. Radiating out from the center were various pathways that extended out toward smaller pockets, each with its own stage. All in all, Nadia estimated there were about twenty thousand attendees. Maya explained that Numinals, Sixers, and Septers from around the world came to celebrate.

"Oh, look!" Maya pointed to a tent where a ritual food and drink service was being performed. "We for sure need to do that. They have this special magic water from Iceland. It's, like, the best B-12 shot you'll ever have."

They headed down rows of vendors selling wares. Trinkets and magical objects such as lamps, knives, and amulets shimmered to entice. Feather and leather clothing magically beckoned, the sleeves of the garments charmed to come to life and wave them over. Whirligigs and puffs of glitter-magic bombs went off, trying to catch their eye. The music thumped. Shopping itself was a party, the beat urging people to dance and buy.

The jangle of a tambourine caught Nadia's attention.

"There's my grandmother!" exclaimed Nadia. She and Maya headed over to the booth where Marina and Avery had set up shop.

They had three long tables set up in a triangle beneath a bohemian shade tent, where Marina and Avery lounged in lawn chairs with cocktails. A large banner bearing the name *The Tambourine Lady's Shoppe* hung across the front. Marina's bottles and pots of cordials, salves, and elixirs were artfully arranged on the tabletops. Old vinyl records played in the back, pumping music out to the area, and Nadia recognized Marina's raspy voice from when she had sung in a traveling band during the Summer of Love.

"These are neat." Maya bent over to get a closer look at a jewelry display case.

"I didn't know you made jewelry too," said Nadia as she inspected a box full of hammered metal wrist cuffs.

"I don't," said Marina. "Avery made those." There was pride in her voice. A Numinal wanted to buy some cordials, and she stood to go ring up the purchase.

Nadia begrudgingly nodded at the craftsmanship. They really were beautiful works of art. "We'll take two of these cuffs," she said to Avery. "Do you offer a friends and family discount?"

Avery sighed. "Fine."

Maya picked up a piece of paper from a stack of flyers next to a tray of bangles. "What's this?" It looked like a crisis hotline flyer for Numinals. "You're involved with the NLA?"

Marina glanced over. "They're a good organization. They really help the Numinal communities. I like to give back."

Maya frowned but said nothing, replacing the flyer back on top of the stack. Nadia glanced at her questioningly, but she merely smiled tightly and indicated that she would tell her later. Nadia gave Avery her credit card, and he swiped it on Square. They waved goodbye and continued on their way.

Down the row, a booth showcased chain mail jewelry. "What's the NLA?" asked Nadia as they stopped to examine the display.

"The Numinal Liberation Army," explained Maya, "is a group of radical anarchists who promote Numinal rights. I used to be involved with them a few years back."

"Not anymore?" Nadia picked up a delicate gold choker and held it up to the light. The salesperson gestured that he would help Nadia try it on, and she turned around so the Numinal could clasp it around her neck.

Maya inspected a tray of jewelry made for elf ears. "They got a little extreme for my tastes. Blowing up test sites, kidnapping people. I used to be down with the eco-protesting, but when you start carrying around grenades and AKs, no thanks."

"What do you think my grandmother is doing with them?" Nadia hoped Marina wasn't doing anything that involved AKs, though she wouldn't put it past her.

Maya shrugged. "Probably just raising awareness. I'm sure it's harmless enough."

"Nadia!" shouted a voice. She scanned the area for the source and spied Miles Kirkpatrick across the row next to a fire spinner, waving an ice cream cone in the air. He looked ridiculous, wearing a large sombrero, sunglasses, and khaki shorts like he was on spring break in Tijuana.

Nadia stifled the urge to laugh. "Hey!"

He strolled over, grinning. "Lovely to see you again." He nodded briefly at Maya. "Hello."

Maya side-eyed Nadia and crossed her arms. Mystics notoriously disliked Pact's CEO in solidarity with Rune.

Miles was oblivious to her hostility. "Glorious day to be out and about, don't you think?"

"Yes," Nadia agreed. "Does Pact have a booth here?"

"We do indeed. Check it out." He waved his ice cream cone toward sandal footprints in the dusty path. In the tread, stamped into the dirt, were the words "Follow me." The footprints led off to a booth where scantily clad nymphs and sirens beckoned to festivalgoers like models at a car show.

"We have something special planned for Numinox tomorrow," Miles continued. "It's all very hush-hush, so I can't really tell you anything."

"Does it have to do with your recent game announcement?" Maya smiled sweetly, but her voice was ice.

Miles waved his ice cream cone at her. "You're a smart one, aren't you? Maya Wren, right? The DJ, The Mighty Troglodyti? Strange name, but I like it. You should come work for Pact. What does Christiansen pay you? I'll double it."

Maya scoffed. "No thanks."

He grinned. "The offer stands. For you as well, Nadia. Shame to keep talent locked away in a dusty old library. Well, ladies, it has been a pleasure, but I must be off. Official Pact business and all that." He waved goodbye with his ice cream and disappeared into the crowd.

After he had left, Maya said, "Can you believe the nerve of that guy? Openly trying to poach Myst employees like we would even think of going there?"

"I know, right?" Nadia agreed. Though really, she didn't see the big deal. Didn't companies do that all the time?

Soon, they found Myst's booth. The startup's logo stretched across the front of a canopy tent flanked with balloons, tinsel, and giant cutouts of misty trees and mountains. Branded swag and display boards with Veil screenshots covered the tables. Music, designed by Maya for the game, blasted out from the sound system.

Out front, Piero was shouting at Kevin, who stood behind the booth's table, inexplicably caressing a T-shirt and rubbing it on his face. Nadia couldn't tell what they were arguing about, but Piero threw up his arms in exasperation.

"Hey, guys," said Maya as they approached. "What's going on?"

"It's a nightmare." Piero sighed dramatically. "We only brought these awful polyester blend T-shirts and not the one hundred percent cotton ones. I don't know *who*"—he glared at

Kevin—"didn't check the tags before they were packed up, but Numinals aren't going to wear these."

Kevin's eyes were dilated, giving him the air of an earnest, slightly high frat bro, with his backward baseball cap. "Dude, no one's going to notice. They feel great."

"I'm going to notice!" Piero screeched.

Maya wrinkled her nose up. "I thought we threw those away after the printing company sent the wrong ones."

"They should have been burned!" Piero shouted. "But for whatever reason, someone saved them in storage. And now, they are here. No Numinal in their right mind is going to take one of our shirts. Everything is ruined!" He slumped over backward like he was going to faint.

Nadia and Maya extracted themselves quickly from that situation and left Piero and Kevin to sort it all out. They spied a neon sign for drinks and headed toward a pop-up Tiki bar perched on a grassy knoll near the lake. Behind the counter stood a humanoid Numinal with a bird head, mixing drinks. Bottles of alcohol clustered behind him, surrounded by red, green, and blue Christmas lights, carved bone talismans, and shrunken heads. Hunched over their empty shot glasses, Carson and Sophie sat on two of the barstools, drunkenly laughing at something hilarious like two old friends.

Maya raised her eyes at Nadia but put on a big smile as they walked over, waving away the miasma of alcohol emanating from them. "Whoa. This is still a company event, you know."

Carson grinned wolfishly and scooted over a seat. "Come join us."

"No thanks."

"Don't be such a buzzkill." Sophie hiccupped. "Rune wants us to have fun. That's the whole point of being here."

Nadia spied a roulotte parked under a shady tree. "Hey, let's go get our fortunes told." She grabbed Maya's hand and pulled her away before she and Sophie could get into it. Carson tried to protest, but Sophie distracted him by ordering another round of shots.

"You know I don't believe this crap," muttered Maya as they approached the rainbow-painted wagon decorated with streamers and lights. A hand-painted sandwich board covered with all-seeing eyes and crescent moons advertised palmistry and tarot card services.

A Romani woman in a colorful headdress and flowing robes sat outside, sipping tea from a porcelain cup. "You want your fortunes told. Come, come." She ushered them inside the small wagon.

Nadia and Maya took a seat around a small table, the interior of the roulette decorated with throw pillows and scrollwork. Books and trinkets littered the shelves next to jars of bones and magic dust. Nadia glanced at Maya and stifled a snort. Maya bit her lip to keep from smiling. The woman slammed her palm on the table, making them both jump.

"Enough of that." The woman gave them a stern look. She seemed to be waiting for something. Nadia pulled out her credit card from her garter purse, and the woman swiped it with a reader on her phone.

Business taken care of, the woman took a theatrical deep breath and gave herself a shake as she let out a long, vibrating sound with her lips. She then ran her hands over her arms and face, wiping off, Nadia assumed, residual bad energy. Ready to perform—it really did feel like a performance—the woman unveiled a clear crystal ball from under a sheer black shawl. Clouds swam in the glass as she peered down, waving her hands about it as if plucking images from the ether.

She glanced up at Maya. "I see a tall handsome man in your future."

Maya side-eyed Nadia. "Uh-huh."

"He is not quite a man. No, he is something else. There is a beast inside him." The woman continued to stare at the crystal.

Maya rolled her eyes. Nadia knew that despite working with seers and mediums on a regular basis, Maya leaned toward the non-believer category. Nadia had pressed her for details on why she was a skeptic, and Maya had explained that psychics could only pick up on probabilities and not definitive outcomes. Things tended to change dramatically before the event happened, leading to faulty predictions unless it was a nexus event—an inevitable event that could alter the trajectory of a realm—and true nexus events were extremely rare.

"I see a road blocked by obstacles," the woman continued. "It will take much effort to remove them, but it can be done."

"Awfully vague," Maya muttered.

The psychic turned to Nadia next. "And you. Hmmm." She paused, staring at the crystal, and waved her hands about the orb. "There is a darkness around you."

"Oh, great." Nadia forced a laugh.

"I see a choice in your future. Two paths. A road diverged."

Maya groaned. The fortune teller shot her a disapproving glance and focused back on Nadia. She hummed and swayed back and forth slightly. And then she started murmuring. Nadia leaned in, trying to catch the words.

"Eights, eights, eights," the fortune teller muttered. "Eight rows, eight columns . . ."

Suddenly, her eyes rolled back, showing only the whites. With a tortured gasp, she threw her head skyward as an awful, choking sound clawed its way out of her mouth. Nadia froze, unsure what was happening.

The fortune teller leveled unseeing eyes on her. "When the pawn becomes queen, the board will turn." The woman coughed, blinked a few times, and shook her head as if clearing a fog. She smiled sleepily and then slumped over, her head resting on her chest as she snored.

Nadia gaped at the woman. Maya stood up quickly, grabbed Nadia, and shuffled her outside of the small caravan, leaving the fortune teller snoring away inside. Nadia blinked in the bright sunlight and pulled her sunglasses down from the top of her head.

"Okay, what the hell just happened?" Nadia laughed nervously.

"I have no clue. That was freaky. Let's get a drink."

Maya spied a mobile bar being pulled on a rickshaw and flagged it down. She ordered them two mixed drinks from a nymph wearing a crop top and a belly chain.

Drinks in hand, they sat under a pine tree by the lake. Nearby, a few other partygoers lounged in the shade with drinks and food from the food trucks.

Maya took a sip of her drink, made a face, and grabbed the flask at her hip. She poured a liberal amount from it into both of their cups. Nadia dipped her pinkie into hers and swirled it around to mix it.

"I knew I got a bad vibe from that psychic," said Maya. "I don't know what she was talking about with pawns and queens, but it sounded like bogus shit from one of those penny arcade fortune tellers."

Nadia absorbed this and didn't mention she had heard those words before.

The last time, she had been out with Rune at Mercurio's nightclub. The goddess of bonds and slavery, Ananke, had gone into a psychic trance, eyes rolled back in her head, and had grabbed Nadia's arm before proclaiming, "When the pawn becomes queen, the board will turn!" It had been odd, but with so much strangeness in Nadia's world, everything seemed odd.

But one thing Nadia had learned was that in the Numinal world, when something happened more than once, it was best to pay attention. Once was a coincidence. Twice was a synchronicity. And three times—well, if something happened three times, it meant something.

This was the second time someone had said the exact same words to her.

Nadia was paying attention.

Chapter 6

After a few mandatory employee retreat exercises and a group dinner, Nadia and Maya retreated to their yurt and changed outfits for the evening. Maya opted for a feather-and-leather look, while Nadia went dark and gothy for the night, borrowing a ripped black shirt from Maya and wearing the hair twists, bangles, and jewelry she had bought from Marina and Avery earlier in the day. They each adorned themselves with glow-in-the-dark glitter and sequins and then headed back over to the music.

They danced. They drank. They dipped their toes into the lake, laughing and splashing each other. It was the perfect end to a perfect day. Nadia was completely in the moment, all her worries and fears about the Blood Oath and Mercurio and becoming an initiate in the Order before Samhain melting away. Nadia lost herself in the beats and the lights and the movement of her body in sync with the music. She gazed up at the Milky Way, the river of stars echoing millennia of stories around her, and she felt at one with the universe and Numinous.

Reality is like the tip of a lemon meringue pie, thought Nadia. *Mmmm, pie.* Had someone dosed her? She was definitely having high thoughts. But she decided that she didn't care because for the first time in a long time, she was happy.

The music changed to a song that all the Numinals around her knew, and everyone started singing the song in rounds, voices echoing up at different musical intervals.

Nadia leaned into Maya and shouted over the music, "What's going on?"

"It's a songline," Maya shouted back. "It is the instructions on how to navigate the pathways to the Other Realms. Numinox is on one of the sites that used to be a Realm Gate." She pointed to the megalithic pillars that created a giant doorway structure under which the DJ was playing. "Singing the song connects Numinals to the Other Realms and keeps the knowledge of the pathways alive. Every Numinal knows the songs. They're like sacred nursery rhymes."

The songline was easy to pick up. After listening to a few rounds, Nadia joined in the simple, repetitive melody. "Through the Gates to down below, fifty heartbeats across the chasm," she sang. She felt her vibrations rising, the knowledge of the Other Realms imprinting itself into her psyche. She closed her eyes and let the sensations wash over her, flashes of myth and archetype and dreamworlds illuminated in her mind like lightning in the clouds.

Maya kept dancing, but Nadia left the floor to go find a drink. Feeling slightly tipsy from the loose energy in the air or the drinks she already had, Nadia stumbled. A cute satyr guy with light brown curls and golden horns caught her.

"Thanks." Nadia smiled at him. He smiled back. A flush rose to Nadia's cheeks. There really were a lot of cute Numinal guys here. The satyr said something to her in Greek. She smiled and shrugged. She didn't understand, but that was fine. They didn't need to talk. It was better this way. He took her hand, and she let herself be led to a dance floor where she lost track of time until the stars were all out and the dance floor had significantly thinned.

Nadia glanced at her watch. Nearly one a.m., though the digits were a little blurry. She left the satyr—he was smelling a little ripe after hours of dancing—and stumbled back to her yurt. Her head hit the pillow, and she closed her eyes and drifted away, falling into a dark slumber.

Her dreams were fevered, figure-eight Möbius strips turning in on themselves, giant chessboards and chess pieces. Gateways opening to other dimensions, dark creatures slithering out from beyond. She tossed and turned, moaning slightly until something took hold of her mind, grabbing her head and turning it so she was forced to look.

The haze cleared. She was in Mercurio's bed chamber, all blood-red and draped velvet, and he was there, naked on his bed. No clothes, no glamour, just . . . Mercurio, in all his well-endowed, *strigoi* glory. With his glamour on, Mercurio tended to look more like a traditional vampire: dark hair, pale skin, high cheekbones. But as an unglamoured *strigoi,* he blended animal with undead man. His hands curled into long-nailed claws, a long hairy tail flicking behind him. His eyes were obsidian black holes, his chest muscled and strong and furred. His black tongue slowly crawled out of his mouth, obscenely, like a snake. The sight of him infected Nadia's mind, chittering insects eating away at her morality and decency and goodness, and she fell into his bed and straddled him. His black tongue slithered out, and she leaned down and sucked on it, grinding her pelvis into him. He slipped inside her, and Nadia lost herself as a yawning, never-ending darkness opened its mouth and swallowed her whole.

Nadia awoke as an orgasm ripped through her body. She lay on her cot, panting at the aftershocks. It was still dark out, the shapes in the yurt a ghostly gray from the moonlight streaming through a hexagonal window. Maya's cot was empty; a thin blanket was crumpled on top of the sheet. Nadia's head pounded. Her mouth was dry cotton.

The wisps of dreams lingered in Nadia's mind, and she ran out of the yurt and vomited into a bush. Wiping her mouth, she panted, gasping for air as she tried to calm her racing heart.

Mercurio was in her mind. She normally had wards up to protect herself, but in her intoxicated state, they must have slipped. The images from her dreams—*were those even dreams?* They had seemed so real. She knew that she and Mercurio were entangled like she and Rune and could mindspeak, but now she was having ... sex dreams about him? *Ew, gross.* She gagged, nearly vomiting again. He was a monster. A sexy monster. But still, a monster. She couldn't—wouldn't—let herself skip down that path and admit that the dreams had turned her on, that the orgasm was more than a bodily reaction to stimulus. It was too much. She had enough on her plate without having to add "undead fetish" to the grab bag of issues she needed to discuss with her therapist.

She needed to cast that Soulwish and break the Oath once and for all.

Rune? Nadia mindspoke to him.

No response.

Rune! she shouted.

What is it? Are you okay? Rune mindspoke back.

I want to do the first test. Right now.

Now? It's the middle of the night.

Nadia squinted at the Psionic on her wrist. 8:88 a.m. She did a double take. It now read 3:33 a.m. Goosebumps broke out over her arms, and she shivered.

Yes, now. Please? I just feel like it's the right time. I'm getting these signs like the Numinous is trying to tell me something. Repeating numbers and shit like that.

The seconds ticked by.

Meet me down by the lake, Rune said at last. *Wear a swimsuit.*

Nadia rushed back inside the yurt. She stumbled around frantically, brushing her teeth, tying her hair up in a bun, and changing into her bikini. She pulled her jeans and a sweatshirt on over it and gave her appearance a once-over in the long mirror propped up in a corner. She quickly cast an appearance charm from her Psionic to cover her burgeoning hangover face. It would have to do. Nadia grabbed her YETI bottle and headed out.

The moon was high overhead, illuminating the path down to the lake. Nadia skipped quickly down the narrow dirt trail that switch-backed down the hill through low shrubs and grasses, swinging the bottle back and forth by the top of the handle. The night was alive with the sounds of insects and the wind rustling through nearby trees. In the distance, the thump of late-night dance music echoed over the water. The path met up with the rocky shoreline, and Nadia followed it until it curved around where she found Rune, waist-deep, in a secluded lagoon ringed with redwood trees. The moon-like pool of water perfectly reflected the stars and the sky above, yet was so crystal clear that Nadia could see the moss-covered rocks peppering the sandy bottom.

Rune's back was turned to Nadia. With the moonlight, she could make out the faint silver crisscrosses of scars down his muscular torso. He appeared to be conducting some sort of ritual. His arms were outstretched toward the water as he chanted in a low baritone. Immense power radiated from him.

He stopped chanting. "Winters," called out Rune over his shoulder. "Stop lurking in the trees. I know you are there."

"I wasn't lurking," grumbled Nadia as she stepped from the shadows and made her way toward him. She took off her flip-flops at the water's edge and rolled up the cuffs of her jeans before wading a tiny bit into the refreshing water.

"We're going to have to work on your stealthiness," said Rune. "You sound like a wildebeest trampling through the forest when you walk."

"Hey!" Nadia kicked her leg up and splashed water in his direction.

He chuckled and lowered his arms, turning toward her. "Are you ready?"

Nadia stripped down to her bikini, folded her clothes and shoes neatly into a stack, and set them on a rock on the shoreline. She waded out into the lagoon, and Rune turned to face her. Nadia's breath caught at the sight of him—the water droplets running down his broad shoulders and pecs, the way his muscles flexed as he moved. She had seen him shirtless dozens of times before, but there was something about the moon and the wild energy in the air and the lingering effects of her Mercurio sex dream that shook loose some of the hairpins Nadia had been trying to hold on to. Her eyes roamed lower down the hard lines of his chest, to his sculpted abs, to his V-line, and then lower to his swim trunks.

Nadia gasped slightly and stifled a juvenile giggle. His swim trunks had duckies on them. She had not expected a man like Rune to wear duckies.

Rune ignored her. "I have not had time to adequately prepare you for this, so we need to do a crash course right now. This exercise will teach you everything you need to know to pass the first test."

"I'm ready," said Nadia solemnly.

"Each year, as part of the agreement to use the retreat center and facilities, I help purify and clean the water in the lake." Rune cupped his hands together, dipped them in the lake, and brought back up a pool of water. Sparkles of snowflakes skipped across the surface as he murmured an ancient-sounding spell. Old Norse, perhaps? Rune blew on his cupped hands and let the purified water drop back into the lake. "Your turn."

"How do you do that breath thing?"

"Visualize the water—all of the impurities coalescing and crystallizing—and that you are blowing them away." He showed her again how to do it, cupping his hands together, bringing the water to his lips, and blowing on it in a steady manner. "When you attune with the spell, you will hear the words to say."

Nadia cupped her hands together and dipped them into the water, trying to attune and hear the magic words. Silence. She blew on the pool in her hands, anyway. Nothing happened.

"Focus," Rune warned. "You are performing the actions with empty intention behind them."

Nadia tried to ground herself in the moment. The moon hung, a gibbous orb glowing in the sky. The water came up to her waist, her dark hair dripping down over her shoulder. She felt herself align with the spell, vibrating at first until her energy slowed into a rhythm and synced with it, like two waves becoming one. She visualized herself blowing on the water, and the words she needed formed in her mind like they were whispered in her ear, her own voice telling her what to say. She mouthed the words with growing force until breath came through her throat, and she vocalized them into the spell. Energy swirled around her like she was in the center of a vortex. She blew on the water, purifying it, sending tiny crystals skipping and twirling into the air like ice dancers, the water now cool, crisp, and pure like an untouched Icelandic lake.

Nadia beamed up at Rune. "Hey, look, I did it!"

Rune nodded. "Good job. Now, get to work." He started wading through the water back to the shore.

Nadia surveyed the scene. Surely, he was joking, right? It would take eons to clear the lake, one cupped handful at a time. She'd be there all night and day and then some and never get to the first test.

"Wait!" Nadia cried after him. He turned and stopped. "I'm supposed to purify this entire lake? That's going to take forever."

There was a mischievous glint in Rune's eyes. "I'll be on the other side of this rock." He pointed to a large boulder jutting up near the shoreline. "There's a hot springs pool and a waterfall. The quicker you finish, the quicker you can join me."

He waded out of the water and disappeared into the shadows.

Nadia stared after him. He was not seriously suggesting that her reward for finishing the drill quickly was getting to frolic in hot springs and waterfalls with him, was he? No, no, no, that didn't make sense. *Focus.* She needed to focus. He was trying to distract her. It was all part of the training. Some stupid test to make sure she understood the boundaries of their relationship as master and apprentice. The real issue she needed to figure out was how she was going to purify this entire lake.

Nadia worked for a while, cupping handfuls of water and purifying them as she tried to figure out what to do next. The melodic DJ set across the water pulsed gently. She got into a musical cadence. Cup, blow, drop, repeat. Cup, blow, drop, repeat. But it was menial work. The magical equivalent of manual labor. Rune was all about efficiency and hacking magic. There had to be a shortcut. Nadia gasped slightly. This. This was the training. She needed to figure out real-world problems using magic. And then that would translate into her knowing everything she needed to know to pass the first test.

She scrolled through her Psionic looking for a spell or charm that might speed up the process. Nothing. A red kegger cup—MOOP from Numinox—floated by, and she grabbed it. She purified a cupful using the plastic cup, noting that it seemed to go faster.

But not fast enough.

Nadia noodled on her predicament. She needed to figure it out soon, or she wouldn't be able to take the first test. Maybe Rune would let her skip this part if she explained she understood the concepts in theory, if not in practice. She waded over to the boulder and climbed up it to peer into the lagoon on the other side.

Rune stood under a small waterfall that dropped about twenty feet into a clear blue pool of water, the water running over his face and down his torso. He ducked his head, letting the water massage his neck and shoulders. Nadia let herself gaze upon him and his masculine beauty for a bit, enjoying the erotic voyeurism and illicit thrill of it all.

He flipped his head back, sending droplets flying. "Get back to work, Winters!"

Busted.

Nadia ducked back behind the boulder, heart hammering, mortified that he had caught her.

She reluctantly splashed back to her side of the lagoon and got back to work. Marina had taught her the importance of creating spells on the fly. Her grandmother used honey packets or little pots of creamer from diners as Numinal offerings if she was stuck in a pinch. She always took stock of the objects she carried in her purse or which herbs she already had on hand. Marina looked for guidance from the universe, synchronicities, patterns, or signs to tell her what to do next. Nadia assessed her available resources. The bikini wasn't going to do much. The Psionic watch might have spells or charms, but she was still going to have to figure out how to use them together. She needed an energy source. Something other than herself to power the spell.

The moonlight glimmered on the water. Bingo. She could use the moon.

Using her Psionic, Nadia checked the conditions: the position of the stars, the moon, and the planets in the sky, the pollen count, the temperature, her own energy levels, and all the other forces that could affect a spell. The conditions were fine, except she was a little dehydrated from the booze. She then cast a quick hydration charm to raise her water levels. Finally ready, she raised her arms to the sky and tried to call down the moon.

There was a block. Some barrier in her mind and body, some shield. It was impenetrable. Nadia focused her energy on dissolving it using the moonlight like a laser through the top of her head. A hole burned through the blockage, the edges crumbling like ash on the wind until the moonlight filled her up. The soft *ting* of a musical note rang out.

She felt free and light. The moonlight flowed easily down into her now, and she took a pebble and channeled the moonlight into it until she felt it stable enough to remove herself from the equation. The moonlight flowed directly into the pebble, and she placed it into the kegger cup of water. She then blew her breath into the water, casting the spell to purify. The pebble vibrated and rolled around in the cup, purifying the water through moonlight-powered magic. She lodged the cup between two rocks, half in and half out of the water, so it could work autonomously on the lake. Satisfied it would hold and pleased with herself for figuring out a work-around, Nadia waded back to the boulder and climbed over to the lagoon.

Rune lay on a rock reading a book. A flame of light hovered over him, illuminating his face and the pages in the darkness. He sat up, closed the book, and placed it to the side as Nadia climbed up onto the rock where he was. She read the title of the book—*Soul Dreaming*—before Rune magicked it and the flame away with the snap of his fingers.

"What were you reading?" asked Nadia as she sat cross-legged next to him. She let her head hang back, and she rotated her head, working out her neck. The moonlight energy had loosened her stiff muscles. A welcome benefit of being able to properly channel and work magic was that it worked some of the energy into the caster's body, effectively healing it.

"Nothing important," said Rune. "Congratulations, you passed the first test."

Nadia jerked her head up, surprised. "Wait, that was it? That was the test?"

Rune chuckled. "You would have become self-conscious and sabotaged your own magic if you had known it was the actual test."

Nadia felt the heat rise to her cheeks, but she shook off the creeping feeling of embarrassment that he knew her so well.

If Rune noticed her discomfort, he hid it gracefully. "There are three tests to become an initiate in the Order of the Sacred Flame. They correspond to the conscious mind, the subconscious mind, and the superconscious mind. You must master each aspect of your mind to be part of the Order. Successfully passing each test attunes you to a certain vibration, and with all three together, it creates a triad: the music of creation. When this happens—when you have all three notes—you bring forth a Soulwish from the Numinous."

"Which part was the test?" asked Nadia. "Purifying the lake?"

Rune shook his head. "It was the dissolving of the false self. You burned away the impurities that blocked you from the Numinous. You should have heard a musical note."

"Wait," Nadia interrupted. "I felt that ... heard that. But what about purifying the water?"

Rune grinned. "Wax on, wax off."

Nadia reached down and splashed water on him. "I thought I was being so smart figuring out that bit, and the whole time it was meaningless?"

"Not meaningless. You saved me a chore I had to do in the morning."

"What are the other two tests?" Nadia leaned back on her elbows, letting her wet hair fall back as she gazed up at the moon.

"The second test will be about attuning your subconscious mind to the second note . . . It's personal for each person, as each person's subconscious is their own. The third test will be about accessing the superconscious—the power of the Numinous—and obtaining the knowledge that the Numinous wishes to bestow upon you at that moment. Usually, some sort of spell. Since you are a Blood Muse, there could be nuances in the tests I am not aware of, so it's going to be important for you to understand more about your Blood Muse powers and how they relate to the Numinous. And I have a list of spells on the Psionic for the Order. You should study those."

Rune scooted over and turned so that they were facing each other on the rock. "Now comes the start of the binding. Are you ready?" Nadia nodded. His expression hardened in concentration as he focused on the space between them, casting a quick series of hand movements as he muttered incantations. A translucent flame, black and smoky around the edges, burning with a black core, burst into being between them.

"This is the Sacred Flame. It represents the magic and knowledge that Prometheus gave to humans. As a Member of the Order of the Sacred Flame, you are duty-bound to honor the three tenets of the creed." He paused, holding her gaze. "One, honor the Numinous above all else. Two, only use the secrets of the Order to protect the bond between Numinals and humans.

And three, only use violence as a last resort. Now, place your hand into the fire."

Nadia stuck her hand into the fire. The fire burned deep magic, pain erupting throughout her being as the Sacred Flame seared into her flesh and core. She winced but didn't pull back her hand. If Paul Atreides could do it, she could too. Rune placed his hand into the fire, as well, grabbing her hand in a secret handshake and pressing Nadia's fingers into symbols that mirrored his own. Their magic bonded in a call and answer. A tattoo blossomed on Nadia's wrist, the outline of the Order's symbol inked into her flesh, one side of the first smaller triangle completed. A second line of the larger triangle appeared in Rune's own tattoo.

Relief flooded her body. She had been pretty sure this was going to happen—she hadn't met a test that she couldn't beat after hours of study before—but part of her had prepared for the worst. For failing. The tattoo on her wrist, magically inked, was a stark reminder that she had set out on this journey. She was the Fool from the tarot, naive and innocent to what dangers might come on this grand adventure.

The world wobbled around Nadia. She and Rune continued to hold hands, even after the fire had died out. She didn't ever want to let go. After several moments, Rune gently extracted his fingers, and Nadia sat back, dizzy from the experience. She took several deep breaths.

"Your energy shifted in a major way to mirror mine," Rune explained. "It might take some time to get used to."

Nadia made a fist, clenching and releasing her hand. The subtle energy lines in her body were shifting to match the blueprint that Rune had placed in her, flexing and pulling as she settled into the new form. She rubbed the tattoo on her wrist.

"It's only temporary," said Rune. "If you pass all three tests, the three sides representing the three tests will be permanently inked into your skin. As we progress through the drills leading up to the remaining two tests, there will be different lessons that the various tasks and exercises will teach you. The point of the exercises might not be what you think. The lessons might be different from what you were expecting. Trust the Numinous. Trust me to guide you. Trust yourself to know what to do." He stood, the bright moon behind him like a halo. "Lesson number one: never waste time and energy doing something that you can magically automate."

"For a minute, I thought I might actually have to do the entire lake myself."

Rune chuckled. "Lesson number two: use the time that you freed up from doing tedious magical labor to enjoy yourself."

He dove into the lagoon, swimming a few powerful strokes under the water before he broke the surface and shook his head, sending water droplets flying. "Are you going to join me?" There was the hint of a challenge, a dare in his voice.

Nadia grinned as she stood up and dived into the water in a graceful arc. She swam in a leisurely circle before she came up for air near Rune. That mischievous look was back. He splashed her in the face.

Sputtering and laughing, she inelegantly pushed water toward him, trying to splash him. He took a deep breath and then disappeared under the surface before he grabbed Nadia's ankle and yanked her under. They play-fought for a while and then stopped to catch their breaths.

Nadia stared up at the moon, trying to stay in the moment. She tried to trust the Numinous and the path that she was now on, with Rune as her master in the Order of the Sacred Flame, she as his apprentice. She would become an initiate before

Samhain, be able to cast a Soulwish to save herself and her family and sever the bond of slavery to Mercurio.

"What are you thinking about?" asked Rune, breaking her reverie.

She smiled at him. "Just enjoying the moonlight."

Nadia surprised herself with how easily the lie slipped off her tongue.

Chapter 7

Pale light streamed in through cracks in the woven twigs of Piero's yurt. Nadia sat in her pajamas with Piero and Maya, blankets wrapped around themselves to ward off the crisp morning air. Steam rose from their coffees. Nadia stifled a yawn. She had barely an hour of sleep last night.

Piero wrapped the blanket over his head like a hood. "Tell me about your night." His knee moved up and down impatiently like he was just asking to be polite and was waiting for someone to ask him about his.

"My night was great," said Nadia vaguely. She took a sip of her coffee and reveled in the first sip of java of the day. Piero had sent a gnome intern to fetch them coffees that morning, and she was grateful for it.

Maya glanced at Nadia's tattooed wrist. "I saw your bikini hanging to dry."

Before Nadia could think of how to explain her frolicking in the moonlight with Rune under the guise of the first test, Piero cut in. "Well, let me tell you about my night." He adopted a regal air. "I think I've found my calling."

Maya and Nadia shared a glance and tried not to laugh.

"It all started when I took what some guy said was just mushroom tea—let me tell you, that was no 'shrooms I've ever experienced—but I had The. Most. Amazing Vision. Quest. Ever."

He stood up, kicking the blanket off, and struck a pose. He then proceeded to regale them in a one-man monologue, complete with wild, theatrical pantomiming of his adventures.

His night had started relatively normally, dancing and exploring Numinox, but after he had taken the 'shrooms, the night took a completely "bonkers" turn. After he got pulled on stage to go-go dance with backup dancers, he was crowned King of the Evening by a group of dryad groupies and hoisted onto a tuk-tuk pulled by human furries who had been transformed into animals. After making several proclamations about whether people were "getting jiggy" enough, he was deposed by a troll, forced into stocks where people could smack his ass, and then rescued by a talking rat. Or at least he thought there had been a rat. At this point, Piero's memory got a little fuzzy. Apparently, he joined the rat camp, became *their* king, but then snuck away when he discovered they wanted him to marry. "If they liked it, they should have put a ring on it," he declared, holding up his hand and flipping it back and forth. He found a lake barge, climbed aboard, and set sail.

"I must have passed out at some point," said Piero, "because when I woke up, there was a heyoka on the barge with me."

"A what?" asked Nadia.

"A heyoka," Piero explained. "Native American spirit. Very renowned. He told me that I needed to stop fucking around and get with the program. He said I have a higher purpose in life, and I'm wasting it."

"The heyoka told you to stop fucking around?" Maya looked skeptical. "Was he even there, or were you still on 'shrooms?"

"Okay, so I'm paraphrasing." Piero rolled his eyes. "But the point is that I've found it! I've found my calling! I'm supposed to be a sacred clown! I'm supposed to say the truths that no one else does. I'm supposed to be a force of chaos and question the status quo!"

Nadia stifled a laugh. "Don't you do that already?"

Piero ignored her. He turned to Maya, towering over her as she sat. He put his hands on his hips and jutted his chin up. "As a sacred clown, my first proclamation is that you and wolf-boy need to stop beating around the bush and just go for it."

Maya feigned distraction.

"Oh my god, what happened?" Piero dropped back down and wrapped the blanket over his head again. "Spill."

Maya grinned. "We kissed last night."

"Whaaaaat!" Nadia threw a pillow at her. "And you waited all this time to tell us! What happened?"

Maya caught the pillow and held it up to her face before screaming into it in a joyful release. Amusement gleamed in Piero's eyes. "I knew it."

"I don't want to jinx it or anything, but I have a really good feeling about it." Maya couldn't help the totally in-love expression on her face. "I just . . . really like him."

"Have you told him how you feel?" demanded Piero.

"He knows."

Piero stood back up. "He's completely dense. He's practically osmium. You can't take chances that he knows. You need to tell him. Right now."

"He's probably still sleeping . . . we were up late."

Nadia grinned. "Uh-huh. 'Up late,' eh?"

Piero hauled Maya up. "You need to tell him. It's now or never."

The trio made their way out of Piero's yurt and over to Carson's, whispering and giggling at how much noise they were making.

"Shh!" Nadia shushed them. "Everyone is still sleeping!"

"I'm being quiet!" Piero boomed out.

That got them going again, and they all dissolved into a fit of laughter.

The wooden door to Carson's yurt was slightly ajar when they got there. Maya tiptoed over, opened it, trying not to laugh, and froze.

On the cot, curled up next to Carson, was Sophie.

She was face down on the bed, topless, sleeping in the crook of Carson's arm. They were tangled together, her arm draped across his bare chest. Her bra was cast to the side on the floor. The blanket was bunched down low across Carson's hips, covering him, but it was clear he was naked. Next to the bed, a glass pipe smoked, a sickly-sweet odor coming from it.

Nadia grabbed Maya's hand to drag her away, but Piero stepped into the yurt.

"What in the Light is going on here?" Piero demanded, hands on his hips.

Carson and Sophie groggily sat up. Carson's eyes went wide and then locked on Maya. "Maya, this isn't what it looks like."

"You disgust me," she spat out.

Sophie glanced back and forth between him and Maya. She punched Carson in the arm. "What the fuck, dude? You said you were just friends."

Carson sputtered, no good excuse coming forth. Sophie grabbed the sheet and wrapped it around herself as she jumped up.

Nadia got a good eyeful of Carson. "Whoa there." She turned her head away. *Now* she understood what all the fuss was about.

Sophie and Maya stood shoulder to shoulder, looking down at Carson. He tried to cover his nakedness with his hands.

"You've been playing us against each other, and it stops now," said Maya.

"I don't even want him anymore," said Sophie. "Liars are so gross."

Maya nodded. "He used to be cute and now he's not."

They both analyzed Carson, tilting their heads and squinting their eyes.

"You're right," said Sophie. "He's not."

"Hey!" he shouted. "What is this? Why are you two ganging up on me now?"

"Because, wolf-boy," said Piero, "you're acting like a dumb human! Get with the program!" Piero hurled a pair of pants at Carson.

Maya linked arms with Sophie. "Let's get out of here. The ideathon is starting soon."

They all left Carson in his yurt as he struggled to pull on his pants.

The Veil event was on a grassy hill overlooking the lake. The area was speckled with picnic tables and circled with poles topped with a rainbow assortment of flags that waved gently in the light morning breeze. As Nadia and Maya passed under a giant banner and archway of balloons that led into the space, Nadia could sense the subtle excitement and ripples of potentiality pulsing from the site. Dozens of Numinals and Sixers milled about, chatting and waiting for it to start, taking advantage of a generous-looking coffee and breakfast service spread out on one of the side tables.

Piero drifted over to Maya and Nadia, rose-tinted circular sunglasses on, carrying a thermos. He was still wearing his bathrobe. He took a large sip of his drink and shuddered, nearly gagging. "Your grandmother's hangover cures are supposed to taste like herbs and honey. Honey, these are not any herbs I've ever tasted."

"I'm pretty sure it says consume at your own risk right on the bottle," retorted Nadia.

Carson stood nearby, hungover and morose. "He looks a little worse for wear," commented Piero.

"Not my concern anymore," said Maya. "He can do whoever or whatever he wants."

Rune called everyone to attention. "Welcome to the first-ever Myst ideathon! Today, we are crowd-sourcing the best ideas to improve Veil. Hit me with whatever you've got. Better interface, better gameplay, any cool elements you'd like to see—you name it. I want to hear it all."

After going over a few more housekeeping issues, Rune broke the crowd and let everyone get to work. Some worked on their own with VR headsets in simulated environments, and some worked collectively at various demo stations. Veil blended augmented reality with live role-playing, overlaying magical elements over various neighborhoods in San Francisco while using Numinals as actors. At Nadia's group demo station, she helped non-Myst participants work through gameplay that included a storyline about finding secret doors on Treasure Island. To start, the players had to climb to the roof of one of the buildings in the Financial District to get a hint from a Corporate Goddess, one of the twelve ghostly statues that adorned the top of the building. The hint then led the players to the Cliff House and down to a dark cave near the Sutro Baths, where they had to solve a riddle etched into the wall of the cave. The prize was a golden key. It was modeled after one of the artifacts in the vaults, a giant skeleton key crusted with rubies that had come to the collection by way of donation from the Levi Strauss family. Nadia was pleased that the programmers had already incorporated her explanations about the history and magic uses of the key into the beta version of the game.

After the testing period, participants gathered to hear the suggestions. Groups and individuals took turns pitching, with Rune, Carson, and Vega as the judges.

Nadia even came up with her own idea on the fly: a module called EyeWish, that magically changed the user's experience based on genie wish magic "in the blink of an eye." She had learned about wish magic in her studies of how to make the Foundation's collection more user-friendly and efficient and had helped the programmers update the search and retrieval system.

It was a half-baked invention. A pipe dream. Nadia didn't even know if the spells she would need existed, let alone if they could interact successfully with Myst's current platform for Veil. It was techy stuff, and she didn't really understand the tech side of things at the company. Rune kept his expression neutral as she pitched it, merely nodding and clapping politely with the rest. Nadia didn't care, though. She was proud of herself for even trying. A month ago, she would have felt completely out of her league in Numinal culture and magical innovation and wouldn't have had the courage to give it a shot.

Soon, the ideathon was coming to an end. Gamers gathered toward the front near Rune to hear the winners. As he was about to announce who won, a dark shadow descended over Numinox. Day turned to night. The sun, high overhead, turned into the moon. Nadia could sense dark magic, heavy and stifling in the air, as a darkness enveloped them in a dome of night. A network of drones in the air powered the spell.

Rune stared up at the sky. Nadia rushed through the crowd to him. "What's going on?"

"It's Pact." He spat out the words like a bad taste in his mouth.

About twenty feet away, a Lovecraftian monster materialized. Covered in tentacles with hundreds of eyes all over its body, it appeared to be a cross between a squid and a potato. Nadia could see the picnic bench behind it through its slightly opaque body; it was some sort of hologram. Various other traditional Halloween monsters—zombies, werewolves, mummies, a Bride of Frankenstein—wavered into sight around them, freezing and unfreezing, like a glitchy video game.

Carson strode over to them. A cartoonish-looking werewolf wearing ripped clothing appeared next to him. "What the hell?" He glared at it. The creature had a crazed look in its crossed eyes, with blood dripping from its fangs and claws. "Now that's just offensive." He took out his cell phone and started recording. Nearby, Miles grinned up at his announcement.

A deep, disembodied voice rang out around them. "This is The Call you have been waiting for! You have been summoned! Find out more on All Hallows' Eve at Impact!" Across the faux-night sky, dozens of lit drones coalesced into Pact's logo, sprinkling magic dust onto the crowd.

And then the drones all caught on fire.

Nadia didn't see which one went first, but suddenly, the sky was filled with flames and smoke. Drones fell from the sky like meteors, striking the crowd below them. Screams erupted as everyone ducked for cover and scrambled away. *Move!* She had to move! Instinct took over, and she threw herself sideways, landing hard on her shoulder and rolling away from a piece of smoldering metal. She crouched beside an upturned table and tried to cast a shield spell to give herself a safety dome. Her hands shook, and her attempt puffed out miserably. She tried again, this time throwing up the purple-tinged dome around her, but her neighbor wasn't so lucky. Her shield spell fell short, leaving him exposed. A drone dropped out of the sky and hit him on the head with a sickening crack. He crumpled to the ground. Nadia screamed. *I didn't make it big enough.* She could have saved him if she hadn't fucked up the first time. The next attempts she made bigger, her hands shaking from adrenaline, and she cast several more shield spells to the people around her.

Rune leaped like a jaguar from falling drone to falling drone, climbing the sky with preternatural speed. Nadia gasped. She hadn't known he could do that. When he reached the remaining drones still hovering in the air, he cast a spell. Reality slipped over the drones like a pocket over a hand, and the drones were gone. Rune landed back on his feet with a loud thump that rattled the earth and sent waves rolling over the nearby lake.

It took a few moments for Nadia to believe it was safe enough to get up. Gingerly, she and others around her climbed to their feet. The ideathon was in shambles: melted tables, grass on fire, injured Numinals. An ambulance siren wailed in the distance. Nadia rushed to the man who had been hit on the head near her. *Thank the gods.* He seemed to be okay, though one of his horns had cracked off into a bloody stump. She looked around for Rune.

He held Miles up by the throat, the man's legs kicking at empty air as his face turned a concerning shade of purple. Barely contained rage radiated from him. Nadia had never seen him so close to snapping.

Sophie stumbled toward her. "Oh my god, Pact's announcement is already trending." She held out her phone. Grainy footage of the spectacle that had just occurred played on dozens of accounts on the Numinal social media site, Woven. "This is awful. Screamforce is going to be the only thing people are talking about for days."

"Hold that thought," said Nadia as she ran over to Rune and Miles.

"Do you even know how much damage you could have caused?" growled Rune. "People could have been seriously hurt."

"I'm sorry! I'm sorry!" Miles squeaked. "Let me down! Please don't hurt me!"

Nadia was pretty sure Rune would have hit Miles if she hadn't been there. With a condescending glare, he threw Miles to the ground and stalked off.

Miles rolled around on the grass, gasping for air. Nadia helped him up. "Are you okay?"

He climbed to his feet, using her arm for support, and rubbed his bruised throat. "Water. I need water," he rasped out.

Nadia manifested a glass of water—one of the more useful tricks Rune had taught her—and handed it to him.

"Bloody hell," he muttered. "That was intense."

"Tell me about it," agreed Nadia. "There were fires everywhere."

"No, no. I meant Christiansen. He's a scary one, isn't he?"

Nearby, Rune and the others started cleaning up the mess the falling drones had caused, their hands waving about in the air as they cast spells to reverse the damage.

"I wouldn't call him scary, no," said Nadia. Powerful, compelling, and ambitious, yes. But scary, no. Nadia felt safer with him than with anyone else in her life.

"I can't believe this happened." Miles shook his head, looking around at the chaos he had caused. "Those drones . . . they weren't supposed to do that."

"I heard the announcement is already trending," said Nadia.

Miles grinned. "There's no such thing as bad publicity. Maybe this will be the bump we need to really get Hacksilver off the ground."

"Unbelievable," muttered Nadia. "Well, I'd better help the crew"—she thumbed over toward Maya and the rest—"clean up. Later, Miles."

She ran over to where Numinals and Septers were trying to

restore order. She joined in to help, practicing minor mendings and spells to reverse entropy.

Rune corrected her form with tiny nudges from his mind, a master helping his apprentice learn.

After so much excitement, Nadia was ready to get the hell out of Numinox.

She went to find Marina and Avery to ask for a ride home and found them tearing down The Tambourine Lady's Shoppe and packing it into the Eldorado.

"Got room for another?" asked Nadia.

"Of course!" exclaimed Marina as she picked up a cardboard box filled with jars and vials. "You might have to sit with supplies on your lap, though." She heaved the box into the back of the car.

Nadia helped load up. "Looks like you sold out on a lot of things."

"We did!" Marina beamed. "Oh, and that nice HR lady of yours at Myst . . . What's her name?"

"Vega," supplied Nadia.

"She wants us to come teach a wellness course at Myst. Something with herbs and the seasons and how to use them to stay healthy. Said it could be a quarterly thing, maybe even monthly." Nadia congratulated her grandmother. She knew how important wellness was to her, and a regular gig doing something she loved was a rare treat.

Soon, they were on their way. Nadia sat in the back seat as the other cars inched along with them. They reached a bottle-neck, crawling to a near stop. She was tired. Exhausted from the late-night and the adrenaline that had worn off, Nadia slumped against the window, trying to catch some shut-eye.

"Did you get a tattoo?" Marina asked.

Nadia's eyes flew open, and she glanced at the beginning of the Order's triangle inked on her wrist.

"Rune took me on as his apprentice in this Order," Nadia explained. "It's a long story."

Marina caught her eye in the rearview mirror. "Look around you. We've got time."

Avery kicked up his heels on the dashboard and tipped his cowboy hat down to shade his face and take a nap.

Nadia explained what had happened, how she had asked Rune to help her become an initiate and get a Soulwish before Samhain, and how she planned on using it to break the Blood Oath.

"I don't know if it's going to work," said Nadia, "but I'm going to try."

"What is the Order called?" Avery mumbled from under his cowboy hat.

"The Order of the Sacred Flame."

"I've heard of them." He snorted. "A bunch of self-proclaimed guardians of humanity and magic. What a joke."

"What do you mean?" asked Nadia.

"What have they ever done for humanity?" he asked. "Locked away, studying theory from afar, 'protecting magic' while there are real Numinals with real problems who need help."

"Well, I'm trying to be one of them," said Nadia in a slight huff. She was tired of justifying herself to everyone.

"Whatever."

"Be nice," warned Marina. "This is Nadia's way of helping."

"Speaking of," said Nadia, changing the subject, "what's up with that NLA stuff you had. All those flyers?"

"I donate a portion of The Tambourine Lady's profits to them," explained Marina. "Tithings, if you will. They're such a great organization."

"You aren't blowing up test sites or anything, right?"

Marina laughed. "No, no, no. That would be crazy."

They lapsed into silence. The clouds overhead were puffy sheep. Nadia let her mind wander. She had passed the first initiation test. Two more to go. She was on the path to freeing herself from a life of servitude to Mercurio. She could do this. She had to. But what if she failed? What if she didn't hear the other two musical notes? Doubts circled around her, like dark birds threatening to attack.

With a single-minded focus to keep the panic at bay, she repeated the mantra in her head: *Anything is possible.*

Chapter 8

The following Monday, Nadia sat at the back of the library with her laptop, trying to learn about Blood Muses and their history. A few other Mystics were in the library, speaking in hushed tones in the vast, echoey hall. Nadia begrudgingly tolerated them. She was protective of the artifacts, as if they were her own children. Carson had sent the gnomes down to pull a few more artifacts to render in Veil, and they had broken only one clay ocarina so far, a success in Nadia's book.

Nadia browsed through various YouScry and Numinal Wiki pages on Blood Muses. Ancient tomes and scrolls littered the table in front of her, source material to verify what she was reading online. Nadia couldn't tell what was real and what was fake news. How the hell should she know if this Blood Muse dress from the sixteenth century was period accurate? How would she know if a recently unearthed diary of a Blood Muse previously thought to be lost in a fire was the real deal, or if it had been created by AI to paint the narrative in a different light? How would she know if these Reddit boards were accurate when it came to the mechanics of how Blood Muses pulled energy from the Numinous, or if a bunch of incels were just messing with each other?

As it turned out, Blood Muses held a specific fascination for Numinals. Countless websites, Wiki pages, message boards, scholarly articles, and the like documented famous Blood Muses and their stories. How they tasted, how they were kept. People had written whole books on them, novels even. Fanfic and fan art ran rampant, much of it very NSFW.

Blood Muses spanned all levels of society, from the highest and most esteemed courtesans, wives, and concubines to lowly blood slaves kept in cages like animals. But the one common thread that ran through each of their stories was a sense of perseverance, determination, and grit. Hope in the face of unerring odds. Even the ones who had faced gruesome hexes and deaths, with beheadings a common theme, managed to triumph in the stories. It gave Nadia a strange sense of camaraderie to be in the ranks of these women.

Nadia was reading about Countess Isabella de Fortibus, a medieval Blood Muse and wealthy landowner who had refused to tie herself to a Dark Numinal, when Kevin interrupted her.

"Oh, hey," he said. "You work in the library, right? Can you help me with something?"

"Sure." Nadia followed him to the search kiosk where Mystics could look up artifacts and books in the startup's database.

"My employee ID isn't working." He typed in some numbers and pressed enter. A box popped up saying no employee found.

"Everyone just got new employee ID numbers. New HR system."

They had received numerous memos reminding everyone, but apparently, Kevin didn't get the message. Not surprising, considering he was half-baked all the time.

Nadia showed Kevin where to find his new ID number and left him searching for magical helmets in the archives. "For skateboarding," he explained.

She returned to her studying, reading up on everything Blood Muse-related that she could find. Rune had emphasized how important it would be for her to understand her powers, so Nadia tried to focus on what was known about the mechanisms by which Blood Muses pulled energy from the Numinous. There wasn't much out there.

Maybe Rune knew where she could find more info. He had said to ping him day or night if she had questions regarding her studies for the initiation tests.

Rune? Nadia mindspoke. The image of a naked Mercurio pushed itself into her thoughts.

I believe you have the wrong frequency, love, Mercurio replied. Nadia slapped a hand across her mouth. *No fucking way!* She had telepathically pinged Mercurio by accident.

Nadia had taken mindspeak for granted and failed to figure out exactly how it worked. Was it like a telephone? A fax? Morse code? Apparently, wires could get crossed—

I'm so sorry, it won't happen again, Nadia mindspoke quickly.

Well, well, well. Entangled with Christiansen? How . . . delightful.

A thousand apologies—Thomas had said that Mercurio loved groveling—*it won't happen again, Master.*

We've talked about this. Drake prefers antiquated customs. I try to, how do they say? 'roll with the times?' You may call me sir.

Yes, sir. Thank you, sir.

There was an awkward silence. Nadia's eyes darted around the vaults as she waited for him to sign off or somehow indicate the conversation was over. Or was she supposed to . . . ? She had no idea what the telepathy etiquette was here.

One more thing, thought Mercurio. *I wanted to ask how your dreams have been?*

Nadia's heart thudded against her chest. The memories of the dreams flooded her body with dopamine. He had been planting them deliberately—the equivalent of unsolicited, magical dick pics.

Nadia kept her tone even to avoid tipping her hand and showing him her true thoughts: how she had liked seeing him naked, dream orgasm ripping through her body.

Uneventful, Nadia lied.

Mercurio chuckled in her mind like he knew the truth.

"Miles Kirkpatrick ought to be shot," declared Rune later that day.

The Veil team was assembled in the Artemis Room, trying to fight the afternoon work slump. Diffusers ran energy charms to perk up their mood and keep them focused. While the original intent of the meeting was to debrief after the ideathon and discuss how to incorporate the winning pitch into the next iteration of Veil, after Pact's disastrous announcement, the more pressing issue was to figure out what had gone wrong and what, if any, the implications were for Myst.

Piero sneezed, and a miniature Halloween zombie flew out of his nose, waving a flag with Pact's logo on it. He smashed it with a rolled-up magazine. "That's, like, the third time today!" he exclaimed. "Rune, we have got to do something about this. I can't keep sneezing up critters."

The magic dust the drones had sprinkled on the crowd turned out to be an airborne viral ad campaign. Everyone there had been infected. Myst's headquarters now gave off the vibe of a Spirit Halloween store full of cheap haunted house décor. Anytime someone coughed or sneezed, new monsters emerged. Myst's magical cleanup crew was in a frenzy trying to contain the virus and rid the space of all things Pact, but it had spread all over San Francisco. Nadia had run into giant spiderwebs coalescing into the letters P-A-C-T outside of her home's wards that morning, and humans couldn't figure out why their pumpkins had moved off their porches, almost like they had sprouted legs and run off.

"Do you think Pact knew there was an issue with the drones?" asked Maya. She coughed, and a bat flew out of her mouth.

Rune zapped the bat with magic, and it dissipated. "It wouldn't surprise me if they did," he said, "but at the very least, it was gross negligence. The way all the drones malfunctioned at once indicates that they hadn't been tested before the announcement." He waved a hand, and one of the recovered drones magically popped into the room. "Carson, I need you to take a look at this and figure out if the issue is with software or hardware."

"On it." Carson picked up the drone and started picking at the body's latch with a claw to open it up. "I can't believe I have to debug Pact's shitty code."

"Maya, I was going to have you help Carson—" Rune started.

"I actually have another project I just got pulled into," said Maya. "With Diego in the labs."

A low rumble came from Carson's throat as he tried to repress a growl. Diego was a rather attractive and flirtatious encantado—a Brazilian dolphin shifter—who headed Myst's bioengineering division. Nadia knew this was Maya's way of getting some distance from Carson. After they had caught him with Sophie, he had doubled down on his fuck-up and tried to convince both women to be in a throuple with him. It hadn't gone over well.

Rune glanced at Carson, who shrugged like he didn't care, though he clearly did. "Fine," said Rune. "But I need you to stay on track for the Veil launch, even if you're helping Diego with something."

"I'm ahead of schedule on the music. I sent you a progress report on Friday."

"Send it again so it's at the top of my inbox." Rune turned to Sophie, who fluttered her eyelashes and smiled. Oh, come on, thought Nadia. So not professional.

"I need you to monitor social media feeds," said Rune. "What's the buzz about Impact? How can we leverage it to our advantage?" Impact was Pact's annual user conference, nick-named "Screamforce" as it coincided with Halloween that year.

A tiny evil jack-o'-lantern with legs ran across the table. Nadia flicked it away.

Sophie scrolled through news feeds on her phone. "I have alerts set up for anything that mentions Impact and am already feeding it through a potentiality spell."

"Good." Rune turned to Piero next, who sat perched and ready for his marching orders, his knee bouncing, his diamond-crusted spats jiggling.

"I need to understand how Pact's announcement impacts Myst," said Rune. "What are they saying? How does it affect our brand? I want focus groups. I want data."

Piero looked smug. "One step ahead of you, boss man. I have a focus group coming in this afternoon. I, unlike some people"—he gave Carson a pointed look—"know how to anticipate the needs of others." Piero and Carson were constantly vying to be Rune's second-in-command.

"Why are you after me, now?" Carson growled.

"Some people—" Piero started.

"Moving on," Rune cut in. He turned to Nadia. She sat up, ready for her assignment. "And, Nadia, I'd like to see you in my office after the meeting."

Nadia answered some emails at her desk while she waited for Rune to return to his office. A request for "Any entries pertaining to hobgoblin blessings for Samhain" had just come in, and she was formulating a response. As it turned out, requests to the library were becoming more frequent the closer it came to Samhain. Dozens had come in that morning, up from the usual one or two a day. It was slightly overwhelming. She felt slammed as it was.

She sneezed. A few miniature witches on broomsticks flew out of her nose, flying around like gnats. The cleanup crew, a pack of brownies in white jumpsuits, rushed over to disinfect her and her desk, waving a magic wand like they were spraying insecticide.

"Thanks, guys," said Nadia as the cleanup crew rushed off to corral several skeletons who were using their own femurs to try to bash Mystics on their heads as they worked.

Nadia didn't have to look up from her desk to track Rune's movements around the floor. With their magic bonded after the first initiation test, she could sense him. Where he was, his general mood and demeanor. It was like a low-key tracking system, his body a magnet pulling on hers. She sensed he was making his way upstairs, done checking in with people. Nadia quickly cleaned up her workstation and rose to follow.

Rune was reading a stack of papers at his desk when Nadia poked her head inside his office.

"Knock, knock. You wanted to see me?" she asked.

Rune waved her in.

"Take a seat." Rune tossed Nadia a stack of papers: a printout of the past three months of library searches from the catalog's search and retrieve functions, tied to each employee ID.

Well, fuck me gently with a chainsaw, Nadia thought. "I didn't realize you could run these types of reports." What had she been searching for during her spare time? Oh, gods . . . menstrual remedies for that time of month, spells to make her hair shinier and her lips poutier and her waist thinner. If Rune had read her searches, he must think she was the most vain creature who'd ever existed. She tried not to make eye contact with him, certain her embarrassment was plastered across her face.

"It's useful to analyze trends to see what employees and contractors are searching for," Rune continued. "In case we should expand the collection in that direction. Remind me and I'll show you how to run the reports. I don't look all the time, but after Pact's announcement, I thought to check to see if anything was amiss. You see, there was something strange about their announcement. I couldn't put my finger on it at the time, but there was something . . . familiar about it. And then I realized I was feeling that way because it was my spell they used."

"Wait, what?"

"Pact used one of my proprietary spells. Not very well. You saw it." He frowned. "I know this may be difficult to hear, but I want to give you a heads-up first since it pertains to the vaults, and that's your domain. We have a thief at Myst, and they've been actively stealing from our files and collection."

Nadia's stomach plummeted. "You're kidding." Did he know? Was he talking about her?

"It's beyond disappointing that I can't trust all my employees." Rune took off his glasses and cleaned them with a cloth. "I will be looking into this personally to find out the extent of Pact's culpability—I think they have someone planted here— but I need your help performing an audit of the collection to see if anything else is missing. Start with the homemade spells, anything that's proprietary, even open source, and go from there. I don't think the thief, whoever they may be, has access to our code. I believe they can only access the vaults."

Nadia swallowed her agony and tried to keep it from registering on her face.

"Now, I'm going to need your discretion," Rune continued.

"This needs to stay private. If others found out about this, it could impact employee morale, not to mention tip off the thief. I want to catch them in the act and get to the bottom of this."

"Understood."

Rune sat back, watching her. She smiled faintly, wondering if she could bolt. Finally, he said, "I noticed you've been looking into Blood Oaths."

Nadia's heart leaped into her throat and threatened to choke her.

"I don't mean to pry," Rune continued, "but can I ask why? Blood Oaths are a very powerful, deep magic and not something to dabble with. I hope this upcoming Soulwish that you want to cast doesn't have to do with that."

Nadia racked her mind for an answer that would get her off the hook. "I overheard someone talking about them and wanted to know more. Sorry, maybe I should have asked before looking. I didn't realize they were taboo."

"Nothing in the collection is off-limits, much to some people's disapproval. But it doesn't mean I won't get concerned when I see something . . . unusual like this." He paused, as if he was waiting for her to say something.

Nadia put on a big, fake, cheesy smile to mask her low-grade panic. "Nothing unusual besides my curiosity apparently getting me in trouble!" She forced a laugh. "Speaking of curiosity," she said, "when do you think we can do the second test?"

Rune glanced at his calendar. "I still don't think it's possible for someone to become an initiate this quickly, but hey, prove me wrong. How about"—he circled his pen in the air at one of the dates—"two weeks from now. That splits the time between the tests and, hopefully, keeps you on track for Samhain."

"Perfect." Nadia programmed an event into her Psionic calendar to save the date.

Rune's eyes softened. "I'll do everything I can to get you that Soulwish."

They locked eyes for a long moment. Words formed on the tip of Nadia's tongue. She longed to tell him everything. But the words died and withered away. She broke away first. "Can we practice the drills for the next test soon?"

Rune checked his watch. "I have an errand to run in North Beach this afternoon. Are you free tonight for dinner?"

She nodded.

"Meet me at the Nike in Union Square, six p.m."

Chapter 9

The cable car chimed as it climbed up the hill in North Beach. Rune held on to a pole on the side of the trolley as it passed through the neighborhood. Tourists drank wine at outdoor cafés, sausages hung in the windows of delicatessens, and bakeries sold fresh bread and tiramisu. When it reached the top of the hill, he stepped down from the car and strolled along, basking in the unusually warm fall day. The weather had been all over the place recently. It didn't bode well for Samhain, but it did make for some nice days in the city.

Rune loved San Francisco. He had adopted the city as his own, made it his personal mission to make it a place where both Numinals and humans could live and thrive. He loved walking through the streets, seeing the color and the history and the improvement over the years. It gave him purpose. He wanted to leave the world a better place than he had found it, give back to the community, and uplift others. If he didn't do it, who would? Imogen had always made fun of him for that—his blind devotion to goodness. "Humans are awful creatures," she had said, laughing at him. "They don't deserve you or your help."

"Everyone deserves a little grace," he had replied.

Thinking of Imogen made Rune miss her. They hadn't talked much since she went back to Dublin. He stopped and shot her a text message: Thinking about you. Let's get a drink when you are in town next. xoxo

What would Nadia think if she read that text? Rune knew she was jealous of Imogen—he had seen the smoldering hatred in her eyes more than once. It was a good sign, he timidly thought. Possessiveness was one of the traits of a mate. But only time would tell . . .

He continued his stroll through North Beach, taking in the sights, smells, and sounds. A *nichnytsia*, a floral-patterned scarf covering her head and hiding her gaunt face, sat on the sidewalk. Humans gave her a wide berth or ignored her altogether, but she stared up at Rune as he approached and held out a liver-spot-covered palm.

"Please," she said in a raspy, dry voice. "Can you spare some change?"

A little way down the street, a Numinal man leaned against a building wall, tossing a gold pocket watch in the air. He kept his face shielded, half in shadows, which wasn't unusual for Numinals who lived in shadows to begin with.

Rune fished out a bill from his wallet. He knew the woman would just spend it on a hit of *ousia—damn Mercurio and his business!* But Rune could not deny a fellow Numinal a little bit of peace and comfort. He squatted down and gave her the money. Her eyes were rheumy, and she had no teeth. The old woman grabbed the money with claw-like hands and scurried off into an alley, cackling.

You can't save them all, thought Rune. Though damn if he wouldn't try.

Ahead was Rune's destination: Vesuvio's. The bar had been a favorite of his back in the '50s, when he would sit in the café and discuss philosophy and life with some of the locals. Jack, Allen, and Rune had been known as the Truth Trio, a joke name that had stuck after too many drinks. The trio spent countless hours there smoking cigarettes, drinking whiskey, and writing, and each time Rune stepped through the wooden doors of the bar, he felt transported back in time.

The spot wasn't crowded in the middle of the afternoon, but Rune glamoured himself to be invisible, nonetheless. The cracked leather booths and the liquor bottles behind the bar wrapped themselves around him like an optical illusion, and he disappeared. At the back of the bar, he tapped on the wall three times and spoke the secret password. The vibration revealed a concealed door. Rune crossed the threshold, stepping through into Vesuvio Duo, a Numinal speakeasy hidden in a pocket reality.

The familiar space was the same as always. Green-papered walls, art deco sconces dimly lit, brown leather chairs. A few Numinals who were hunched over their drinks glanced up as he entered. Rune's eyes adjusted quickly, and he took a seat at the bar next to an androgynous Numinal with short spiky white hair.

Rune clapped them on the back. "Pheme. It's good to see you. How long has it been now?"

They ruffled their wings. "Much too long, my friend."

Rune and Pheme exchanged pleasantries before Rune got to the real reason for the meeting. He leaned in close, keeping his voice low. "Someone's been stealing spells and artifacts from Myst's vaults. I think it was Pact. Have you heard anything lately?" Pheme dealt in rumors and secrets, and over the years, had been an asset to Rune when he needed the latest in Numinal gossip.

Pheme shook their head. "Nothing about Pact or Myst, but I'll keep an ear to the ground."

"Thanks."

"But I have heard something about you," they said.

"Whatever it is, it's probably not true," Rune joked.

"Rumor has it you're slated to be this year's Prophecy King."

Rune groaned. "Not this again."

"Not many contenders. You check all the boxes." Pheme shot back their whiskey.

"When will people understand the whole thing is a hoax?"

"It doesn't matter. They believe it's true. Belief is a powerful drug."

Rune rubbed his throbbing temple. The Counter-Prophecy was a conspiracy theory that had, sadly, gotten traction over the years. Its so-called instructions claimed to show how to save the world if the Dark tipped the Light in the Other Realms, triggering the prophecy of end times and the Realm Gates opening once more. The whole thing had grown into a Pizzagate of a myth, taking over the world. Everyone wanted to predict Armageddon and the players involved: a king and queen, meant to perform *hieros gamos* and save the world. Each year, bookies took bets on people's lives. Prediction markets abounded. It was a twisted popularity contest that raised unwilling contenders to the ranks of Numinal celebrities and thrust them into the public spotlight.

But the Counter-Prophecy was most likely a sham. It had impossibilities in it. Every now and then, it roared back to life in the public's consciousness, usually around some celestial event, and with this year's Samhain coinciding with a lunar eclipse near midnight, the story had taken on a life of its own.

Pheme slapped Rune on the back. "People are looking to play, and they have their eyes on you." They leaned in, looking about themselves to make sure no one was paying attention. "Something is going down on Samhain. You've felt it in the air. And with the increase in attacks . . ." Pheme wheezed and coughed. They patted their pocket, took out a little pipe, and took a hit of *ousia*. The crystallized magic stabilized them.

With the Realm Gates closed, true magic from the Other Realms was drying up. With each generation, the magic died out even more. Magic was Numinals' connection to the Numinous. Without magic, they would be cut off forever. They'd waste away, becoming ashes on the wind without it. How long that would take—well, anyone's guess was as good as his. *Ousia* and other ways to imbibe magic were only temporary fixes. Ways to relieve the pain. Until Numinals could create new magic from the Earth Realm, they were all at risk unless the Realm Gates were reopened. And that was looking to be more and more of an impossibility each year, especially as the magic waned.

"I'll keep an eye out. Thanks for the heads-up." Rune checked his watch. Five-thirty. "I've got to run. Let me know if you hear anything about Pact."

"I'll send a smoke signal." Pheme grinned.

As Rune left Vesuvio's, a shadow caught his attention as it disappeared into an alley. He was pretty sure it was the same man he had seen earlier, the one who had been watching him talk to the old woman.

Someone was following him.

He turned back to confront whoever it was and demand some answers, but the man had already slipped away.

Union Square bustled with tourists weaving in and out of stores and restaurants. A wedding party took pictures on the cable car tracks, the groomsmen making goofy faces for the camera in between taking swigs from a flask. Nearby, guerrilla filmmakers videoed a group of skateboarders doing tricks off benches before the cops could stop them. Nadia had a few minutes to spare, and she perused the Halloween window displays at one of the pop-up stores. Several small Numinals had taken up residence in them, posing as part of the scenes. A family of sprites was living in one of the pumpkins, looking like glow lights.

Around San Francisco, the city itself was under the ancient

holiday's claw-tipped thumb. Masked as Halloween, Samhain was slowly taking over the vibe of the city. It didn't help that Pact's viral ad campaign was still loose in the air, adding to the general Halloween atmosphere. Grinning jack-o'-lanterns turned up on the neighborhoods' stoops and walk-ups, cardboard cutouts of witches and black cats and Frankenstein's monster appeared at small businesses, and spiderwebs floated through on the wind, getting caught in buckeye and cypress trees. Restaurants changed their menus and décors to fall, pumpkins, acorns, and nutmeg featured heavily. It seemed all candy-drenched fun and games, a countdown to merriment, mischief, and revelry, but a darker undercurrent wove its sinister web throughout. Samhain's wild energy thrummed, snaking around and infecting the entire city until it was boiling like a frog in a fat black cauldron, realizing too late that its warm bath was not a bath at all.

Nadia was appreciating a Louis Vuitton window display—they had brought back their Circus Halloween theme with harlequin elephants—when Thomas popped into existence next to her.

"I hate when you do that," Nadia grumbled, looking about herself furtively to see if anyone had seen. It didn't look like anyone had, pedestrians continuing on their way down the sidewalk.

"Meeting Christiansen for a training?" Thomas asked.

Nadia narrowed her eyes. "How do you . . . you know what? Never mind." She was pretty sure that Thomas tailed her on a regular basis.

"I know that you are trying to become an initiate in the Order of the Sacred Flame." He motioned to the tattoo on her wrist. "It's not a good idea to bond your magic to his. Lord Mercurio will not like it."

"I don't think it's any of his business," Nadia snapped.

Thomas leaned in conspiratorially. "He's been asking about

you. I haven't told him anything, of course. Like I said, I'm on your side. But I'm just giving you a heads-up. Let you know how I'm looking out for you."

Sure you are, thought Nadia. She had the vague notion that Thomas was stirring up problems. Planting ideas about her in Mercurio's mind. Keeping her—and himself as her handler—as part of Mercurio's inner circle. He liked to pop up every now and then and proclaim how helpful he was being, without Nadia seeing any proof that he wasn't somehow stabbing her in the back.

"You're my hero," said Nadia. "Now, go away. I have a training." She shooed him off.

Thomas waved goodbye, an impish grin on his face, and popped out of existence.

Nadia crossed the street and made her way over to the plaza. Rune sat at the corner of the base of the Nike statue, waiting for her. The monument, a tall column with the goddess of victory at the top holding a trident and a wreath, was covered with a fine dusting of spiderwebs, silvered by twilight. Nadia climbed up the steps and joined him.

"For a minute I thought you meant Nike, the shoe store." Nadia gestured over to the Nike San Francisco on the corner.

Rune grinned. "Nope. I meant the goddess." He stood up and evaluated the darkening sky that threatened rain. "The conditions aren't great, but they will do." A storm hadn't been on the forecast that evening; earlier in the day, it had been beautiful out.

"To pass the second test," said Rune, "you will need an energy source to power the spell to access the subconscious world. In the first test, you used the moon. That was good. But it's not going to be enough. You're going to need to access the energy of the Earth. A ley line should be enough to power you up with energy to cast the spell."

"Can't I use the Numinous itself?" asked Nadia. As a Blood Muse, she had the power to directly tap into the energy of the Numinous and pull from it. It gave her an unlimited source of energy to power spells—or survive a Dark Numinal feeding from her—if she could keep the channel open and constant.

Rune shook his head. "You need to let yourself go to access the subconscious, and you won't be able to sustain a link to the Numinous and let yourself go at the same time.

"Now, the protectors of a location are the loa. They're spirits, and in San Francisco, they guard the ley lines. To access the ley lines, you need their blessing."

"Make friends with the locals," said Nadia. "Got it."

"It is best to give them offerings." Rune gestured to a nearby street vendor selling street tacos. "They like the local food. Are you hungry?"

Rune bought tacos and bags of chips from the man. They each placed a taco at the base of the Nike statue and sat back on a bench to eat the remaining ones.

"What happens now?" asked Nadia.

"We wait," said Rune. They ate in silence, enjoying people watching. Tourists milled about, shopping bags in hand. Pigeons scavenged under bistro tables at nearby outdoor restaurants. Nadia glanced at Rune's profile. It was surprising how easy it was being with him. So natural.

Rune wiped his mouth with a napkin. Nadia tried not to look at his lips and focused instead on her food. Get a grip, Winters, she told herself.

"There are ley lines all over the city," said Rune, "but the major ones connect the seven hills. Once the loa grant you access, the lines will help amplify your power. You can tap into them at will. It will feel different from pulling it from the Numinous . . . It's Earth energy, tied to this planet and realm."

"What does the energy in the Other Realms feel like?"

Rune thought for a minute. "They are different in each realm. Some are more electric, some are more grounded. Why do you ask?"

"You had mentioned that you have been to the Other Realms, and I was just curious."

"Curiosity is a good thing. It keeps you engaged."

Nadia decided to go out on a limb. "Does that mean I can ask you questions?"

"About what?"

"About you."

Rune chuckled. "Why do you want to know about me?"

"I think it's a little crazy that our magic is bonded, and I don't really know anything about you."

The corner of Rune's lip curled up. "Okay. What do you want to know?"

Everything, Nadia thought. "I don't know. What your family is like. What you were like before becoming a Numinal, if you were ever human. What you've done for the last few centuries."

"You want the CliffsNotes version?"

"Sure."

Rune thought a minute and then said, "My parents were human—you would call them Vikings—as I was, before I was turned. My mother was from what is now Turkey and had been captured by raiders and brought back to my village. My father was a warrior. He fell in love with her, and they started a family."

"What were they like?"

"They were good people. Kind. My mother loved the finer things in life—spices from her homeland, jewels, furs. We used to sit around the hearth, and she would tell me stories she had learned from her grandmother, stories about wild djinn and dragons. Numinals"—he gave her a wry smile—"though I didn't know it then. My father was fearsome to some, but I loved him. He taught me to fight. I have some of his weapons still. I was a warrior, like him."

Nadia wasn't surprised. Being a warrior was on-brand for Rune. "How did you become a Numinal?"

Rune threw some chips to gathering pigeons. "That is a story for another day."

Nadia could tell she had hit a nerve. She needed to keep things light. Keep him talking. "How did you start Myst?"

"I started with MystOS, the operating system. I'd tried different ideas before, but they had all failed. I've failed countless times, until one day, I didn't. I grew it from there."

Nadia thought about that. She often felt like a failure. She hoped that one day, she wouldn't. "Are you ever self-conscious about your abilities?"

He shrugged.

"Never?"

"I try to eradicate my weaknesses so I am not vulnerable."

"What makes you vulnerable?"

Something in his eyes flickered, and he smiled slightly. "Beautiful women."

Nadia tried to keep her voice light and breezy. "I've found your Achilles' heel, it seems."

"Don't use it against me." Rune brushed her shoulder with his, and Nadia nearly jumped out of her skin at the contact. He chuckled. "You seem nervous."

"I am nervous."

"It's cute." Rune's smile was teasing, and Nadia blushed despite herself.

An older woman in sneakers and a loud floral-print shirt ambled over to their bench. Nadia scooted closer to Rune so the woman could sit. She took off her shoe and started rubbing her feet.

"You two make a cute couple," said the woman.

Nadia wasn't sure if she should deny that she and Rune were a couple, but Rune graciously accepted the compliment and thanked her. The woman wandered off a little later, babbling on about "young love."

A couple, eh? The world saw them as a couple. The thought gave Nadia a sense of buoyancy and lightness. There was hope after all. She would soon be able to break the Blood Oath and—

There was a shimmer near one of the tacos as a few loa bubbled up.

"Hey, look!" Nadia pointed to the base of the statue.

The loa gathered around Rune's offering and started devouring it with tiny translucent mouths. They refused to touch Nadia's.

She glanced at Rune. "That's not good, is it?"

He frowned. "It looks like they don't accept you as a San Franciscan yet."

"Ah." Well, shit. How was she supposed to convince a bunch of the local energy spirits that she was devout?

When the street taco was gone, the loa bowed in thanks to Rune and disappeared.

"I'm not sure you're going to be ready for the next test as scheduled," said Rune. "And I won't let you try it if you aren't ready. It's too dangerous."

Nadia tried to shrug off her mounting panic. "I'll be ready. This was just a minor setback."

"I wasn't anticipating that they don't accept you as a San Franciscan yet. You really need some practice with ley lines before the second test."

"I'll keep giving them offerings, and I'm sure they will accept me soon."

He frowned. "Okay, but if I think you aren't ready, we will have to push back the test."

"Understood."

Nadia stared at the uneaten offering, sending silent prayers up to the Numinous that everything would work out as it should.

CHAPTER 10

"Knock, knock," Nadia said as she poked her head into Rune's office the next day. He and Carson glanced up from where they sat huddled at Rune's desk. "Should I come back later?" She held out papers for the library audit she was working on to figure out what else, if anything, the thief had taken.

Rune waved her inside, and Nadia took a seat.

"We were talking about Pact's announcement at Numinox," said Rune.

"I debugged the code from the drone," said Carson, "and it looks like the issue is that the spell wasn't compatible with the drone hardware."

"What does that mean?" asked Nadia.

"My energy spells are specifically designed for the intended function," Rune explained. "Like the Psionic. The spells that power it were specifically designed, coded, if you will, with that watch shape and size and functionality in mind."

"Cinderella problem," said Carson. You can't just shove any old foot into a shoe and expect it to fit. Has to be the right foot and the right shoe."

"We need to figure out how my spell ended up being used in the first place," said Rune. "I'm hoping the announcement itself holds a clue." He swiveled his computer monitor to face them and pressed a button. Viral footage from Pact's announcement filled the screen. The images were grainy and pixelated in the low light of the spell, but showed the Halloween creatures moving about, blinking in and out of the picture.

"Sloppy programming," Carson growled. "Rush job. And Jesus Christ!" He gestured at the monitor. "Look at this. Oh god. He's butchered it. This is awful. I can't watch." He didn't turn away, his eyes fixed on the screen.

Rune continued, "Pact does not have in-house developers with Carson's capabilities to do this type of complex design work"—Carson dipped his chin, acknowledging the truth—"so they usually outsource their work. Whoever did the tech work used in Pact's announcement might have more information about how they got my spell. And I'm pretty sure I know who designed this." He typed on his keyboard and pulled up the video from the announcement again, fast forwarding to when a bunch of mummies had materialized. Rune froze the video and zoomed in. A small key-shaped image was embedded on the side of a mummy in its folds and wraps.

"Key," said Carson. "I should have known."

"What's key?" asked Nadia.

"Not what," said Rune. "Who. He's a Septer. A hacker. Runs the Hades Market from his base of operations somewhere in the southern part of Docktown. He always signs his handiwork with that symbol."

"The Hades Market?" asked Nadia.

"It's an online Numinal black market," said Rune. "You can find almost anything on there. *Ousia*, Numinal artifacts, black magic spells."

Mercurio's digital stomping ground. Great.

"There's some weird, dark shit on there, man," said Carson. "I don't freak easily, but some of that stuff is downright freaky."

"And what is Docktown?" asked Nadia. She hated that she knew so little. Why wasn't there a handbook for all this?

"Docktown is a predominantly Numinal underground neighborhood beneath Hunters Point," said Rune. "Carson, you free for an off-site? We can get a drink at Mami Wata's, for old times' sake. See if she knows where we can find Key."

"You know it." Carson stood and stretched. Rune went for his coat, hanging on the hook.

Nadia realized she was about to get left behind. She jumped up and ran to the doorway before Rune could get there, arms outstretched to block him. "I'm going, too."

Rune shrugged on his coat and scowled. "No."

"You're telling me there is a whole underground Numinal neighborhood in San Francisco, and I'm not allowed to go? Get real. I'm coming with you."

If Nadia wanted to break the Blood Oath and escape Mercurio and his weird, freaky sex dreams, the loa would have to accept her. She had to learn everything she could about San Franciscan Numinals and their culture and figure out how to assimilate herself into the community.

In high school, Nadia had been on varsity lacrosse, and while she hadn't been the star of the show (that honorific went to her high school best friend, Rebecca "Legs" Murphy), she made sure she was always on the starting lineup. Lately, she felt like she had benched herself in life. Taken out her own kneecaps. It was time to get back in the game.

"It isn't safe." Rune stared down at her.

Nadia crossed her arms. "There are two of you. I'm sure you can protect one of me."

"She has a point," said Carson. "No one's going to mess with anyone if they're with you." He feigned a right hook. "Pow!"

Rune shook his head, resigned. "Fine. But you will need to

wear this." He magicked a blue cloak out of the air. It shimmered with obscuring spells. She swung it back over her shoulder and swooped it around, clasping the ruby brooch at the throat. It settled around her, the magic a miasma that blurred her figure.

"There aren't many humans in Docktown," Rune explained. "And you tend to draw attention to yourself."

"I'll take that as a compliment," Nadia said.

"As you should," he replied with a wink.

Nadia seriously doubted that Rune was aware of the effect he had on women. One look, one smile from him turned her into jelly. Master-apprentice, boss-employee relationship be dammed. As Nadia followed Rune and Carson down to the vaults, she recited over and over in her mind one of the core contradictory tenets of the Order of the Sacred Flame: *I shall not want that which I cannot have. I can have everything I want.*

"The easiest way there is through the tunnels," explained Rune as he opened the large circular door to Vault Four. The heavy door swung open, and they hopped through into darkness. Rune cast a torchlight and floated it in front of them so they could see. The light sent ghostly shadows flickering along the wet rock sides of the tunnel, rivulets dripping. Rune then cast some sort of protection spell over Nadia with a rapid series of hand movements and incantations—bits of Old Norse and druid magic. The incantation settled into her skin, tight at first like spandex, but then loosening as she moved so that it felt like nothing at all.

"What was that?" Nadia followed the two men as they picked their way through the tunnels.

"It will protect you from radiation," explained Rune.

"Come again?" Nadia sidestepped something gray and icky.

"Docktown sits under the old naval shipyard at Hunters

Point. It's highly contaminated from years of nuclear testing in the area."

"Keeps the humans away," added Carson.

"That's where that giant crane is, right?" Nadia always thought the giant crane looked like something out of *Stargate*. She slid on something slippery and grabbed Carson for support.

"Careful, little lady," said Carson as he righted her.

"The Hunters Point gantry crane," continued Rune, "was at one time the biggest in the world. It was first used as a shipyard crane at the dry docks and then for other purposes like catching missiles in Operation Skycatch. Later, it was used in top-secret experiments to try to open the Realm Gates."

"You're kidding me." Nadia splashed through a puddle. "Wouldn't people notice?"

Carson whistled. "They did. Lots of weird glowing shit in the night sky, big energy bursts that fried electronics in the area. I lost a couple of transmitters to it."

"Sorcerers thought if they could focus enough energy through the crane," said Rune, "using its shape and capacity to move objects, they could use it as a sort of crowbar to wedge open the gates. The crane works as a sort of prism that condenses and amplifies energy."

"Did it work?" asked Nadia.

Rune shook his head. "The Realm Gates can't be opened. People have been trying for hundreds of years. All attempts have failed."

"Doesn't mean it can't happen," Nadia pointed out.

Rune stopped in front of an old sewer pipe. "True. After you." He gestured to the pipe. Nadia stepped up into it, years of graffiti on the wet, dripping concrete sides. Trash and needles floated in the murky water. She tried to pick her way around the puddles, but Rune and Carson had to help her through the worst parts, carrying her across to dry bits of ground. Nadia was glad it wasn't raining. One of those atmospheric rivers would flood the place.

They chatted more about the history of the area as they walked a couple of miles through the labyrinthine tunnel system. Rune had some choice opinions about the government's failure to protect Bayview residents from radiation poisoning, a problem that had spurred Myst into developing cleanup technology. When they reached a fractal graffiti marking, the symbol of the Numinous, sprayed on the side of the concrete wall, Rune stopped. He pressed his palm against the symbol and muttered an incantation. The wall dissolved, revealing another smaller tunnel.

"Move quickly," he said. "The portal only lasts a minute or so."

Nadia grabbed onto the back of his shirt as she stepped over a bunch of rocks and into the passageway.

"Stay close," said Rune as they entered Docktown.

Docktown sprawled beneath the old naval shipyard like a half-sunken pirate utopia, a subterranean neighborhood stacked on itself inside an immense, dimly lit cavern, sporadic natural light pouring down holes in the surface. Wires and rickety rope bridges crossed a maze-like mess of winding streets, narrow alleys, and open-air markets. At its heart sat a massive dry dock, transformed into a gladiatorial arena for fights, bets, and whatever passed for sport among Numinals. Neon banners shimmered next to enchanted plasma screens broadcasting the results of various fights and races, bloodied victors mid-roar. Giant concrete slabs and filled stadium seating floated slowly around the arena, suspended in the air with magic, the cheers of the crowd echoing among thumping hype music. Nadia tried not to gawk.

Despite everything she was learning, large displays of magic still caught her by surprise.

They passed a WW2 bomber plane that had been hollowed out into a curry stand. An elf beckoned them to sit and eat, the smell of exotic spices tempting, but they kept moving. All around them was abandoned military equipment. Rusted-out hulls of naval warships and tanks were piled haphazardly on top of each other and secured with magic, creating rickety, multi-story structures that served as both businesses and homes for Numinals. Strangely enough, there seemed to be a lot of haberdasheries in Docktown.

"You've got a little pep in your step," Rune commented as Nadia took everything in. "It's probably the ambient magic in the air. Gives you a bit of a buzz."

Nadia sidestepped some sort of crawling, green Numinal that looked somewhat like a gecko. "I didn't know a place like this could exist." She tried not to stare at the creature. That would be rude. Above ground, Numinals tried to hide their existence, and many used glamours to blend in. Here in Docktown, they thrived in the open. Hardly anyone had a glamour on. Ogres, elves, and were-creatures walked about freely, going about their day. There also seemed to be numerous types of incorporeal Numinals. Air spirits shaped like whales, jellyfish, and schools of fish drifted under a canopy of bioluminescent mushrooms that shimmered across the top of the cavern like stars in the night sky.

From a hole in the top of the cavern hundreds of feet above them, natural light rained down on a waterfall that poured out of the cliffside. Numinal children frolicked in the pool of water at the bottom, splashing and playing and diving for coins that appeared to tumble from the light. A beautiful, naked Numinal man playing a fiddle—Nadia was pretty sure he was a fossegrim—sat off to the side on a submerged rock. Rune stopped at the pool and threw coins in as an offering.

They turned down a narrow cobblestone alley crisscrossed with wires. Laundry hung out on ropes, drying. Cat-like Numinal creatures with multiple tails darted from shadow to shadow, the scent of fish and smoke heavy in the air. Dirty Fae children followed them, trying to sell human teeth. Rune explained they were the "Tooth Fairy Boys," a street gang of orphans who sold collected baby teeth like Chiclets.

At the end of the alleyway, they reached a small courtyard where a colossal open-mouthed skull sat, water pouring through its single eye socket in a curtain. Moss and wetland plants grew up all around. A crudely painted sign indicated it was The Balor. Nadia glanced at Rune to check if this was their destination. It was like something out of a video game—the next step in the quest.

Nadia followed Carson and Rune over a small wet footbridge into the mouth of the skull.

"Can I take my hood off?" Nadia asked Rune when they entered. He nodded, and Nadia lowered her hood to get a better look at the place.

They were in a poorly lit room carved into the side of a cliff, with a bar made from a broken airplane wing along one side. Upturned barrels, slabs of concrete, and bits of broken metal siding served as makeshift tables and chairs. Sconces cast ghostly patterns along the stone walls. Hunched over their tankards, a few patrons watched Nadia warily. With a start, she recognized two of Mercurio's henchmen, burly blue djinns she'd seen before at Alchemy. They both stared at her, and she quickly flipped her hood back onto her head to obscure her features once more, hoping they hadn't recognized her.

They took a seat at the bar on rickety wooden barstools.

Behind the bar, running the length of it was a fish tank. Nadia prayed Rune couldn't hear how loud her heart was thudding in her chest. Mercurio's guys were right behind her.

The bartender swam over with a splash, her green-and-purple fish tail flipping up and down. A writhing green water snake slid around her neck, wrapping its tail around her bare chest. Bits of shells and shiny metal jewelry adorned her wrists and dark hair.

"Mami Wata," Rune said, addressing the Numinal. She had brilliant, otherworldly purple eyes. Rune bowed his head in respect, pressing his palms together and touching them to his forehead. Nadia and Carson did the same. Nadia risked a glance behind her to see if the djinn were watching her, but they appeared to be engrossed in some sort of dice game.

"Rune Christiansen," said Mami Wata in a thick African accent, nodding back at them in greeting. "I haven't seen you 'round these parts in ages."

"I don't come down to Docktown very often anymore," said Rune. "How have you been?"

The Numinal goddess shrugged a bare shoulder in a sexy, calculated maneuver. The snake around her neck slithered and flicked a forked tongue in and out. Carson seemed enchanted by her presence.

"Carson Ross," she said with a flirtatious wink. "Always a pleasure."

A drop of drool threatened to fall from Carson's lip. Rune kicked him in the leg, and he quickly rolled his tongue back into his mouth.

Mami Wata chuckled and turned back to Rune. "No more fighting for you, eh? Have we seen the last of the Demon Slayer?" She grabbed four shot glasses from a shelf above her and set them down on the bar.

Nadia raised her eyebrows. "The Demon Slayer?"

"That was Rune's nickname when he used to fight," explained Carson. "I told you he was a beast. I made a lot of money off that one match with Chiyou."

Mami Wata gestured to a wall of UFC-like fight posters. They had to have been there at least fifty years, the edges of the papers yellowed and worn. One had a photo of Rune, shirtless with long hair, facing off against a Numinal with four eyes and six arms. Rune's eyes were obsidian, blazing with fury. Nadia almost didn't recognize him. It didn't look like *her* Rune. This Rune was dangerous. Deadly even, simmering with barely contained rage.

Mami Wata poured four shots of rum and raised one. "To the Demon Slayer, may he rise again."

"Those days are long gone." Rune cleared his throat. "Mami Wata—" he began.

"I take it you aren't here to chitchat," she said.

"We were hoping you could help us with something."

Her eyes flicked down to Rune's gold watch. "That's a nice piece you have there."

Rune unclasped his watch and placed it on the bar. She picked up the Rolex, holding it to the light, and nodded her approval at the offering.

"We are looking for a Septer named Key," said Rune. "We were hoping you could find him for us." He flicked his gaze past her to the small hand mirror hanging on the wall among trinkets, tokens, and other gifts she had collected.

"What makes you think I can find him?" She glanced back at the mirror and crossed her arms. The snake raised its head and peered at them with slitted eyes.

"Mami Wata." Rune's voice turned seductive. "You are beautiful beyond measure. Mortals bow down to you. I'm sure you've crossed paths with this Septer once or twice. I'm sure he has made an offering to you at some point in time."

She wagged a finger at Rune. "Tut-tut." But she pulled the mirror down from the wall. "Come to the back."

Mami Wata shifted into human form, her fish tail splitting and morphing into legs. She climbed out of the pool of water behind the bar. Her back to them, she tied a red and white cloth around her hips, knotting it at her side. With the snake still draped around her bare shoulders, she ushered them behind a tarp partition and led them to a small windowless room.

They took seats around an old wooden barrel. Mami Wata placed the mirror in the center. "If he has ever gazed upon the mirror, then I will be able to find him. But the price of using the mirror is that you must gaze upon it now as well, and I will forever be able to find you."

Nadia glanced at Rune. Surely, he wouldn't want someone to be able to permanently locate them, like tagging them with GPS for the rest of their lives?

Rune gave a wry smile. "You know we've gazed upon the mirror before." He gestured between himself and Carson.

She chuckled. "How could I forget?"

Nadia fingered the evil eye amulet hanging around her neck, the feelings of jealousy dissipating.

"That's a lovely piece of jewelry," said Mami Wata.

It seemed like Mami Wata expected her to give it as an offering. Nadia unclasped it from around her neck. Rune frowned slightly. It had been a gift from him to prevent jealousy after a disastrous night at a charity gala. It had worked wonders around the former head of the Foundation, Imogen. But now Imogen was back in Dublin, and Nadia wasn't too keen on letting a Numinal have a permanent tracking and surveillance ability on her face.

Nadia held out the necklace. "I would prefer not to look upon the mirror, if that is okay."

Mami Wata chuckled. "Your toy is keen to make deals, Rune."

"I am not his—" Nadia started.

"Toy," Rune finished. He glanced at Nadia, and she managed to keep the embarrassment from her face.

Mami Wata laughed and pulled the sheer cloth covering the mirror off. She closed her eyes, settling in, and waved a hand over the mirror. She opened one eye, her pupil rolling back and forth between them. "What is his name again?"

"He goes by Key," supplied Carson.

"Key . . . hmmm." She settled back in and took several deep breaths. "I believe I know who it is you want."

Nadia hung back, watching Carson and Rune gaze into the mirror. Shapes began to coalesce and emerge in the glass like shifting fog.

"Is that the end of Ablution Alley?" asked Carson.

"I think so," said Rune. "It looks like he's home right now, so we may have the element of surprise if we move fast."

Ablution Alley was a dark street that wound along a narrow canal in the red-light district. Mice and rats and strange Numinal-animal hybrids chittered in corners, their yellow eyes blinking from the shadows. Signs and ads from defunct stores like Blockbuster's, Mervyn's, and Bebe had been repurposed and hung above pawn shops and nightclubs. Red neon lights lit up windows where sex workers advertised their bodies to the patrons who prowled the cobblestone street. A nymph in a window blew a kiss to Nadia as she passed, and she blew one back, shrugging at Rune's amused glance.

Nadia kept close to Rune and Carson, the hood of her cloak covering her face, as they picked their way along the canal.

Nadia was pretty sure nothing would happen to her—people here seemed friendly enough, and her cloak seemed to repel people from coming too close—but the red-light district of any city was one to be careful in.

A few blocks down, there was a small brick coffee shop where a few patrons sat behind dirty glass windows. Strange, twangy, exotic music came from inside. Above the shop were apartments, the alley below crisscrossed with wires leading to and from windows. A faint buzz of magic and electricity hummed in the air. Carson pointed to a window where a glowing neon Fry's Electronics sign hung, and Rune nodded.

"We need to move fast," said Rune in a low voice. "He'll have wards around the place and will know as soon as they are disarmed. Carson, you watch out for Nadia."

Carson nodded.

They moved around to the back of the building to the exterior stairs on a fire escape. As they started to climb the stairs, they were repelled by wards. There was a slight gonging sound, like an alarm going off. They stopped, and Rune closed his eyes, holding a hand up to feel the wards, his fingers twitching like he was trying numbers on an invisible keypad. The wards dropped. Rune jumped up to the top of the stairs in one tall bound and disappeared inside the building.

Carson swooped an arm under the back of Nadia's knees to carry her. With a low grunt, he jumped up to the top of the stairs in a whoosh like Rune had and set her down. He put a finger to his lips, motioning for her to stay quiet. Nadia nodded.

They quickly made their way inside, Nadia's heart pounding. The building appeared to have been used as a military facility, with mint-green trim painted over weathered concrete. Broken ceiling tiles and typewriters littered a hallway that was crawling with mold and mildew from the damp environment. Drips of water and the scuffling of their footsteps echoed in the silence. Nadia tried not to touch anything and suppressed a cough. She hoped that Rune's protection charm against nuclear radiation also worked for black mold.

Carson kept Nadia behind him as they picked and side-stepped their way around pockets of already-triggered booby traps: clouds of poisoned gas floating in the air, invisible local-ized tornados, magical sinkholes in the floor.

"Looks like he disarmed the place already," Carson whis-pered. He held an arm out to keep Nadia back while he made sure the coast was clear and then pointed to a door.

The door had been blasted open and hung on its hinges. They carefully entered a small apartment. Rune was nowhere to be found, but the window overlooking the alley was open.

The room was barely bigger than a dorm room, with a small kitchenette tucked to one side. Metal shelves covered the walls, cluttered with circuit boards, batteries, and household appli-ances haphazardly mixed with rusted talismans, broken wands, chipped mirrors, and other antiquated Septer supplies. A desk dominated the space, outfitted like a cyberpunk hacker's dream, with giant monitors, computers, and soldering equipment.

Nadia picked up what appeared to be a puzzle box from the desk. Judging by the still-warm welding tools that lay nearby, he had been working on it when they interrupted him.

Scuffling sounds came from outside the window. "I'm sure he'll be back soon," said Carson as he eyed the computers. He cracked his knuckles, leaned over the desk, and started typing on the keyboard. "Password protected. Should take me just a few minutes."

Nadia picked up a notebook from the jumble of electronic equipment and hacker junk. It was filled with random, insane rambling—schizophrenic beat poetry, Cy Twombly-like scribble drawings, arrows leading off one page and squiggling to another. Nonsensical words were boldly circled, and there were pages and pages of numbers and letters, like he had been trying to break a code. Clearly, this guy was nuts.

Rune hopped deftly back in through the window, dragging a thin man by the collar. He deposited the man into the oversized gamer chair.

The man glared at him. He was weirdly pale, like he hadn't seen daylight in eons, with long curly hair and a weird little pedo-stache. One eye was clouded. "You didn't have to accost me on my smoke break."

"My apologies, I thought you were fleeing," said Rune.

"I was." Key slumped down in his chair as if trying to shrink from Rune. "What do you want?"

"You keep information about your customers?" asked Rune.

Key shrugged. "My clientele knows they have my full discretion. They know I won't reveal any information about their identities or the nature of the work."

"Oh, come now," said Rune. "We know you did the work for Pact's Numinox announcement. You left your signature in the code."

Key rolled his eyes. "Okay, you caught me. I did it. Now what? It isn't a crime to take a job."

"What's a crime is how sloppy the coding was," growled Carson. "Don't you have any pride in your work?"

"They wanted it in forty-eight hours. If I had the time, it would have been perfect."

"Did Pact ever mention where they were getting their spells?" asked Rune.

Key picked a piece of lint from his shoulder. "I would get a packet with the instructions and materials at a specified drop point. I never saw the customer. Of course, I put two and two together and knew it was Pact, but we all like to play the anon-ymous game and pretend we don't know who we are working with."

"Where's the drop point?" asked Rune.

"At Odette's. You know the place, in Nob Hill? I would say hello to the girls, get the packet, and leave."

Nadia continued to flip through Key's notebook as Rune questioned him. She turned to a page that contained a scribbled cross, or maybe it was a compass, with two names written at the top of each point. She gasped. At the top of one of the north points was her name, Nadia Winters, next to Rune Christiansen.

Nadia whirled to Rune. "Take a look at this." She handed the notebook to him, open to the page with the compass and their names.

His eyes flicked back and forth over the page. "Why is my name in your book?" he asked slowly.

Key shrugged nonchalantly. "Sometimes I hear things. Numbers, probabilities, patterns. I write them down and decode them. I heard numbers, and your name came out. Lots of names came out." He tilted his ear up slightly like he was picking up reception or hearing voices and eyed Nadia. "Nice to meet a fel-low Septer."

Nadia hadn't met many other Septers. Humans with true magical powers were few and far between. She regarded this one with his uncombed hair and slightly manic energy. Being a Septer didn't seem like a benefit to him. He gave the impression of having a few screws loose, barely functioning at all. She didn't know why her name was in his crazy number book, but whatever the reason, it probably wasn't good.

Rune seemed ready to press further, but Carson interrupted him by swiveling one of Key's laptops toward them, an Excel spreadsheet on the screen. "I'm in. Looks like he takes meticulous notes about his customers."

The spreadsheet listed each client, the job, and the payment amount.

Rune scrolled down to the entries that involved Pact as a client. "The Numinox job, work on The Call . . . did you keep records of the specific spells used?"

Key glared at Carson, seemingly annoyed that he so easily bypassed the security systems. "Maybe."

"All of Myst's spells are tagged on the blockchain," said Rune. "Run me a list of any of our spells that you've used in your engagements."

"What'll you give me in return?"

Rune smiled dangerously. "Your life."

Nadia wasn't sure if he was play-acting or not.

Key swiveled his chair over to the laptop. "Okay, you're the big scary guy. Got it." He ran a report and printed it out. Rune took a quick glance at it and then disappeared it into a pocket reality that he used to carry things.

Carson perused the work that Pact had outsourced to Key. "Remarkable. Just remarkable. This is all basic stuff. I'm surprised they don't have someone to code this."

"They have a few." Key shrugged. "I get a lot of the overflow work."

Rune peered at the list. "It looks like there was an uptick a few months ago in the amount of work Pact was giving you. Is this all because of The Call?"

Key leaned in. "I heard that their programmers refused to implement some of the spells. Too dangerous, or unethical. Something like that. There was some sort of attempted uprising. I don't know the details."

"But you had no problem doing that work, did you?" demanded Rune. "What were the spells? What do they do?"

Key shut his mouth and gestured locking it. "All I can say is . . . read the fine print."

Chapter 11

"And then Rune comes back holding this guy who was a dead ringer for Weird Al," said Carson. "You could tell he hadn't showered in days." He wrinkled up his nose.

They were sitting around the Artemis Room, giving the Veil team a recap of what they had learned about Pact from Key. Nadia sipped her morning coffee, eager for the caffeine. After getting home from Docktown, she had slipped out under the guise of a late-night walk to Union Square and had spent hours, with no luck, trying to make friends with the loa. Marina had commented on the dark circles under her eyes that morning, and Nadia felt like a walking zombie, running on only a few hours of sleep.

Rune pulled up The Call's terms and conditions on the conference room screen and zoomed in. "Pact's early business model was a way to make binding, magical contracts. It's how they got their start and their name."

"Like a Docusign for magic?" asked Nadia.

Rune chuckled. "Something like that. I've warned you all before not to download Pact's app. There were a few instances in the past when Pact used unscrupulous and unethical practices to bind people, unknowingly, to contracts. They supposedly don't do that anymore, but I don't trust them." He scrolled through the legalese. "Key said to read the fine print. I've given this to our lawyers to investigate further, but at first blush, I'm not seeing anything out of the ordinary."

Sophie held up her cell phone. "Pact was robbed last night. It's all over Woven."

Carson ticked off his fingers. "First Kami, and now Pact. Does it say what was taken?"

Sophie shrugged. "It just says confidential information relating to Impact. That could be anything."

Piero adopted his sacred clown persona. "This smells like a PR stunt to me."

"Miles Kirkpatrick did say that all publicity is good publicity after the Numinox announcement," Nadia supplied.

"I wouldn't put it past him to stage something, but all we have now is speculation." Rune glanced down at the meeting agenda. "Okay, next up we have the status report on the battery issue. Where are we on that?"

As Carson gave a quick overview of the current status, Nadia's cell phone vibrated. She picked it up and read a text from Thomas: I'm outside. Mercurio wants to see you.

"Fuck," Nadia murmured.

"Is everything all right, Ms. Winters?" asked Rune.

Nadia glanced up guiltily. The team eyed her with a mixture of boredom and interest. Sophie popped her gum.

Nadia tried to think of an excuse to get out of there. "I, uh, need to use the facilities?"

"Is that a question?" asked Rune.

"No. Statement . . . of fact." Nadia got up quickly and pointed to the door. "I'll be right back."

Thomas sat on a bench outside of Myst's wards, peeling an apple with a knife.

"What's going on?" Nadia asked as she sat next to him. She

glanced about. A few Mystics were within sight, but Thomas was glamoured to be invisible to everyone but her.

"He wants to see you."

"About what?"

"Someone saw you in Docktown. With Christiansen. It somehow angered him. I don't know more than that."

"Great," Nadia mumbled. What use was Thomas if he wasn't going to give her information? "Do I have a choice here? I'm kind of in the middle of work." She checked the time on her Psionic. Rune and the others would notice her absence if she were gone much longer, or they'd think she was doing something weird and unmentionable in the bathroom.

Thomas sliced a piece of apple off and offered it to her on the end of his knife. "You may choose not to go, but I don't think you'll like the consequences."

"For someone who technically isn't on the hook yet as his *slave*, he sure has a lot of demands of me."

"My dear, you are in his high esteem. The rest of us . . . in the gutter." He smiled tightly. "I do enjoy these little exchanges we have." He gestured between the two of them. "The verbal sparring, the 'Will she? Won't she . . . ?' So much fun. Truly. But we both know how this is going to end. You're coming with me. Now." He was right. When Mercurio said jump, Nadia said how high.

"Fine." She shot off a quick email to HR and cc'ed Rune, saying that she wasn't feeling well and was going home to rest, citing vague "human problems." The dirty deed done, she turned back to Thomas. "We're stopping for Philz on the way."

Mercurio's private office at the back of his warehouse was disgustingly opulent and entirely suited to him. Filled with rococo furniture, crystal chandeliers, and exotic furs, both animal and Numinal, the office was also a collector's showroom. Gold Fae crowns, antique scrolls, and preserved mermaid skins gleamed in glass displays illuminated by spotlights around the room. Classical and contemporary nude paintings and photographs, ranging from art to the obscene, hung on crushed-velvet wallpaper. Nadia couldn't tell if Mercurio's taste was cutting edge and hip, or extremely crude and gauche.

Nadia dutifully followed Thomas to Mercurio's desk—an oversize gold-embossed brick—where the vampire lounged with his feet up. His cronies and groupies chatted in clusters, some relaxing on gilded divans, others gathered around hookah-like *ousia* pipes. Mercurio's eyes lit up when he saw her, his fangs descending.

"There you are," he drawled, his hairy tail flicking up behind him. "The witch." Conversation around the room died. The Dark Numinals all eyed her.

The last time Nadia had seen Mercurio, he had almost snapped her neck. The memory flooded through her: his crushing grip on her throat, the fear and panic coursing through her veins, the small bit of power she had knowing that her pain had turned him on. She stood up a little straighter and steeled her nerves. Fake it until you make it. She plastered a big smile on her face. "Thomas said you wanted to see me?"

"You were spotted in Docktown." Mercurio examined a pointed black claw, affecting boredom.

Nadia wasn't sure if he expected a response to that. "I was there," she said finally.

"Were you selling your energy?" Mercurio demanded. "Was Mami Wata brokering a deal?"

"What? No . . ."

"Because I want exclusive rights, if you are."

Nadia cleared her throat. "My energy is not for sale, thank you." She inhaled deeply, forcing herself to stay calm.

His fingers drummed rapidly on the arm of his throne. "Shame. I suppose I will have to wait then."

Until the Blood Oath passed to her—and he could compel her to do whatever he wanted. Nadia swallowed the thought, her throat tight.

Mercurio kicked a leg up onto the armrest and took a sip of Ambrosia. "And how are things at Myst?"

He sure was feeling chatty today. "You told me to infiltrate Myst and get close to the CEO," said Nadia. "I have done so."

Mercurio's eyes, black pinpoints ringed by pale blue, fixed on hers. "And bonded your magic to his, I hear. As his apprentice?" He held her in a relentless stare.

Nadia broke away first. Did Thomas really have to tell Mercurio *everything*? All that bullshit about being on her side . . . She glared at the demon, but he mouthed, "It wasn't me."

Mercurio chuckled. "Christiansen is part of that Order . . . what is it called?" He snapped his fingers, trying to think. "Ah, yes, the Order of the Sacred Flame. A bunch of self-righteous Boy Scouts, if you ask me. Running around like vigilante super-heroes, tasked with protecting humanity, blah blah blah. It is *so* boring."

The Dark Numinals around Mercurio all chuckled politely.

Nadia sucked in a breath. Of course, Mercurio would know about the Order of the Sacred Flame. Why did she think her two worlds—Myst and Mercurio—were separate?

"But they do," Mercurio continued, "hold a rather extensive collection of magical artifacts. Some very powerful spells. And surely lots of arcane knowledge that my clientele would pay top dollar to get their hands on. I commend your initiative, witch. You've set things up for me rather nicely. I wish you all the best in your endeavors. Please let me know if there is anything I can do to help you with your studies."

Nadia smiled tightly. She wanted to tell herself that there was no way in hell that she'd let him use her as a spy again, but who was she kidding? She was powerless and at his mercy. And when the Oath passed to her, then she really would be in trouble.

Might as well swing for the fence, Nadia thought. She cleared her throat. "Actually, there is something you could help me with."

Mercurio seemed a little surprised but delighted she had spoken up, and he sat back to hear her request. "Pray, continue."

Nadia stepped lightly over to his throne. Shakily, she dropped down slowly onto her knees in a sort of supplicating, begging position. "I would like to understand my powers as a Blood Muse better. For you, and for . . . the future. I don't understand them. I don't know how to control them. I am afraid of another . . . incident. If you had any guidance or advice, I would be . . . so appreciative."

Nadia held her breath. Mercurio peered at her kneeling figure with keen interest. She tried to find something to fix her gaze on—not the leering face of a wraith next to her, nor the bulge of fabric covering Mercurio's crotch, and certainly not his glittering gaze. She focused instead on a tassel of one of the gold-and-eggplant-purple throw pillows that he leaned on.

"You have attracted some interest lately," Mercurio said at last. "A few of my more . . . *elite* clientele noticed your reaction at the 'incident' the other evening. They thought it could be indicative of something else, something . . . *prophetic*. There hasn't been a Blood Muse with your kind of power in quite some time."

Nadia kept her face impassive, unsure of where this was going.

Mercurio regarded her. "You aren't like the other pitiable humans I see out there, cluttering the world. You crave excellence. That, I admire. You have initiative. I commend you for wanting to be the finest Blood Muse you can be for me. But to become that will require sacrifice. Are you up for the task?"

Nadia nodded. "Anything," she said, slight Marilyn Monroe breathiness in her voice. Sultry, innocent, playful.

A dark smile played on his lips. He went to a nearby antique desk and rummaged around. "Where did I put that . . . ? Ah, yes, here." The metal tool he pulled out resembled something like a citrus squeezer. "Handy little thing, if I do say so myself. My own invention. I'm patenting it." He approached her, invention in hand. "Exposure therapy. It'll do you wonders."

Nadia's mouth went dry. That thing was a harvester. He wanted to harvest her energy, and she had just willingly agreed to it. "Anything," she had breathed, like a fucking idiot. She could have slapped herself for walking straight into his trap.

But exposure therapy *could* help, she reasoned. It helped people face their fears and deal with trauma and PTSD. And by the look on Mercurio's face, he wasn't going to let her say no. Nadia squared her shoulders and slowly tilted her neck back, exposing her throat. She was ready. She could handle this. Bring it on, she thought.

Mercurio's eyes fixed upon her. She closed her own eyes, unable to look at him, at his devastating features. Deep breaths. She needed to take deep breaths. She dropped into her body, aware of every sensation, every sound. There was a slight buzzing sound near her neck. Her eyes fluttered. Energy left her body, up through her toes, up her legs, through her abdomen, and out through a hole in her aura. She felt herself wobble, polarities threatening to flip.

The buzzing stopped. "We'll start off slow," said Mercurio, his voice a low purr. Nadia opened her eyes. The vampire opened the contraption and pulled out a small vial, shimmering pearl twirling about within. He held it up to the light, admiring it. "Brilliant color on this. Like a prism." He labeled the bottle and tossed it to a nearby nymph, who caught it and dropped it into a basket filled with others.

"Thank you for your contribution," said Mercurio. "Regular donations will only help you master your powers and display your devotion. To me."

Nadia, lightheaded either from the surrealness of the whole experience or the harvesting itself, let herself out.

Chapter 12

Dusk descended over the city. On one of Myst's loner bikes, Nadia pedaled behind Rune as they headed toward Golden Gate Park, navigating through city traffic on the streets. She didn't often bike, scared of being hit by distracted drivers, but Rune had protected them with a magic safety bubble that repelled cars, and Nadia got to relax into the ride and enjoy it.

In the few months that Nadia had been in San Francisco, her experience of the city had changed. While at first everything had seemed scary and new, the people strange and intimidating, Nadia was starting to think of them as her brethren. But the loa still did not accept her as a San Franciscan. She had tried one last-ditch effort, plying them with offerings of Ghirardelli chocolates, but they hadn't taken the bait. To keep her spirits up, Rune had suggested they meet with the White Lady of Blue Heron Lake, who was rumored to have an "in" with the loa and might know what it would take.

As they waited for a red light to turn green, Nadia had the strange craving for Pavés de Genève, this special chocolate truffle from Geneva that her father used to bring home after his travels. A smooth, rich chocolate cube with a hint of hazelnut that melted in her mouth. She hadn't thought of that taste in years. And then, over at the nearby corner store, lo and behold, was an advertisement for Chocolats Rohr in the window! She had thought it was only available in Geneva. She made a note to go back and buy some.

They entered the park and pedaled along the paved roads. Up ahead was the Conservatory of Flowers, an elaborate Victorian greenhouse on a grassy knoll, stark white against the purpling sky. They turned off the road onto a narrow bike trail that led to a picturesque lake, misty fog rolling along the top.

Rune pulled over and parked. "The White Lady lives on Strawberry Hill, there," he said, pointing to a foliage-covered is-land in the middle of the lake.

Nadia pulled up her bike and parked next to him. An owl hooted in the distance. A nice sitting bench was nearby, and they took a seat to wait.

Rune pulled up Myst's dossier on the White Lady on his phone and let Nadia scroll through it. Piero had prepared it; he made one each time they were courting new talent. They'd been in talks for months about bringing the White Lady into Veil and using Strawberry Hill as one of the quest stops. The dossier gave a basic rundown of the Numinal: her skills, areas of expertise, suggested roles in various Myst consulting engagements, as well as ideas for her as a character in Veil. She was a *momokē*, a water spirit from the Cook Islands, who had taken up residence in the lake after immigrating. Her American name was Betty Parker.

Rune checked the time on his watch. "If she's not out in fif-teen minutes, we'll leave. No point in sticking around. She's usually only seen at dusk when it's foggy, and it doesn't look as foggy as it should be."

"What happens if she doesn't show up?" asked Nadia.

"We pivot," replied Rune. "There's always a solution if you think hard enough about it."

They sat in comfortable silence for a bit. The wind rustled

the nearby trees. Thunder rolled ominously in the distance. Fog crept in over the glassy surface of the lake.

"We haven't talked about Key's book," said Nadia at last. In the rush of everything going on with the thefts and Pact, they hadn't a moment to touch base on what the hell was going on with that.

Rune glanced at her. "This is true. We haven't."

"What are we going to do about the fact that our names were in it?"

"Nothing."

"Aren't you concerned?"

"No."

Nadia pressed on. "Well, I'm concerned. I don't think it's a good thing that our names came up in some crazy guy's weird number book."

"Probably not," Rune agreed. "But what would you have me do?"

"I don't know. Care, at the very least!"

"I care."

Nadia was about to argue more with him—*he was* so *frustrating*—but a moaning wail echoed hollowly over the lake. A ghostly figure emerged out of the fog.

Rune stood and waved. "Hello, there! It's Rune Christiansen. From Myst. Do you have a moment?"

The figure on the hill nodded.

Rune and Nadia took the little footbridge over to Strawberry Hill. The White Lady waited for them near the bank of the lake, a pale figure in a long white dress with dark hair. She was more corporeal than Nadia had originally thought. Up close, she didn't really look like a ghost, but Nadia could see how people would make that mistake, especially from a distance.

Rune and the woman exchanged pleasantries. Her voice was surprisingly deep considering how ephemeral she seemed.

"We were actually hoping to get your help with something," said Rune after they had exhausted the small talk.

"If I can help, I will," said the woman.

"Nadia here," said Rune, gesturing to her, "is having trouble with the loa. They aren't accepting her offerings. We were wondering if you had any ideas."

She thought a minute. "You've tried Boudin?"

"Everything," said Nadia. "Mt Tam cheese, fortune cookies, Ghirardelli, fernet, Mission burritos, sushi . . ." She had even chartered a boat out to one of the city's floating islands, hidden magical hot spots in the Bay where magicians could cast bigger magic. She had been sure that an acceptance spell and offering boosted by the hot spot would help when she attempted to offer It's-It ice cream sandwiches. "Nothing's worked."

"The loa are as hard to crack as a *karikao* shell," said the woman. "I think you're going to need to prove yourself. Gifts are not enough. You need to plant roots here. Invest your energy into the earth. The loa will not accept you if they suspect you are transient."

"I fully intend to stay here," said Nadia. She did. Or, at least she thought she did.

"Your mind might say that, but your soul says otherwise," said the White Lady.

Well shit.

Rune frowned at this. "I know you made this island your home . . ."

She nodded. "I suggest she do something similar. Garden, or maybe plant a tree. Or put up some public art. These are just some ideas." Nadia had been hoping there was a quick fix, some sort of charm or spell for this. Planting an entire garden and waiting for it to grow would take forever, and she didn't have the luxury of waiting forever.

"Thank you so much for your time," said Rune. "And we'll be in touch with the paperwork to bring you on."

The woman's eyes clouded over. "'When the pawn becomes queen, the board will turn.'"

Rune startled. He grabbed the woman's arm to steady her as she swayed.

Her eyes cleared. "Great," she said. "I look forward to receiving the contract."

They made their way back over the footbridge to their bikes, Nadia's heart thumping in her chest. That was the third time someone had said that to her! The universe was trying to tell her something, and she was listening.

"That bit about the pawn and the queen . . . is that from something?" asked Nadia. "Like a reference to a poem or a line from a play about chess?"

"It's related to the Prophecy. It's . . . complicated."

Nadia's eyes went wide. "Like, *the* Prophecy? That whole Dark tipping the Light thing?"

Rune hopped back on his bike and gazed up at the stars. "Strange."

"It's just that I've heard that bit about pawns and queens before. Twice." Nadia told him about how both Ananke and the fortune teller at Numinox had repeated the exact same thing to her.

Rune stared at her. "Why didn't you tell me?"

"I didn't know it was relevant information! I didn't know it was about *the* Prophecy. I thought maybe it was a song lyric or a well-known Numinal poem that everyone knows. But now three different people have said that to me, and some weird underground hacker guy is channeling my name with a strange cross or compass or whatever, and I'm a little bit concerned."

Rune sighed. "We need to pay a visit to my friend Rocky."

The following evening, Rune and Nadia zipped over the Golden Gate Bridge in his black McLaren to visit Rocky. The sun sat low and heavy, a yellow slab of butter melting into the blue of the Bay. It was an unusually warm fall night. Rune had put the top down as they left Myst headquarters, driving fast through the city and traffic, his dark aviators reflecting Nadia's laughter and gasps. If he was trying to scare her or get her to value her life, he had succeeded, but she suspected he just loved driving like a maniac and making her scream. When they got to the Golden Gate Bridge, Rune tossed a coin into the glamoured Numinal toll booth—a giant troll head with a wide-open carnival mouth—and the human-driven cars on the road moved magically to the side, giving them a straight shot across the bridge.

Nadia lolled back and let herself have this moment. The wind tossed her hair about, the sunlight warm on her face. She raised a hand up, the wind ribboning between her fingers. The sun's rays sparkled on the water in a fairy dusting of light, as little boats bobbed along on the waves. Nadia turned the music up, summertime lo-fi Tiki beats. Rune put his own hand out the window to feel the air rush through his fingertips when he saw Nadia enjoying herself.

Her cell phone vibrated, and she fished it out of her satchel to check the caller. It was her mother. She sent it to voicemail. She hadn't talked to her family much over the past few months, unable to tell them about her day-to-day. Working at a magical startup wasn't exactly the easiest thing to explain. But despite her silence, they kept calling, trying to check up on her. She made a mental note to send them an email.

After they crossed the bridge, Rune exited the freeway into Sausalito and drove along the seaside town's small streets. Families sat outside old-fashioned ice cream parlors while joggers ran past antique stores and flower shops. Down toward the harbor, ramshackle houseboats lined the shore. Rune pulled over and parked next to a streetlamp.

Nadia opened the car door and stepped out. The houseboats were all eccentric, colorful artist retreats, with potted plants spilling out onto the pier and outdoor lights crisscrossing the path. Rune made his way down the pier, Nadia hurrying to keep up with him. He stopped in front of a dilapidated houseboat.

While the other houseboats all had their whimsical quirks—tulips and vintage ship wheels abounded—this one seemed as if it had been outfitted for a telecom recon mission. Various antennae and satellite dishes stuck out from the flat top of the boat. Power cables snaked in between telescopes and radio receivers. It was heavily warded and glamoured with various charms and spells, patched together like a quilt. African drumming music blasted out from the window.

Rune picked up a navy-blue frog statue sitting outside the boundary of the wards, turned it three times counterclockwise in his palm, and set it back down. The wards dropped, and they walked over a creaky little bridge that connected the pier to the houseboat before the wards went back up again.

Rune knocked on the door.

"Coming, coming!" a man's voice called out. The peephole slat slid open. Two eyes peered at them before it slammed shut and the door opened.

A well-tanned man in his forties wearing a tribal vest, cowboy hat, and aviator sunglasses stood in the doorframe. He ushered them in quickly, looking furtively out the doorway like the neighbors might be watching.

"Rocky, this is Nadia," said Rune as they entered. "Nadia, Rocky. Nadia works in Myst's library and vaults."

"A librarian, eh?" Rocky grinned a big car salesman smile, hands on his hips.

Nadia glanced around the houseboat. The inside was filled with an eclectic jumble of junk. Fishing tackle was propped up in the corner next to mountains of books and magazines and bongo drums. The common area had been turned into a command center with a dozen screens tuned to various broadcasts and news reports. Giant flat-screen computer monitors made a semi-circle around an L-shaped workstation.

"I was just doing a radio broadcast." Rocky clapped his hands together in a prayer-like fashion. "Mind if I finish?"

"Not at all," said Rune.

Rocky jumped into the armchair at his workstation, donned headphones over his cowboy hat, and pulled over a microphone on a boom stick. He pressed a button, and a red "On Air" light came on above him. "We are back, boys and girls, to The Beacon Radio. The last bastion of truth in an increasingly false world. Wake up, Sheeple! Bah! Bah! To wrap up what we've been talking about, all signs point to something happening on Samhain. No, it won't be the big one—I know what y'all are thinking with the eclipse and all, but there is a disturbance in the Force. The demon attacks, the weather. And now, I'm seeing strange patterns in the various markets around the world. Something is up, and it ain't anything good. I'll keep y'all updated as the situation progresses. In the meantime, be vigilant, be truthful, and most of all, be you. Rocky out."

He switched off the "On Air" button and swiveled around to face them.

"Rocky is one of Myst's seers who helps us power MystOS,"

Rune explained to Nadia. "He specializes in using global consciousness to form predictions."

Rocky glanced back at the screens behind him. They all showed news reports from around the world, stock market prices, Top 40 playlists, earthquake and seismic data, weather and astrological maps, and various social media feeds.

"This is where all the magic happens." Rocky kicked his feet—he was wearing pink Crocs—up on the desk.

"How do you read all this?" asked Nadia. Some Sixers had amazing predictive capabilities, but this was next-level.

"It's just intuitive. I look at the data, crunch the numbers, come up with predictions." Rocky pointed to a few of the screens, drawing arrows with his fingers. "I've been focusing on the latest Taylor Swift concert tour as a bellwether. Those Swifties touch everything from weather patterns to the stock market."

"Rocky also happens to be an expert on the Prophecy and the Counter-Prophecy." Rune magicked Key's notebook from somewhere and handed it to Rocky, open to the pertinent pages. Rocky flipped up the clip-on shades attached to his eyewear and adjusted the lenses so that one magically telescoped out like a slinky. He inspected the text. "Who wrote this?" he asked as he scanned the pages.

"Key," replied Rune. "Runs the Hades Market down in Docktown."

"I'm familiar with his work. Mostly seems to pick up on probabilities. Not very accurate as far as predictions because he weighs everything the same, but he sometimes hits gold. He's clairaudient?"

"He said he hears numbers and decodes them," Nadia supplied.

Rocky nodded, his eyes flicking back and forth as he mouthed the numbers and corresponding cipher. He took a couple of pictures of the pages with his phone camera, snapped the notebook shut, and handed it back to Rune. "It would appear that you two are potential players in the Counter-Prophecy. As the Two, the king and queen of the Earth Realm. Rune, of course, has been tagged as the king many a time, but this is the first time I'm seeing a partner."

Nadia glanced at Rune, trying not to scowl. He hadn't mentioned that not only was he familiar with all this, he was intimately involved. As the king, whatever the hell that meant. Nadia seethed. What other bits of information had he withheld from her?

"What does that mean?" Nadia asked, trying to keep the surliness out of her voice. "What's this 'Counter-Prophecy'?"

"How much do you know about *the* Prophecy?" asked Rocky.

"Not much."

"Okay, let's back up," said Rocky as he settled in to tell a story. "Prophecies are predictions. Glorified riddles for the initiated. One of the most famous, well-known prophecies is believed to be about the Myth of the Two Sisters, a Numinal myth about two warring courts in the Other Realms, the Light Court and the Dark Court."

Rune cleared his throat. "Let's stress here that this is all myth. Much of what is in the Other Realms is confined to the land of archetype and myth in the Earth Realm."

Rocky conceded the point. "The Prophecy, true or not, is so dire, so pivotal to the future of Numinals here that it has its own Counter-Prophecy: a way to counteract the Prophecy if it ever were to come true. The problem is ... the Counter-Prophecy is most likely not real. No one knows where it came from. It just appeared one day and spread into everyone's consciousness, mostly through Reddit boards."

"So, this Counter-Prophecy is just ... fake news?" asked Nadia.

"Could be," said Rocky. "An elaborate internet hoax that everyone believes now."

Fucking idiots, thought Nadia. They really were sheeple.

"I consider it to be a viral piece of apocalyptic folklore," Rune added. "There have been stories like this passed down through the ages, time and again."

"And to make matters worse," Rocky continued, "the whole thing has spurred a deluge of so-called 'prophets' who are supposedly channeling linked prophecies. Most are easily discredited, though some like Celextina are considered legit and have amassed quite the following, thanks in large part to OnlyFans."

"How many linked prophecies are there?" Nadia asked.

"Hundreds," said Rocky. "Thousands. I don't know. I only track the trends."

Nadia had a flash of herself doing a Jennifer Lawrence impression and saying, "Can't set down a prophecy without knocking over another prophecy, you know what I mean?" She cringed and, thankfully, stayed silent, hoping Rune hadn't noticed.

Rocky swiveled to his computer screen and pulled up a website that was dedicated to the Counter-Prophecy. The lines of the text scrolled across the top of the site.

When Saturn joins Jupiter and the Moon in the House of Sex and
    Death
And the wheel rounds the eight,
Hell will be unleashed from an open mouth.
When the pawn becomes queen, the board will turn
Two will unite in sacred union to heal the rift.

"This is supposedly a little-known prophecy of Nostradamus,

first included in his 1555 work *Les Prophéties*, but later repressed and erased from human knowledge like all his other Numinal prophecies. But, like I said earlier, we don't know where it came from. I've tracked it to the '80s, to an early online chatroom, but I don't know where it was before that. And whoever wrote this didn't do their homework. Nostradamus wrote his prophecies in quatrains. This has five lines.

"Just for fun," Rocky continued, "let's pretend this *is* real. What does it mean?" He pulled up a star map of the night sky on one of the computer screens. "The Counter-Prophecy is basically thought to be about when the Realm Gates will be opened and how to seal them back up. The House of Sex and Death is the Eighth House in astrology. It rules sex, death, rebirth, transformation, the occult, secrets, taboos, taxes, inheritance. The first line references a point in time, or a window I should say, when Saturn, Jupiter, and the Moon are all in conjunction in that part of the sky. The Saturn-Jupiter conjunction happens every twenty years or so. The problem is that houses are uniquely tied to a person's birth chart. And we don't know whose. Big red flag.

"The second line is generally thought to be about Samhain," Rocky continued, "'when the wheel rounds the eight,' with Samhain being the eighth sabbat of the wheel of the year."

"Every Samhain, someone thinks that it will be *the* Samhain and the Gates will open," added Rune. "But even if the whole thing were true, which I assure you it is not, what the Counter-Prophecy is saying couldn't come true for millennia."

Rocky nodded. "Saturn, Jupiter, and the Moon won't be in conjunction with each other on Samhain for thousands of years.

"The third line," he continued, "is generally believed to be about the Prophecy—the Myth of the Two Sisters. That one little line packs a punch. That whole hell from an open mouth bit covers the war between Light and Dark forces in the Other

Realms, the Dark triumphing over the Light, and the Realm Gates opening once more. A stretch, I know. The fourth line is thought to be about a chosen one, a pawn transforming into a queen, like in chess, to perform the Counter-Prophecy."

Nadia's heart sped up. She tried to remind herself that no, she wasn't the Chosen One. This whole thing was made up. She peered at the text. "What does that last bit mean, 'two will unite in sacred union'?"

"You're familiar with *hieros gamos*?" asked Rocky. "The sacred marriage in alchemy—or, in many Numinal cultures, a ritualistic sex act done by a king and queen to symbolize and promote fertility, crops, and abundance."

"And . . . people think Rune and I could be this king and queen?" asked Nadia. She tried to keep her face impassive like, yeah, this happens every day.

Rune cleared his throat. "The point is that despite none of this being true or even possible, people think it is. It's led to this whole massive predictive gambling scheme. People take bets, make lots of money."

Rocky nodded. "People try to forecast who the pawn is and who the 'Two' are, the king and queen who would have to perform the ritual. Even though the event never comes true, the Realm Gates haven't opened, they mine the collective consciousness for *potential* players. Who *could be* the king and queen, not who *are* the king and queen. They pick a pair every year."

"And the worst part is not just that people are profiting off unwilling contenders like me," said Rune, "it's that they are endangering people."

"Every year, some yahoo who believes in the Counter-Prophecy and doesn't understand how math or the stars work tries to open the Realm Gates on Samhain. It never works and sometimes causes big problems. They are working with dangerous energies they can't control, and people get hurt."

Nadia peered at the screen. "I still don't understand why people are speaking lines of the Counter-Prophecy to me," she said. They explained to Rocky how Nadia had heard the verse with the pawn and the queen three times now.

Rocky's eyes went big. He held up his fingers to make a little window for one eye, peering at Nadia through it. "I think I can see it."

"See what?" demanded Nadia.

"Let's test you." Rocky took out some sort of magical apparatus: a weird pogo stick covered with wires and electrical circuitry. He aimed it at Nadia, arm outstretched like he was shooting a gun, pressed a button, and then pulled it back quickly to read the dials. "Well, you are throwing off major pawn energy. That's for sure."

"Thanks, I guess," Nadia mumbled. She pointed to the text. "It says right here that a pawn will become queen."

Rocky shrugged. "Anything unique or special about you?"

"Uh . . ." Nadia tried to think about anything this guy would consider unique or special. Her resume-building activities like debate club and lacrosse that she had worked so hard to develop in school had little value in a world dripping with magic.

"She's a Blood Muse," Rune offered.

Rocky let out a low whistle. "That'll do it."

Nadia's pulse jumped. "Why? What does that mean?"

Rocky's eyes flicked over her like he was taking various calibrations and measurements on her hair, her face, her magic aura. "I could see it. Everyone loves a good Cinderella story. A Blood Muse pawn turning into the queen. How did you become a Blood Muse? Did someone create you?"

"Create me?" asked Nadia. "No, no, no. I wasn't created. I think it was just a random fluke. My grandmother bound my powers when I was young—it's a long story—but when I broke the chains and learned about magic, it turns out I'm a Blood Muse."

Rocky looked skeptical. "Uh-huh. So, this grandmother bound your powers, and now you're a Blood Muse." He cocked a trigger finger and pulled it like he was shooting a gun. "Boom! That's what happened. That shit backfired. The energy built up threefold and turned back on itself, making you a Blood Muse. You're an ouroboros, eating your own tail. A pawn ouroboros, of course. But an ouroboros, no less."

Nadia gasped and turned to Rune. "Is that even possible?"

Rune shook his head, at a loss. "I can't find fault in the reasoning."

"I could see it all checking out," said Rocky, spreading his fingers in the air like he was visualizing the scene in front of him. "The story of the Blood Muse pawn and how she became a queen, how her grandmother's binding changed her. The Eighth House—the House of Sex and Death—also rules inheritance, bonds, and the things we pay for in our lives that were passed down by our ancestors. The whole thing checks out. I can see why your name is coming up." He swiveled to his computer. "Just for fun . . . when's your birthday?"

Nadia told him, and he plugged it into his algorithm. He peered at the data and cringed. "Nope . . . not you this year. Very low, low probability. Sorry, chica."

A simultaneous sense of relief and sadness washed over Nadia. It had been fun to make-believe she could rise to the ranks of Numinal celebrity, destined to have some sort of cosmic role in a grand, multi-realm prophecy. That she was important and special enough, that she and Rune were fated to be together. But the Counter-Prophecy was a fake, and she was a pawn. End stop.

Rune made noises about having to get back to the city, and he and Nadia returned to the McLaren. Rocky waved goodbye from the front door as he reactivated the wards around his house with a tennis racket.

Rune settled into his seat. "You okay? I'm sure that was a lot to take in."

Nadia climbed in. "I'll be fine."

"Every year, someone throws my name into the hat to be king. You get used to the attention. I have some anti-paparazzi spells that will help keep the tabloids away from you. It'll die out."

"Thanks," said Nadia. "Kind of crazy, though, right?"

"What is?"

Nadia gestured between the two of them. "Us. You know."

Rune chuckled. "Why? Am I too old for you?"

"Shut up," said Nadia. She hated his teasing. "You know what I mean."

Rune pulled away from the curb. "Yeah, I know what you mean. Crazy." He glanced at her, something unreadable flickering in his eyes, before turning back to the road and driving in silence, leaving her alone with her thoughts.

Chapter 13

Nadia floated down a long hallway. Blood-red velvet lined the walls, sconces flaring up, a magnetic pull drawing her in. A door opened, and she was in Mercurio's bed chamber again. Like last time, he was naked and unglamoured. His black forked tongue flicked out and slithered toward her like a tentacle. It wrapped around her wrist, capturing her, and pulled her to him. She fought, trying to free herself, but his tail wrapped around her waist and rubbed between her thighs.

Nadia almost succumbed to the sensation, let herself be devoured by him, but she thought about Rune. She thought about the Order, being a Blood Muse, and the stories of all the women who had come before her.

She could fight this.

"Get out of my mind!" she screamed. Mercurio hissed, fangs out, but she managed to wiggle free. He tried to pull her back, claws trying to grab at her dress and legs, but she ran and ran—

Nadia! Rune mindspoke. *Nadia, wake up!*

With a start, Nadia snapped to. The waking dream dissipated, and Nadia found herself in Myst's gardens. Rune had her by the shoulders. He peered down at her, a concerned look on his face.

"H-how did I get here?" Nadia closed her eyes, trying to shake off the wisps of the awful, awful dream. Last she recalled, she had been in the vaults working.

"I think you were sleepwalking." Rune frowned. "Well, sleep-running, more like it. I haven't seen anything like that before."

Nadia tried to still her racing heart. "I have somnambulism," she lied.

"You should make an appointment with Moon Rabbit," said Rune. "He can mix up an elixir for you to help with that." Moon Rabbit was Myst's on-site herbalist and naturopath; Mystics could see him for all sorts of health issues.

Nadia nodded. "Sure, will do."

Rune led them over to the bench next to the labyrinth. Big leafy plants moved out of the way as Nadia and Rune sat down. He magicked a worn leather book and handed it to her.

"What's this?" she asked, looking at the object in her hands, still dazed from visions of a naked Mercurio haunting her mind.

"One of the books from the collection." Rune turned the book open to a blank page. "There used to be a spell here, a rare, very powerful energy amplification spell, called The Wolf and the Ram."

Nadia fought the urge to throw up.

"It looks like the thief somehow bypassed the security systems and managed to steal this without leaving a trail. There is no log of this being called up in the system."

"H-how could that happen?" Nadia's voice was hollow and small in her ears. She stared at the blank page, remembering the last time she had seen it. She had snapped a picture of it and sent it to Thomas before realizing that the spell only existed with one copy; it disappeared from the book.

"I don't know. It's like they knew where to look." He sounded weary. "Some of these items we have are priceless. Irreplaceable. And extremely dangerous if in the wrong hands. I'm pretty sure this was the spell used by the oni demons when they attacked Myst. I'm running forensics to compare the spell signatures, and I should know for sure later today."

Nadia did not want to think about what would happen if Rune found out she had stolen from Myst and caused the oni break-in. He'd fire her. He'd hate her forever. He'd—

"I know you have your plate full with the upcoming test," he continued, "but I need you to do a complete audit of the collection. Not just what's in the user logs. If there are other missing items, we need to know what they are so we can look for them on the Hades Market and hopefully get them back. Key ought to be able to help with that."

"No problem," said Nadia. "I'll get right on it." She forced a smile. He needed to leave so she could finish her panic attack.

Rune stood. "And do make sure you see Moon Rabbit. Employees are more than welcome to use the nap rooms, but we can't have you running in your sleep all over Myst."

When he had left, Nadia exhaled. *Screwed.* She was so screwed. Now she was having waking dreams of Mercurio? How was he getting past her mental defenses? This was bad. Very, very bad. If she couldn't control herself while dreaming, who knows what she would do?

She could only think of one solution: she needed to start over and rebuild. There was a defect, a crack in her mental fortifications that was letting Mercurio in. She didn't have time to sit and debug it. She needed to bulldoze and start again. But rebuilding would take all afternoon.

She'd better get to it then. Nadia sat for the rest of the afternoon in the gardens and rebuilt her mental wards, one shining brick at a time.

*   *   *

The next morning, as soon as Nadia passed through the wards protecting Marina's house, Thomas appeared, visibly flustered, with bloodshot eyes and rumpled attire.

Nadia stopped short and took out her AirPods, glancing around to make sure the coast was clear and none of the neighbors were watching. "What do you want?" She checked the time on her Psionic smartwatch. If she didn't hurry, she was going to miss her bus. "Walk with me. I don't have time to chitchat."

Thomas fell into step with her. "You need to come with me to Mercurio's. Right now."

No thanks. Memories of a naked Mercurio flooded Nadia's mind, and she tried in vain to squash them out. She flipped her hoodie up over her head as if the fabric could protect her. "No can do, buddy boy. I'm going to be late for work."

"Nadia," Thomas said in a singsong voice, "I don't have time for games."

"Who's playing games?"

His smile tightened. "Listen, Mercurio is demanding your presence. I told him I'd collect you and we'd be back, *tout de suite.*"

"That sounds like a 'you' problem," said Nadia sweetly.

They reached the Muni station at the end of the block. A couple of other passengers stood around fiddling around on phones or listening to music in headphones. A hipster-looking man wearing skinny jeans and a slouchy gray beanie held a coffee.

"Don't make me beg," Thomas pleaded. He followed her gaze to the man's coffee. "Coffee? I can get you a coffee." He walked over to the man and charmed him with his demon magic. With glassy eyes, the man handed his cup to Thomas.

"Ew, gross," said Nadia, shooing it away. "I don't want that guy's used coffee. Give it back."

Thomas grumbled something about "ungrateful humans," but gave it back, a confused expression on the man's face.

"Listen," said Nadia. "I'm not going. Last time I was there, I missed almost an entire day of work. People noticed. Tell him I can come after work." Part of Nadia's workplace training included a module on "managing up," and she was taking those lessons to heart. Boundaries, she thought. It was all about boundaries.

"We don't have time for this." Thomas grabbed her arm, and Nadia was teleported across town, popping into the space in front of Mercurio's warehouse in SoMa.

"Ever heard of consent? You asshole," Nadia hissed at him, her stomach woozy. Folding gave her a queer, disturbing sensation, and it was better if she mentally prepared for it. Surprise folding often ended with her vomiting in the bushes.

Thomas opened a side door to the building and shoved her inside. "Let's go."

Tall aisles of stacked crates and shipping containers towered over Thomas and Nadia as they navigated through the maze-like warehouse. A few pallid demons inventoried boxes and moved things about with forklifts. Mercurio appeared at the end of one of the aisles and strode purposely toward them when he spotted their arrival.

"Goodbye, Drake." Mercurio dismissed Thomas, who disappeared into a shadow. The vampire turned his attention to Nadia, his eyes cold. Nadia took a step back, unsure of what was bothering him. Last time, he had been a lot friendlier. She forced a smile.

He took out the harvester and waved it in her face. He wanted her energy. Of course.

Mercurio brushed Nadia's hair back behind her shoulder, his

fingers lingering a bit too long on her skin, and held the harvester up to her neck. Her energy zigged out of her body, and she squeezed her eyes shut, trying to swallow the rising panic.

"That'll do for now." Mercurio snapped the machine off. "Walk with me." He tossed the harvester to one of his goons and set off on a leisurely stroll through the crates, his hands clasped behind his back. Nadia hesitantly joined him.

"I don't know if you are familiar with my personal history, my dear," he started, "but let me illuminate my humble beginnings for you. You see, my father was a sea merchant, mainly trading with the Orient. Spices, silk, medicines. Trade is in my blood."

Oh gods, he's such a narcissist, she thought. She tried to adopt a serene, interested expression.

"I used to wait for months for my father to return," he continued, "until I was old enough to go with him. He taught me everything he knew—about sailing, commanding a crew, about the sea, and how to navigate difficult waters. But the most important thing he taught me was about loyalty.

"My father had a large crew, hundreds of men. He had to trust each one of them. And he provided for them, gave them food, generous wages. I watched him take care of them, treat them like brothers. Like . . . family. But one day, he realized that his second-in-command was stealing from him. He had trusted this man, saved his back more than once. What was my father to do?"

They stopped in front of a large crate filled with smaller boxes. Mercurio picked up one of the boxes and opened it. It was empty.

Mercurio continued, "These boxes are supposed to be full of elf ears. Fresh ones. As I said, I am"—he pressed his hand against his chest—"but a humble merchant. If I have no goods to sell, how am I supposed to provide for my staff, for my employees?

What kind of merchant am I if I have no wares?" He crushed the box in his fist, splintering the wood with a loud crack, and tossed the broken box to the side.

He stared at Nadia intently, and she shrank under his gaze. "Nadia, my sweet, do you know about supply chains? A supply chain is the entire system and network of people and companies that are involved in the production of goods." Jesus Christ, she thought. Now he was mansplaining economics to her. "Raw materials to finished products. In a chain, there are crucial linkages. If you remove a link, there is a disruption in the connection. You will have what is called a 'supply chain disruption.'" Mercurio abruptly walked away, and Nadia hurried to catch up. She had a sinking feeling this whole conversation was going nowhere good fast.

"One of the crucial members of my team is the supply chain manager," he continued. "He is supposed to be making sure we have enough of everything we need, at all times. I have very demanding customers with extremely particular needs. They pay a lot of money for my services because they know I can deliver on time. I am number one for a reason. But if I do not have the items that my customers require"—he paused for effect—"if someone *takes* them from me and causes a supply chain disruption, then I won't be able to stay on top. I won't be number one. And that is something I *will not* tolerate."

They reached the end of the aisle and entered a large open area in the warehouse. Mercurio had removed his turbo-charged car collection that usually sat there. Instead, the space was filled with a large gallows-like platform. A metal vat sat on open flames, liquid boiling and hissing, hot embers flying out. It was a surreal tableau, medieval torture devices centuries out of place.

A bulky green ogre dragged a blindfolded and handcuffed human man up the side stairs to a platform above the boiling vat. Nadia's stomach tightened. The ogre ripped the blindfold off the man. He blinked in the sudden light and started screaming.

"Please, let me go!" the man begged. "I swear, I don't know anything!"

Nadia flinched when the ogre punched the man in the gut to shut him up.

"This here is Fred," said Mercurio, waving at the ordinary-looking man doubled over in pain. "Fred is responsible for my supply chain logistics. I didn't even know his name until recently. Until I had to learn it to figure out who grandly fucked up and had an entire shipment of elves just . . . disappear."

The ogre raised Fred up and hooked his handcuffs to a rope. A pulley and rope system raised the man into the air, his feet kicking. Fear gripped Nadia by the throat.

"Someone help me!" Fred screamed. "It was the witch! The witch tricked me!"

Nadia's eyes went wide, and she backed away from Mercurio. "I don't know what he's talking about."

Mercurio grabbed her by the shoulders and moved her a few feet until she stood on a glowing square. "Stay here, and do not move." He snapped his fingers. An ogre scurried over carrying a gilded throne chair and placed it a few feet away from her. Mercurio collapsed into it, throwing one leg over the side. A siren sauntered over and handed him a small flute of effervescent Ambrosia, the top of the drink bubbling red. He took a sip.

"Now Nadia, dear, I do not think—no, I *know* you were not involved. You would not be so . . . *foolish* as to double-cross me. As my future Blood Muse, you know better. But another witch did double-cross me, silly creature. And I intend to find out who. Now, over the years, I have learned that witches are like toadstools, popping up here and there, but connected like a . . .

fungus to one another. If I put pressure on one witch, I know the message will be received down the line. And you, my sweet, are shaping up to be quite the interesting specimen. I want you to be my ally. Part of my family." His gaze locked on hers. "Humans are like coal. Most turn to dust under pressure. But some turn to diamond. Which will you be?"

Nadia opened and closed her mouth, unable to answer. He nodded to the executioner, who released the pulley system and lowered Fred into the boiling vat. Fred's screams doubled.

"No! Please! I didn't do anything!" he sobbed.

The bottom of Fred's shoes bubbled and started dripping as the soles melted. The scent of burning meat filled the air.

Nadia stood agape, frozen to the spot on the glowing square. Thomas lurked in the shadows, watching the scene, and she shot him a pleading look to do something, half-convinced this was a trick like before when Mercurio had pretended to torture him, but he merely shrugged, apparently at a loss himself.

"I'll relay the message," begged Nadia. "Please, just release him."

Mercurio threw back his head, laughing, his fangs flashing in the light. "Oh, I cannot do that. What kind of leadership and strength would that show if I just released my prisoners every time a pretty face begged me to do so? When my father found out what his second-in-command did—how he stole from him—he uncovered an entire ring of deception. And he killed each and every one of those traitors. He cut out the rot before it could infect the entire crew."

The executioner continued to lower Fred into the vat, the pulley system squeaking. His screams were met with the hissing of melted flesh until his head slumped over his neck, and he cried out no more. The vat popped and sizzled.

Nadia wanted to throw up. Her breath came in shallow gasps, the world a smear of color. Thomas appeared by her side and grabbed her arm to steady her. Her gaze swiveled and landed on Mercurio.

"I assure you, the effects are only temporary." He grinned evilly at her.

Thomas dragged her away, Nadia unable to walk on her own, Fred's screams echoing in her ears.

Chapter 14

Nadia gasped and shot awake in bed. The remnants of the nightmare—the soles of her feet melting off—clung fiercely to her mind, and she ripped the covers away from her legs and slapped the skin around her ankles as if the fire had been real. Tears streamed down her face, and she sobbed with terror and helplessness until she managed to still her racing heart.

She wiped her face. It was still dark out. The digital clock on her nightstand—blurred through her tears—read 8:88 a.m. *That's not right.* She looked closer: 3:33 a.m. A chill went down her spine. That was the second time that had happened to her.

She wished she knew what it meant.

Nadia couldn't tell if she was manifesting synchronicities or if they were signs from the Numinous. And if they were signs, she couldn't tell if they were warnings or if she was on the right path. But either way, she didn't know how to read them. The language of the Numinous was just beyond her grasp.

Nadia clutched the blankets to her chin and tried to will the memories of the nightmare away. After Mercurio's, she had come home in a complete state of shock and panic and had gone numb, refusing to speak or meet anyone's eyes for hours. Marina and Avery had gone into triage mode to rouse her out of her state: walking her back and forth around the living room, alternating between hot and cold compresses on her meridians and energy points, practically force-feeding her healing tonics and elixirs. Gradually, the trauma started abating until Nadia could tell them what happened. Marina's eyes had gone hard when Nadia told her what Mercurio did to that poor man and how it was a message to other witches.

After Nadia had calmed down enough to listen, Marina explained that Mercurio's choice of torture method was calculated to create the maximum damage to Nadia's psyche. Marina took her hands and said, "Listen to me. Witches for centuries were persecuted and tortured. They were burned at the stake, with their feet going first. The past trauma is ingrained in our collective unconscious. Generational trauma. Seeing that would be horrible for anyone, but Mercurio knew it would especially impact you as a witch, the bastard."

"He needs to be stopped," added Avery. He said it quietly, but Nadia had sensed the anger rolling off him in waves.

Marina shot him a silencing look. "He'll get his comeuppance in due time." Nadia doubted that. Mercurio had been tormenting victims and ruling his empire with an iron fist for centuries. He was practically invincible.

Nadia rose from her bed and drifted toward her mirror, her reflection thin in the silvery light of the moon. Tears threatened to fall, but she twisted up her face in anger instead. *Smack.* She slapped herself across the face. *Stop being a coward. Stop being a baby.* She was letting fate push her around, acting powerless, and playing the victim. If she had learned anything, it was that determination and willpower could move mountains if she wanted them to. She could have anything she wanted in this life or the next. She would become an initiate in the Order before Samhain and cast her Soulwish on that eve, when the veil was thinnest. Nadia couldn't comprehend an existence where she resigned herself to being Mercurio's slave.

But she would never break the Blood Oath if she just lay around feeling sorry for herself. Nadia clicked on the lamp on her nightstand and pulled out Rune's chapbook.

She worked on the drills for the next section: various exercises to bring her brain waves into an alpha state, ways to recognize manifestations that were not her own bleeding into her magic, methods of energy manipulation. They were the basic building blocks that she would have to combine and apply on the fly. They were so familiar by now, Nadia could have done them in her sleep. She repeated them a few more times for good measure, her nightmare forgotten.

Putting the chapbook to the side, Nadia pulled out a leather-bound book she had checked out from Myst's library: an ancient Numinal tome on opening portals titled *Portails et Passerelles: Une Belle Histoire*. Nadia ran her hand over the gold-embossed lettering on the front and opened the book to the title page. Printed in Geneva, in 1749. Goosebumps. There was Geneva, again. She was onto something, the forces aligning.

The ink was faded, the pages yellowed, but Nadia had a passable knowledge of French, and she could pick out the gist of what the text said, though it was rather dense and archaic. She had to look up numerous occult terms in the Psionic's glossary. The text appeared to be a primer on the philosophical concepts and nature of doorways and portals. Portals were spaces of transition and contained a duality: they were both a path and a place. A beginning of one space and the end of another.

Various structures around the world had served as portals at one time or another. Stonehenge in England, the Gateway of the Sun in Peru, and *torii* at various shrines in Japan were all discussed as examples. Something glistened in her consciousness. Words rose to the surface. Another magical text, underneath the one she was reading, burst to the surface. The page was a palimpsest, something written underneath the inked pages. The erased words still held their magical potency.

She concentrated on discerning the words, sensing them with her Sixer powers, feeling them out like she was reading braille. It was a spell. The words formed in her mind. Something was happening, some magic releasing. Patterns and swirls emerged. Vibrations settled into song. Slowly, hovering a few inches from the page, a pinprick in reality opened. One of those teeny-tiny portals that she had heard about before. It looked like a speck of . . . well, nothing. It wasn't black, like she had seen on TV, like what she expected a wormhole or black hole to look like. It was reflective. The sides of space and time warped in on each other like a doughnut.

Nadia gasped. What had she done? She reached out to touch it but snatched her fingers back before they met the void. What if it sucked her in, or worse, turned her inside out? The black hole—or whatever it was—pulsed and started to grow bigger. Now, it was the size of a grapefruit, with blackness in the center. Nadia scrambled back and grabbed the book, paging through wildly for anything that might help. Surely, if there was a spell, there was a counterspell, right?

The portal pulsed again. Something was trying to break through. Fear gripped Nadia by the throat. The portal wobbled again, time slowing, Nadia's heart pounding in her ears. And then, the portal erupted with thousands of winged flying things that swarmed around her like locusts. She swatted them away, crying out. Sharp, gnashing teeth bit at her hair, her ears, and her arms, drawing blood. A few flew at her with stingers out, ready to strike.

Nadia cast a protective shield tight around herself—those stingers were no joke—and grabbed a broomstick from the corner, swinging wildly. She hit one midair, and it fell to the ground.

She squatted down quickly to get a closer look and . . . *what the fuck?* It was only about three inches long, with leathery wings, a woman's skull-like face, and a scorpion's body. Several of the chimera creatures landed on her doorknob and started to twist it open. *Oh gods, they were smart enough to figure out basic mechanics!*

"No!" Nadia lunged at them, but it was too late. The creatures wrestled the door open and took flight into the rest of the house.

"Shit, shit, shit!" Nadia cried as she went after them. Marina and Avery were going to kill her for letting a . . . whatever-the-hell-this-was infestation into the house. The house and grounds were warded against pixies and other winged Numinals who loved to feast on Marina's garden, often leaving nothing but stems after they had mowed through the herbs and flowers. She had no idea what kind of damage these things would do or if their stings were poisonous. She ran downstairs, her footsteps thudding heavily on the creaky wood. The second-floor hallway buzzed with the creatures as they swarmed in drippy bunches on the walls and the ceiling. Avery's bedroom door was completely covered with them as they worked the doorknob.

Avery's bedroom was strictly off-limits. He hadn't needed to tell Nadia that; it was clear he was a secretive person. They didn't have the kind of relationship where she could go in there to borrow something. She had never even been in his room. But the creatures managed to turn the knob and open the door to his bedroom. She ran over to stop them, but it was too late. They swarmed inside.

"Motherfucker," Nadia muttered. She had to go after them. She slipped inside through the swarm and slammed the door behind her. The room was dark. She sensed the creatures flitting to the ceiling, their chittering disappearing into heavy silence. A pungent, earthy smell hit Nadia's nose like she had entered a damp, moss-covered forest. Nadia cast a small ball of witchlight and let her eyes adjust to the dimness.

The entire bedroom was covered in vines and foliage. In the center of the room, hanging from the ceiling, was some sort of Fae nest. An old four-poster bed hung from the ceiling, twisted branches wrapped around the posts and under the bottom of the bed for support. Moss, lichen, and forest wildflowers spread out across the top like a blanket.

Nadia slowly crept toward the bed. The bottom hung about eye level, swaying slightly like something was breathing and moving it. Nadia couldn't find a step stool or ladder. Instead, she gingerly climbed onto a chest of drawers and peered up into the bed.

Avery was sleeping on his back, his face serene and angelic. His wings were splayed out underneath him, propped up in some sort of healing splint. Nadia could sense restorative magic cocooning the bed. She barely had time to register what she was looking at before one of the winged scorpion creatures appeared and slid down the headboard onto Avery's pillow. Avery's dirty-blond hair was splayed out around him, and the creature wove in and out of his hair like it was looking for a place to roost or lay eggs.

Nadia muttered a binding charm, palm outstretched, her fingers twisting into symbols. She lassoed the creature and hogtied it with the charm. Avery's eyes flew open, and he grabbed her wrist.

Their eyes locked. "What are you doing?" Avery demanded, squeezing painfully.

With a shriek, the creature sank its teeth into Avery's cheekbone.

"What the fuck!" he yelled, bounding up. Nadia fell off the chest of drawers and hit the ground with a loud *thump*.

"Get out!" Avery flicked his wrist to magically unlock his bedroom door.

"No!" cried Nadia. But it was too late. The bedroom door flew open. Thousands of the creatures flooded the room and joined the swarm from the ceiling, biting and pinching and stinging. Avery, clad only in boxers, cast a protective shield around himself, a few of the creatures sizzling and falling to the ground as they got caught inside the shield.

"What did you do?" he demanded as the creatures swarmed around the shields, trying to get to them.

Nadia picked herself up off the floor. "It was an accident! I didn't mean to!" Avery's eyes went wide as they entered the hall. The creatures had secreted some sort of substance and were building what appeared to be a hive on the ceiling.

"What in tarnation's name is all this racket?" Marina called up in an old man's voice. Her head appeared as she walked up the stairs. One of the creatures flew into her face, and she screamed, "Aaahhhh!" before almost losing her balance, arms pinwheeling out. She grabbed the banister and glared at Avery and Nadia.

"Don't look at me!" shouted Avery as he cast a protective shield over Marina. He unfurled his wings, grimacing, and fluttered them, beating the creatures away in a wide arc.

"It was an accident! There was a hidden spell in a book I was reading on portals, and one opened!" Nadia zapped the bugs one at a time, little lightning strikes that fried them, the creatures fluttering to the ground dead.

Several of the things slipped into a storage closet, flattening like octopi to get under the door. Nadia grabbed the doorknob and tried to open it, but it was locked. She prepared to zap it open with magic, but Marina pushed her away. "Don't!"

Nadia stumbled back in surprise. "Why?"

"I don't want that door unlocked!" Marina whirled to stand in front of the door, blocking Nadia from it. "Trust me, you don't want to know more."

"Okay, fine! But let's get them out of here!"

It took several hours to round up all the creatures into glass jars and send them back through the portal in Nadia's room. She had wanted to just kill them all, but Avery insisted they save them, a horrified and angry look on his face that she would dare suggest such a thing. "They're Numinals, whatever they are," he had said.

Then, Nadia was forced to figure out how to close the portal. She stumbled through several failed attempts before she managed to reverse the spell just after daybreak. Work was going to be painful with so little sleep, and there was no time to take a quick nap before she was due to meet Thomas for their weekly check-in.

Marina put the kettle on. "You march that book right back to that library and put it back," she said as she poured herself a cup of coffee. "I can't believe that they let anyone just flounce in there"—Nadia rolled her eyes—"and check out whatever they want. That book was dangerous! A random portal just opening up, with no controls . . . It's beyond reckless."

"Anything could have come out," said Avery. "Parts of the Other Realms are so completely unimaginable that it's impossible to know what creatures might emerge from its depths."

"Wait, I thought the Realm Gates were closed," said Nadia. "How did I open a portal to the Other Realms?"

Avery frowned. "I'm not sure that you did. It could have been a pocket reality in the Earth Realm. But those creatures . . . they seemed to be from the Other Realms. Do not—under any circumstances—tell anyone about this. If the Fae knew that a Septer had opened a portal to the Other Realms, one that allowed corporeal entities through . . ." His voice trailed off, and he gave himself a shake. "If anyone knew, Fae or not, they'd be after you."

Nadia covered her face with her hands, hiding from the world and the weight of yet another life surprise.

"Don't worry about the Other Realms," said Marina. "They're a mythical land to Numinals. Some think it's Valhalla, and some think the Boogey Man will get you. But don't go opening up any more portals, got it?"

Dolores Park was surprisingly busy for the early morning. Joggers, people walking their dogs before work, and a few unhoused people passed Nadia as she sat on a bench near the grass waiting for Thomas. She checked the time on her Psionic, knee jiggling in annoyance. She'd be late for work if he didn't get his ass there soon.

She still couldn't believe she had opened a portal. These things weren't supposed to happen. And certainly not to her. A few months ago, the biggest problem in Nadia's life was a shitty boyfriend and worrying about whether or not she felt fulfilled working a customer service job. Accidentally opening a portal and releasing a swarm of flying death scorpions hadn't been on her bingo card this year.

Nadia futzed around with her phone while she waited, browsing various shopping apps for deals, scrolling through her social media feeds, and checking her work email and Slack channels. After a while, Thomas popped into existence next to her on the bench.

"Took you long enough," Nadia grumbled.

"Top o' the morning to you too, my dear," said Thomas, affecting an Irish accent instead of his normal British. "I trust there are no lingering effects of Mercurio's little . . . display the other day?"

Nadia paled. Her hands threatened to shake, but she clasped them together. "All good."

"And how is apprentice training with the esteemed CEO going?" asked Thomas.

"Fine."

He gave her a look of mild annoyance. "Are you sure you want your magic to be tied to his?"

"Why do you care?" Nadia snapped.

Thomas leaned in. "Look, Christiansen has enemies. He's not a good guy. There are lots of people—Numinals and Septers alike—who would rather see him dead. Binding your magic to his would put you in unnecessary danger. I'm just looking out for you."

Sure you are, thought Nadia.

Thomas continued, "Rune isn't what he seems. He pretends he's Mister Nice Guy, some stand-up bloke that cares about everyone, but I know better."

Nadia narrowed her eyes at him. "Do you know him or something?"

"Everyone knows Rune Christiansen." Thomas shrugged. "But I wanted to check in on you." He nudged her with his shoulder playfully. "Come on. What's going on?" Thomas adopted an air of complete devotion and attention to her. "You look awful. Are you not sleeping?"

Nadia side-eyed him. Did he know about Mercurio haunting her sleep? "I don't get you. Why do you serve Mercurio?"

"The same reason you do," he said. "Lord Mercurio rewards loyalty handsomely."

"I serve him because you tricked me," hissed Nadia. "All of this"—she waved her hand about herself—"the Blood Oath, all of it, is your fault."

"Blaming me doesn't change things."

"But it sure as hell makes me feel better." Nadia crossed her arms in a huff.

"Listen, if it hadn't been me, someone else would have found you, eventually. You're lucky I am nice. Not many are. And you should know, I'm here to help you. I know you want to get a Soulwish and use it to break the Blood Oath."

Nadia shot him a look, annoyed that he knew that.

"I don't fault you," said Thomas. "I would do the exact same thing if I were in your shoes. Many have joined the Order just to get a Soulwish. Only the devout stick around. But you need to be careful. If you obsess about something, you could turn into a demon, like I did."

"What, a Blood Oath demon?" Nadia scoffed.

"Often, what you think you are obsessing about is not the actual thing. I don't know what you'd become. But it wouldn't be pretty." He bumped her shoulder again. "And you, Nadia, are pretty."

Nadia tried to decide if he was putting her on. "Thanks, I guess."

"That's why Christiansen *likes* you," he continued. "You remind him of someone."

Nadia frowned. "How do you know that?"

"It's my job to know things." Thomas stood up and stretched. He pulled out a gold pocket watch and checked it for the time.

"All right," said Nadia, "what's going on with the demon attacks around the city? Are the deaths really from over-harvesting, like Mercurio said?"

"That I cannot say."

"I thought you knew everything."

He gave a smile just shy of a smirk. "Just because I know everything doesn't mean you get to."

Later that day, Nadia had an energy healing session with Rune in one of Myst's private workout rooms next to the gym. Rune lay face up on a blue massage table, calming aerial scenes from various tropical islands and coastal towns on the wall-to-ceiling video screens. A soothing soundscape reverberated around them, blending with the sound of waves crashing gently on a beach.

Nadia rubbed her palms together to activate her energy and gently placed her hands on Rune's shoulders. Taking a deep breath, she pushed thoughts of how intimate and weird this was out of her mind and focused on the steady thrum of power coursing through her veins, out through her fingertips, and into him. He had shown her how to keep the flow constant, using her powers as a Blood Muse to pull energy from the Numinous, but she still hadn't figured out quite how to do that without nearly giving herself a hernia. Sweat beaded her brow as she concentrated on keeping the flow steady.

"Stop straining so much," said Rune, his eyes still closed.

"I feel like I'm trying to thread Hoover Dam through the eye of a needle," Nadia gritted out.

Rune chuckled. "Relax. It's like a muscle. Contract, and then release, contract, and then release."

Nadia tried to relax, tried to trust the magic would just do its thing, but it was hard to let go and not force it. Release and surrender were difficult concepts for her.

She moved her hands from Rune's shoulders to his heart chakra in his chest, caressing him with sensual, featherlight touches over his skin and down his muscles. He twitched slightly at the contact. Nadia sucked in a small breath. She hadn't meant to touch him like that, like it was foreplay. It had just . . . happened.

"Sorry," Nadia mumbled. She shook herself slightly. What was wrong with her? *Master, apprentice, master, apprentice.*

Rune's heart energy pulsed under her fingertips. "No need to apologize."

"I didn't mean to . . . you know . . ."

"It's okay. You're still learning."

Yeah, learning how to make a fool of myself, she thought.

They fell back into silence. Seagulls cawed through the sound system, layered over the crash of waves projected onto the LED screen walls.

"How's it going with the loa?" Rune asked after a short while. "Have you thought of a way to build roots here?"

"I started a garden at my grandma's," Nadia lied. She planned to do it. She really did. She just hadn't had the time yet.

"I'm worried that you aren't ready for the second test," he said, his tone gentle. "And it would be exceedingly irresponsible of me to test you and put you in danger if you aren't."

"I'll be ready," she said firmly. She had to be.

"I know that you want to cast your Soulwish on Samhain," said Rune, "but a Soulwish isn't a magic wand to solve all your problems. Often, they cause more problems than they're meant to fix."

"You speak from experience?"

Rune was silent for a moment. "I cast my Soulwish in the depths of despair," he said quietly. "I was in a bad place. And my wish hasn't come true yet. At least, I don't think it has. All it's done is bring me confusion and pain." Rune opened his eyes and abruptly hopped up from the massage table. It was clear he no longer wanted to talk about it. "Your turn."

Nadia climbed onto the table and lay face up, closing her eyes and settling in. Deep, steady breaths, she told herself. The music shifted to darker, faintly tribal beats. Nadia peeked to see that the video montage on the walls had turned to underground volcanic settings: black rocks crested with molten lava, jagged stalactites hanging from cave ceilings, primeval Jurassic forests sticky with life. The music and images in the room were spelled to sync with the caster's disposition, and it seemed Rune found serenity in darker wavelengths.

What had happened with Rune's Soulwish? Nadia had felt his pain, felt the agony in his heart. His confession had been one of the most real and raw things she'd ever heard. She let out the breath she'd been holding. He was sensitive and in touch with his feelings, too? *Why did he have to keep getting so perfect?*

Rune's fingertips gently caressed her shoulders before he slipped his hands under her back. He applied a slight pressure, searching for tension points and skillfully massaging them out. Nadia melted under his touch, turning to jelly. *And he was an expert masseuse?* She was done for.

"As a magician, it is important to have regular bodywork. Energy and magic flow better if there are no maelstroms in their path." He pressed a sore spot, and Nadia relaxed into the sweet pain and release as he worked out a knot.

To say that things with Rune had become more intimate would be an understatement. With their magic bonded and the amount of time they spent together training, it was to be expected they'd become closer, but never in a million years would Nadia have thought this could happen when she had started at Myst: that she'd be on such familiar terms with the CEO. He was impressive. A genius. A visionary. A powerful Numinal, known around the globe in both the human and Numinal worlds. And there he was, giving her a private massage, his fingers expertly and professionally moving over her skin and never lingering long enough to give her pause, though she desperately wished that they would.

After the massage, Rune scanned Nadia's energy for knots, moving his hands over her aura, her body acutely aware of his. She tracked him around the table, her ears burning as she listened for his soft movements. When his hands hovered above her sacral chakra, she involuntarily flexed her pelvic muscles, hoping he didn't notice her body was practically screaming, "Touch me!"

Rune moved on to her heart. He paused, his hands hovering a few inches from her body. "I sense an imbalance here."

"What kind of imbalance?" Nadia asked, her eyes still closed. "I'm not going to implode or something, am I?" Despite Mercurio's exposure therapy, she still thought of herself as a ticking time bomb, about to go off at any moment.

"Not that." His tone was delicate, understanding. "You have an abundance of guilt. It's building up in your heart."

Nadia's blood pressure spiked. Her Psionic pinged. "Oh, just that?" she said jokingly. Mercurio's face popped up in her mind like an evil jack-in-the-box. She tried to keep her face neutral.

"I can't begin to understand the complexities of your personal situation and life and why you might be feeling guilt," Rune started. "Being a Blood Muse is a whole new identity for you to shoulder, one that you did not choose for yourself. I recognize that. I, myself, fought against my Numinal identity for many, many years before I finally came to accept it."

"You were turned against your will?" Nadia asked, surprised. "What happened?"

"Remind me and I'll tell you some day. But the point is that no matter what the cause of this guilt is, you need to figure out how to release it, or it will eat you up and eat up your magic. I can see them—three little smudges, interrupting your flow like rocks in a stream. They weren't there after you passed the first test. You burned away everything that stood between you and the Numinous. These have formed since then."

Nadia thought about telling him everything. Confessing it all: Mercurio, the Blood Oath, how she'd been planted at Myst to get close to him and steal secrets, how she had stolen the spell from the library and had caused the attack on Myst, how the thought of the repercussions of him finding out terrified her. But the weight of her lies hung around her neck, choking off her voice, and she stayed silent. She imagined the guilt in her heart calcifying and hardening, three dark pebbles marring her light. She had the sense it would start spreading like hard coral, and she flinched, scratching and rubbing her chest.

Rune took a step back, and Nadia sat up, suddenly feeling naked and exposed. She clutched her shoulders, holding back tears.

"Hit a raw nerve there," he said. "Why don't we call it a day? Veil meeting this afternoon. I'll send out a calendar invite."

Nadia nodded, unable to meet his eyes.

Chapter 15

"Where are we on the new battery specs?" Rune asked Carson that afternoon at the meeting. Nadia sat at the table with the others from the Veil team. Piero—who had been very vocal that this meeting could have been an email—sat with Sophie poring through social media feeds. Maya had declined the meeting, claiming she was needed in the labs.

Carson hung his head. "We . . . haven't figured it out yet."

Rune frowned.

"But we are really close," Carson continued. "The entropy is still eating the energy at too fast a rate, but I've been working on those possible kinetic workarounds—a self-powering loop. I just haven't been able to grok it yet."

Rune narrowed his eyes at Nadia like she was a puzzle to figure out. She shifted uncomfortably in her seat.

"You need a self-powering loop?" Rune asked. "Like . . . an energy ouroboros?"

"That would be ideal," said Carson. "If I could find one to model after, we'd be set."

Rune wanted her energy. *No, no, no, wait. Let's talk about this first,* Nadia mindspoke to him.

You're not scared, are you? His eyes twinkled.

Of being your lab rat while you run weird tests on me? Why would I be scared of that?

This might help you understand your powers better. Prepare you for the next test.

He had her there. If she wanted to use her Blood Muse powers properly, she needed to understand how they worked. A little bit of her energy would be a practical sacrifice. "I'd be happy to help," she said, forcing a smile.

Myst Labs was always on the verge of exploding. Magical and mundane equipment—boiling cauldrons, alembics, weapons, spinning centrifuges, and flying drones—littered the underground room where employees in white lab coats worked, conducting experiments. Magic puffed and zinged. Lightning flew down from the sky and struck a nearby sandbox; someone was making fulgurite. Nadia spied Maya in front of a large silver tin and headed her way.

Maya looked like she was playing dress-up in lab clothes, her neon rave wear visible under her white coat. She pushed her goggles up, waving a pipette in greeting. "Ahoy!"

"What are you working on?" Nadia asked as she strode over to the tidepool tub filled with sea anemones and starfish.

"I'm helping Diego speed up coral reef growth with an exponential growth spell. It's for that engagement with the Australian government." They had contracted with Myst to help with restoration efforts, part of Myst's push into sustainable solutions for ecosystems around the world. Diego, who could have been a telenovela star in a lab coat, had taken the lead on the project and was pipetting magic into a nearby basin.

Maya smiled and waved at him. He flashed a brilliant, sexy smile before returning to his coral.

"We missed you at the Veil meeting," said Nadia.

Maya rolled her eyes. "I just needed a break from Carson and all his bullshit. He's so needy. Did I tell you he's been leaving me these pathetic voicemails where he's crying and begging forgiveness? I saved them. I'm thinking of using some in a new track I'm working on."

"Nice," said Nadia. "I always appreciate a good revenge track."

"Oh, it's not a revenge track," said Maya. "More like a commentary on the state of masculinity and bro culture."

"Ah," said Nadia. She picked up a pipette and inspected it. "Well, hopefully, bro culture can figure out how my energy works." She explained how they were going to run tests on her to determine the biomechanism by which she channeled energy from her surroundings as a Blood Muse. "Speaking of, I'd better get over there."

"Good luck," said Maya.

Rune and Carson were deep in conversation with a bearded dwarf in a white lab coat at the back of the room. Near them, a strange machine sat on a table, a heavy coil bristling with dials, cords, and cables, all feeding into a row of small humming boxes.

Rune waved her over. "Nadia, this is Artie. He's one of our scientists."

The dwarf reached out and shook her hand. He had a hipster fade haircut, a pointed beard, and he wore a bow tie under his lab coat. Gold-rimmed spectacles completed the look. "Boy, are we excited to meet you, Nadia. We've been running simulated tests on Kevin here"—he gestured to Kevin, who lay in a nearby beanbag chair with a Nintendo Switch—"but now with a real, live Blood Muse, we can really map out the loop and finally solve this battery issue for good."

"Happy to help. What is this thing?" Nadia pointed to the coil machine.

"It's a crystal set," said Rune as they gathered around the table. "We use them in energy experiments. Right now, the world's energy resources are being depleted. Fossil fuels are running out.

We're working on ways to harness alternative sources of energy. The battery system in the Veil plugin stems from this."

"We've been working on various sources," added Artie, "kinetic, thermal, wind. But the most abundant source of energy is cosmic energy, the energy of the Numinous. It's all around us, radiating throughout the universe. If we could find a way to tap into that and harness it, we could solve mankind's energy problem. We could have unlimited energy."

"Now, we do a lot of experiments related to collective consciousness," said Rune. "The 'hive mind,' so to speak. As you know, nerve impulses in the human brain are electrical energy signals that create energy fields around the body."

Nadia knew where this was going. "So, you want to use humans as electrical generators to harness cosmic energy or whatever?"

"Precisely," Rune said.

A slight thrill ran down Nadia's spine. She could be the reason Rune solved mankind's energy problems! Her: Nadia … a savior. Well, not quite. Rune would be the savior. But she could be a muse. His muse …

"As a Blood Muse," Rune continued, snapping her back to reality, "you can act as a conduit for the energy around you. Your energy cycles like an ouroboros, feeding on itself as it pulls from the Numinous. We're going to run some tests. If we can pinpoint the biomechanism that allows you to pull energy from your surroundings, then Carson can model it in code, and we can understand how you do what you do."

"Sounds good," said Nadia. "Where do you want me?"

Artie motioned to a mess of little sensors nearby. Nadia held out her arms as Rune and Artie placed sticky nodes all over her body.

"We will start with taking some measurements," said Artie as he peeled off the backing on a sticky and placed it on Nadia's wrist. "Then see what sort of energy signals we can read from your body. We'll measure heart rate, vitals, and energy levels. Once we discover the general mechanism, we can run some tests to pinpoint it, and Carson will translate it into his program to map it out."

"Reverse engineering," called out Carson, his head buried in a laptop.

They got to work. Artie, Rune, and Carson took a seat at the workstation where an army of laptops and computers stood, ready to capture the data. Deep breaths, she told herself. She could do this. When they were about to start, Rune gave her a thumbs-up, and she gave him one back. Carson initiated systems go. A slight tingling sensation spread through her, a heightened awareness of her body and energy as the sensors captured the data.

"How's it going?" Rune called over.

"I'm fine!" she called back. A wave rolled through her, but she took a deep breath, centered herself, and the nausea passed. They were doing something to her energy, manipulating it somehow, a slight push and pull of calibration that sent waves through her flesh.

Rune was glued to the screens. He pointed at something. "See there? That's the quadrant. Just hold on a few more minutes," he called out to her. "Artie's almost pinpointed the mechanism."

Nadia took deep breaths, settling into her body. She closed her eyes, rolled her head around on her neck, and stretched.

"There she is," called out Artie. "And . . . got it."

Nadia's eyes fluttered open.

Carson's fingers flew over the keyboard. "Initiating capture system." He grinned. "I've always wanted to say that."

"Okay, Nadia," called out Artie, "we are going to simulate a demon feeding from you—"

"Wait, what?" she cried. This had *not* been disclosed up front.

"We need to see how your body keeps the energy levels constant," Rune called out. "The crystal set will absorb your energy, similar to a feeding. Just . . . walk toward it. We're monitoring your levels, and if anything is off, we will shut everything down immediately, okay?"

Oh hell no. Nadia put on a smile and nodded agreeably. "Got it!"

The crystal set sprang to life, buzzing. Deep breaths. It's just a machine, she thought. Nothing scary about machines, right? She walked toward it, the wires from the nodes connecting her body to the machine looping in on themselves and nearly tripping her. Jesus, this thing was a death trap. There were safety issues all over the place—definitely not OSHA compliant. As Nadia neared the machine, the familiar feeling of her energy being depleted from her body sprang to life. She wobbled for a second, woozy.

"You okay?" Rune called out. "Your levels dipped, but you're back up."

She fought down nausea and panic. "I'm okay." She took a few more tentative steps toward the crystal set. Her energy was being sucked away, but it was being replenished at a constant rate. So far, so good, she thought. No death yet.

"Okay, got the first part," said Carson.

Rune's face glowed from excitement. "Okay, Nadia," he called out, "we've got phase one. We've pinpointed and captured the mechanism by which you replenish your energy wells. Now, phase two. We want to capture the reverse of that, to see if you can act like a battery and power something else." Rune pointed to a screen next to the crystal set, covered in hundreds of tiny

LED lights. "See if you can send that energy back out and light up the screen."

She nodded that she understood.

"And . . . go!" Carson called out.

Nadia imagined the energy zapping through her arm and out toward the screen like a bolt of lightning. The LED lights on the screen flickered, and she held her breath, thinking she had done it. Her arm sagged, suddenly tired. Nadia felt overextended, sluggish, her wells starting to dry up. Her lizard brain kicked in, and she felt something in her flip upside down and inside out, pulling the energy back into her body in a survival response. The influx of energy overwhelmed the system, and she detonated like a bomb.

Everything went silent. Time slowed. In a blinding flash, the room erupted with the smell of ozone. The energy around her disappeared into a vacuum. She flew backward in an arc through the air, her feet leaving the ground. Rune moved with preternatural speed to catch her, and she thudded hard against his chest, her teeth clacking painfully in her mouth. He wrapped his muscled arm around her and cradled her into his body as they landed hard on the ground. He quickly cast a protective shield around them, covering her body with his to protect her from the blast.

Nadia lay stunned for several moments, breathing heavily. Rune lay on top of her, heavy and solid, his arms and legs wrapped around her like he never wanted to let her go.

"I can't breathe," Nadia panted after a minute. He loosened his grip. She squirmed around under him until they were face-to-face. "You're going to have to get off me, or you're really going to have an injured Septer on your hands. You have to be, like, double my weight. Seriously, dude? I'm dying over here."

The corner of his mouth turned up. "She almost kills us. And all I get is attitude." His voice was teasing, but there was that flicker in his eyes again.

They were so close, Nadia could taste the minty warmth of his breath. Her lips parted, their eyes locked on each other. For a breathless instant, she thought he might kiss her.

"Nadia!" Maya cried out as she rushed over, interrupting their moment. Rune released Nadia, and they gingerly sat up.

Artie and Carson leaped over the upturned tables.

"Is everyone okay?" Artie's eyes were wild.

"I think so." Rune rubbed the shoulder he landed on, maneuvering the muscles in circles.

Maya lunged at Nadia, placing a hand on either side of her face, and patted her down, assuring herself that Nadia was in one piece. "Thank the Light you're okay. Nadia! I was so scared." Maya picked the nodes off Nadia's body. "Let's get these things off you." She scowled at Carson. "What kind of experiment was this? You could have killed her!"

It looked like a hurricane had come through the room. The crystal set lay shattered, the room a wreck of overturned tables, splintered chairs, and broken equipment.

Carson's eyes blazed, his hands furry, his ears pointed. He needed to shift soon, the excitement making him lose control over his glamour and magic. "We got it. We got the mechanism." He shuddered, a pulse of energy running through him. He cracked his neck. "Sorry, I, uh—" He gave a sheepish look.

Rune nodded. "We're fine. Go."

Overexcited by the experiment's results, Carson tore through the lab as he started shifting into his wolf form, shedding clothes as he went. The others in the lab cautiously emerged from where they had ducked behind tables and supply cabinets, hiding from the blast.

Maya helped Nadia to her feet and turned to Rune, a defiant look on her face. "Permission to take Nadia to the healing baths for the rest of the day?"

Chapter 16

"A girl could get used to this," said Nadia as she soaked naked in one of Myst's magical healing tubs, a giant barrel that easily could have fit twenty. Maya lolled across from her, cucumber slices on her eyes. Steam rose around them as *miengus*, African mermaid-like water deities, poured scented oils from alabastrons. The deities sang healing songs as they worked, calibrating Nadia's and Maya's energy levels with strong vocal magic, their voices echoing throughout the Roman-style bath.

When Nadia had started at Myst, she knew there would be benefits, but she hadn't explored the extent of what the startup offered. Each employee was allowed ten full spa days per year and accrued wellness points that could be used on massages, herbal treatments, energy healing, and chakra rebalancing. Most of the wellness treatments focused on Numinal health, but a fair amount were beneficial to humans, as well. Nadia vowed to look back through the employee handbook that Vega had given her when she started to make sure she wasn't missing out on anything else.

Maya stood up, water running down her body. "I'm too hot," said Maya. "Let's go to the mud baths."

She and Nadia headed to the neighboring vat. A miengu wrapped a towel around Maya's dreadlocks and another around Nadia's ponytail before they sank into the dense blue mud bath.

"Did you see Carson start to go all wolf in the labs?" asked Nadia.

Maya snorted. "He can't control himself when he gets excited about code."

"He's totally jealous of you working with Diego."

"Good."

A miengu placed cucumbers on Nadia's eyes. She leaned back, enjoying the slight tingling sensation of the blue mud. The mud was magically enhanced to buff, hydrate, and smooth skin.

"How are you feeling?" asked Maya. "Better?"

It had taken Nadia a good twenty minutes to stop shaking after the explosion in the labs.

"I'm fine. Really."

"Rune looked so concerned. He totally thought he broke you."

"I think he was worried I'd file a workplace injury suit," Nadia said lightly. Rune had seemed concerned, though, his brows knitting together as he scanned her body for both physical and psychic damage. The almost-kiss lingered in her mind, but she decided she'd made it up, letting her imagination get the best of her.

Maya's watch pinged, and she glanced at it. "Hey, do you want to watch the Women in Tech keynote? It's about to start."

"Sure."

Maya waved over a miengu. "Solange, would you mind turning the screen there to pairing mode?"

The miengu pressed a button on the wall, and one of the LED screen walls of the baths, usually depicting calming nature scenes, switched to black. Maya pulled up the keynote on her phone and Bluetoothed it onto the screen.

Diane Robbins stood at a podium, addressing a packed auditorium.

"Is that the CFO of Pact?" Nadia asked. She had previously met the woman at a charity event.

Maya nodded. "I hate Pact, but I have to admit that the woman is impressive and knows her shit. When she got to Pact, it was nearly failing, but she turned it around."

Diane smiled at the audience, throwing off distinct Michelle Pfeiffer vibes in a blue pantsuit and blouse with a blonde blowout.

"—most important thing I've learned from my time working in this industry," Diane said, "is that the relationships you make are key to your career. And as women, we often are not afforded the same networking opportunities as men. Deals are closed over golf or in men's clubs. How many of you have turned down drinks after work because you had to go home to your family? How many of you have lost out on opportunities due to not being even invited in the first place? Women need to support each other, create networks of women, and share opportunities. Younger women, the leaders of tomorrow, need to find opportunities to learn from their elders. Mentors need to teach what they have learned from their struggles to the younger generation so that their hardships weren't in vain. We need to stop tearing each other down and instead, work to build each other up!"

Maya took the restorative fizzy drink that Solange handed to her, nodding in thanks, and turned the volume down on the TV so they could chat. "She says something similar in her book. It's all Sisterhood propaganda."

"She wrote a book?"

"It's supposed to be the next *Lean In*. I haven't read it."

Solange handed Nadia a drink as well. "Thanks, Solange." She was trying to do better with names. "What do you know about the Sisterhood?" she asked Maya. "Meredith Vincent told me I was 'goddess-blessed.'"

Maya rolled her eyes. "She told me the same thing. I think she's told half the female employees here that."

"Why's she trying to recruit everyone?"

Maya took a sip of her drink and made a face at the taste. "My understanding is that it's a little like an MLM scheme. The more people each Sister brings in, the more power and standing they get in the group. They want to have the female leaders of tomorrow loyal to their cause. They use their influence to help their own get ahead in life, stacking the ranks of corporations and boards of directors, politics, and the arts with loyal converts. I went to a recruitment event once. It wasn't for me."

"Why's that?"

"They were hosting a comet watch party. It was pretty fancy. Black tux shit. They'd rented out the Palace of Fine Arts, and there were these model-looking guys serving cocoa with marshmallows and sprinkles. Like, each looked like a friggin' Abercrombie model. And they had these insanely powerful telescopes that let you practically see the space dust from the comet. It was pretty awesome, to be honest. But they started to get all woo-woo about the Goddess on me, talking about personal connections and signs from the Numinous and all that crap. After I had my cocoa and saw the comet, rubbed elbows with some people, I left." Maya shrugged. "Didn't stay for the attunement ritual. I don't believe there is some super goddess out there"—she made woo fingers in the air—"in the ether watching out for women and helping them out when they pray to her."

"Yeah, that would be crazy, right?" Nadia laughed along with Maya, though the idea of a super goddess sounded kind of nice. Like all the goddesses rolled into one. "But the Sisterhood believes that?"

Maya nodded. "Yeah. They're true believers. Some even claim to hear Her voice. The voice of the Capital G Goddess. They act in Her name. Do anything to advance their cause, things that she *tells* them to do. Their devotion is unmatched. It's scary when you meet people who are such avid believers in something that's so markedly untrue. You wonder what reality they've been living in."

"They're not, like, kidnapping people or doing weird sacrifices, are they?" asked Nadia. She didn't want to get wrapped up in a cult if she could avoid it.

"It wouldn't surprise me," Maya said. "They're kind of like the female version of the Bohemian Club."

The rest of the keynote rehashed the same points about women supporting women. Nadia had to admit that Diane Robbins seemed like a great role model. Successful on her own terms, navigating the corporate and tech world, raising the profile of others. When Nadia had first met her, she had seemed cold and condescending, full of microaggressions. She hadn't seemed like this warm persona on the screen, akin to a favorite aunt, one who had aged gracefully with the help of lots of Botox and a regimented skin routine.

What else had she gotten wrong on first impression? The Numinal world wasn't what it was before to Nadia. When she had first arrived in San Francisco, the city had been overwhelming, magic and Numinals visible and abundant. But she had assimilated, bit by tiny bit, into the community and culture. She was starting to see the people as her people, the city as her city. The tiniest roots had sprouted, mycelium on a witch's toadstool. There was hope for her yet.

When Nadia got home, Marina and Avery were outside in the garden, doing something with the giant iron cauldron they kept in a gravel clearing. Avery held maracas and was keeping beat as he and her grandmother chanted menacingly, Marina chucking dried herbs into the iron pot.

"What's going on?" asked Nadia as she took a seat on a tree stump to watch.

"We're cursing City Hall," said Marina.

"What'd they do now?" asked Nadia. Marina often took out her frustration with government inefficiency and incompetence by lobbing curses at them. The parking division received the brunt of the attacks.

"Did you know you need a business license to operate a home business?" Marina huffed.

"The Tambourine Lady got fined by the city," explained Avery. "Might have to go to court."

"Sucks," said Nadia.

"Misdemeanor, my ass," grumbled Marina. She grabbed another handful of dried plants from the bags on the nearby wooden picnic table and threw them in. "Staggerweed should do the trick."

"What's staggerweed do?" asked Nadia.

"General, all-purpose curse and banishment weed. Inspector Kim better think twice about coming 'round here again."

"Aren't you worried about karma?" asked Nadia. What you put out into the world was supposed to come back to you three-fold.

Marina's eyes flashed. "I'm the one who was wronged here. I'm providing a valuable service to the community. These stupid laws don't apply to me."

Nadia didn't argue. It was pointless to disagree with Marina, especially when it came to whether she was answerable to the law or not. To Marina, rules were arbitrary and meant to be broken. Nadia wished she had the same freewheeling view of morality.

Are you free tonight? Rune mindspoke.

Nadia startled at the sound of his voice in her mind and nearly fell off the stump.

Avery glanced at her like she was a mental case.

Um, let me check, she mindspoke back.

"We aren't doing anything tonight, are we?" asked Nadia.

"Not unless you want to get in on this curse action," said Marina. "I'm making plenty. Anyone you want to curse? Mercurio?"

Tempting. But Nadia didn't want any other ties to him, and cursing tended to build a psychic connection. It was probably why Marina kept getting so many parking tickets. Like attracts like.

"Thanks, but maybe some other time," said Nadia. "I'm trying not to hex anyone, even if they deserve it."

"Suit yourself." Marina threw a handful of something into the pot, noxious blue fumes wafting up as the concoction crackled and sizzled.

I'm free tonight, Nadia mindspoke to Rune. *What's going on?*

I've been thinking about your ... predicament, after what happened in the labs today. I think I know someone who can help. I'll pick you up in twenty.

Chapter 17

The gray sky threatened rain as Rune pulled his McLaren over to the curb.

"This place is a tearoom?" Nadia asked, peering out the car window at the stately Victorian boarding house off Fillmore. In the distance, thunder rumbled.

"It's one of Myst's projects. You'll see." Rune grinned as he opened the car door and got out.

After Rune picked her up from Marina's house, he explained that the data from the experiment in the labs showed that when Nadia's energy was harvested, it caused a panic attack that started a chain reaction and ended with the magical equivalent of a bomb going off. Rune assured Nadia that the woman they were going to see in Japantown, apparently named Aiko, could help Nadia control that panic response.

As they headed up the front steps to the door, fat raindrops fell from the sky. Nadia held her purse over her head to protect her hair. "I wasn't expecting rain today."

Rune glanced up at the sky. "It wasn't on the forecast."

Nadia knew what that meant: dark forces were aligning, impacting the weather, the countdown to Samhain ticking.

He rang the bell at the door. The pings echoed around them. Nadia shifted from one foot to the other. Her nervousness was hard to hide.

Rune glanced down and gave her a comforting smile. "It will all be okay, I promise."

The door opened. A beautiful blonde nymph dressed in a nude slip dress answered. Her makeup-free face lit up when she saw Rune. "How good to see you again," she said warmly.

"Cora, this is my assistant, Nadia." Rune gestured toward her.

Cora smiled and opened the door wider. "Please, do come in. Aiko is expecting you."

They followed the nymph into an elegant parlor, decorated with antique Japanese pieces from the Edo period mixed with contemporary furniture. Cora chatted pleasantly about the newest additions to the collection, and Nadia had to suppress her inner art history nerd who wanted to inspect everything: Samurai swords, hand-painted vases and teapots, woodblock printings. Cora gestured to a door partially covered by a beige-and-gold hanging tapestry that depicted various scenes from Japanese folktales.

"I know my way around, thanks, Cora," said Rune.

The woman dipped her head and left.

"Where are we going?" Nadia asked.

"To the Floating World," said Rune as he held back the tapestry and performed a series of incantations at the lock. It opened like he had produced a key, swinging back into the dark. Rune snapped his fingers, and a torch hanging on the side of the space burst into flame, and then another and then another, revealing a narrow, curved concrete tunnel.

Rune grabbed the torch. "Under Japantown is a massive cavern and tunnel system that we're turning into a Numinal community space. It'll be an artistic interpretation of the Edo Floating World. Teahouses, geisha, Kabuki theater, various sensory experiences. Many Numinals hail from that era, and we anticipate a great demand for entertainment that reminds them of it."

Nadia stepped after Rune into the tunnel. "It sounds like an amusement park."

"More like an interactive art installation that people live in."

"And this Aiko designed it?"

Rune nodded. "She is a brilliant artist and visionary."

After walking for a few minutes, the tunnel system promptly spat them out in front of an Edo-era tearoom, still under construction. Some of the walls had been erected, but others were only half-completed, parts held together with loose magic that sparkled like spiderwebs in the dusk. Rune knocked on the door and slid it open.

A woman rose from a sitting area where she had been working with a laptop. She was Japanese, dressed in a classy knee-length skirt and a wrapped silk top with kimono-like details. Her glossy dark hair fell straight like a waterfall down her back.

"Rune," she said, smiling. He kissed her on the cheek in greeting.

"Aiko, this is my assistant, Nadia," said Rune.

Nadia stepped forward.

The woman clasped her hand warmly with both of hers.

"Please, take a seat," said Aiko. "I was so happy to hear you wanted to come inspect the progress on our little project."

"I thought Nadia might want a tour of the Floating World," said Rune.

They took a seat around a low coffee table. The woman typed a few keystrokes on her laptop and laid it flat, pulling both halves down so that it became a tablet. A purple 3D hologram of a city projected out from a pinpoint on the screen.

"This is the Floating World, as it will be," said Aiko. The 3D model rotated slowly.

Nadia leaned in. "That's amazing."

"The space will be augmented with both magic and tech,"

explained Rune. "It's the same 3D overlay system we use in Veil, but on a much larger scale. Parts will be pure simulation, but all the senses will tell you otherwise, even touch."

"Do you want a closer look?" asked Aiko.

"Absolutely."

Aiko hit a button, and the hologram expanded, growing larger until it surpassed the size of the tearoom and enveloped them. Nadia felt a rush as the magic overtook her senses, a *whoosh* as her mind tried to keep up with what was happening, a blur of color and light, and then suddenly they were back, sitting where they had been in the tearoom.

"It's a sensory spell." Rune stood up. "It's like being inside a memory. We are physically still sitting where we were, but our minds are detached from our bodies and allow us to roam inside the model."

Nadia made a fist and then released it. She had the vague sense of detachment from her physical body, but she could feel a faint pull from an attached tether.

"The tearoom serves as the cornerstone to anchor the space," Rune continued. The three of them went out to the cobblestone street. "It's the only space that's been built out so far, but someday everything you see here will be reality."

They strolled down the winding street past little wooden buildings and footbridges that arched over bubbling streams. Lanterns cast a haunting glow. Cherry blossoms floated about them like snow. Studio Ghibli-like spirits clustered around *shinboku*, twisted trees that were sacred dwelling places of *kami*.

In front of them, a *yōkai* blinked in and out of existence.

Rune frowned. "Looks like some of the settings are off. I'll take a look at that for you when we get back."

They reached a giant empty spot where the shaded outlines of a 3D blueprint were superimposed on the space. "We plan on populating the narratives with AI until enough Numinals move in and start playing out their own stories," explained Aiko. "The centerpiece will be an arena, right here. A place where people can come together to see something wonderful. A cumulation of storylines."

Nadia couldn't help feeling a tiny bit jealous of Aiko. Here she was, creating worlds for others, inventing new and wonderful ways of pushing technology and magic forward. And instead of just designing it, she had actually taken the steps to make it real. Aiko wasn't stuck, lamenting her fate. She was changing it, bending the world to her will. Nadia decided she could learn a thing or two from this woman.

After exploring the simulation, they exited and returned to the tearoom. Nadia blinked her eyes open, lightheaded and woozy from the spell.

"The marigold will help with that." Aiko poured Nadia a cup of steaming herbal tea. Nadia gratefully accepted it.

"If you both will excuse me." Rune stood. "I'm going to check on the control panel. Fix that blip we saw earlier." He left, shutting the screen door behind him.

Aiko sat back in the lounge settee and casually draped her arm over the back. "Rune told me that you're a Blood Muse, but you weren't traditionally turned. Your grandmother bound your powers, and they came back thrice and made you who you are. It is unfortunate that you did not have a choice in the matter as I did, though historically, not many of us did."

"I didn't realize you were a Blood Muse," said Nadia, heat rising to her cheeks. Now it all made sense why Rune wanted her to meet the woman. "Why would you choose this, if you don't mind me asking?"

"I was trained in the art of geisha and had reached the pinnacle of my career. I was desired by all. The living embodiment of beauty." *Sheesh. No false modesty here.* "One day, a demon came to me and told me about a way to become even more. If I transformed into a Blood Muse, I could be a geisha to Numinals. It opened a whole new world for me. I underwent the ceremony."

Nadia took a sip of her drink. "What is the ceremony like, if you don't mind me asking?"

"It's painful," said Aiko. "It feels like your soul is being ripped apart and sewn back in a different way. One closer to the Numinous. You are lucky you did not have to undergo it, that any pain you felt from your grandmother's binding you was absorbed into your infancy, and you have no memory of it."

"Even if I don't remember it, it doesn't make what she did okay," Nadia huffed. They were treading in dangerous water, Nadia still trying to navigate how she felt about her grandmother's betrayal. "Sorry. I'm just trying to understand it all."

"I know it's difficult. You are wearing the mantle of the thousands who came before you. Even if you don't want it, you are a Blood Muse now and must accept what that means. It impacts your place in the world and how you navigate it." She clasped her hands and leaned forward like they were finally getting down to business. "Rune says you have a fear of feedings."

"That's one way of putting it," said Nadia. "More like I completely freak out and cause an explosion."

The Blood Muse gave Nadia an understanding smile. "I take it your experiences have been somewhat . . . traumatic."

"You could say that."

"Have you heard about reaching flow?"

Nadia shook her head.

"When a Blood Muse truly wants and allows a Numinal to feed from her, the two will reach a state of flow. The first time is the Eights Ritual. The experience can be quite life-altering."

"What do you mean by a state of flow?" asked Nadia. She only knew it to mean being in the zone.

"A state of flow is a mingling of energies. It happens when both parties consent to the feeding. It can be quite pleasurable."

Nadia narrowed her eyes. "Pleasurable like a bath . . . or like . . ." Her voice trailed off at the woman's amused expression. "Ah. That kind of pleasurable."

"I once had thirty orgasms in the span of an hour."

Nadia choked on her tea. "Wow! Thirty, huh?" She coughed into a napkin, trying to appear unalarmed at the woman's blunt confession. She hadn't known that geishas could be so forthcoming.

Aiko smiled indulgently. "I see I have made you uncomfortable."

"No, it's fine," Nadia said. "I just . . . wasn't expecting you to say that."

"As a Blood Muse, you will eventually grow into your sexuality. You won't be squeamish talking about your own pleasure."

Nadia smiled politely. That day was not today. "Why's it called the Eights Ritual?"

"When a Blood Muse and another reach flow together, their energies mix, and they forever carry a piece of each other. The Eights Ritual honors the first time, the energies the most pure and undiluted by another."

"And they have to have sex to do this Eights Ritual?"

"Not always, but it does help get into flow."

Aiko explained to her that the throat chakra and the sacral chakra were intimately connected. "Like infinity—a figure eight—the energy flows from the throat chakras through the solar plexus chakras to the sacral chakras. The sacral chakra is where life and creativity stem forth, while the throat chakra communicates your spiritual point of view, speaking your own truth. The solar plexus chakra is all about your personal power. How you see yourself. Activated all together, it brings forth this beautiful, profound moment between two people where they cease to be separate and instead are one." Aiko gestured to a tray of colorful, tiny pastries sitting between them. "Would you like to try? They are my own recipe."

"Oh." They were onto pastries now. Nadia timidly reached out and took a small circular pink-and-green cream puff decorated to look like a mushroom. "Looks too good to eat!" she said awkwardly, turning it this way and that as she tried to figure out the best angle to take a bite. She took a small nibble from the side and nearly melted as the taste exploded on her tongue. "I think that's the best thing I've ever had. Is that marshmallow?"

Aiko smiled. "Blood Muses live their lives as art. The things that they do, the way they move through the world, how they present themselves and use their bodies, being in flow with another, it is all meant to inspire beauty, passion, and innovation. I've inspired countless creations, inventions, and masterpieces. And even though I am a muse, I am a creator as well. I build entire worlds like this one"—she gestured to the 3D miniature hologram of the Floating World—"but I also love to make perfect little cakes. Poems for the mouth. One is not better than the other, not more worthy. You will figure out your path as a Blood Muse—your art—whether you find it with your body, or your mind, or both." She leaned in, a twinkle in her eye, and whispered, "I recommend both. Much more satisfying."

Nadia was sure it was. "I wonder where Rune's gotten off to."

As if he'd been waiting outside the door for his cue, Rune knocked and poked his head into the room. "I fixed the projection boundaries. You're all set."

Rune and Nadia walked back through the tunnels to the

surface. She kept sneaking glances at Rune, indulging a guilty pleasure, imagining what it would feel like to reach flow with him.

He glanced at her. "How was Aiko's?"

Certain her thoughts were written all over her face, Nadia forced herself to keep a neutral expression. "Illuminating."

"Did you learn anything that might help you control everything? Help with the second test?"

Had she? She wasn't sure what to make of all the information the woman had given her. She had meant to ask specific questions about how to control her fear. But she had gotten sidetracked with all the talk of this Eights Ritual and creativity orgasms, and she had forgotten everything she wanted to talk about.

"Oh yes," said Nadia. "It was super helpful. Thanks for introducing us."

They stepped out onto the sidewalk. The rain had let up already.

Rune held the door open for her as she slid into the supple leather of his car. "I'm worried you aren't ready for the second test," he said hesitantly. "Even with Aiko's help."

"I'll be ready," said Nadia. She would. She had to be. There was no other option.

<h1 style="text-align:center">Chapter 18</h1>

Test day. Nadia spent the entire afternoon in the vaults preparing. She meditated and tried to clear her mind of the constant chatter and self-doubt. She worked on energy spells and drills until she was confident that she could do them in her sleep. Nadia hoped the extra exercises would make up for the fact that the San Francisco loa still did not accept her as one of their own.

The tiny roots she had sprouted had not been enough. The loa had never given her their blessing, so she couldn't use the city's ley lines. And she wasn't skilled enough or immoral enough to take the energy by force. Without the extra energy to sustain the spell, she would have to do it with her own energy and not drain herself too much in the process or freak out and have a complete meltdown.

During their last practice, Rune had tried to keep Nadia's hopes up and asked her to think of a time that something improbable had happened. Her mind had jumped immediately to the Dartmouth game in high school, the time she had made the winning shot that led to her school winning the state championship. She wasn't the best on the team. Not by a long shot. But that day, everything had gone in her favor. Nadia had been the crowning achievement of her father, who had called her "beautiful and brilliant" at her celebration dinner.

"That wasn't a lucky shot," Rune told her. "You made that

happen by force of will. You wanted it, so it became reality." He had taken her hand in his. "You are more powerful than you can imagine."

He held her gaze for too long, and Nadia snatched her hand back. Hurt had flashed across Rune's face, but then his stoic mask slipped over. Master, apprentice. Nothing more.

When Nadia came upstairs at the end of the day, there was a commotion on the floor. In the center of the room, among the coworking spaces and habitats, a small crowd had gathered around someone. Nadia's pulse quickened as she recognized who it was.

Imogen.

The Fae's eyes were sparkly and bright as she greeted everyone. She was even more lovely than Nadia remembered, wearing a kelly green sweater dress that contrasted nicely with her red hair, pale skin, and smattering of freckles.

"What are you doing here?" asked Piero, giving her a hug.

She hugged him warmly back. "I'm in town for the Women in Tech conference. I thought I would stop by and say hi to everyone."

Maya and Sophie came over to hug her as well.

"Well, we missed you," said Maya. "It's just not the same with you gone."

"Rune's been a monster without you," said Carson, giving her a hug that lifted her off the ground. A pang of jealousy lodged itself in Nadia's heart, nuzzling next to the guilt.

Carson set Imogen back on her feet. She turned to Nadia, smiling, her expression warm. "Hi, Nadia. How have the vaults been?"

"Great," Nadia murmured. She wished she could go hide in them. Imogen was supposed to be in Dublin. With her fiancé. Nadia had thought she'd never have to see the woman again, never see her strutting around in her Louboutins, but here she was, Louboutins and all.

Rune stood on the second-floor balcony hallway, looking down on them, his eyes locked on Imogen.

Imogen followed Nadia's gaze to Rune. "There he is! Come say hello," she called up to him, smiling.

Rune came down to the fray, joining everyone. He gave Imogen a warm hug and a kiss on the cheek.

"I was hoping you were free to grab a drink right now?" she asked him.

He nodded. "I'd love to."

Nadia startled at his response. *I thought we were going to do the second test this evening?*

Rune kept his expression neutral. *You aren't ready. I can't put you in danger like that.*

But I—

No, Nadia. Final answer.

They walked off the floor together, Rune's hand on the small of Imogen's back. They looked like a couple. His height fit hers. Her body moved in tune with his. Nadia tried to look nonchalant and breezy, leaning back against one of the open coworking tables and fiddling with her phone like she was responding to an important email, but she seethed inside. How *dare* he treat her like this!

Rune didn't even look at Nadia as he and Imogen passed by. But Imogen glanced down briefly at her. Nadia could swear there was a smug smile on her red lips.

Piero adopted his sacred clown persona and wisely assessed the situation, his eyes flicking back and forth between the three of them. When Rune and Imogen had left the floor, he gave Nadia a pitying look. "I think you need a drink as well."

*   *   *

Piero, Sophie, and Nadia sat at a dingy dive bar near Myst, getting a drink. They hadn't wanted to go to The Bell, Myst's in-house bar, in case any coworkers overheard them, instead opting for somewhere where they could sit in anonymity and talk freely. Nadia had thought that drinking might be a distraction from Imogen and that look she had given her, but the more she drank, the worse she felt. The green-eyed monster had reared its ugly head and taken control of her senses. Rune hadn't even *looked* in her direction when he left with Imogen. Like *she didn't even exist* when Imogen was around. And he had blown off the second initiation test. Said she wasn't ready. If she didn't take it soon, she wouldn't be on track to pass the third before Samhain and get her Soulwish. She hated herself for feeling this way. Angry. Helpless. Powerless. Dependent on Rune.

"Would you like to unburden yourself, my child?" Piero asked Nadia as he leaned back on his barstool, settling in like a dirty priest awaiting a salacious confession. "What's been going on with you and Rune?"

Nadia took a large swig of her vodka soda and grimaced at the taste of the well liquor. "There's nothing to tell."

"Then why are you all hunched over like a sour crow?" asked Sophie. "Seriously, you're making me so depressed even looking at you, I'm going to need to drink just to be around you right now." Sophie slammed a shot of whiskey followed by a pickleback and wiped the corners of her mouth with a bar napkin, careful not to smudge her purple lipstick.

Nadia knocked back the rest of her vodka soda and signaled the bartender for another round. He nodded and grabbed a bottle from the shelf and the soda hose to mix her a fresh drink.

"Sorry, guys. I'm just dealing with some personal stuff, that's all."

"By 'personal stuff' do you mean 'totally inappropriate crush on your boss'?" Piero wagged his eyebrows.

"NO!" she said, a little too forcefully. "I mean, no."

"You're still training with him, though, right?" Sophie gave Nadia a faux-innocent look and batted her eyelashes.

"Training, eh? Is that what the kids call it these days?" Piero dissolved into a fit of giggles and almost fell off his chair. That made Sophie howl with laughter, and they tried to shush each other, glancing around the mostly empty bar to see if anyone cared about their hysterical outburst. No one did.

Nadia glared at them. "You two aren't as funny as you think you are."

Sophie wiped the tears from her eyes. "Yes, we are."

Piero patted Nadia on the shoulder. "I saw your face when Rune left with Imogen. I know what you're thinking, but it isn't like that with them."

"I have absolutely no interest in Rune's social life." Nadia tried to say it with conviction.

"You know what you need?" Sophie dug out her cell phone from her pocket. "You need a distraction. San Francisco is just crawling with cute tech guys with lots of disposable income right now."

Piero's eyes lit up. "Excellent idea! When was the last time you had a proper date?"

Nadia finger-combed a tangle from her dark hair, frowning at the snag. "It's been a while."

Sophie scrolled through her phone. "There are heaps of cute guys on Tinder you could bang to get over your slump."

"Whoa, whoa, whoa." Nadia held up her hands. "Who said anything about banging anyone?"

"Don't be a prude," said Sophie, still engrossed in her phone.

"You don't have to Foxtrot Unicorn Charlie Kilo," said Piero. "Unless you want to, of course. But you need to go out and forget a certain irritable CEO who we all know you're trying to convince yourself that you aren't into."

"He's too uptight, anyway," said Sophie. "I'll find someone fun for you."

"Isn't that your profile?" Nadia gestured at her phone. "Won't you be matching with guys, not me?"

She shrugged. "You're pretty enough. I doubt they'd care if you showed up instead of me."

"This seems like a bad idea," Nadia started. The last thing she needed was more complications in her life. And dating online randos seemed entirely complicated. The start of a wish spell formed in her mind, a manifestation emerging from her psyche. "Seriously, guys. I'm not into online dating. I'm more into the whole organic-meeting thing."

Sophie and Piero shushed her. "Ooh," said Piero, pointing to a picture on the phone. "Nice happy trail."

Nadia silenced her thoughts and focused. The Numinous thrummed in her mind.

I wish . . . I wish I didn't have to go on a date with a random guy on the internet. The magic coursed through Nadia's veins as she sent her plea out to the universe. She glanced about the bar for items she could use to amplify the spell. There was a No Smoking sign near the door, and she used that to focus her intention to banish unwanted internet dudes.

Someone behind Nadia chuckled, and she glanced over her shoulder to a cute guy who was eavesdropping on their conversation. He appeared to be in his late twenties, lanky and tall, with a mop of sun-kissed brown hair and a slightly punk style, leather jacket and plugs in both earlobes. Nadia checked for a glamour and found none. A human. He stepped up to the bar and ordered a PBR, flashing her a boyish grin. "Hey."

Nadia spun her barstool over to him and smiled back. "Hey." Game on.

Sophie held up her phone and shoved it in Nadia's face. "How about this guy? He's shirtless in his pic."

Piero nodded. "That means he's DTF."

Nadia pushed the phone out of her face. "Pass."

The cute guy next to her cleared his throat, a touch of amusement in his voice. "Not always."

Sophie's and Piero's heads both swiveled at the same time. They looked him up and down, their eyes narrowing as they both assessed him.

"What are you, like, a Tinder expert or something?" Sophie crossed her legs, flashing him a fishnet-covered thigh.

"That would be a negative. I don't do online dating." He stuck out his hand to Nadia. "I'm Connor, by the way."

She took his hand, his touch vibrating her own magic back to her.

"Nadia," she said, suppressing the urge to shout from the rooftops that her off-the-cuff spell had worked. "I don't do online dating either."

"Hey, I have an idea. How about you and I go out sometime?" The corner of his mouth quirked up in a decidedly adorable manner.

Nadia thought for a moment. She was thrilled her impromptu manifestation spell had worked. She had been presented with a problem and had quickly figured out a solution. Maybe she would be able to pass the next test, after all. Too bad it would never work out with this Connor guy, though. He'd been caught in the crossfire, lured in by the siren song of magic. Nadia would never know if it was just the magic that made him ask her out, or if he actually liked her, and she could never be with someone if she wasn't sure.

On the other hand, he *was* kind of cute, in a skinny, punk, skater-boi way. Who cared if magic helped her get a date? She wasn't looking for her soulmate or anything like that right now. She could get a drink with the guy, for crying out loud.

Piero nudged her. Sophie mouthed, *Do it!*

She smiled flirtatiously. "Sure, why not?"

He grinned and pulled out his cell phone to get her number. Nadia typed it in, and he saved it.

"I'll text you. Bye, beautiful." Connor took her hand and kissed her palm briefly before he grabbed his drink and returned to his friends.

Nadia turned back to Piero and Sophie.

"Now, that is what I call manifestation!" Piero gushed. "You did that, didn't you?"

Nadia shrugged, trying to look nonchalant. "I don't know what you're talking about."

She sat back and took another sip of her drink as Sophie and Piero discussed manifestation and what they would do if they could wish for whatever they wanted. Nadia tried to wish thoughts of Rune and Imogen on their fancy date out of her mind.

She failed.

Rune and Imogen stepped out of a cab and into an Irish bar off Union Square. The smell of cheap beer spilled on carpet hit Rune as they entered the dingy room. He put up shields at once, blocking the full-on assault on his senses.

The crowd was rowdy and boisterous—both tourists and locals busy getting drunk and watching a soccer game. Rune ushered Imogen through the throngs of overgrown frat bros and drunk coeds to a corner booth in the back. Sparkly green shamrocks, permanently up since Saint Patrick's Day, peppered the wall.

"I don't know why you always insist on going to these Irish bars," Rune grumbled. "Can't you get better bangers and mash in Dublin?"

Imogen scooted into the worn vinyl booth, making herself at home. She threw her purse to the side and placed the tabletop basket with ketchup and mustard at the far edge. "Nonsense. I love going to Paddy bars in America. It's like going to Disneyland. The American version is always so . . . tacky." She pulled out the pins that were holding her hair up in a neat bun. Her red locks came tumbling down, and she tousled them with a sexy hair flip. A few nearby frat bros playing pool stopped what they were doing and openly gawked at her.

"Stop that," growled Rune.

Imogen winked at the bros and turned back to Rune. "You're no fun."

"How's Loch?" asked Rune, referencing her fiancé. Rune raised a hand and signaled to the server to come and take their order.

Imogen pulled the neck of her sweater dress down to reveal the pale, creamy skin of her shoulders. Rune averted his eyes.

"Are you really not going to even *look* at me?" she demanded.

Rune turned his head back to her and gave her a long, appreciative glance. "Better?"

She opened the menu. "It will have to do."

The waitress came over to take their orders. Rune ordered them two pints of Guinness.

When the server had left, Imogen said, "Lochy's fine. He sends his regards."

Sure, he does. He hadn't talked to his best friend in decades. They had served together for many years before their falling out over the direction of the Council, when Rune had relinquished his seat. He seriously doubted Loch would send him anything except a dagger in the back.

Rune settled into the worn vinyl booth and surveyed his surroundings. The room was full of drunk humans, trying to escape their meager existences by drowning themselves in alcohol. The room reeked of desperation and worry, recklessness and bacchanalian revelry tainted by the incessant mind-chatter of trying to pay bills, dealing with idiotic bosses, and the endless noise of politics, social media, and pointless news consumption. In the darker corners, a few demons passing as humans fed off the room's energy. Rune ignored them. Where there were lush humans, there were demons feeding on their sloppiness.

The waitress brought over their pints of Guinness. Imogen ordered a plate of fries and sent the server on her way with a warm smile. When she had gone, she turned to Rune. "Could you?"

Rune cast a shroud around them. The spell made them almost invisible to the patrons at the bar and muffled the bar noise.

Imogen glanced about and decided that the spell was adequate. "The Council had an emergency session—"

"You shouldn't be telling me this," Rune cut in.

Imogen's nostrils flared. "You know as well as I do that they need you. I've said it once, and I'll say it again: you were the heart of the Council."

"Not anymore."

"Stop with the ego." Imogen pursed her lips. "You and Loch are practically the same person. Both stubborn as hell. At least he doesn't run and hide from his past."

Rune narrowed his eyes. "These are new sentiments coming from you. You sound like your parents."

"Low blow." Imogen sat back and crossed her arms. "What's going on with you and Nadia?"

"Nothing."

"Does she know that? The girl is completely enamored with you."

Rune looked away. "Not my problem."

Imogen scoffed. "You would be so much happier in life if you would just accept your vulnerabilities, Rune."

"They teach you that at Trinity?" Even to his own ears, he sounded condescending and sarcastic.

"Fuck you," Imogen snapped.

"You've already done that, sweetheart." He smiled darkly.

"And you enjoyed it thoroughly, if I remember."

At that moment, the waitress brought over the plate of fries. She spun in circles, looking around. Rune lowered the wards so she could find them.

After the waitress had set the plate down and left, Imogen took a fry, popped it in her mouth, and stood up. "I feel like playing some pool. You sit here and think about the best way to treat a person who is trying to help you."

She strutted up to a group of frat boys and challenged them to a game. The young men didn't know how to react to such a confident and voluptuous woman. They didn't stand a chance. Imogen sashayed around the pool table, showing off her ass as she bent over and hit every ball into the pockets. She winked at Rune. He chuckled. It was the game they played with each other, teasing each other but never crossing that line.

Not anymore, anyway.

Rune and Imogen had once been an item. But that was centuries ago, when they were different people. Now, she was with Lochland. A High Fae who had sided with the Council when everything had gone to hell. The thought of getting wrapped up in Council business once again infuriated him. They'd been trying to lure him back into their corrupt folds for decades. Rune wished he could ignore what they were doing, but their actions affected the entire world, rippling throughout the Numinal communities. One of these days, they would do something rash, incite reckless mayhem and violence in their relentless quest for power and magic. If Rune could do something to help the situation, he was duty-bound to try. And if Imogen was coming to him with information, she was right—he was going to want to hear it.

Imogen finished the pool game, blew the boys a kiss goodbye, and sauntered back over.

Rune engulfed them in a shrouding spell once more as she took a seat. "Tell me what the Council said."

"It appears that they are interested in our very own Nadia," said Imogen. "Her name came up in several recent predictions from various sources. She's a player in the Counter-Prophecy now, tied to you as your queen, and that makes her interesting. You know they keep tabs on all that."

Rune swore under his breath. "I've been trying to keep her out of the spotlight."

"They seemed to know about her even before her name came up in connection with yours."

"Simon might have said something about her. He met her at a board meeting."

Imogen raised an eyebrow. "She's going to board meetings?" She tsked. "Oh, Rune."

"I know what I'm doing."

"Do you? Because it looks like you're handing over the castle keys to a human who is little more than an intern."

"She's a Blood Muse," Rune said softly. The words hung heavy in the air.

Imogen sat back. "Does she know about . . . ?"

"No."

"You're going to have to tell her at some point."

"I know."

Pity swam in Imogen's eyes. "I don't *think* they would do anything to harm her, but . . ." She let out a long breath. "They would do anything to get you back. And once again, they think the Realm Gates are going to be opened this Samhain . . . They're going to make it happen. There are murmurings that they've been pulling strings, putting pieces into play—pieces they control, mind you."

"I know how they operate," said Rune. He scanned the bar scene. All around them, humans were living out their little lives, unaware of the powerful players that stacked the deck.

"You need to protect Nadia. She's in danger. Because of you." She pointed a finger at him. "You got her into this mess, and you'd better get her out of it."

"I know, I know," said Rune. "I'm working on it."

Imogen took his hand and massaged his palm. She traced her finger over the second side of the triangle on his wrist. "That's a good place for her to be. Your apprentice. You can protect her that way."

Rune hoped that was true.

"The next Council meeting is in a few days," said Imogen. "You might want to . . . drop in."

Chapter 19

Night descended over San Francisco. Rune stood in the shadows as the neighborhood around Nadia's house wound down for the evening. Cars found parking spots on the street or pulled into driveways. People returned home, a few coming out again briefly to walk their dogs, before locking their doors, turning off their porch lights, shutting windows, and closing blinds. It all seemed so pastoral, so picturesque, so human.

Rune had followed Nadia home from work, trailing her to the bus stop and onto the 48 to Noe Valley, where he sat hidden in the back under a cloaking spell. She had seemed jumpy, like she sensed she was being followed, but he was sure she hadn't seen him.

Nadia was in danger. The Council could use her to pressure him, to get him to bow to their will. And they were rather fond of using unscrupulous and painful methods to get what they wanted. Rune had taken it upon himself to watch over her personally. He couldn't trust that she would be okay on her own. The few times that Rune had already followed her home, he had done so at a respectful distance until she crossed safely behind the wards, and then he had headed back to Myst.

But that night, Rune posted himself as a sentry over the house. It was something in the air, or some internal intuition. A nudge from the Numinous that said he should stand guard.

There was a demon lurking in the shadows, tailing Nadia, and Rune had sensed Mercurio's network in action. The demon was following Nadia. Rune just didn't know why.

Rune settled into a curve of the sycamore tree across from Nadia's window, blending in with some dryad magic he had picked up in the Balkans. The wards around her grandmother's house were adequate, but not especially advanced spellwork, and they glimmered faintly in the twilight around the aged Victorian.

He listened to the night, sensing the comings and goings of the quiet residential neighborhood. The light in Nadia's bedroom window flicked on. From his vantage point, he could see her moving around her room and changing for bed through the sheer curtains. He glanced around at the other houses warily for any Peeping Toms or fetish demons that might be watching. Humans were often blind to the fact that others could see into their houses when they left the shades and curtains open, though San Francisco seemed to have its share of exhibitionists who seemed not to care what the neighbors saw.

Changed into pajamas, Nadia opened her window and leaned out, watching the street. She seemed to focus on the tree he was leaning against, resting her chin on her folded arms. She had a melancholy expression on her face, like something was weighing on her. She really was beautiful, with her wide-set eyes, high cheekbones, and full lips. She had one of those timeless faces. A classic beauty. Rune let himself have this moment—tucked it away like a precious pearl—of the view of his girl.

His girl. He could finally admit it to himself.

Nadia took out a notebook and sat in the open window, writing. Occasionally, she would stop, ponder something while chewing on the tip of her pen, and then continue. She reached down for something—a wine bottle—and she took a swig straight from it. Rune chuckled and then shook his head, resigned. He was so gone. Everything she did was charming and ridiculously adorable. After a few minutes, she closed her notebook, hopped down from the windowsill, and her room went dark.

One by one, the lights in the neighborhood flicked off, and the night stilled. Only the light in Nadia's living room stayed on. Nadia's grandmother peered out the living room window as if looking for someone. The Fae they lived with flitted around, moving furniture. They were up to something. Nadia's story about her grandmother binding her powers didn't quite add up, though Rune didn't know why. The elderly witch and the Fae were performing some ritual, arms thrown to the air, Nadia's grandmother consecrating the cardinal points. And then the unimaginable happened: the wards around the house dropped. One by one, the lines of a geodesic dome of silvery magic fell to the ground like a curtain dropping.

Rune tensed, ready to pounce. The air was still. No sign of dark creatures yet. The old woman and the Fae scurried about inside doing something. But Rune was focused only on Nadia's window.

From the tree he blended into, Rune sensed Nadia's energy radiating from her, that sweet honey nectar of Blood Muse energy perfuming the air. The wards had not only kept unwanted creatures out of the house, but they had also been keeping Nadia's energy in, sealed up where Dark Numinals could not smell it. It wasn't a problem during the day. He hoped it wasn't, anyway. Her somnambulism was . . . concerning. But during the night, though—well, that was a different matter. Her mind's wards were loosened like in a dream, her energy like a siren's call. A slight buzz in the air developed, and Rune sensed dark creatures flitting from treetop to treetop, edging closer. Anyone would think that it was just a night breeze ruffling the trees, but Rune knew the inevitable: Dark Numinals were coming to feed.

Glamoured to be invisible, Rune crept around to the back of the house and jumped the wooden fence. He extinguished a couple of imps that had come sniffing around, hitting them with a carefully calibrated magical strike. The Dark Numinals dissipated like tar smoke. Rune started up the old wooden porch that wrapped around from the front to the back of the house. There was a rustling in the bushes, and he ducked low, crouching beside the stairwell.

The back door opened, and Nadia's grandmother poked her head out. She made a low whistle with her two fingers, and from a bush, a small humanoid figure emerged.

It was a Curupira, an Amazonian Numinal with bright-orange fur and backward-facing feet. Except this one was missing a foot, one leg tied off with a bloody rag. It hobbled along the garden path up to the porch, using a broken-off mop as a makeshift crutch. The old woman and the Fae rushed out and helped it up the stairs. The door closed.

Rune sensed the wards were about to be raised again. He hopped quickly back over the fence and outside just as the wards burst back into existence, fire on an oil slick. Safe. He wouldn't need to escape the wards and risk triggering an alarm.

The living room light went off. The night was still once more.

Nadia's grandmother and the Fae must be running some sort of healing and trauma center. Rune knew that the old woman was an herb witch. It made sense that she would be running some sort of clinic. He didn't have a problem with that. It was admirable, in fact.

But he did have a problem with the fact that Nadia's grandmother was bringing strangers into the house. The Council could send someone to harm Nadia and use this to get to her. They'd planted agents in the field before to do their bidding. Rune couldn't be sure they didn't have people watching her already.

But if she were a full initiate in the Order, she would fall under their protection and be able to call upon the other members to help her. Rune had called upon the others before to help him deal with the Council's meddling. It was part of their code of honor to help a brother or a sister in need. It wasn't much, but it was something. And if the Council was involved, they would need all the help they could get.

Rune had told Nadia that she wasn't ready for the second test. She wasn't, that was for sure. Without the loa's acceptance, she'd have to power the spell to access the subconscious by herself, and with her fear of feedings and of her energy being used up, she'd risk setting off a chain reaction with her fight-or-flight response. It was a risk he wasn't willing to take.

But there was a solution. There always was. Rune did not like to admit failure, not when they were so close. As the pale streaks of sunrise lightened the sky, Rune formulated a plan for her second test.

Nadia arrived for her morning workout and training session at the gym, carrying her gym bag and a change of clothes. The echoey changing room and showers were empty, as was expected that early. She threw her bag into a locker in the changing room, slamming the locker door behind her.

Rune intercepted her as she walked out onto the floor, pouncing on her like an overeager puppy. He jogged back and forth on the balls of his feet as he said, "Winters, there you are. I have a surprise for you today."

"More reps?" she joked, throwing her towel over her shoulder.

"We're going to do the second test."

Nadia blinked. "I thought you said I wasn't ready."

"I think you are."

Nadia bit her bottom lip. She sure as hell didn't feel ready. But this was it. She had to step up to the plate and take a swing. "What do I tell Piero and Carson? They have me on deadlines."

"Tell them you're doing an off-site with me today. They'll understand."

"What about the loa?" she asked. "I've been trying . . ."

A grin broke out over Rune's face. "There's always a workaround. The loa in Yosemite are a little more . . . accepting."

Chapter 20

The four-hour drive to Yosemite was picturesque and pleasant. Once they had left the Bay Area, it was like a fog had lifted. The air was clean, with less ambient magic all around. The weather was warm and sunny. The lightning storms that had plagued the city that morning cleared. Nadia hadn't ever been to Yosemite before, and she felt a sense of awe and wonder as they drove through the giant sequoias that lined the twisting road into the park, light dappling the wet earth. Rune usually liked to drive fast, but he drove slower than normal, like he was savoring the time and didn't want it to end.

Once they arrived in Yosemite and parked, they grabbed their hiking backpacks and water bottles and set off for the Cathedral Lake trailhead. The air smelled clean and earthy. Leaves crunched under their feet. Nadia followed slightly behind Rune, allowing herself the luxury of really looking at him: the slight sheen of sweat on his muscular torso, the stupid way he had knotted his shirt around his head to ward off the sun, the way his teeth shone a dazzling white whenever he smiled, her reflection smiling back at her from his mirrored aviators.

Rune scanned the land. "Make sure your shields are up so you aren't leaking any energy. Yosemite and other uninhabited places often have wild demons, and they won't think twice about attacking."

"There was something in the news about an increase in animal attacks out here," said Nadia.

"It isn't bears or mountain lions," said Rune. "Authorities don't know what to make of the remains they are finding, so they assume it's rabid animals."

Nadia climbed over a large boulder. "Is it strange that there have been so many demon attacks outside the city?"

"It's definitely not normal," confirmed Rune. He stopped for a pause at a breathtaking vista and took a sip from his water bottle. "There's some wild energy in the Numinous, stirring things up and egging them on. Demons can't help themselves."

"It must be awful for them." Nadia shuddered.

"For whom? The demons?"

"Yeah, I mean, I know some demons used to be humans." Thomas had told Nadia that he had once been human, but his obsession with something had eaten away his humanity and turned him into a demon. She knew that demons were turned many ways, but that had always struck her as a particularly bad way to go: a slow realization and sense of powerlessness, knowing that he was succumbing to darkness.

"I didn't know you had any sympathy for the devil, so to speak," Rune remarked.

"Well, even if they are Dark Numinals, they are still Numinals."

"Many are not as compassionate and kind as you are."

Nadia shrugged. "I suppose it's like dealing with an addiction or a disease. They can't help what they are—how their soul was twisted—and how they are lured by the darkness."

Rune stared at Nadia, and she wondered if she had said something wrong.

They fell into silence, enjoying the majestic sights around them: eagles soaring high overhead, granite peaks rising into the endless blue sky, tall trees bathed in golden light. They walked through springy meadows of moss dotted with yellow and purple wildflowers, little white butterflies flitting among the verdant green grass. Nadia knew John Muir had thought of Yosemite as a living church, and, indeed, the place felt sacred and holy.

Before long, they reached Cathedral Lake, the glassy pool spread out before them like a mirror. Rune jutted his chin at one of the nearby mountaintops. "That's Cathedral Peak. There is a powerful nexus of energy in Yosemite, and we can tap into the ley line at the top. The loa here have given magicians a blanket pass to use it if they first give back to the wilderness with three drops of their magic."

The pointed top of the mountain loomed at a dizzying height. "We don't have any rope or climbing gear," said Nadia.

"We're magicians," replied Rune. "We don't need it."

As they ascended the gradual slope, the forest started to thin until they reached the face of the cliff. Nadia almost had vertigo as she looked up at the daunting cliff face, pinpricks of fear poking holes in her confidence.

Rune patted the granite. "You going to be able to do this?"

"I have a fear of heights," Nadia confessed. "And I've never free-climbed before, magic or no magic."

"Lesson number three," said Rune. "When faced with a challenge, always assess your own weaknesses and limitations first so you can overcome them."

Rune showed her a list of spells in her Psionic to help with free-climbing, including spells for increased grip strength, eagle vision, and goat-like agility. He also showed her some personal body charms for sun protection and to prevent dehydration. He then led them in a brief grounding and centering activity. Nadia cast the spells and charms, the spells puffing into the air like perfume, the miasma of magic settling over her skin.

Rune went first, leading the path for Nadia to follow. He moved quickly and efficiently, pausing for her every few feet so she could keep up. Nadia's muscles burned from the exertion, but she settled into the rhythm of the climb, enjoying the sun beating down on her back and the view of a shirtless Rune grinning down at her as she climbed up toward him.

When they reached the top, they sat for some time, soaking in the panoramic view. Eagles soared gracefully through the air before they nose-dived into the lakes, pulling up trout in their claws. Air currents pushed the high-altitude clouds, alpine taffy being pulled in the sky. Sunlight sparkled over the crystal lake like pixie dust. Nadia closed her eyes and let her other senses take over, her magic heightened by the energy at the pinnacle. She heard the echoing sounds of the canyons, smelled the earth beneath her feet, and felt the warm fall air and sunlight on her face.

"For the second test," Rune said, "you will need to master your subconscious mind and find the second musical note. To access the subconscious, you will need to use the ley lines as a source of energy."

He kneeled on the granite, his arms outstretched, palms faced downward. He closed his eyes and took a deep breath. His fingers curled slightly like he was pulling something up with his palm. A ley line appeared, a shimmering golden stream, fuzzy at the edges.

"Some ley lines have energy valves, like geysers. Extremely violent. Cathedral Peak is a nice, easy ley line." Rune traced sigils on one of his palms with a finger, and three drops of his magic fell from his palm into the ley line like three silvery tears. Rune took Nadia's hand in his, and he traced the same sigils into her palm. It burned, searing her, magic welling up under the lines. She let three tears of her magic drop into the ley line as well.

They kneeled across from each other, palms stretched out

to the golden river. It was like dipping her hand into a warm, slow-moving stream. A liquid-honey feeling spread up her arms and dripped down her back until she was filled up with energy and love and power. The energy flowed into Nadia, patching up the weak spots, filling the cracks in her soul.

Rune circled around behind her and performed a series of quick hand movements above her head, dropping the spell to access her subconscious into her mind. Nadia felt the symbols seep into her brain, and the words rose in her mind and flowed out of her lips as she began to chant.

As the energy from the ley line and the Numinous flowed into her body, an island formed inside her. A dark spot that would not allow the light in. The three pebbles in her heart had become a large boulder.

Rune sensed the blockage. "You must surrender to that darkness to dissolve it."

Nadia's fingers trembled, and her breath became uneven and shallow. She tried to surrender, to accept, but there was a wall, rock hard. One she'd painstakingly erected to hide all the dark parts of herself. The nasty little pieces of shame and unworthiness that she masked daily as she pretended to be someone she was not: a good apprentice, a good employee, a good person.

Nasty, evil thoughts took over her mind. What if Rune found out about her family's ties to Mercurio? What if he found out that she'd been lying to him this entire time? How bad a person she was deep down inside, how worthless and twisted and un-lovable? What if being Mercurio's blood slave was the best she could hope for in life? Worse, what if she *liked* it? The thoughts spiraled upward, and she was lost in the maelstrom.

Rune grabbed her back, away from the ley line. "That's enough!"

Nadia cradled her hands like they'd been scalded. She sobbed quietly for a minute, breathing fast, tears streaming down her face. Rune quickly and methodically gave her magical first aid, calibrating her energy levels, and her magic calmed.

"You were about to spark a chain reaction," said Rune. "You need to be very careful near ley lines. It would be like an atomic bomb went off."

Nadia made herself meet his eyes.

"I pushed you too quickly," he said. "You aren't ready for the second test." He swept his hair back from his brow and squinted up at the sun, disappointment on his face. "We'd better get going."

"I'm not giving up," said Nadia quickly. "Let me try again."

"That darkness . . . I didn't realize you had so much. It's going to manifest in the subconscious."

She stared at him. Part of her wanted to confess it all. Open Pandora's Box and let out all the nasty little monsters that she kept hidden. Hope that he had his own monsters too and understood. But the look on his face stopped her. He looked . . . pained. Conflicted. She was certain he was questioning her worthiness for the Order, a dark stain upon her.

"I can do it." Nadia wasn't going to let some hidden part of her shadow and a couple of monsters stand in her way.

Rune shook his head slightly, resigned. "When you dissolve that darkness, it's still going to be there. It just will be . . . everywhere. I don't know what you're going to face. Just . . . be careful."

Nadia held her hand out to the ley line once again, feeling the energy flow upward and into her. She reached the boulder, calcified emotion, and tried to figure out what to do. Rune had said she must surrender. Surrender and accept, she repeated in her mind. Surrender and accept. She mentally wrapped her arms around the boulder. Maybe it just needed a hug. Stupid, but it worked. The darkness dissolved, casting everything slightly gray, a fog descending.

Her world tilted backward and threw her upside down. She was entering her subconscious. When she opened her eyes, she was in front of a temple. The small building shifted shape depending on how she looked at it. From one angle, it was like a cathedral. From another, a Greek temple. Others appeared more Hindu or Thai. There was a dull hum in Nadia's ears, a strange vibration. Everything was a murky gray, and she couldn't tell if the flat plains below were sand or sea. Tentacled creatures like the ones she had seen floating in Docktown burbled up and floated in the sky like clouds. She felt removed, like she was in a dream.

Her eyes adjusted to the darkness as she entered the temple. Flames from torches lined the stone walls. A narrow path led up some rocks to a golden chalice, pale light streaming down from nowhere like a spotlight. She was wearing a flowing white dress here, her hair loose and wild. She wondered if she could change her outfit. It would be a pain in the ass to climb those rocks in that dress. She tried to will more of a Lara Croft look, but nothing happened.

She set out for the chalice. An abyss was on either side of the path, a black void into nothingness. Oil-slicked black hands reached up and tried to grab her, catching her ankles, her dress, and her arms, threatening to pull her down with them. She struggled, kicking at them, but they were strong, and she was unable to shake them off. They pulled her down, grabbed her ankles and her wrists, covered her mouth so she couldn't scream, covered her eyes so she couldn't see, smothering her. Failure and disgrace and shame flooded her body.

The tether to the ley line snapped. Nadia shot back into her conscious mind, back to the top of Cathedral Peak, back to Rune. He had her by the shoulders, and she gasped, struggling for air as the remnants of the black hands sank back down, slick black oil cooling into tar pits in the recesses of her mind.

"Are you okay?" Rune demanded. Nadia sobbed involuntarily, a release of emotion, and then brought herself under control.

"Again," she said, her voice wobbly. "I need to go again." She held her arms out and started the spell.

"Nadia." Rune grabbed her hands and pulled them down. "You can't. You're not ready."

"I need to go again." She stared at him, unwilling to admit defeat.

Admiration flashed briefly in Rune's gaze. He bowed his head, accepting what she was going to do. Nadia held her hands out and closed her eyes.

Like before, she found herself outside the temple. She rushed in, ready to face the hands. Black appendages bubbled up from the darkness and slid across her skin, prying into her nose, her ears, and her mouth, threatening to choke her. She gagged, fighting the urge to claw them off, telling herself to accept it, to endure the violation. Shame burned in her chest. Some part of her believed she deserved this, that her weakness had brought her here. She tried to surrender and let the punishment wash over her, but her body rebelled, panic surging, and she fought. The hands clamped down, pulling her under, smothering her, pressing oily palms against her face, her chest, and her legs, until the darkness swallowed every trace of her.

She opened her eyes. She was in front of the temple again.

"No!" She ran back in, again let the hands pull her down, and again found herself outside the temple. She tried one more time, but again, she found herself where she started, no closer to finding the second note and passing the second test.

She was caught in a loop.

Shame and guilt spiraled up around her, inky monsters

bubbling up from the pits of despair. Who was she kidding? She wasn't worthy of being in the Order. Not when she wasn't willing to face her fears. Not when she was being dishonest and deceitful. Not when thoughts of being Mercurio's Blood Muse kind of turned her on and made her slut-shame *herself*. Why did she always have to do things the hard way? Maybe this was meant to happen, what she deserved. Giving up would be a hell of a lot easier than figuring out how this puzzle worked.

Nadia walked to the side of the temple. She put her hand on it like she had Cathedral Peak. Rune knew she could climb the cliff. He had faith in her. And she had faced her fear of heights and surprised herself. If she could free-climb a mountain, she could do anything. She activated the quick charms from her Psionic, hoping the magic worked the same in her mind, and heaved herself up, climbing up the vertical wall of the temple one footstep and arm pull at a time.

On the roof of the temple, she had a bird's-eye view of the land. Inky monsters speckled the gray clouds and sea, lightning cracking in an approaching storm that swallowed everything in its path in darkness. Soon, the storm would hit, and she'd be lost.

Rune had said there's always a solution. She looked about herself wildly, and then there it was: a golden slipstream upward into the clouds. She didn't have to face her darkness, after all; she could rise above and embrace the light. Whatever the chalice was, whatever it represented in her mind . . . she didn't need it. The slipstream shimmered out of reach, and Nadia had to make a jump for it. The distance and physics were all off, but fuck it. No guts, no glory. She ran and took a flying leap out into the air before she could chicken out.

Nadia soared above the gray and hit the slipstream. It shot her upward in a spiral, and she flew through the clouds, through zinging lightning and rolling thunder, until the air cleared. She landed on a white, puffy cloud, the sky blue and bright, the light of the Numinous shining through to her.

A golden gong and mallet lay in front of Nadia. She swung the mallet, and a single note reverberated out. The sound rolled through her body, and her mind attuned to it, the vibrations syncing together.

She had done it. She had passed the second test.

Her world spun once more, and Nadia found herself back on top of Cathedral Peak with Rune. She stumbled, and he caught her, steadying her.

"Whoa, there," he said, bringing her down to sit on the rock. "Easy now."

The second line of the triangle inked itself on Nadia's wrist. She hung her head between her knees, taking deep breaths. Rune hadn't warned this would be so intense.

"Congrats," said Rune. "How was it?"

"I feel like I might throw up."

"That happens. Here, take a seat."

Nadia sat, hanging her head between her legs as her mind calibrated to the dizzying effects of the second note. Rune rubbed her shoulders and her back. After a few minutes, she felt in control enough to stand.

"Where was the note?" Rune asked.

"Up on a cloud. Golden gong. Is it the same for everyone?"

He shook his head. "Mine was a birdsong in a tree, a note from a lullaby my mother used to sing. My master said his was the sound of a waterfall cascading over rock."

They made their way down the cliff face. Her thoughts turned inward. Those hands, pulling at her, trying to take her down . . . was that her darkness? Why hadn't she had to surrender to it? Were there pockets of darkness all throughout her mind? What did it mean that she couldn't reach the chalice?

"Winters, your shields," Rune warned from below her.

Nadia looked down at him. "Huh?" *Oh fuck.* Her mental shields were loosened, and she was leaking energy all over the place. She quickly fortified them and then continued her descent, one foot then the other.

Below her, Rune froze. Nadia immediately tensed up, their magic linked stronger than before. He sent out psychic feelers, mentally scanning the area.

"There's a demon nearby," Rune said calmly. "Not a humanoid. Most likely an animal. We need to move fast."

They moved quickly but carefully down the cliff face. A moving shadow appeared, jumping after them from ledge to ledge, hunting them. Nadia couldn't get a good look at the demon. It was all snarling fangs and smoky scales, like a wildcat crossed with a gargoyle. It disappeared, but Nadia kept moving.

"We're about fifty feet from the bottom," Rune called up.

Nadia sensed the shape flying at her face before she saw it, and it swooped in like a bat, clawing and snapping. She screamed as she lost her grip on the granite and slipped down the mountain, her fingers trying to find a hold. Her fingers caught the ledge, held for a second, and then lost their grip again. She slammed into the side of the rock, scraping the shit out of her face, and pinned herself to the rock with arms outstretched.

Rune leaped past her to the demon and killed it. Its body dissipated like a dirty wisp of smoke.

"Nadia!" Rune called down to her. "Just breathe. You're okay. I'm coming to you."

She squeezed her eyes shut, her fingers and grip slipping. The magical enhancements dissolved as her fear took over. "Oh my god, I'm going to die! I'm going to die!"

Rune was above her now. "Remember what I said about fear?

Your fear is killing the magic. Believe you are going to be okay, and you will be."

"Please, just help me," Nadia sobbed. She opened her eyes, and there he was, watching her, making no moves to help. "Seriously, this isn't funny!"

"I'm not always going to be there to save you," he said gently. "You need to save yourself."

She could have strangled him. "Rune! Just help me, okay?"

He stared at her and . . . smiled. *Bastard.* Nadia steeled her resolve. This was all part of the training. He wouldn't let her die.

Nadia recast the finger grip spell and slowly lowered herself to a better perch, her foot searching until she found a good wedge to work with. She allowed herself a few moments to breathe and then scowled up at Rune. "I really hate you right now."

"Oh, I'm sure by the end of this you'll loathe me," Rune replied, a sardonic smile on his lips. "I cursed my master many a time."

They made their way safely down the rest of the way. When she was about five feet from the bottom, she dropped the remaining way down, whirled around, and tried to punch him in the face. He easily dodged her fist and sidestepped around her.

"What was that for?" he demanded.

"For making me so angry at you!" Nadia lunged at him again, hands outstretched, preparing to throttle him. He ducked behind her, enveloping her in a straight-jacket bear hug.

"Get off me!" Nadia snarled.

"Not until you calm down," Rune replied evenly.

Nadia tried to wrestle him off, twisting this way and that, but he was too strong. Resigned, she stopped fighting, stilling in his arms. They paused there for a moment, both catching their breaths, Rune's arms encircling her in an embrace. She felt something—the brush of his lips, perhaps—against her earlobe. She froze, unsure of what was happening, not daring to hope. She felt it again, and this time she was sure, his breath hot against her neck, his arms wrapped tight around her. Heat pooled low in her body, and all rational thought flew from her brain as she succumbed to sensation. Instinct took over. She rubbed his muscles, his arms, his thighs, arched her back, exposed her neck. Breathed in his rich, masculine scent: spices and wood and smoke and mint. His lips were on her neck, his heart pounded against her back. She reached behind her, felt him hard in his shorts. His breath hitched. Her own breath came in shallow gasps as he caressed her abdomen and her hips. His fingers dipped into her waistband while the other hand snaked up to her throat. Please, Nadia thought desperately. She wanted it so bad . . . she *needed* him to touch her. But then, as strangely as it had come, it was gone. Rune released her and stepped back. Nadia was acutely aware of his absence, the void between them. She blinked hard, her mind reeling.

Time stretched, and they stood like that until Nadia calmed her racing heart. She plastered a smile on her face and turned to face him. In an overly chipper manner, she said, "We should probably get back, don't you think?"

She couldn't read the expression in his dark eyes.

Nadia prattled on about this and that on the hike back, mainly to fill the silence. She asked him questions about the history and ecology of Yosemite, and Rune obliged her, telling her stories about John Muir, Theodore Roosevelt, and others he had known during their time.

They were silent on the car ride back to Myst. Nadia's thoughts swam with feelings of guilt, confusion, denial, skepticism, and incredulity until she started to question what had even happened. She could be having some sort of solipsistic crisis, imagining the entire thing. Rune gave no indication that anything *had* even happened, as professional and courteous as always. He kept glancing over to check on her, but Nadia pretended she didn't notice, fixing her gaze on the passing blur outside the window.

Nadia was on pretty good terms with her old friends Denial and Avoidance. They'd gotten her through a lot of her childhood, giving her survival advice when she needed it. It was the easy way out, the chickenshit way, but she didn't care. As they crossed over the Bay Bridge back into the city, the lights of downtown twinkling across the water, Nadia decided the best way to handle the situation with Rune was to pretend that it didn't exist.

Chapter 21

Nadia ran through the rain, splashing mud puddles with her rain boots, and ducked inside the Musée Méchanique. Filled with hundreds of antique slot machines, the building near Fisherman's Wharf was a respite from the deluge outside. At the door, she shook herself off and gazed up at the dark sky. Lightning flashed in the wet gray clouds. Thunder ominously rolled through. There was a wild, electric energy in the air, and it wasn't a good sign.

She scanned the room for Thomas, but he didn't appear to be there yet. Only a few people milled about the slot machines, pushing quarters into machines to make automaton dolls dance and pinball machines light up. Nadia shrugged out of her dripping coat and squeezed the water out of her hair. Holding her coat draped over her arm, she wandered through the machines as she waited for her demon handler to arrive for their weekly check-in.

An old gypsy fortune-telling machine caught Nadia's eye. The automaton wore a wrapped headscarf, and her hands hovered over a crystal ball and tarot cards. Nadia stopped in front of it and fished in her purse for some quarters.

She pushed a coin into the machine, and it turned on. The gypsy waved her hands, and the machine spat out a little white card. Nadia grabbed it and held it up to read.

You are a very powerful queen. Eight rows and eight columns. Checkmate is only the beginning.

Nadia blinked and then read it again.

What.

The.

Fuck.

The universe was seriously messing with Nadia. Like, in a weird, fucked-up, about-to-cause-a-mental-collapse sort of way. She hunched down like a rat caught by a flashlight, sure someone was watching her. What did it mean? Was she the Prophecy Queen after all? Was any of it real, or was it all one big fucked-up game? If it was, she was playing fairy chess. The rules changed mid-game, Fate laughing, as she stumbled about.

Someone tapped Nadia on the shoulder, and she nearly jumped out of her skin. "You scared the fuck out of me!" she said when she saw it was just Thomas.

He peered at her. "What's going on with you? You're practically vibrating." He led her over to a corner away from the chaos of the whirling and *bings* and *bongs* of machines. Nadia closed her eyes and took several deep breaths to calm down enough to have a normal conversation.

"I'm fine," she said. "It's nothing."

Thomas grabbed her wrist and turned it to reveal the second side of the triangle tattoo. "I see you've passed the second test."

Nadia snatched her arm back. "Did you doubt I could?"

He shrugged. "You seem determined enough, but to pass all three tests is notoriously difficult."

"I'm going to do it."

"I believe you believe that."

"Fuck you."

Thomas chuckled, and they took off walking between the rows of machines. He zapped a change machine with his demon magic, and quarters spilled out, plinking into the metal cup. They grabbed a few handfuls, went to a nearby machine with an automaton marching band, and pushed in some coins. The machine lit up and started playing, cymbals crashing, band members marching.

"What do you think?" asked Thomas.

"Kind of fun, I guess," said Nadia. To make their weekly check-in sessions more palatable and less like meeting with a parole officer, Nadia had suggested they meet at all the tourist sites in the city. The boat trip to Alcatraz for their last session had been downright pleasant, all things considered.

They moved on to another machine, one with spinning ballerinas. Their pink tutus flared out as they spun. The sight tugged at something deep with her, a memory she had thought long-buried: the sharp slap of her pointe shoes hitting the stage, the fire in her muscles as she overextended her legs. Nadia had once chased the dream of being a dancer, a short-lived fantasy she'd indulged after her father had taken her to see her first ballet in New York City. She'd been okay at it. Not great. And to be a dancer, you had to be great. But she had loved to spin, to watch the audience rush by in one big blur as she lost herself in the dance.

It seemed like a lifetime ago.

Nadia dropped a quarter into the machine. "What's Mercurio been up to lately?"

Thomas glanced down at her. "Going on the offense?"

She shrugged, trying to look nonchalant. "Trying to be a good and docile servant and learn about the business."

His expression said he wasn't buying it.

"Come on," Nadia said, whining slightly. "Give me something. I know you wish you could escape working for him, too. Give me something I can use."

"Wrong," Thomas called out. "I enjoy the perks of being in Mercurio's employ."

"I know it isn't all about money for you. You aren't a money demon."

"Astute."

"What kind of demon are you, anyway?"

"Oh, ho!" He laughed. "That's the oldest trick in the book."

"What are you talking about?"

"If you know how a demon was turned, you know their weakness. Their vulnerability."

Nadia studied Thomas's face, trying to figure out what his weakness could be.

"Stop looking at me like that," Thomas warned, holding his hands up to block his face. "Seriously, stop!"

Nadia menaced Thomas a bit, wagging her eyebrows and making faces. "But seriously, though, what's Mercurio up to? What's he doing on Samhain?" If Nadia was going to cast a Soulwish that broke the Oath to him, she needed to know what he was doing that night, as well as any extenuating conditions that could impact the casting.

"Just the usual, I suspect," said Thomas. "Bacchanalian revelry. Blood orgies. And he'll probably make money off it."

"Lovely."

"What's Christiansen up to on Samhain?"

They moved on to another machine, one with a giant claw to pick up toys. Nadia shrugged. "Probably going out somewhere. I don't know." She didn't want to think about Rune. Didn't want him in her thoughts any more than he already was.

"I need you to find out what he's doing."

"Why?"

"People want to know where he's going to be."

Nadia glowered at him. "Stop being so cagey."

"Stop being so uncooperative." Thomas dropped a quarter in the machine and activated the claw, moving the joystick around as he tried to line it up to catch something. He tapped the glass of the machine with the signet ring he wore on his pinkie: his good luck charm. The claw descended, picked up a ball, and dropped it before Thomas could win the prize. "Oh, bloody hell."

"What's going on with your magic?" asked Nadia. Apparently, his luck had run out.

Thomas scowled. "Mercurio's gone and rationed everyone's magic. 'Cutbacks,' he said. Perfect timing, too, with Samhain coming up."

"Wait, he can ration your magic?" This was new information.

He nodded. "You didn't think I naturally had this much magic, did you? How do you think I can fold?"

"I don't know. I figured you practiced a lot or something."

He shook his head. "Um, no thank you. I do not have time for such trivialities like studying. That is Christiansen's domain, not mine. No, Mercurio gives everyone a monthly stipend. An allocated amount. Or at least, he did. Before a certain someone decided not to let him harvest from her anymore."

"What does that mean?" Nadia snapped.

"Your energy is extremely concentrated. One vial of you is like forty regular humans. I think he scaled up, thinking you were going to keep up your 'exposure therapy,' and when you didn't come back, he had to cut back on operating expenses."

Well, shit. "Is he mad at me or anything?" She didn't want to be the next Fred.

"As far as I can tell, no," said Thomas. "Like I said before, he's taken an interest in you. He seems to be playing the long game, seeing if you will come around. That's why he hasn't called you back yet after the last time."

Like a spider lying in wait, thought Nadia. He was trying to give her a false sense of security, and then *Bam!* He would get her.

"Say, I have an idea," said Thomas, his eyes lighting up. "Why don't you willingly come back and donate a little of your energy? A little good faith demonstration."

"You just had that idea, huh?" There was always a favor with him.

"It really would help me out. Show that I can keep you in line. He might let me have some magic this month. I'm itching not having it."

Nadia understood that. She couldn't imagine not having magic anymore. It would destroy her. "I'll think about it."

Thomas grinned smugly. They both knew she would find herself in front of Mercurio again sooner or later. She fingered the piece of paper in her pocket that the fortune-telling machine had given her. *Checkmate is only the beginning.*

Inky smoke from burnt offerings snaked up in front of Rune as he sat cross-legged in his underground ritual room. Dark blood marked the stone floor. Surrounded by chalked pentagrams and occult symbols, Rune lit a black candle with his mind. The flame burst into being and wavered in the darkness.

He closed his eyes and took a deep breath. His brain waves settled into an alpha state, and he disconnected his consciousness from his body, floating up. It was a duality. He was simultaneously aware of watching himself and being inside himself.

If they could see me now, thought Rune. He'd never told his buddies at Project Stargate he used magic. They thought the remote viewing truly had been some sort of ESP. He tried not to use this ability and magic very often. It was rather draining. But to spy on the Council? Well, he'd risk the repercussions on his body. He had to know what they were up to and how to prepare for their eventual attack.

Rune's body sat motionless in the ritual room as his mind and soul took off into the sky and shot over to Europe. The Earth turned beneath him, continents blurring past. In minutes, he was already above the Alps, the journey little more than a heartbeat on the astral plane. He located his target and descended, flying through the clouds, a kiss of rain coating his skin. A stone castle surrounded by snowy peaks and trees came into view. He shrank down, flew in through a window, and wove his way through velvet-lined hallways and dark passages to the Council's secret meeting room.

Sconces flared on the stone walls. The Council members sat in a circle, each in the throne that corresponded to the domain they represented. Shadows pooled between them, as if even the firelight hesitated to touch the space where so much power gathered.

"She's the key to Christiansen," said Senator John Conrad from his seat for North America. Rune bristled at this remark. The senator was in his human form: clean-shaven, short-cropped hair, hard eyes. But he was a doppelgänger; he could take any form, shifting fluidly with deep, dark magic. Like Rune, he lived primarily among humans. He had quickly risen in the American political ranks to advance Numinal issues, callous to a fault about human life.

"The girl is not the queen," said Lady Bai, the representative for Asia. The older woman sat demurely sipping tea, her white snake-like tail coiled behind her.

"It doesn't matter if she is or if she isn't," said Dieter, sitting in Rune's old chair for Europe. The tall, thin *Feuermann* had glamoured his skeletal features and wore half-moon sunglasses to cover his fiery eyes. "He cares for her, and that's enough. He'll bend to our will to save her."

The hell I will, thought Rune.

Lochland sat back in his chair for the British Isles. The High Fae prince wore silver battle armor, its surface encrusted with magical gems and Celtic knot protection spells. His russet hair fell loose about his shoulders. He was bored with the proceedings and stifled a yawn. Rune couldn't help it. He flicked him on the back of his ear. Loch startled, his eyes widening as he glanced about the room for whoever was there.

"She plays a part," said the senator. "How big of one . . . well, only time will tell."

"What are we to do with the Septer woman?" asked Carmina in her high-pitched child's voice. The elemental who represented the sky Numinals wore all white, her pale face peeking out from swaths of misty clouds. "She doesn't know what she's doing. The repercussions could be . . . devastating."

Rune's consciousness fuzzed for a moment with an influx of power. The edges went soft, the Council members' faces blurring and warping, as the senator magicked a leather-bound tome into the room. Rune almost lost his grip and shot back into his body, but he held fast to the remote view.

The book pulsed with dark magic as John Conrad held it on his lap. "We will gift this to her. She will take care of the rest." The man opened the book, and the power was too much. Rune flew back into his body.

He'll be the death of us all, thought Rune as he started to clean up and put things away. The senator had been one of the reasons Rune had left the Council in the first place. They were never going to see eye to eye on any issue as skewed as the man's perception was.

Back in his study, Rune sat in an armchair with his laptop, scanning the dark web and the Hades Market for Myst artifacts when his cell rang. He wasn't surprised to see the caller.

"Loch," said Rune when he answered.

"Come over," said Loch. "I have something to show you."

Rune folded over to Loch's country estate outside of Edinburgh. The Avalon House, a large stone manor set amid rolling green lawns, had been in Loch's family for generations. It had been decades since Rune had visited, but the estate was more or less the same. Ivy crawled on the walls while cherubic faeling statues burbled in fountains. Loch had put in a new rose garden and croquet field, though. The grass around both was brand-new.

The Fae prince answered the door at Rune's knock. "I thought you'd fold in. You know how to enter the wards." He wore his glasses and a tweed vest, the battle armor stored away in favor of his familiar professor look.

Rune stepped inside. "I didn't know if you changed the locks to keep me out."

The two men made their way through the sumptuously decorated living room. Portraits of Loch's ancestors lined the wall, antiques tucked away into corners.

Rune glanced at the décor. The walls were cream, the curtains frilly. "The chandelier is different," commented Rune as he eyed the gold and crystal monstrosity hanging from the ceiling.

"It's bloody awful," said Loch. "Imogen redecorated."

Rune chuckled. He had guessed as much.

Loch's study was the same as it always had been: dark mahogany, walls lined with books, mystical artifacts displayed on the shelves. Loch picked up an open book from his desk and handed it to Rune. "I've been reading up on Roseland."

Rune scanned the page. "I'm familiar with his work. Seventeenth-century mystic. Hid many of his dangerous and most potent spells within other texts, weaving them into prayers and poems, philosophical treatises, and even recipes. I have a few of his books."

Loch nodded. "The book that Conrad has supposedly contains one of his spells. One to open a portal to the Other Realms. Apparently, he sprinkled that spell over. I've tracked down dozens of copies."

"Does it work?"

"Not for me."

Rune doubted any spell that claimed to open a portal to the Other Realms was real. "Who was the Septer woman they were talking about?"

"Diane Robbins."

Rune's head snapped up. "The CFO of Pact?"

"Many are in the Council's pocket."

"Are you?"

Loch's gaze was unwavering. "You know how I feel about the Council. It's better to be on the inside where I can be involved in what they are doing than outside, watching them."

"As you've said before."

Loch floated over a bottle of Glenfiddich and two crystal glasses from his bar and poured himself and Rune a drink. The two men took a seat, the book open on the coffee table in front of them.

"Do you think Diane Robbins is skilled enough to open a portal?" asked Loch.

"Highly doubtful." The woman had charlatan written all over her. Septers with true power were few and far between, Nadia being one of them. Or she would be, once Rune taught her how to control her gifts.

"What's that look?" asked Loch, an amused expression on his face.

"Nothing," said Rune gruffly.

"Imogen said you were smitten." Loch held up his hands in mock surrender. "Her words, not mine."

"I am not 'smitten.'"

"The Council will be after her. They see her as your weakness."

"I know."

Rune would just have to make sure that the Council thought Nadia meant nothing to him.

Chapter 22

"Now that Carson's solved the battery issue," said Rune, "we're on target for the launch." The Veil team clapped their hands and banged them on the conference room table, cheering.

"I'm ordering a cake. Can we have cake?" asked Piero.

"Of course we can have cake!" Rune grinned. He slapped Carson on the back. "Thanks, friend. I couldn't have done it without you.

"Aw, shucks." Carson feigned embarrassment.

They were sitting around the Artemis Room at the weekly team meeting. With Nadia's help in modeling the self-sustaining loop, Carson had figured out how to power the battery for the game without draining the users too quickly. It was a relief. With the disastrous start at Numinox at the ideathon, they had all been afraid they'd fall behind schedule and miss the target date.

Nadia had proudly entered the spell into Myst's spell repository. They'd allowed her to name it, and she had decided to call it "The Pawn Ouroboros." Take that, Fate. Nadia had helped do some good in the world, inspired a spell to help solve the world's energy crisis. If she succeeded at nothing else, at least she had that.

She joined the gang in the celebration. They ate cake, popped glitter bombs, and took shots. When Nadia went to refill her Diet Coke, Rune sidled over.

"How are the artifact overlays coming?" he asked. One of the modes of Veil was "learning mode," where people could get an in-depth look into ancient artifacts, San Francisco history, and mythical lore. Nadia was responsible for drafting the text for the informational pop-ups designed into the game.

"I'm about ninety percent done." Nadia took a sip of her drink. "Maybe ninety-five."

"Wonderful," he murmured, goosebumps breaking out over Nadia's skin at the sound of his deep voice.

They hadn't talked about what had happened in Yosemite, both conveniently sweeping the day under the rug and pretending that nothing was different. They worked and trained together like usual, keeping things strictly professional.

But things were different. There was no unringing of that bell. Every time Nadia looked at Rune, memories of his lips on her neck flooded her mind. Had that moment even happened? Had she imagined it all? Having a Numinal like Rune Christiansen—*the* Rune Christiansen—want her was something she never would have dreamed of. It was a wild wish, something she never thought could come true. Other people lived the fairytale. Not her. She never thought she would get a happily ever after. And certainly not with a Numinal *man* who looked like *that*. All washboard abs and brooding masculinity. His hungry gaze, the feeling of his body pressed against hers . . . She clenched her thighs. Just thinking about him was going to send her over the edge.

But she was getting ahead of herself. Nothing had happened. Not really. One moment, just one moment. One sweet, stolen moment where the forces perfectly aligned to bring them together. *Oh gods, did I just peak?* What if that was the pinnacle of her existence—rubbing up against a sexy, centuries-old magical Numinal—and it was only downhill from there?

Nadia stuffed a large piece of cake in her mouth, mimed

needing to chew, and walked away before Rune could figure out what she had been thinking about.

Piero grabbed her by the shoulders and peered into her face. "Are you okay? You look like you're about to choke."

Nadia managed to swallow without killing herself. "I'm okay."

"Well, easy on the cake, okay? It's cake *or* death, not cake *and* death."

After a bit, Rune brought the group back to the table to finish the team meeting. "Settle down, everyone." Rune dropped into his boardroom chair and glanced at the itinerary. "We're almost through. Piero, what's the latest on Impact? Any way we can leverage it?"

Piero scrolled through social media feeds on his phone. "Screamforce is the big-ticket party on Samhain. Everyone's excited to be there. Rumor has it Tiesto is headlining."

"Tommy Lightning is playing," said Sophie, stars in her eyes. "I would literally kill to be there." She shot Rune an apologetic look that said, "Sorry, not sorry." Sophie was the vampire rockstar's number one fan.

Rune shrugged. "I get it. Everyone loves a good party. Anything we can use?"

"I have some interns seeing if they can bootstrap some potentiality spells," said Piero. "See if we can ride the wave. Slingshot from the amassed energy and gathering of people. There's supposed to be like twenty thousand people there. It's going to be wild."

Sophie leaned forward excitedly. "I'm launching an ad campaign that pushes Myst front and center in people's minds."

Rune narrowed his eyes. "That sounds like black magic."

Sophie's eyes went wide. "No, I would never. Nope. This is definitely . . . gray at worst."

"Clean it up," said Rune. Sophie nodded. Rune continued, "I know several big VCs are going to be at Impact. Pact is going to use their party to showcase the tech and design in The Call. We need to make sure that people know how derivative it is of Veil."

"There's that VC event on Thursday," said Carson. "The one at The Battery."

"I was invited," said Rune. "I originally wasn't going to go, but this might be the perfect opportunity to get investors' attention before Pact does. I'm sure it's all the same people."

"If you want, I can tweak the demo we used at the ideathon," offered Carson. "Make a two-minute elevator pitch you can show people."

"Perfect." Rune glanced at Nadia. She sat up in her chair. Was he going to ask her to be his date to the event? It wouldn't be the first time they'd attended a work function together. He pressed the intercom on the table. "Anya? Can you come here, please?"

They chatted for a few minutes before the leggy nymph who worked the front desk and as Rune's personal assistant appeared in the doorway.

"What can I do for you?" she asked in her sultry voice.

"What are you doing Thursday?" he asked.

"No plans."

"Great. Change the RSVP to two for that VC thing at The Battery. I'll send you a dress."

Heat rushed to Nadia's cheeks. Apparently, Rune sent dresses to every date he took to events. Nadia had thought she was special when he had sent her that dress for Artumnal, but as it turned out, she was just one of the herd.

Anya smiled, her gorgeous face lighting up. "Pick me up at six?" And he knew where she lived. Great.

"I'm also going to the VC mixer." Piero smiled cheekily at Rune. "Do I get a dress too?"

Rune snorted. "I saw your expense report last month. When did I start paying for your personal tailor?"

Piero brushed a speck of lint from his shoulder. "I renegotiated my employee contract. Ask Vega."

When Rune dismissed everyone from the meeting, Nadia stared at him.

"Anything I can do for you, Ms. Winters?" he asked.

They held each other's gaze. Unspoken words flowed between them, electricity crackling in the air. Neither one wanted to mindspeak first, so they let their eyes carry the weight of everything unsaid. *We crossed a line*, said the look he gave her. *You're running away*, said hers back. Rune was the first to look away.

Back at her habitat, Nadia scrolled through her contact list to find that guy from the bar's number. She considered texting him. They'd exchanged a couple of messages here and there but never made firm plans to hang out. He'd for sure go out with her if she asked. But she hesitated. It wouldn't be enough to make Rune jealous. He wouldn't care about a human rando she met at a bar. But then, she found another guy to text: Miles Kirkpatrick.

I'd love to cash in my rain check for a jaunt around the Bay. How about Thursday? xo. She typed out the message and hit send.

Two could play at this game, thought Nadia. She wanted to hit Rune where it hurt, and going out with the CEO of Pact would definitely hurt.

If Rune was going to pretend nothing had happened between the two of them, she would show him that nothing did.

The next week flew by quickly, and then it was Thursday.

"Where do you think you're going?" asked Piero as he moseyed over to where Nadia sat at her habitat, putting cherry-red lipstick on in a compact mirror. He watched her for a second before he seized the tube. "Child, who taught you to put on makeup?" He grabbed her chin and applied it to her lips.

Sophie flounced over and jumped up to sit on Nadia's desk, perching like a kawaii kitten. "Looks like Nadia has a hot date."

"A hot date, huh?" said Rune behind her.

Nadia spun around in her chair as he dropped a stack of papers on her desk. "I'm actually going out with Miles Kirkpatrick tonight," she said. Her heart thumped wildly in her chest. She ignored Piero's and Sophie's incredulous expressions. "Are those the specs you were talking about?" *Breezy and casual, breezy and casual.*

The corner of Rune's lip turned up in amusement. "Yes, but this can wait until tomorrow. I wouldn't want you to be late for your *date*." Nadia thought she detected sarcasm in his voice when he said the word "date," but couldn't tell if she had just imagined it.

Rune nodded to employees as he made his rounds. "Have a good evening, everyone." Near the front, he stopped and shot Nadia a heart-stopping smile and wink. Her knees buckled. What did that mean? Did that mean he was jealous? Did she get under his skin? Or was he just fucking with her? His way of reminding her that he would always dominate their relationship, keeping it on his terms and keeping her guessing?

Piero fanned himself. "This is a new development. PDA?? Ooh la la!"

Sophie smirked. "That's one way to get a promotion, I guess."

Piero settled his face into a wise, all-knowing expression of a sacred clown. "If you and Rune are an item, why are you going out with Miles Kirkpatrick?"

"We are *not* an item," said Nadia. "Miles invited me out on his boat and to some art show, that's all. I thought it would be good recon. You know, to see if we can use anything about Impact to our advantage."

"What are you doing?" asked Sophie in a singsong voice.

"Sometimes it takes a woman's wiles to get information," said Nadia. "I'm just helping Rune."

Piero narrowed his eyes. "Hm. Well . . . you do have a point. Miles seems like the type who would spill the beans the second a woman paid him any interest. And we do need to figure out how to use the fallout from Impact. I'll allow this. Where are you going? What're the deets?"

"We're taking out his yacht, *The Empress*, for a little . . . *jaunt*"—Nadia wiggled a bit like she was being fancy—"around the Bay. And then there's an art show. Nothing crazy. I'll be back before eleven, Mom." Nadia stuck her tongue out at him. "It's completely harmless. But I've watched enough true crime shows to know that you never go out on a boat with a guy, harmless or not, without telling someone. So, I'm telling someone. If I don't make it to work tomorrow, you'll know why."

"Oh, wonderful," said Piero. "We'll just dredge the Bay. Make sure to keep your GPS on." He crossed his arms. "I don't think this is a good idea. I once heard a story about Miles and some model-escort slash working girls who wound up dead, floating in the Bay. They had some sort of orgy and did too many drugs and fell overboard, and no one noticed because they were all too high on *ousia* and the Light knows what else. He was arrested, but all charges got dropped."

It didn't surprise her that Miles had a sordid history. He seemed to type who would have rich parents to pay off the district attorney each time he fucked up. "I'm not going to do any drugs with him. Or have sex with him. There's nothing to worry about." Nadia mock saluted. "I'm off. Wish me luck."

"It's not luck you're going to need," said Piero with a giant sigh. "It's common sense."

The Lilihana Yacht Club was in an unassuming yellow houseboat on the waterfront next to the Chase Center where the Warriors and the Valkyries played. Despite the club's outside appearance—rundown, aged, and in desperate need of a fresh coat of paint—several very expensive yachts and sailboats were parked in the harbor next to it.

Unsure where exactly she was meeting Miles, Nadia walked up the ramp to the front and rang the doorbell. After a minute, a man with a thin mustache and a white tuxedo coat opened the door.

"Yes?"

"Oh, hi. I'm supposed to meet Miles Kirkpatrick. Is he here?"

The butler opened the door wider, allowing her to enter. He led her to a podium with a large logbook open on top of it and told her to sign. As she wrote in her name, she couldn't help but notice that most of the entries were logged by women visiting Miles. Inviting chicks out on his yacht must be his one big move, she thought. He seemed the type to recycle his efforts.

After Nadia signed in, the butler led her down a hallway. Vintage black-and-white photographs of beautiful people on boats lined the walls. They entered a gilded lounge with a wooden bar to one side, where dozens of nautical flags hung. Leather couches and wooden lounge tables were scattered around the room, and about eight or ten club members sat in the lounge as waitstaff in white tuxedo jackets served them.

Miles stood at the bar, talking to the bartender. His golden hair was haloed around him in the overhead spotlight, giving him a Golden Age of Hollywood vibe. His eyes lit up as Nadia approached.

"Mr. Kirkpatrick. Your guest has arrived." The doorman gave a small bow and backed away, taking the butler thing to a whole new level.

"Thank you, Henry." Miles leaned down and kissed Nadia on the cheek. "You look wonderful. Would you care for a drink? Or better yet, care for one on the boat?"

Nadia shrugged, smiling. She felt removed from the situation, like she had walked onto a movie set and found herself the star. They made a grand exit, with half the club waving bon voyage and popping confetti at them. The whole thing was slightly ridiculous, and she didn't know if they did this every time someone set sail, or if Miles had brought out the big guns to impress her.

They emerged into the daylight onto a pier. Miles swept his hand toward a large navy-blue cruiser yacht with pristine white trim and blond teak decking. It practically sparkled in the sunlight. A crew worked on deck, efficiently and expertly loading supplies and provisions as they readied the boat for its trip out.

"This is *The Empress*," said Miles.

"Wow, she's gorgeous." Nadia took a minute to enjoy the luxury of it all, feeling a little like a princess.

They walked up the ramp to the boat and stepped onto the deck. "Let me give you the grand tour," said Miles. He placed his hand on Nadia's lower back, a tad too low for her comfort, as he led her to the master stateroom with a lounge and a bar. It seemed brand-new with no scratches or wear on the mahogany and brass accents, though there were a few stains on the carpeting. She was pretty sure a black light would reveal a lot more.

The bartender poured flutes of Veuve. Miles handed her one.

"Cheers to new adventures." His blue eyes sparkled as they clinked glasses.

Nadia took a sip of champagne. "This boat is amazing. I used to sail a little, but never on something quite like this."

Miles beamed. "Thank you. I've always been a fan of the sea." Nadia tried not to wince at his stupid proclamation. Miles gestured to the stairs. "Let me show you the rest of *The Empress*."

After Miles showed Nadia around the boat and introduced her to the staff, they settled in on the viewing deck as the captain nudged the boat out of the harbor and headed north, passing under the Bay Bridge.

"Where are we going?" Nadia held up her champagne, and a waiter refilled it. She promised herself that she would cut herself off after three.

"I thought we would just sail around and have dinner, and then we'll go to the art show around eight p.m. or so. Don't worry. We aren't leaving the Bay."

Nadia leaned back on the teak deck chair to watch the waves. They made their way north through the water, the Golden Gate Bridge to their left. The sun was low in the sky, casting brilliant watercolors of orange and pink across the sky. It was like the sunset she had seen with Rune when they went to Rocky's. She tried to push all thoughts of Rune from her mind, but he kept creeping back in. What was he doing with Anya right then? Was he thinking about her and Miles?

Miles must have noticed she was distracted because he went below deck for quite some time. Nadia was almost starting to worry when he reappeared with a fresh bottle of champagne and a crew member carrying a rather impressive cheese plate, a cornucopia of dried fruit, nuts, cheeses, and crackers.

Miles sat back down, a little jumpy and twitchy. There was a sweet smell about him. Tobacco? No . . . something sweeter. *Ousia.* Nadia was slightly miffed that he hadn't asked her to partake. Did he think she was a square? Did he only do *ousia* with model slash escorts?

But she quickly forgot about all that as she lay out in the wind and the waves, watching the sun set over the Bay. They headed up past Tiburon and made their way under the Richmond Bridge. Nadia found herself relaxing, laughing, and all the events of the last few weeks melted away as the boat sailed through the last light of the sunset. She found herself enjoying Miles's company. Rune and Mercurio and all her problems floated away into the sky like balloons.

As Miles explained the history of the area and pointed out landmarks they passed, Piero's and Sophie's warnings about him fell by the wayside. He was good-natured, flirtatious, and easy-going. He was pretty much the exact kind of guy Nadia used to think she wanted. The perfect boyfriend and maybe future husband material if she played her cards right, as her mother liked to say. For a hot minute, Nadia had thought that her ex, Keith, had been what she wanted, but that was until he blew it by cheating on her. But he hadn't been what she really wanted, not deep down. He wasn't ambitious or intellectual enough for her. She always felt like she was debating a guppy when they tried to discuss politics, his mouth opening and closing as his neurons tried to fire and form a cohesive argument.

"What are you thinking about?" asked Miles, bringing her back to the present.

"Oh, nothing important. So, tell me about Pact. It seems unusual for a human to be running a magical company. I wasn't aware of . . . *everything* until only a couple of months ago."

Miles splashed more Veuve into Nadia's glass as she grabbed a dried apricot to nibble on.

"If by 'everything' you mean the fact that there's a whole different reality that most people are oblivious to?"

Nadia nodded.

"My eyes were opened after college. I used to be like you: young, unaware, totally naive about the existence of Numinals."

Nadia fought the urge to roll her eyes. "How did you learn about them?" She shifted slightly to get comfortable.

Miles's gaze flicked down briefly to her cleavage. "Purely by accident. You see, my father started the Stonewell Group in DC." Nadia knew of the Stonewell Group. They were big military defense contractors who supplied weapons to the government. "He always envisioned that I would take over after I graduated. He went to Yale, too, and thought I was following in his footsteps. I never wanted to do that, you see. I was somewhat of a disappointment to my family. Partying, spending time traveling around, doing everything I could to avoid real responsibility. I was backpacking in Thailand, doing a lot of the whole 'avoiding responsibility thing,' when one night, this old man told me this tall tale about spirits and how they are around us all the time, passing as humans. He told me that if I smoked this special drug, I would be able to see them like he does. Now, I know what you're thinking. Spoiled rich kid on a spiritual quest doing drugs. How original."

Nadia shook her head, laughing. "What I was thinking is that I wish I had done that drug so I would have known about everything sooner."

Miles chuckled. "Me too! Anyway, the old man said he would act as my spiritual guide. For a fee, of course."

"Naturally."

"He led me to his house, this awful hut in this squalid neighborhood. I sat down on this mat, and he got out a tiny foil-wrapped figurine of what looked like crystal or ice, molded into the shape of a winged creature with a long tongue and clawed feet. He placed it in this pipe and lit it, taking a few puffs himself before he passed me the pipe. I took one hit and started hacking up a lung."

"What was it?"

"*Ousia.* Supposedly, it is crystallized magic made from Numinals."

"Imagine that." Nadia feigned awe.

He laughed. "The more you know, right? The second I stopped coughing, the veils were gone. It turned me into a Sixer. And the old man wasn't a man at all. He was a demon. A drug demon, to be exact. And he had decided I was his next victim." Miles paused for effect, taking a sip of his drink before he continued, "The drug demon was terrifying. A hulking, rotting gray corpse, with skin falling off in lesions. His breath smelled like ass. He tried to get me to keep smoking, but I knew that if I did, that would be it for me. Miles would be pushing daisies. I learned later that he was trying to get me addicted so I would turn into a demon like him."

"That's awful. How did you get away?"

"I bolted. I've never been so scared in my life. I ran through the streets of Bangkok, high on *ousia*, mind you, demons and other Numinals everywhere. Ghosts and these weird bug-creatures that were like . . . bunny beetles. The whole thing was frankly quite unnatural and extremely terrifying. After a while, the *ousia* wore off, but my world had been turned upside down. I was a Sixer. I knew I couldn't go back to pretending everything was normal. And I couldn't go work for my father. I found others who knew of the creatures and started Pact, getting funding from them. I was determined to find a way for humans and Numinals to work together. To bridge that gap and foster mutual understanding."

Rune had said the same thing about how he started Myst. Once again, Miles was ripping off Rune, this time with his motivation to start a Numinal startup. Nadia's thoughts spiraled back to Rune. He was out with Anya. She was sure they were cozying up together.

"I've got some *ousia*, if you want to try it," suggested Miles. "As a Sixer, it sort of 're-ups' the ability to see Numinals."

Nadia hesitated. This was exactly the sort of thing she should avoid.

"You don't have to if you don't want," said Miles. "I just thought you might be the kind of girl who's down to try it." He smirked, his expression a dare.

Nadia had always been a "good girl." The kind of girl who toed the line but never crossed it. How many times did she go home early to study while her friends went out? Turn down drugs at a party? Where had that gotten her in life? *Make good decisions*, said her father's voice in her mind. All she'd done was make good decisions, and that had gotten her exactly nowhere. Her life had been thrown off track, even doing everything "right." Nadia let Miles pull her up and lead her downstairs.

He ushered her into the master bedroom, whispering and tiptoeing like he was hiding from the staff. Nadia was pretty sure they knew exactly what Miles was up to. Once there, they lay on the bed and passed a small pipe back and forth, lounging in hedonistic bliss among feather-down pillows. Each time Miles took a hit, he was lost for minutes in a drugged fugue. But Nadia didn't feel nearly the same euphoria she had the first time she had tried it. Her magic had grown stronger, and the drug—being itself magic—didn't have the same effect on her anymore. Nadia regretted doing this. She'd probably have an awful hangover chasing the dragon and never feeling high.

Miles rolled toward her on the bed and tried to smother her in a full-body bear hug. Nadia removed his wandering hands. He snuggled in anyway.

"You feel so nice," he murmured. "You should have been with me at Artumnal, not Rune Christiansen."

Nadia pinned his roving hands down again. "Tell me again,

how it is that you and Rune know each other? Forgive me, but it doesn't seem like you like each other very much. Seems almost personal, and your mutual business goals are so aligned."

Miles murmured into her neck, "You picked up on that, eh?"

"It's a little hard to miss." She shoved Miles off her. Coming down here had definitely been a mistake.

Miles rolled onto his back, cradling his head in the crook of his arm, oblivious. "Rune and I discussed a joint venture a few years ago, but it didn't work out. I went my way and started Pact, and he went his way and started Myst. Did you know he started a few companies before Myst? They failed, of course. The landscape wasn't ready yet, the technology not advanced enough. Investors just couldn't believe anything he was promising was true. Everything did just seem like magic. And it was, of course. That's his whole business model. Hiding magic as technology. But Rune is so shortsighted. He didn't want to allow black magic! Can you believe that? Never mind that the most powerful men in history have always used black magic to get where they were. My philosophy is that if the universe provides it, it's just another tool that you can use. You just have to make sure that you are sufficiently prepared to wield the power. No one wants to give an AK-47 to a monkey."

Nadia chuckled appropriately. "Do you practice black magic?"

"Me? God, no! No talent for magic. I'm only a Sixer. I know that Diane, on the other hand, is a Septer and dabbles in the occult."

"How did you start working with Diane, if you don't mind me asking?"

"She worked with my father for years, mostly in R&D in the weapons sector. When she heard I was starting Pact, creating a startup that used magical blockchain, she came on board. Even though she's old-school research and development, she really supports my vision for crypto."

Nadia listened for a while to Miles wax on about Pact's crypto, Hacksilver, as they went back up to the viewing deck and settled back in. From what she could tell, their game, The Call, mined crypto as users played. They paid them minimal rewards for their efforts, while keeping most of the profits, and enticing them to spend the crypto they earned at Pact through their various game offerings. As he spoke, Nadia became more and more confused about what Miles actually did at Pact. He seemed to have almost no understanding of day-to-day business activities and seemed to rely heavily on Diane for most strategic decisions. Nadia got the impression that he spent a lot of time telling people he was the CEO of a company, without doing any real work.

"Does Rune ever tell you what they're up to in the labs?" asked Miles. "Or does he just keep you locked away in those boring vaults minding the database? No offense if that's your thing. I could never just sit in front of a computer all day like that."

"I actually helped out with an experiment the other day," said Nadia, slightly offended that he would think the vaults were boring. She explained how she was a Blood Muse and Rune had done experiments on her, focusing on energy cycling. Miles didn't seem to know the implications of being a Blood Muse, but he was impressed that she had used her own biomechanics to solve a company problem. At one point, he had to answer some important emails, and Nadia proceeded to drink more champagne by herself as he wrapped up business.

The sky darkened. Miles glanced at his watch. "I think it's about time to head to the art show." He stood up, placed his cell phone on his deck chair, and stretched. "I'm going to hit the little boys', but I'll be back in a minute."

Nadia didn't mean to look at his cell phone. She really didn't. But he had left it unlocked and open to where he was messaging someone on the Hades Market. She did a double take. The bastard had asked for energy conversation blueprints from Myst! Miles was working with the thief!

His voice drifted up from below, and Nadia returned his phone to the table before he could see, fumbling and nearly dropping it in her worry about getting caught.

When Miles came back, he slipped his phone back into his pocket. "I've told the captain to head to the show."

"Wonderful," Nadia murmured, her heart still racing.

Chapter 23

Rune stepped with Anya into the spotlight on the red carpet and pulled her in for a picture. *Flash! Flash! Flash!* They smiled, her hand on his chest, his arm around her waist. He turned Anya's cheek and playfully gave her a kiss. She giggled vapidly, acting like a minor celebrity in a Swarovski crystal dress with her billionaire boyfriend. The photographers snapped several more pictures, and he knew that the image of him and Anya together as a couple would soon be splashed throughout the human and Numinal world on social media.

It wasn't much, but he knew that who he was seen with and who he dated was always tabloid fodder. He hoped being seen with Anya would throw the Council off the scent so they would leave Nadia alone. Anya hadn't minded when he asked her to play the part of his girlfriend. It wasn't the first time he'd called in a favor from one of his oldest and dearest friends to help hype up the media. Going out with Anya would sway the odds and throw a wrench into the algorithm that had him and Nadia together as the king and queen, and he loved messing with gamblers who were betting on his actions and life.

Rune had come up several years in a row as the king, requiring various long-term magical spells to remove the stain of empty celebrity. It was tedious spellcasting that required constant updates. Social media was notoriously difficult to wrangle.

Too many influencers used charms to boost their visibility, and all that conflicting magic and intention tended to bubble up and clash.

That evening's event at The Battery was an informal networking event limited to the very elite. Only the Who's Who of the tech world was there. Attendees mingled around the lounge, sipping cocktails and chatting as a DJ played unobtrusive house music in the corner. Rune had been to a few events like this before. They were generally dull, but a good way to network. Inventors could get access to VCs, float ideas, and start putting together deals, no pressure, with alcohol to lubricate the conversations. He recognized several people he knew and mimed that they should catch up soon.

Rune and Anya stepped up to the bar and ordered Japanese whiskeys, neat. In the corner, Piero was having an animated conversation with a bald man who looked like a Russian oligarch. He wiggled his fingers to say hello when he saw Rune.

Anya scanned the room. "Who's the first target?" Rune tipped his head toward Ted Brinkley, a VC known for investing in eco-friendly technologies. "I'm on it," said Anya as she slinked off toward the man in full-on nymph mode, hips swaying with each calculated step. Within minutes, she had brought the man over to introduce him. Rune took over, charming him into investing in Veil after he told him about the self-charging battery technology used in the design.

They worked the room like that, Anya giving Rune layups that he could slam-dunk. Soon, they'd met everyone they wanted to meet. Rune had given dozens of informal pitches, secured investments or further talks, and spread the knowledge that Myst was the forerunner in humanitarian and eco-friendly tech.

"My feet are killing me," said Anya as she took off one of her high heels and rubbed her foot. "Unless you need me longer, I'm going to head out."

He followed her gaze to an attractive human woman with auburn hair who stood in a corner, making eyes at Anya. "Go," said Rune. "I'll wrap up here."

Anya floated off toward the woman, and the two of them left together.

Rune leaned against the bar, trying not to think about Nadia. She was out with Miles Kirkpatrick, of all people. He thought she might retaliate for him going out with Anya, maybe give him the cold shoulder or make some snarky comment, but he hadn't anticipated she'd go for the jugular and go out with the CEO of Myst's biggest competitor. She had balls, that was for sure. Not many women would dare to try to make him jealous like that. Rune didn't get jealous. At least not when the other contender was a mere mortal boy like Miles. It wasn't a fair comparison; the idea wasn't even worth humoring.

There was some commotion at the front of the room as a group entered, and Rune locked eyes with Mercurio. A slow, evil smile crept over the vampire's face. The last time Rune had seen him, Mercurio had attacked Nadia and drank her blood. It wasn't a scene that Rune cared to dwell on. The look on her face, the panic, the horror of what he was witnessing, the helplessness he felt . . . it was all too horrific. Pure hatred coursed through Rune's veins as Mercurio flashed his fangs at him, taunting him with the memory.

Rune turned away. If he kept looking at Mercurio, he wasn't sure he would be able to keep it together. He itched to pummel the man's face, for more reasons than just his feeding on Nadia.

"Christiansen," said Mercurio as he sidled up to him at the bar. "What a pleasant surprise. I didn't know you went to these kinds of industry events."

Rune forced a smile, aware of others watching the interaction. "I heard you're designing a new product."

Mercurio pulled out a handheld device similar to a forehead thermometer. "A nifty little gadget, if I do say so myself. A portable harvester." He covered his mouth like he had said too much. "I mean, a portable crystal healing diffuser."

Rune raised an eyebrow. "You're marketing it as a crystal diffuser?" That was a new one.

"Wellness is 'in' right now. Humans will buy anything if you tell them it makes them look younger or slows aging."

Rune took a sip of his drink. "Preying on the fears of mortals."

Mercurio chuckled. "We aren't that different, you and I. We are both pioneers, game changers trying to build a better future." He gestured around himself. "All of this is meaningless unless we figure out something sustainable. You say that yourself. The fact is, we need energy, and humans have it. I am merely building a symbiotic relationship, a win-win for everyone."

The vampire prided himself on alternative techniques to harvest energy from humans. He thought of them like a cash crop, something to exploit and use, not as animals for the slaughter. He skimmed energy out of the air at his nightclubs, harvesting humans to the edge. Rune didn't condone it, but at least it was preferable to the alternative: using humans as fuel and straight up killing them.

"Good to see you." Mercurio clapped him on the back and leaned in, speaking low. "And thank you for bringing that sweet little Blood Muse to my attention. She was . . . *exquisite.*"

It took all of Rune's resolve not to punch the vampire's smug face. "Leave her out of this."

"You are the one who brought her to me," he replied. "Have you had a taste yet?" He laughed, throwing his head back, fangs out. "Of course you haven't. So strict. So buttoned up. All work and no play makes Rune a dull boy." Mercurio spied several swords and sabers on display on the wall. He plucked two off and threw one to Rune. "Have I offended your honor and manhood? Are you going to duel me?"

Rune threw the sword to the side. "I'm not going to fight you." He was no stranger to duels, but it was neither the time nor the place for a big public display that was sure to make the tabloids, as well.

Mercurio grinned and attacked, bringing his sword down in a wide arc. Rune deftly sidestepped. It didn't surprise him in the least that Mercurio would attack an unarmed man. He had no morals. No honor.

"Stop," snapped Rune. A crowd developed around them. A few people held up cell phones, recording. So much for keeping this out of the papers.

Mercurio swung again. "You're positively boring, you know that?"

Rune circled out of the way. Mercurio struck again, and Rune retrieved the saber he had thrown to the side and used it to block the blow. Metal on metal rang out as their swords clashed, and they pushed up close against each other.

Mercurio flicked his tongue in an obscene gesture. "What's it like, knowing I had a taste of her? That I had her blood. Did you think about it after? Did you think about *me*?"

Rune clenched his jaw. That was it. The gloves were coming off. He shoved Mercurio away and then struck with a forward blow. Mercurio dodged it and parkoured off a lounge table into a somersault. The crowd gasped. Showoff, thought Rune. It was all a game to him. A fucking performance. The vampire sliced his saber toward Rune, who deftly sidestepped and parried. He wanted to skewer him. He wanted to stab—

"Think about it now," said Mercurio, grinning wildly, "my fangs sliding into her neck, sinking into her flesh, that sweet Blood Muse energy all mine for the taking."

Okay, fuck this guy. Rune threw the saber to the side and tackled Mercurio to the ground, bone crunching under his fist as he pummeled the vampire's face. Shouting broke out in the crowd.

Black blood from a busted lip smeared across Mercurio's face. "It appears I've gotten under your skin."

Rune hit him again.

"You know," continued Mercurio as Rune hauled him to his feet, "I've always seen you as a bit of a Boy Scout. A Goody Two-shoes, high on your own supply. But you fight dirty, like me. Another reason we are the same." He grinned, a crazed joker, his teeth stained black from the blood.

Security guards rushed over. "We are nothing alike," Rune spat out as two of the guards pulled him off Mercurio to break up the fight. "I'm fine. Get off me!" He shook off the guards and straightened his suit coat.

Mercurio dabbed the blood on his face with a handkerchief, a satisfied glint in his eye. "Always a pleasure to see you, Christiansen."

Nadia and Miles docked at the harbor on Treasure Island and disembarked from *The Empress*. Dark storm clouds formed overhead. Miles gave Nadia his hand to help her onto the ramp, and she gingerly took it, Miles going on about something or other.

She couldn't believe he was working with the thief! All this time . . . that entire story about Bangkok, getting her to open up, human to human . . . he had been using her to get information about Myst! What had she even prattled on about, her tongue loosened by so much champagne? She needed to play her cards better. Hold them closer to her chest. She had let her guard down thinking he was kind of an idiot, and he had turned out to be more devious than she originally thought. It wasn't like Nadia had been a saint. She was using him to get back at Rune, after all. But her deceit at least didn't involve corporate theft. Not in this instance, anyway.

The art gallery was inside one of the whitewashed stucco buildings on Treasure Island that had once been used for the military. As they approached, they could hear the music from a DJ inside thumping through the walls. Outside the door, spotlights shone into the sky, lighting up the gray clouds. Nadia considered ditching Miles, but she kind of wanted to see where this was all going. Was he going to try to sweet-talk information out of her? Could she plant misinformation and throw him off the scent? And she was already here. She'd gotten all dolled up for this. Might as well stay for the party and drink some more champagne.

Inside the gallery, dozens of humans and Numinals milled about, talking in clusters, drinking cocktails, and examining the art on the walls. Miles ushered them over to the bar and ordered drinks from a bartender in a black tux.

The bartender handed Nadia a vodka soda and a napkin. Pact's symbol was on the corner of the bar napkin along with another she didn't recognize.

"What's that symbol?" asked Nadia. It looked like a torii or maybe a dolmen.

"Pact is partnered with a startup called Pyli to put on this event," said Miles. "Here, let me show you." He led her around the art gallery, his hand on her lower back, introducing her to several Pact and Pyli people as they perused the art on the walls. A few of the girls there sized up Nadia like they too had once been Miles's date to an event.

"What am I looking at?" Nadia asked as they stopped in front of a large piece of art. It was about fifteen by twenty inches, bordered by a gold frame, and appeared to contain some sort of live video feed. The images showed dark foliage of a jungle moving slightly and rustling in the wind.

Miles grinned. "I'm sure you've heard about the Other Realms. These pieces are a sort of live video feed from other worlds."

"You're joking."

He smirked. "Pact developed a technology that creates a small rift into the Other Realms. Each of these pieces here shows a pinhole, so to speak, into a different world. We never found a use for the technology—not much you can do with it if you can't communicate with the other side or send anything through—but we licensed the technology to Pyli, who makes art pieces with it. Here, take a closer look."

She moved from piece to piece, examining the images, Nest Cams into the Other Realms. It felt sacred, like looking at stained glass inside a cathedral. Each portal was unique, ranging from only a couple of inches wide to several feet, in custom frames to match the scene being portrayed. And each image inside was something entirely different.

The video feeds showed images of exotic worlds, alien landscapes, and Martian rubble. In one, bits of stone corners floated by like broken-off sides of buildings. Another showed a cloud-like structure, crystalline and fractal in nature. Inside, the clouds vacillated, the image in the frame moving like a breathing thing. Like an alien, something foreign. It was a rare glimpse of another world. Another plane of existence.

"Isn't it marvelous?"

Nadia turned to the woman's voice behind her. It was Diane Robbins, the CFO of Pact. She smiled at Nadia.

"Diane," said Miles, "you remember Nadia from Artumnal."

She held out her hand, and Nadia took it. "Of course. So nice to see you again."

"Good to see you again as well. I was just telling Miles how impressive this show is."

Diane gazed at the image in front of them, a sense of pride in her expression. "It really is an amazing technology. It can only receive images right now, picking up on signals. We aren't able to triangulate location in the quantum realm yet. But hopefully soon, we will be able to send data through."

Miles finished off his vodka soda. "I'm going to get another drink. Nadia, can I get you a refill?"

"I'm okay for now, thank you."

Miles left her and Diane in front of the art piece. Diane glanced over to Nadia, a serpentine smile creeping over the woman's collagen-injected red lips. "I sense the Goddess is strong in you."

"That's funny. Meredith Vincent said the same thing," said Nadia.

"Then it must be true." Diane's kohl-rimmed eyes bored into her, and Nadia shifted uncomfortably at the attention.

At that moment, Miles rejoined them, champagne in hand. Diane made excuses and floated off, but Nadia kept catching her staring. It was flattering but slightly unnerving to have someone watching her every move. It was like being on stage. Nadia found herself putting on a bit of a show, sashaying her hips and touching Miles on the arm as she smiled coyly at him. It could have been all the champagne making her feel bolder, but Nadia leaned into the feminine energy—*Goddess energy? Sure, why not?*—as she worked the room and chatted with people. Miles basked in the attention Nadia was giving him, caressing the small of her back and trying to grab her ass as he showed her off as his date, the new flavor of the week. Nadia even let him kiss her briefly behind one of the art exhibits, but he just shoved his tongue in her mouth and let it sit there like a dead fish. She pushed him off and pretended that she didn't want his coworkers to see them making out. If there had been any chance of her being attracted to Miles, that kiss had snuffed it out.

While Miles was using "the little boys' room," as he called it, Diane materialized next to Nadia, startling her.

"I'm having a women-only get-together at my house," said Diane. "Why don't you come?"

"For the Sisterhood?"

Diane nodded, smiling. "Just some gals getting together to honor the sacred feminine. We won't get too crazy, I promise."

"Oh." Nadia was taken aback. All that woo-woo stuff Maya had talked about gave her pause, but she was pleased that the woman saw potential in her, even if she didn't exactly know what the potential was for. "Sure, that would be great."

"Come with an open mind. The Goddess can be extremely generous to those she deems worthy." Diane took out her cell phone and took down Nadia's contact information. "I'll have my assistant send you the details."

Rune walked home to give himself time to cool off. The night air was chilly, but he took off his suit jacket. He had ripped it in the back when he had been pummeling Mercurio's face into a pulp. There was a homeless man sitting against a building, and he gave the jacket to him. The man had seemed surprised but pleased, taking off his threadbare coat and shrugging on Rune's Tom Ford.

He headed west through Chinatown. Lanterns and colorful flags were strung over the streets. Numinals and humans alike roamed around fruit markets that spilled out onto the sidewalk.

Neon signs for trinket shops and dim sum buzzed in windows. Rune wished they still had opium dens. Drugged-out bliss would be a welcome diversion from his feelings.

He had walked right into Mercurio's trap. The vampire had baited him and managed to provoke an intense reaction. Video of Rune and Mercurio's fight would reach the Council, if it hadn't already. If they suspected that Rune had feelings for Nadia, he had proved it by getting into a fucking duel over her. What was *wrong* with him? He never lost control like this. Never was so sloppy. Scrubbing the internet of all those videos would be a massive pain in the ass. He needed to use his resources and energy more wisely and not waste them on pointless brawls.

He stopped in front of Grace Cathedral. The French Gothic building was lit up at night, the façade towers glowing. Rune said a quick prayer to the Numinous, asking for strength. He felt weak, powerless, at the mercy of his temper, at the mercy of his impulses. He needed to numb the feelings. Numb the pain. Numb the urges. There was a corner store nearby, and Rune popped in for a bottle of whiskey, drinking straight from the brown paper bag as he continued his walk home.

Nearby on the street, a human was acting erratically. The girl couldn't have been more than sixteen, with matted hair and a baggy sweatshirt. It appeared that she was doing some sort of ritual dance, from the way she was shuffling around in a circle, as she held her cell phone in her hand. When she noticed Rune watching, her eyes flashed red.

Inhibiti. Rune sucked in a breath. She was possessed.

He couldn't leave her like that. She was just a child. If there was a demon inside of her, it was only a matter of time before she turned into one herself. Rune placed the brown paper bag of whiskey to the side and cautiously approached.

"Excuse me," said Rune. She looked over warily, her eyes clear. The demon was hiding now. Rune caught a glimpse of the screen on her cell phone. She was playing Pact's game, The Call.

"What is that game you are playing there?" he asked. "Can I see it?" He cast a quick persuasion charm over her, and she readily handed over her cell phone.

Before Nadia knew it, the night was coming to an end. She and Miles left the party, reboarded *The Empress*, and set off back toward the Lilihana Yacht Club. Miles escorted her off the yacht and waited with her while she ordered a ride, though he kept being a tad handsy, forcing her to keep swatting him away.

Nadia's cell phone vibrated as she was holding it. She glanced at the text from Piero.

The VC thing was lame. At the Hemlock with Sophie. Ditch the playboy and come join us!

"Everything okay?" asked Miles.

Nadia tucked her phone back into her purse. "It's just some coworkers trying to get me to come out tonight. They're at a show at The Hemlock."

"The Hemlock? On Polk?"

"Yeah. Have you been?"

"No," he said quickly. "But you need to stay away from there tonight."

"Why?"

A pained expression crossed his face. "Just, please, promise me you won't go out on Polk Street tonight. Stay away from that whole area."

Nadia's pulse quickened. "Miles, you're scaring me."

He took Nadia's hand. "I don't mean to. It's just . . ." He struggled to find the right words. "We've been tracking the demon attacks around the city with The Call. It's all very complicated, but there's going to be an attack on Polk Street sometime tonight."

Nadia shot off a quick message to Piero.

Not safe!!! Demon attack on Polk tonight!!!

Piero responded right away. ???

Leave NOW!!!

Miles kissed her on the cheek as Nadia distractedly climbed into a Waymo. Her mind swam with what Miles had revealed: Pact knew when there would be demon attacks. Myst had suspected its own tech was somehow involved, but it seemed like something in Pact's technology could predict—or was the cause of—the demon attacks around the city. She hoped Piero and Sophie would leave before anything happened. She tried calling them both, but neither picked up.

Back at home, Nadia lay in bed with her cell phone, repeatedly refreshing her news feed and scouring social media for any indication of an attack on Polk Street. She was just about to give up when she found something: someone had posted a grainy video from The Hemlock of a man jumping from the stage during a concert. At first, it looked like he was just trying to crowd-surf, but screams and chaos broke out, the crowd scattering. The video went shaky and then dark.

Horrified, Nadia tried calling Piero and Sophie again, but both phones went straight to voicemail. "Please call me back and let me know you're okay," Nadia pleaded to them.

It took her a long time to fall asleep that night.

Chapter 24

The next morning, Rune pinged the Veil team over Slack to meet in the Artemis Room. Everyone except Rune was already assembled by the time Nadia got there.

Sophie assessed Nadia's yoga pants and the dark circles under her eyes. Nadia had tried to freshen up with some appearance charms but, apparently, had done a piss-poor job. Sophie wagged her eyebrows lasciviously. "Someone kept you up all night long."

"Dude, I thought you were dead," Nadia snapped. "Why didn't you call me back? I was so worried."

"Sorry," said Sophie. She didn't sound sorry at all. "Met someone."

Nadia turned on Piero next. "You didn't call me back either!"

Piero gave a long sigh. "My cell got stolen last night. It's a long story. Never trust a lutin."

"Morning, everyone," said Rune as he entered the war room. He walked behind Nadia and placed a hand on her hip as he brushed by. The physical contact was searing, a reminder of what had happened in Yosemite. Nadia tried to keep her expression neutral.

Piero witnessed the interaction. He gave her a look that said, *I know what this is, and we are going to talk about it later, and holy fuck, did you guys . . . ?*

Nadia gave him a look back that said, *Do not say a word or I will hex you.*

Rune quieted them. "I'm sure you've all heard. There was another attack last night, at The Hemlock."

"We were there," said Piero, gesturing between him and Sophie. "Complete. And. Utter. Chaos."

"I'm glad you both are okay," said Rune. "What happened?"

"It was wild," said Piero. "This guy ran on stage and tried to attack the band!"

Sophie held up her cell phone. "I got video." They all peered at her screen. The video showed a bulky guy in a hoodie jumping from the crowd, the crowd's screams stopping the music. The band scattered, the drummer diving offstage. Sophie zoomed in on the attacker and paused when his face was turned to the camera. His eyes glowed red.

Maya gasped. "*Inhibiti.*"

"I ran into one myself last night." Rune pulled up Pact's terms and conditions on the overhead from a cell phone that had anime stickers on the back. "It appears that Pact's game is causing possession. Apparently, there is a different clickwrap for humans and Numinals. Our lawyers were looking in the wrong place." He read from the screen, "'User allows Pact and its agents, subsidiaries, and third-party contractors temporary authorization and control of User's faculties, mind, body, and soul while using the app, at the complete and sole discretion of Pact.'"

Nadia's jaw dropped. "Mind, body, and soul? How is that even possible?"

"Unfortunately, it's a binding magical contract," said Rune. "The user must accept the terms when using their software. And since this clause is overbroad, it's been leading to demons possessing users. They are slipping into bodies and causing havoc—the violence we've been seeing."

"Pact must not know about this," said Maya. "I have a hard time believing they would knowingly harm their user base."

Nadia glanced at Rune. "Miles Kirkpatrick said Pact knows the locations of attacks in advance. They've been tracking them. They're aware."

Rune pinched the bridge of his nose. "It's just so . . . disappointing. Miles is generally an idiot and has little business acumen or common sense, but I didn't think he was just callous about human life."

"They might not know that the clause is overbroad," countered Carson. "Maybe they thought it was doing something else."

"I mean, the text is pretty clear about what they intend," said Piero. "Control of 'User's faculties, mind, body, and soul'?" That can only mean one thing. They're wearing people like suits!"

"But why?" asked Maya. "That's so freaky."

Rune navigated to The Call's interface and clicked into a module. A pop-up box with instructions appeared: a pair of disembodied hands demonstrating the steps to a ritual. "This is the gameplay. Humans perform energy-generating spells, capturing power like using a windmill. I'm sure they're storing the energy on a server somewhere."

"They're doing double duty," said Carson, begrudgingly impressed. "Mining crypto by users playing the game and also generating energy they can use to power the spells."

"Is that even legal?" asked Maya. "I mean, that's like slave labor, right? They're mining crypto and ritual energy on the backs of unsuspecting humans who think they are just playing a game."

"I bet they are using this temporary possession clause to nudge players to use the app more, to mine crypto faster, and to create more energy," said Carson. "It's genius, really."

Maya scowled at Carson. "Don't defend them."

He looked shocked. "I would never."

"Guys, this is crazy," said Sophie. "Like, total batshit." She had that right.

"What are we going to do about Pact causing the attacks around the city?" asked Maya. "We have proof of that, with the clickwrap. We have to do something. We have to tell someone!"

"There's no one to tell," said Rune. "California is outside Council dominion, and human authorities would think we're insane." He thought for a minute. "Here's what we're going to do. Send these T&Cs to legal to see if they can find a loophole or workaround. And then figure out who has the bandwidth to whip up a quick software update. Some sort of protection spell, or shield magic. Maybe we can counteract Pact's shady corporate policies with preventative magic in Veil and at least protect our overlapping user base."

"I have the gnomes combing Veil for bugs," said Carson, "but I can pull them off and we'll coordinate an update."

"Great." Rune sat back, rocking in his chair. "If no one has anything else, then I'm going to call the meeting." He dismissed the group, and everyone scurried off to work.

Nadia tried to focus on her assignments throughout the day, but she was distracted. She kept scrolling through posts on Woven and searching YouScry and Google for any information about the demon attacks. Articles rehashed outdated theories, though the fentanyl crisis was still a popular one. Reddit boards, fringe websites, and conspiracy theorists' blogs tied the demon attacks to the end times, the Prophecy and Counter-Prophecy coming true on Samhain.

In the afternoon, an email popped into her inbox with the subject line "Invitation from the Goddess." It was all the information for the Sisterhood event, sent by Diane Robbins's assistant.

Nadia didn't know what to do. Should she go? What kind of woman knowingly harmed their user base? As CFO of Pact, Diane had to know what was happening. Miles was the CEO, but it was clear Diane was the brains of the operation. She had probably designed the spell to nudge and mine more crypto herself. She was a Septer, after all. If Nadia had any common sense, she would run the hell away from the whole situation.

But something niggled at the back of Nadia's brain. Diane had said that the Goddess was generous to true believers. What if this Goddess could help her? The third test was coming up, and Nadia could use all the help she could get. She glanced at the time on her laptop. 8:88—no wait, 3:33. Another sign from the Numinous. She was on the right path. She was sure of it.

Nadia clicked "Yes" to RSVP.

Diane Robbins's house, a white, boxy, modern structure made almost entirely out of glass, was like something out of *Architectural Digest*. Perched on the cliffside with sweeping vistas of the Bay, it had to cost at least ten mil, if Nadia had to guess. Maybe more.

Her ride pulled over, and Nadia stepped out onto a circular driveway and smoothed down her outfit. She had opted for a pink Chanel skirt suit with a cropped jacket, a little-used gift from her mother when Nadia had graduated from college and was entering the professional world. She was happy with her decision when she saw other young women wearing similar attire to the event.

She entered the foyer with two others. The waitstaff wore black tuxes and greeted them with glasses of champagne. Nadia decided to detach herself from the two when they started giggling. They seemed young and immature, unused to attending networking events. Nadia slipped away into the living room to get her bearings.

The house was elegantly decorated in a California coastal style. Live-edge tables, cream furniture, and a slight Zen feel added to the sense of understated luxury. Nadia walked to the glass wall overlooking the water and took in the enviable view. The sun was setting, painting the sky and the water in pinks and golds against a twinkling San Francisco city skyline. Strike ten mil—this place had to have cost twenty.

"Nadia!" Meredith Vincent strolled over and air-kissed her. "I didn't know you would be here. What do you think of this place? Isn't it just fabulous? Diane manifested it."

"It's gorgeous," said Nadia. "Her keynote at the Women in Tech conference . . . that bit about manifestation. It was so inspirational."

Diane stood across the living room, chatting to a group gathered in a semicircle around her. She was dressed in a cream dress and seemed completely at ease. A queen holding court.

"I'll introduce you," said Meredith as she led Nadia through the throngs of women. Nadia tried to tell her that Diane had been the one to invite her, but Meredith seemed not to hear.

"Diane, dear, I want you to meet Nadia Winters," said Meredith.

Diane laughed. "Oh, Meredith. I'm the one who invited her."

Meredith cringed. "Oh. I didn't realize. My mistake." Maya had mentioned that the more prominent young women a member sponsored, the more power and prestige they amassed in the Sisterhood. It appeared that Diane had scooped Meredith when it came to Nadia. Meredith retreated like a kicked puppy.

Nadia searched for some small talk to have with Diane. "Your house is lovely. Thank you so much for having me."

Diane sighed contentedly like she had not a care in the world. "I saw it and just had to have it. It's a Frank Lloyd Wright."

"Gorgeous," Nadia murmured. "I wasn't aware there were any Frank Lloyd Wrights in Tiburon." Her mother had a certain fascination with them, and Nadia knew entirely too much about his designs and legacy.

Diane winked. "The Goddess is generous to true believers."

Nadia blinked. The Goddess could fabricate and give you entire architecturally significant mansions if you believed hard enough? Sign her up!

She took a second to admire Diane's collection of what appeared to be original Monets and Degases—she even had a Ming vase—with symbols of the Goddess sprinkled throughout. Pomegranate statuettes and eight-pointed Stars of Ishtar were on pillows and on gold-and-cream wallpaper. Diane followed, giving her an impromptu tour of the house and the art, and she nodded approvingly at Nadia's appreciation and admiration, almost like she was the Goddess herself watching a worshipper in a temple.

After the tour, Diane gave her shoulder a light squeeze. "If you excuse me, I must make my rounds. We have a special treat later. I do hope you stay."

"I wouldn't miss it," said Nadia. Diane moved on to chat with other people.

Nadia mingled and networked with the members and prospective members of the Sisterhood. The young women who had been invited to attend were all like Nadia: ambitious, starting out their professional careers, wanting to make a difference in the world. The Sisters she spoke with were all titans in their fields. Politicians, engineers, doctors, lawyers, physicists. One woman had even won a Nobel Prize in Chemistry. A lot of the chitchat was about the Sisterhood in general: their mission, the benefits, and their impact on women in STEM. Buzzwords flew around the room like candy. "Like-minded," "empowerment," and "strength of community" were popular ones.

Nadia tried to steer the conversation to glean information about Diane Robbins. She was dying to know if this supposedly amazing role model was a mass murderer, but everyone seemed to know only minimal information about the woman. They all parroted the same inspirational stories about Diane's work in tech and to honor the Goddess, and no fewer than five people told Nadia that she had manifested the house. Nadia got the impression that Diane Robbins was strict about how she cultivated her image, controlling the information that was known about her. She supposed there was some sort of spell for ensuring the information on the internet was sanitized of anything potentially unbecoming or scandalous, but she hadn't given the topic much thought before. She made a mental note to investigate spells to alter one's digital footprint.

As Maya had predicted, the conversation turned a little woo. The event that evening was to honor the Dark Goddess: one half of the Capital G Goddess. The Dark Goddess appeared to be an umbrella archetype for goddesses around the world associated with the left-hand path and the occult, shadows, and darkness. Hecate, Lilith, and Circe all came up as powerful sources of inspiration. The Sisters found power by tapping into the subtle energies of various goddesses, invoking whichever one the moment called for, and many found the dark goddesses were especially beneficial for navigating the corporate world and the patriarchy.

After about an hour, Diane called everyone to attention by striking a large golden gong with a mallet three times. Nadia had the strange sense of déjà vu as she remembered the golden gong from the second test.

"It's time to introduce our new recruits to the Dark Goddess," said Diane.

Two of the waitstaff carried in a trunk and set it down off to the side. One of the Sisters opened it and started passing out black robes. Nadia snagged one and held it up to her body. Crepe. Not her choice of fabric, but it would have to do.

"We try to refrain from wearing street clothes while invoking the Goddess," Diane continued. She reached behind her and unzipped the back of her dress. "There is no shame in the female body."

They were supposed to just strip down, right there, in front of each other. No locker room or anything. A couple of the potential new members exchanged nervous glances with Nadia, but they all started removing their clothing and donning the black robes.

From her time in a sorority, Nadia was familiar with various rituals involving robes, scythes, and bells. It had been silly, akin to playacting, many of her sisters using the initiation rituals that involved wine as an excuse to get drunk. She had never taken it that seriously. But as she stripped off her clothing down to her bra and panties and put on the toga-like robe, she felt like she was partaking in something holy. Vials of essential oil were passed around, and the older Sisterhood members showed the recruits how to anoint themselves, elders passing along sacred knowledge. Nadia dabbed oil along her chakras: on her third eye, her throat, between her breasts, and below her navel.

Clad in the black robes, the furniture pushed to the side to create space, the Sisters and recruits stood in a circle. The lights dimmed. Candles were lit. Meredith stepped up beside Nadia and gave her a wink as they joined hands.

Diane stood across from Nadia in the circle. "The Goddess is neither Dark nor Light. She is both. When she gave birth, she became something else, splitting herself and her powers. She became her own two daughters, one Dark and one Light. Tonight, we are here to honor one of the Two Sisters, the Dark Goddess."

Nadia was pretty sure Diane was still speaking metaphorically, but it was hard to tell. She was speaking as if the whole thing were real. It made Nadia uneasy listening to it all. Like the time she had talked to Keith's mom about the Bible, only to find out that she truly believed that the dinosaurs became extinct because Noah didn't have room on the ark.

"I will now lead us through the incantation," continued Diane. "Please close your eyes."

Nadia closed her eyes and took a deep breath. A bell chimed three times. Diane began chanting in Latin and then switched to Greek and then switched again to a Norse language. Icelandic, perhaps. She was invoking the Dark Goddess archetypes from various parts of the world, and each time she switched to a new language, the air became denser with magic, making it harder to breathe.

Nadia found herself swaying slightly to the cadence of Diane's voice, her rhythm changing as Diane moved from language to language. A dark fog settled over Nadia's mind. Diane instructed them all to take a deep breath and open their third eye.

Nadia's third eye activated and calibrated. Her vibration aligned with the spell as waves synced up. She blinked a few times. She was in a dense forest, the canopy of trees overhead shadowing the moist earth. Female voices called to her, echoes all around, and she spun in circles trying to figure out which one to follow. "This way!" called one. "No, Nadia, this one!" called another. There was a tug on her magic, and she knew the one for her. She followed the sound of Her voice, stumbling over slippery rocks, splashing through shallow pools of water. It was compulsive. She couldn't have stopped her feet even if she had wanted to, caught in the tractor beam of the Dark Goddess's power.

She came to a cave, barely bigger than she was, and she pushed her body against the earth and tunneled through, loose dirt falling down the hole with her. Everything was wet and dark, but she pushed through, tumbled out, and rolled to a stop next to a shallow pool of water.

She lay there for a minute to catch her breath. Moonlight rippled on the water from a dark, unseen moon. She was in a large cavern that extended into a black void of nothingness. It was impossible to gauge the depth or size of the space by sight alone, and she sent out her psychic tendrils to explore the space. It was massive, layers upon layers of tunnel systems bent in on each other like arteries in a heart, compressing and condensing the farther in it went. The shadow of the Dark Goddess was all around her, enveloping her in a luscious velvet fur.

She stood, soaking up the Dark Goddess's power. She was Mystery, she was Chaos, she was Forbidden Desire. But then . . . she felt something . . . off. A slimy feeling washed over her, something oily and sinister. Nadia's heart raced. There was something else in there with them. Something foreign. Something dangerous and unnatural. It slid from shadow to shadow, blending in and hiding itself, slithering and eel-like. Watching, waiting, urging her to reach out a hand and touch it.

Nadia bolted.

It hunted her, jumping from rock to rock. Nadia scrabbled back up through the hole, but dirt poured around her, and she slid backward. She fought her way up again, willing her hand to just reach through to the surface before she was trapped down there forever with . . . that *thing*. That entity. It grabbed her ankle and yanked her back—

A bell chimed.

"And come back to us now," said Diane.

Nadia's eyes fluttered open. Her heart thudded in her ears. The ghost remnants of the experience lingered, and it took a few seconds for her to remember where she was. All around her, the other women stirred like they were coming out of a trance.

"I hope you enjoyed that," said Diane. "You will know if you and the Goddess are a good fit. You'll feel it, the pull of Her. Some of you will return to future events. Some will not. But we welcome those who will join us and pledge themselves." The group broke up and changed back into their clothing, handing the robes back to the Sisters.

Meredith turned to Nadia. "I love these tune-ups. I always come back feeling rejuvenated and refreshed. Sometimes a little sore, like from a good massage. It's that deep shadow work, attuning our bodies with the Goddess."

Nadia slipped the black robe off her shoulders and pushed it to the floor, uncertain about what had just happened. No one else seemed to have had a bad experience. After she had changed back into her skirt suit, she leaned over to Meredith and said, "I had a strange thing happen."

"Oh?"

"I was in a dark cave, and I started feeling the Goddess—attuning like you said—but I felt there was ... something else there."

Meredith's brows knitted together. "It should be just you and the Goddess."

"It felt ... bad. It's hard to describe."

"Hmmm. I wonder if you unconsciously brought something negative into the meditation, and it manifested."

"I-I'm not sure," Nadia stammered.

They said their pleasantries and departed as rideshare drivers pulled up and the valets returned people's cars.

For the initiation tests, Nadia had been working with Rune on knowing her subconscious patterns, in case something manifested in her magic. She was keenly aware of what her imagination and manifestations felt like. When she shook that cute guy from the bar's hand, her own magic had reverberated back at her. She knew when someone or something had come from herself.

And that thing had not come from her.

Chapter 25

The strange experience at Diane's diminished in Nadia's mind until it could fit into a nice little box. She tucked it away in the back closet of her memory until the predominant feeling about the Sisterhood event that she was left with was one of awe, inspiration, and gratitude. The Goddess was kind. The Goddess was giving. And the Goddess loved her.

She had finally found her tribe.

It was the first real religious experience that made sense to Nadia. She had tried on other religions, explored various aspects of Christianity, Judaism, and Buddhism, but nothing had stuck. But that experience in the cave . . . she had met a goddess. And not just any goddess. *The* Goddess. She had felt Her presence, been absolutely sure of Her existence and blessings. Nadia had magic, but to touch a god . . . that was different.

The concept of God had never really made sense to her. The Bible was a story, one used to keep certain narratives as the predominant ones. But now she had experienced a Sister / Mother / Best Friend / Role Model / Mentor Goddess. A Super Goddess, all goddesses rolled into one. A master archetype for all women, especially Septer women. And Nadia wanted to embody Her. She wanted to stop being a pawn and force herself to metamorphose into a queen. And not just any queen. The Queen. The Prophecy Queen that everyone was talking about, a celebrity who was a vitally important part in the fate of humanity and Numinals and the very realm they existed in. Even though Rocky and Rune had both said that the Counter-Prophecy was a sham, Nadia felt in her bones it was real. Something that powerful would not just pop out of nowhere. There had to be truth in it.

It was a wild dream. The thought of escaping Mercurio and the Blood Oath seemed so trivial in comparison. The Order—child's play. When she was the queen, she would be able to do whatever she wanted. She could bend Mercurio to her will. Make him her docile slave, her bitchboy. She could keep *him* in a cage and bleed him to death, if that's what she wanted. She didn't want that—*gods no!*—but she liked the idea of being a strong enough woman to be able to handle Mercurio and render him harmless. The Blood Oath would be a nonissue in the grand scheme of things.

The Goddess was giving. All Nadia had to do was ask, and it could be hers. She just needed to figure out what she wanted. But what *did* she want? The question plagued her. She paced back and forth in her bedroom, practically wearing holes into Marina's rugs, racking her brain, trying to figure it out.

She went to her supply closet, a vintage medicine cabinet that Marina had picked up at the flea market and refinished, and opened the cabinet door. She rummaged around and pulled out witchy supplies that spoke to her in that moment: wax votive candles, red rose incense, a jade sculpture of a dragon she had bought in Chinatown, a statue of Ishtar, a gold art deco hand mirror. At her desk, she pulled out her jewelry box and adorned her fingers with rings and her arms with bangles. She tried to put on a pair of earrings, gypsy witch, boho ones she had stolen from Marina, but she couldn't get them on. For some reason, she couldn't find the hole in her earlobe.

Not meant for this, thought Nadia. She put one feather earring in one ear and a rhinestone-studded hoop in the other.

Nadia sat cross-legged on the floor and activated her Myst Zisurrû—portable technology to help set up a sacred space. The sensors placed strategically around the room lit up and cleansed unwanted energies. The tech-savvy equivalent of smudging with sage. She set up the altar in front of herself and settled into her body, closing her eyes.

She listened.

Meditation had not come easily to Nadia. She had a hard time just *being*. Existing. It was easier and less painful to distract herself with mindless scrolling, watching television, reading, studying, cleaning the toilet . . . anything except just sitting with herself and her thoughts. But meditation improved her magic. Even a little bit of sitting still, by herself, with no sounds or distractions, did wonders. It gave her space. The walls of reality were not so suffocating when she pushed them back and made room for herself.

After a bit of just existing, she was ready to ask the Numinous a question. She thought about a direct connection, a golden rope that dropped down from the sky and her higher self—her better, more aligned self—sliding down to come talk to her.

What do I want? She tried on different hats, considering the possibilities. It was like shopping for a new reality. She imagined different life trajectories, different combinations, ones with Mercurio in them and ones without. Ones with Myst and Rune, and ones without. The ones without Rune in them seemed like impossibilities. She had to have Rune in her life. He was her master, she his apprentice. Their magic was bonded. There was no reality in which Rune wasn't in her life, in some form or fashion.

A thought tumbled out of the sky and hit her on the head.

She flinched. The universe was just lobbing sense at her now. But now, Nadia knew the answer to what she wanted all along.

She wanted Rune.

Nadia was tired of being his apprentice and living in his shadow. She wanted to be his equal. Prove herself to be worthy of his esteem. He would never respect her as a woman, would never go for her unless she made the first move. He was too up-standing. Too good. He wouldn't try to seduce an employee and use his position of power to cross a line.

That moment in Yosemite had been one of pure potential. She and Rune . . . it could have happened. And she had chickened out.

Next time she wouldn't chicken out, she told herself.

She needed to set a trap. Lure him in, unsuspecting. The power of the Goddess filled her, giving her life buoyancy and hope.

Rune, Nadia mindspoke.

Yes?

You know I went out with Miles, right?

A pause. *Yes.*

He kissed me.

Silence. Would he take the bait? Nadia grabbed the half-empty wine bottle sitting on the nightstand and took a large swig. The label bore a pomegranate: a symbol of the Dark Goddess. Nadia flicked her wrist toward the candles on her bed-side table, and they sprang to life. She waved a hand toward the ceiling lights, dimming them. She asked her Psionic to play dark, sensual music on her nightstand speaker.

Why are you telling me this? Rune asked finally.

I thought you should know.

Another pause. *Are you trying to make me jealous?*

Is it working? Nadia held her breath.

No.

Goddammit. She needed something more.

Nadia fell to her knees in front of her altar to the Goddess. With a flick of her wrist, she lit the candles and incense. *Help me with Rune*, she pleaded in her mind. *Help me make him mine.* She studied her reflection in the mirror, trying to see the Goddess's eyes in her own.

After a few minutes, Rune mindspoke to her again. *The next test is in just a few days. Want me to show you dreamshifting? It might help you access your superconscious.*

Well, thank you, Goddess. She was listening. *What's dreamshifting?*

It's similar to what you experienced at Aiko's with that sensory spell for the Floating World. Let me show you.

Nadia went to her bed and lowered her mental defenses. She felt herself spinning, shrinking, and then expanding back out again. When her mind cleared, she was in the exact same spot where she lay on her bed in her pajamas, except Rune had joined her in the room. He was bare-chested and wore joggers like he had been relaxing at home.

"Whoa, what is this place?" Nadia held out a hand and flexed it. She felt detached, suspended in a waking dream. The air shimmered slightly like translucent soap bubbles.

"Your mind creates a copy of the physical world on the astral plane. We are inside that copy. Advanced practitioners can create worlds without needing a material source. That is dreamshifting."

"I need to know how to do that. Now."

He chuckled. "That's why we're going to practice."

Rune showed her how to cast the spell. It turned out to be rather simple, creating threads that grew into larger pieces on their own, vines crawling and expanding. It reminded Nadia of those magic pills she had as a kid, the ones that grew into sponge animals when doused in water. She just had to plant the seed of the world, and the spell took care of the rest. Nadia repeated it for a while, weaving miniature dreamworlds into large glass marbles. They were crude imitations of reality, stick figures and wobbly lines compared to Rune's detailed masterpieces, but he was encouraging. She kept sneaking glances at him, her courage waning. Was she really going to have to do drills the entire night? It was much easier to be all bravado and confidence before he was right in front of her.

After some time, they stopped practicing and fell into easy conversation.

Nadia leaned back on a pile of pillows on her bed. "Why's magic so tricky? Every time I think I have it pinned down, it goes sideways on me."

Rune gazed up at her from where he was lounging on the floor. "I sometimes think I'm being too hard on you. But I'm pushing you because I know you can handle it and you're insanely talented."

"Really?" She was slightly incredulous that someone who was so successful and talented themselves would consider her so. She glanced at the pomegranate wine label, and it gave her a small boost.

"I'm not sure I've ever seen such raw potential and talent before. In the Order or outside of it. It scares me a little," Rune confessed. "I worry that I won't be able to help you, that I'm not the right person. I know my limitations. I may not be powerful enough to help you control it. I know that you are struggling to accept the Blood Muse identity, wondering how to reconcile the old and the new person you are, and that's impacting your magic. I know what that feels like, to face the different parts of yourself. I've done a lot of soul-searching over the years, and I know how difficult it can be to take a long, hard look at yourself in the mirror."

"You know, I've never seen you without your glamour."

He smiled a small sad smile. "Maybe someday I will show you."

Had something happened to him? Was he disfigured and ashamed of it? "Show me now."

Rune shook his head. "It's getting late."

"Please?" she begged. "I don't want to go to bed yet. This is way too fun."

He laughed, and Nadia let him wiggle off the hook, though she vowed to herself that she would get him to lower his glamour and show her his true appearance someday.

They said good night. Nadia tried to think of reasons to keep him there, but before she could come up with anything, he dissolved the dreamworld and returned her mind to her physical reality. She wanted to kick herself. Once again, he had been moral and upstanding, and she had chickened out and had failed to make the first move.

Nadia scanned her bedroom. Four powder-blue walls, vines creeping in through the window. Her dumb altar to the Goddess. It was all very empty without Rune there. She hated herself for failing. There had been plenty of moments she could have acted on to make her interest in him obvious. But fear had taken over, and then it had been too late.

She looked in the mirror and pouted. She grabbed her breasts, pushing them up. Pulled up her shirt, revealing her flat stomach, her jutting hipbones, her curves. She was sexy. Anyone would want this. The Goddess hadn't abandoned her. It was never too late to make the first move.

Nadia climbed on her bed and took some selfies, all tousled hair and glossed lips. She sent one to Rune.

What was that for? he texted back.

That's me without my glamour on. What you see is what you get.

Nadia sent him another selfie, slightly sexier. A little more pout in her lips, a little more shoulder, a little more tousled hair.

What are you doing? Rune texted.

She sent another. You should send me a pic.

That would be inappropriate, he texted.

Why? Are you naked? she asked.

The text bubble popped up and disappeared. Nadia held her breath as she stared at her phone.

Maybe ;-P, he finally texted back.

With a start, Nadia realized that—*fuck yes!*—they were flirting. Rune was flirting with her. He had taken the bait. It was on. But she couldn't scare him. He needed to be comfortable with the idea of being with her. It was like trying to break a horse in, not let it spook away. She needed to tame Rune into thinking they could be together. But the whole thing was so . . . *wildly inappropriate.* And totally hot. He was her boss and master in their apprenticeship and, like, a million years older than she was.

If you want to be a queen, you'd better start acting like one, she told herself.

Nadia snapped a selfie of her naked back, hair tumbling down in long silky waves, just the hint of her breast peeking out behind her clasped hand as she covered herself. There was no doubt this was a "more than just friends" pic. She shot it off to him before she could chicken out.

Time stretched, and Nadia nearly drove herself mad. She had opened Pandora's Box. There was no putting the genie back in the bottle. She had jumped without a parachute, thinking the Goddess would provide one, and was beginning to suspect she had been very, very wrong.

Her phone vibrated.

Rune had sent a photo. He was shirtless, lying on black silk sheets, one arm behind his head, his dark hair mussed, the other hand holding the phone out. A book lay face down across his hard stomach like he had been reading in bed. He grinned seductively at the camera, a five-o'clock shadow on his chiseled jaw. It was a smoldering invitation. He knew exactly how sexy he looked and was asking her to jump into bed with him. Nadia emitted a little shriek and slouched down into the covers.

She couldn't contain her smile. This was really happening. The shadow of the Goddess filled her with power.

Come back to me, Nadia mindspoke. She closed her eyes, lowered her mental wards, and spun into the dreamland. She opened her eyes to her astral bedroom and stood up from the bed to face him, his expression guarded.

Nadia reached out her hand and tried to touch Rune's arm. Her hand passed through him. She had to remind herself that he was little more than a hologram, a projection of his mind into her own.

"This is freaky," said Nadia.

"You're telling me," Rune replied. "Imagine doing this without a guide. Just finding yourself sucked into someone else's mind." Nadia knew exactly how that felt. She had been waking up in Mercurio's mind nightly.

"Is that what happened to you?"

"My master was not so patient as I am with you."

"You don't have to go easy on me. I can handle it."

"I know you can." He looked down at her, a flicker of heat in his gaze. Nadia licked her lips.

He brought his hand to her neck and gently caressed her. "You don't have to touch to be able to feel." His fingers trailed lightly over her skin.

Nadia's nipples hardened, and she caught her breath. "Oh,"

she exhaled. Now she understood what he was saying. There was no difference in the mind between reality and the projection. If she focused, she could feel every touch, every sensation, her body on fire for him.

Rune brushed her collarbone. Nadia closed her eyes, reeling from the sensation. He bent down, and she arched her neck to his lips. He gave her one featherlight kiss, and her knees buckled. She had forgotten to breathe.

Nadia stared at his eyes. She brushed a lock of his dark hair from his face and relished the look he gave her: naked, hungry, and vulnerable. Nadia wanted to lose herself in that look forever. But he took her hand in his, flipped it over, and kissed the inside of her wrist.

"I'm sure I'm going to regret this immensely," he said, rubbing his thumb over the partially finished tattoo on her skin, "but I'm going to stop us here." He took a step back and dropped her hand. Nadia wanted to grab him, bring him back close to her body. But with a lingering last look, his face the embodiment of longing, he dissolved the dreamworld, and Nadia was left alone back in her bedroom.

Rune skipped their morning workout session the next day. Nadia ran through her exercises quickly, the drills tedious and boring without him. When she arrived at her desk to start work, she searched for him, but the light was off in his office, and he wasn't on the main coworking floor.

He was avoiding her. She was certain of it.

It was a rotten feeling to have put herself out there only to have him disappear on her. It hurt. Confusion clouded her brain. What had even happened? Had it all been nothing because it was a dreamworld? *Why does he keep running away?*

Her mood spiraled downward as the day went on and she

failed to see him. She snapped at people. Told a telemarketer to fuck off. And work was a nonstarter. There was no way she could concentrate in her state. The only thing she could manage was visiting and chatting with coworkers.

Maya wasn't at her desk, and neither was Piero. Sophie was, but Nadia wasn't that desperate for a diversion as to open that rat's nest of drama and ridiculousness. Her entire life belonged on Overheard San Francisco.

Carson was at his desk, however, and Nadia grabbed two lattes from the goblins at the tree and headed over.

"I brought you some caffeine," said Nadia as she handed him one of the cups.

Carson took it gratefully. "Java, java, java. Mmm, gracias." He took a sip.

"How's the patch coming?"

"Swimmingly," he responded, swiveling back to his triple screen setup. "I've isolated the bug to the CSS, and now I just need to bisect the regression and create a hotfix."

"I have no idea what you just said."

He grinned. "Basically, their shit sucks, but I can create a patch to protect our users."

"Got it." Nadia dallied, watching him work. He really got into it, extremely focused, with these excitable outbursts when he figured something out or caught a bug. "Can I ask you a question?" she asked finally.

"Shoot," said Carson, without looking away from his screens.

She didn't know how to phrase this properly. "Do you think Rune is the kind of guy who runs scared from women who come after him?"

Carson glanced up. "Uh-oh, what happened?"

"Nothing." It was practically nothing.

"Did you make a move at him?"

"I might have . . . sent him a few pictures."

"And he bolted."

Nadia nodded.

Carson winced. "Listen, it's not you. It's him."

"Why is this not making me feel any better?"

Carson scratched the back of his neck with a furry hand. "He's had a lot of shit happen to him. He uses it as fuel to motivate himself. But it makes him closed off, afraid to let anyone in."

"What kind of shit?"

"I don't know specifics," said Carson, "but there was a woman. I think she died or left him or something. He doesn't talk about it that much."

"Ah, I see." Thomas said that Nadia reminded Rune of someone. She wondered if it was her. "How did you and Rune meet, if you don't mind me asking?"

"I've known him for a long time. We were on the fighting circuits in Docktown together, way, way back. We lost touch after he stopped fighting. Rune is the best guy I know. Hands down. I was really messed up after Vietnam. Aimless. There was always some war I was fighting that wasn't even my own. Even though we hadn't seen each other in ages, Rune reconnected with me. Paid for my first coding lessons. I couldn't believe the things computers could do when I first saw one. Back in my day, steam trains were the height of technology."

"That's wild that you've seen the rise of technology like that." Every day, it seemed like there was some new technology, some new AI thing that was threatening to take over the world.

"You have no idea."

"Why did Rune stop fighting?" Nadia asked.

He shrugged. "I think he was tired of being a puppet for the crowd."

Maya walked across the floor. She waved to Nadia. Carson lit up when he saw her and waved at her, but she ignored him.

He seemed crestfallen. "I don't think she's ever going to forgive me."

"Any progress at all?"

He shook his head. "The worst thing is that I completely ruined our friendship." Tears pooled and threatened to fall, and he looked away quickly, rubbing his eyes. "I just miss her. I miss talking to her. I just keep thinking how stupid, stupid, stupid I was! I can't believe I messed up so badly. I'll never forgive myself."

"You never know," said Nadia. "She might forgive you. It might take time, but if you two are meant to be friends again, it will happen."

"Maybe."

"It's Samhain soon. A time for new beginnings. Anything's possible."

Carson nodded distractedly at the screen. "What the—"

"What is it?" Nadia asked.

Carson was silent, focused on the screens. Eventually, he seemed to remember that Nadia was still there. "Sorry."

"It's okay. What's going on?"

Carson's jaw clenched. "Pact used my code in this."

Chapter 26

"I didn't know Rune had a man cave down here," said Nadia as she and Carson walked over to Vault Three. The door to Vault Three had always been closed, and when Nadia had first started at Myst, Rune had said it was "restricted access" and left it at that.

It was closed now. Carson pounded on the door with his fist. "Bro! It's me! Let me in!"

They stepped back, and after a minute, the seal to the heavy circular door broke with a *hiss*, and the door swung open. Rune stood at the entrance. He seemed surprised to see Nadia.

"What's going on?" he asked.

Carson held out an iPad. "Dude, I was running lines and saw that Pact is executing my Veil shield code in their pipeline."

Rune closed his eyes, his jaw tightening. "People are going to think it's our tech causing the demon attacks."

"We know it's because they implemented it wrong, but the public doesn't know that."

"I know," Rune snapped. He caught himself and took a deep breath. "Come in." Nadia and Carson followed him into the room.

Sleek black furnishings offset by custom-designed lighting filled the space and reflected his minimal, sensuous taste. It was about what Nadia expected, though she hadn't thought Rune would be an all-black furnishings kind of guy. But this is where he had run to, to avoid her. This was his sanctuary. She silently seethed.

Rune went to a wet bar and poured three drinks into crystal glasses. He handed Nadia and Carson theirs and then dropped into an armchair and took a deep sip.

Carson leaned against Rune's desk. "Do you think that Pact is using their overbroad possession clause to puppet a Myst employee around the headquarters to steal things?"

"That would mean the thief is human," said Rune. "It would narrow things down significantly." There were only a handful of humans besides Nadia who were full-time employees at Myst, but outside contractors had access to the vaults, as well.

"Miles posted on the Hades Market for Myst energy conversion blueprints," said Nadia. "If he could just puppet someone to go get it, he wouldn't need to post jobs for it."

Rune looked at her, incredulous. "Miles is working with the thief? Why didn't you say something earlier?"

"It slipped my mind," said Nadia. "Sorry." More like, she wanted to steer Rune clear of anything related to the thief because she was one.

"I'm actually impressed," said Rune. "He doesn't seem smart enough to pull something like this off."

"Posting on the Hades Market is hardly a master plot." Carson typed on his cell phone. "Just logging in . . . searching for 'Myst' and . . ."

"Energy conversion," supplied Rune.

"Bingo." Carson held out his phone for them to see. "His screen name is EdgeLord69. Lame-o." He scrolled through all the postings that Miles had made. "Helmet of Hades, Chintamani Stone, Peach of Immortality . . . Kvasir's blood . . . all very specific. Those are things we have in the vaults, right? I just modeled that helmet for the new push. He must have a list of our inventory."

Rune zapped something on his desk with magic, and a fidget spinner floated over to him. "I'm going to set up an alarm on our blueprint files. If anyone accesses them to get those energy conversion prints, we'll know. I want to catch the thief in action."

He cast a spell over the fidget spinner and handed it to Nadia. "I've got to make a few calls, but I want you to monitor this. If it goes off, we'll know someone touched the blueprints."

She took the spinner and looked up at him. He looked like he was waiting for her to say something, to do something. There was a glimmer of amusement in his eye, and the corner of his mouth twitched almost imperceptibly. He was calling her bluff, seeing if she would make the first move after their heavy-petting dreamworld session. Nadia repressed the urge to kick him.

Carson cleared his throat, interrupting their staring contest. "I'm just going to . . . yeah." He pointed to the door and stood up to leave. Nadia stood as well.

She smiled tightly and saluted, the good little soldier she was. "I'm your girl Friday." Girl Friday? *What is wrong with you?*

She couldn't read the expression on Rune's face. She followed Carson quickly out.

Back upstairs, Nadia put the fidget spinner on her desk and got to work. She wrote a few of the artifact write-ups, answered some emails, and responded to a couple of Slack messages asking for status updates on various projects. She tried to focus and knock it out of the park, make her inbox read zero new messages, but her mind wandered.

She couldn't stop thinking about Rune. Thinking about the look in his eyes in the dreamworld. It had been possessive. Carnal. It had scared her to be fully owned like that. And then, he just ran away, immediately after. *Coward.* He had hidden from her. Pretended nothing had happened . . . again.

And what about her apprenticeship? Did this change anything? She needed to take the third test soon. Samhain was only days away. She was back to the Soulwish plan. Her brief shining moment of thinking she could be the queen had died on the vine.

"Hello?" Piero snapped his fingers in front of her nose. "Earth to Nadia."

Nadia came back to reality with a start. "Sorry. Hi. What's going on?"

"I need help," he whined. He held up a stack of blank papers. "Everyone thinks they're an office prankster around Samhain. Someone spelled all printer ink to be invisible ink. Real funny, whoever you are!" he yelled out to the floor. Nearby Mystics chuckled and snorted.

Nadia scrolled through her Psionic's spell list for ones tagged as office spells. HR had been forced to compile a list after someone had turned everyone's computer mouse into a live mouse. She cast a reversal one so the ink turned back to black.

"Thanks," said Piero. "What are you working on? Have the bandwidth to help me with the slush pile today? I'm putting together a new pitch. A project in Antarctica. We need to find people with experience in subzero temperatures. No yetis. I'm not going to have a repeat of Tibet. These all need to be entered and tagged in the system." He held out the stack of papers to her.

Nadia eyed them. A solid two or three hours, if she worked fast. "I can tomorrow. I'm slammed today."

"That will have to do, I suppose." Piero dropped the papers on her desk and flounced off to harass someone else.

Nadia returned to her work.

A little later, a loud ringing like a siren went off. Interrupted from her thoughts, it took Nadia a minute to figure out what was going on. She pulled out her AirPods. The fidget spinner! It was hovering a few inches off her desk, spinning wildly, flashing a red strobing light.

Rune! Nadia shouted in her mind. *The thief triggered the alarm!*

I'm on my way, Rune thought back immediately.

She hurried to the back elevator and pushed the button repeatedly to call it up. "C'mon, c'mon!"

The elevator seemed to move at a snail's pace. Finally, it reached the vault floor, and the door slid open. Nadia squeezed through before it had fully opened, and she ran to the open door of Vault One.

At the back of the room, next to an open blueprint file cabinet, Rune held Kevin by the collar of his shirt. Kevin's feet kicked in the air as he gasped for breath. Nadia ran through the library. Kevin went slack, his eyes closed.

"Fainted," said Rune. He threw him to the ground.

Nadia dropped down to the crumpled heap of a human. She felt his neck for his pulse and checked his breathing. "What did you do to him?" she cried out.

Kevin twitched unnaturally, having little seizures.

"He's under possession," said Rune with disgust. "Look at his eyes."

Nadia pulled up one of his eyelids to reveal a spot of red in milky white pupils. "Ack!" She shuddered and scooted back.

Kevin's eyelids fluttered open. His pupils were still red and clouded. Rune bent down. "Can I please talk to whoever is driving this human?" he asked. "I promise I won't harm you or Kevin. I just want to find out what's going on."

Whoever was inside Kevin nodded and hauled him to his feet like a puppet on strings. He moved herky-jerky, like whoever was inside him was losing control. Rune magicked a glass of sugar water to stabilize his energy and held it out. Kevin gulped it down.

The three of them stared at each other. "Well?" asked Rune.

"I'm Kevin's roommate," said Kevin. "Dougie."

"You'd better start talking," Rune growled.

"First off, I'm a total fan," said Kevin/Dougie. "I saw that piece in *Wired* about you."

"Flattery isn't going to get you anywhere."

Kevin/Dougie hung their head. "Please don't fire Kevin. He has no idea I can do this."

"Do what, exactly?" asked Rune.

Kevin/Dougie held up the Pact app. "It's this app. It lets me go inside Kev. I figured out a way to slip into him when he was at work."

Carson was right. Someone *had* been using the possession clause to puppet a thief around Myst.

"I knew that Kevin worked here," continued Kevin/Dougie, "at Myst. And I know that Myst is a Numinal startup. I figured there'd be a lot of information about magic. Study material. I'm not a formally trained Septer. I figured no one would notice if I studied in the library."

"I thought Kevin was just taking an interest," said Nadia, grimacing at her mistake.

Kevin/Dougie nodded. "Nadia, right? You were super helpful. I started off just studying, for personal reasons. But then, I realized that some of the stuff I was looking at was really valuable. Like, super valuable, on the Hades Market. I started posting to see if anyone else thought so, and I started selling to buyers."

"What can you tell me about Miles Kirkpatrick?" Rune demanded. "EdgeLord69?"

Kevin/Dougie scratched his head. "I don't know who Miles

Kirkpatrick is, but I've sold some stuff to EdgeLord69. I've never met him. I just leave a packet at a drop point."

"I need a list of everything from Myst that you've taken."

"Are you going to press charges?" asked Kevin/Dougie. He typed on his phone, pulled up a file, and sent it to Rune and Nadia. Nadia received the file and opened it on her phone, scrolling quickly through the spreadsheet. He had taken meticulous notes, documenting the date, item, buyer's screen name, and price. It always surprised Nadia that criminals were such excellent bookkeepers, though she figured that level of organization was probably what made them successful in the first place.

"I won't press charges," said Rune calmly, "if you return all of the items you've taken from me."

Kevin/Dougie's eyes went wide. "That's impossible! I don't know half the buyers."

Nadia scrolled through the list of items that he had sold to Pact as Rune continued to interrogate the human. Spells, talismans, various magical objects. And then her heart rate spiked. Three weeks prior, he had sold battery specs to EdgeLord69. It looked like they were the battery specs for the Psionic—it was hard to tell for sure. But they had only figured out how to make the technology work the week before. The ones that Dougie had sold were faulty. And wasn't the problem that they drained users at too fast a rate? If Pact somehow used this Myst tech in their game, it would certainly implicate Myst . . .

Nadia held up her phone to show Rune. It took him a minute to realize what he was looking at.

He closed his eyes, eerily calm. He took a deep breath and then focused on Nadia. "I'm going to fix this," he promised her. "All of it."

Nadia swallowed, hoping he was talking about more than just the stolen tech.

*　　*　　*

"Is this thing on?" Simon Davies said into the video camera. He poked the screen a few times, his gold sunglasses taking over the entire screen in the conference room where Nadia was sitting with Rune. Simon appeared to be videoing in from a yacht. He was shirtless, lying on a deck chair, with thick Sean Connery-esque chest hair and a heavy gold chain hanging around his neck. Meredith looked like she was in the middle of a spa treatment—white towel tied around her head and bathrobe on—while Curtis appeared at his desk at NASA. David Song had a Zoom background of Buddhist temples behind him until Nadia realized that it wasn't a background, and he was indeed in front of Buddhist temples.

"We can see you," said Rune patiently. "Can you see us?"

The board members nodded.

"Great, let's get started," said Rune, shuffling some papers on the table. "First off, I'd like to thank you all for meeting on such short notice—"

"Cut the crap, Rune," said Simon. "What's this all about?"

Rune smiled coldly at Simon. "It has come to our attention that a thief has infiltrated the company and has been selling our secrets and equipment to Pact."

"How could this happen?" demanded Curtis. "Don't we have security?"

"We do," said Rune. "Pact has an overbroad clickwrap agreement in their app that allows for the temporary possession of humans. The thief, a kid by the name of Dougie, figured this out. He got his roommate, who is one of our employees, to use the app, and he's been taking items from the vaults."

Meredith pantomimed wildly.

"You're on mute, Meredith," said Rune. "The button at the bottom."

Meredith fumbled around before she finally unmuted herself. "We need to go after this Dougie character then!"

"He will be dealt with," said Rune. "But the real issue is that he's been selling company secrets to Pact. To Miles Kirkpatrick, specifically. Kirkpatrick has been making requests, showing that he knew he was getting the information from Myst. And now, Pact has some of our proprietary tech. Very dangerous proprietary tech."

"An accusation like that without proof would be damning to Myst," said David Song. "What proof do you have that Kirkpatrick knowingly bought our stolen goods?"

"Miles Kirkpatrick posted specific jobs on the Hades Market to retrieve Myst items," Nadia interjected. "I believe the thief gave him a list of what's in the database, and he basically used it to go shopping."

"What is she doing here?" Simon Davies scoffed. "Really, Rune."

"Nadia is head of Myst Foundation," said Rune. "As such, the thefts fall under her domain."

Nadia tried to keep her face from registering shock at Rune's announcement. Head of Myst Foundation?

"Climbing the corporate ladder," murmured Meredith. "Well done, Ms. Winters. Congratulations on your promotion."

"More like she's been climbing something else." Simon laughed, leering at her. Nadia blinked, refusing to give him the satisfaction of seeing her shock. He'd actually said that out loud. To her face. *What the fuck?*

Easy now, Rune mindspoke to her.

"You need to talk to Miles," said Curtis, "before you publicly accuse him and Pact of anything."

Chapter 27

The sun set on the horizon, casting a warm glow over Highway 280 as Nadia and Rune sped along on his Ducati toward Pact's headquarters in Palo Alto. She sat behind him on the seat, clutching his abdomen, her cheek pressed against his back. She squeezed her eyes shut, bracing herself against the wind whipping her face and the breakneck speed at which they were traveling, leaning with him into the curves of the highway. They wove in and out of traffic, cutting it entirely too close to some of the cars for Nadia's liking, but she trusted Rune. He would never let her get hurt. But she still sent a silent prayer up to the Goddess for keeping them safe when Rune pulled in front of Pact and her feet hit solid ground once more.

Pact's headquarters were modern and corporate, big reflective glass sides framed by eucalyptus trees around several boxy buildings. The inside was light and airy, with pale wood furniture and white walls. While Myst looked like a bustling startup, Pact was more like a venture capital firm. It wasn't exactly warm and friendly. Employees moved quickly in hushed tones, their heads down in papers or their phones.

Rune and Nadia checked in with security, a no-nonsense woman who could have been a professional weightlifter, and jumped through all the hoops to get inside. Biometrics were taken. IDs were logged. A young woman in a skirt suit came to collect them and led them to Miles's office. She was human, like most of the employees at Pact. Nadia assumed they all were Sixers, but everyone was normcore, and she found it difficult to tell.

The assistant dropped them at Miles's large glass-walled office. Like the rest of the headquarters, it lacked any personal touches save a few college trophies, Lucite awards, and Marvel action figures that lined a wooden shelf on one side. Miles sat behind a large maple desk, and he rose to greet them as they entered his office. "Nadia . . . and Rune Christiansen. To what do I owe this pleasure?" He walked around to the front of his desk and leaned back against it, crossing his arms.

Rune walked to Miles's bar, uncorked a bottle, and poured himself a drink. "I hope you don't mind."

Miles gestured toward the bar. "Mi casa es su casa."

Rune took a seat on one of the couches and settled in. Nadia took a deep breath and took a seat. She had a feeling this wasn't going to go well. Miles smiled tightly, waiting for Rune to speak.

"I came here as a professional courtesy," said Rune, "before I take this to the authorities. It's come to my attention that you have been stealing Myst's trade secrets and looting our vaults."

Miles didn't even try to look surprised. "That's quite a bold accusation, my friend."

"We have proof." Nadia held up her cell phone to show screenshots of Miles's posts on the Hades Market. "One of the items, blueprints to an energy device, is faulty and extremely dangerous."

Miles's expression hardened. "Well, well, well. Now I know why my VPN was open when we were on *The Empress* together." Nadia was pretty sure he had left it wide open, but whatever. "I knew he"—Miles gestured toward Rune—"was conniving. All Numinals are. But I thought you were different."

"You don't deny it?" Rune sat back, relaxed, crossing a leg over his knee. "I thought you'd at least give me the fun of beating it out of you."

"Deny that I took advantage of the situation?" Miles laughed. "Old man, if it wasn't me, someone else would have bought the stolen goods. You are the one with a leak. Don't blame me for realizing it."

"The leak only happened," Rune growled, "because of your overbroad clickwrap agreement that allows for possession. All the attacks around the city—all the deaths—caused by your app."

Miles's brows knit together. "I don't know anything about the attacks."

Nadia scoffed. "You warned me not to go to The Hemlock."

He shook his head. "We've noticed a correlation between the attacks and Pact users, but I never thought for a moment that Pact was *causing* the attacks." He walked to the bar and poured himself a drink, shooting it back. "No, no, no. Pact is not responsible for the attacks. You can't blame me for this one. In fact, Rune, you owe me—"

"You entitled little prick," Rune snapped. "Do you know what I had to overcome to get where I am? What I had to sacrifice? You, on the other hand, are given the world, and what do you do? Piss on it. I owe you nothing."

Miles paled at Rune's outburst. Nadia was a little scared herself. He usually kept himself so calm and collected. There was an awkward silence.

"And you," said Miles finally, shifting his attention to Nadia as he took a seat across from them on the couch. "Nicely played. I thought we had a real connection. All that about energy conversion and your past . . . I thought maybe you were helping me. That you understood my vision."

Rune stared at Nadia.

"I don't know what you're talking about," Nadia lied. She kept her gaze focused on Miles, not daring to look Rune in the eye.

"Oh, come on, you were practically throwing yourself at me, with the cleavage and the hair." Miles shook his head. "Watch out for this one, man. She's not what she seems."

"Don't talk about her like that," snapped Rune.

"Like what? Like some seductress vixen sent to infiltrate me and my company?"

Rune stood up. Miles's eyes widened. "Looks like I hit a nerve. What, you don't have feelings for her, do you?"

"That's enough, Miles," warned Nadia.

Miles looked like a kid about to rattle the lion's cage just to see what would happen. He stood up and grinned. "Have you done *ousia* with her yet? I have. *Quite* the experience. She's a moaner, that one."

Rune decked him. Miles flew backward over the couch and tumbled to the floor.

"Rune!" Nadia cried out as she scrambled to her feet. Rune stood, breathing heavily, his eyes dark obsidian.

Miles touched his lip, his fingers coming away red. "Get out."

Rune parked the Ducati in front of Myst. Nadia hopped off and removed her helmet, placing it on the back of the seat. He took off his own helmet and magicked them both away.

He glared at her as he stalked toward the front of the building.

"What?" demanded Nadia. She grabbed his arm to stop him.

"You told him about our work in energy conversion."

"So?"

"That's a trade secret," Rune bit out. His expression was stony.

The enormity of what he was accusing Nadia of sank in. "You think I've been feeding him information." She exhaled, tired from the weight of her life. She looked away, unable to meet his piercing eyes. Overhead, a plane soared, tiny at 30,000 feet. Nadia felt very small, shrinking under Rune's hard gaze.

"There's evidence of a second thief," Rune pressed. "The Wolf and the Ram spell wasn't on the list that 'Dougie' gave us. And now I learn that on your 'date' with Miles, you were dallying on his boat, telling him about energy conversion, and doing *ousia!*"

"I didn't know Myst had a policy against employees going on boats," said Nadia flippantly.

"Goddammit, Nadia! You know how this looks? How this makes *me* look?"

"I assume it makes you look like a fool. Or else you wouldn't be quite so upset right now." Nadia turned to leave. Air. She needed air. The walls of reality were tightening in around her.

Rune was suddenly in front of her, moving at his freaky preternatural speed. She stopped short before she ran into his chest.

"I wasn't done talking to you," he growled, suddenly too much in her space.

"You don't get to do this!" Nadia snapped. "I'm not your goddamn property!"

They were in their own little world, a maelstrom of emotion circling around them. Nothing else mattered. She had a vague sense of people walking by and staring at the lovers' quarrel, but it was all fogged and blurred, so focused was she on his face and his words.

Something dark and undeniable gleamed in his eyes. Nadia's stomach tightened as she realized what it was: desire. The fight was turning him on. The flame of lust burst into being between the two of them, hot and consuming. Nadia focused on that fire, the power of the Goddess flowing through her. Breathing heavily, she stepped forward. Her hips brushed the front of his pants, a light tease. Heat and hunger smoldered in his gaze. She saw herself in his eyes, powerful beyond belief, capable of bringing him to his knees if she tried.

Nadia cocked an eyebrow in question. Was he going to make a move?

She thought for a second that he might. She thought that she would finally get to taste and experience the force that was Rune Christiansen in shining Technicolor. They could continue what they had started in the dreamworld in real life. Magic swirled in the air between them. She licked her lips, staring at his. This was it. The moment that she had been waiting for all these months.

But he stepped back, breaking the spell.

"I . . . I can't." His shoulders slumped. Nadia wanted to cry.

She moved closer and whispered, "Why are you fighting this?" She had to try, had to reach him somehow. He was locking himself away from her. Closing himself off. Nadia wanted in.

"I just . . . can't."

Her hand snaked up the front of his shirt, and she grabbed him, pulling him closer to her. "Anything is possible," she breathed, their mouths warm on each other.

His lips met hers. The shock of it stopped the entire world from turning. For a second, she was too stunned to move.

And then she exploded in desire.

Her hand was in his hair, yanking him closer to her, her other hand around his back, under his shirt, feeling his muscles ripple beneath her fingers. His hands were all over her, touching, feeling, his silken tongue lapping in her mouth, the kiss deepening, becoming more passionate. Nadia moaned, grinding her body into his. They had crossed a threshold, an invisible barrier, and there was no going back. Nadia couldn't have even if she wanted to. She threw herself headlong into danger, not caring about anything except her mouth on his, his hands on her, and the exquisite anticipation of what could happen next. If he kissed like this, she could only imagine what else his tongue could do . . .

Nadia lost herself in that kiss. Nothing else mattered. Time fell away until she suddenly became aware of a tingling sensation moving up her spine.

Rune's eyes opened at the same time Nadia's did, and they froze, staring at each other. Nadia reacted first and pushed him away. Her blood, moments ago hot and searing for him, ran cold.

"You're . . . you're a demon," she whispered.

"Nadia, I can explain," he started. He took a step toward her, and she shrank from him. He flinched at her reaction, his expression pained.

"How could you . . . ?" Her breath came in rapid bursts. She couldn't handle this. Not now. Not after everything that had happened.

Without another word, she dashed away down the street.

He didn't come after her.

Chapter 28

Nadia slammed the door behind her and took the stairs up to her bedroom two at a time. Avery was coming down the stairs, and she nearly ran smack into him.

"Hey, watch it!"

"Sorry," she mumbled. In her bedroom, Nadia shut the door and threw herself onto the bed.

Oh gods, Rune was a demon! How had she missed it? Was she that much of an idiot? All those times he said he never lowered his glamour ... The fact that he was so adept at fighting demons ... His fighting name "Demon Slayer" ... He'd practically been broadcasting the truth, and she'd completely ignored the signs!

And she had bonded her magic to his ... She didn't even know the implications of what that meant. Was her magic now demon magic? Was her darkness growing?

Big fat tears slid down her face. She closed her eyes, trying to shrink down and disappear and stop her heart from being ripped out and shredded.

There was a knock on the door.

"I'm busy," Nadia called out, her voice wavering.

The door opened anyway, and Marina poked her head through. "I heard you come in. Why are you stomping around?" Her expression softened when she saw Nadia's tear-streaked face. "What happened?"

"R-Rune's a demon," Nadia managed to get out.

"You're kidding." She didn't seem that surprised. Her eyes flicked up like she was thinking of something, and she nodded slightly. "Avery says he knew there was something wrong with him when he met him."

"Can you please stop mindspeaking to him?" asked Nadia. "I'm in the middle of a crisis here."

Marina took a seat on Nadia's bed and patted the spot beside her. "Come here." Nadia sat up and let Marina rub her back comfortingly. "There, there. I'm sure this isn't the first time a man has lied to you. Your father . . ." She snorted. "Not exactly a role model of good behavior in men."

"This isn't helping."

"Okay, sorry," said Marina. "I'm just trying to say that . . . maybe he had a good reason to lie."

Nadia took a deep breath. "It isn't the lying. It's that . . . I had no idea. I trusted him. I thought he was a good guy. But I was wrong." She closed her eyes, the weight of the world heavy on her shoulders. "And if Rune isn't a good guy, then I don't know who is."

"All in favor of informing the Council?" asked Simon. The members of the board, assembled virtually as before, all voted. Curtis, in his NASA shirt, Simon, on his yacht, and David Song, floating cross-legged in front of his temples, all raised their hands. Meredith, in silky loungewear on the screen, and Rune, in the conference room, kept their hands down.

"That's three to two," said Curtis. "Looks like we'll be involving the Council in the event we need arbitration with Pact."

Rune slammed his fist on the conference table, cracking it. "You are giving them too much power! This is an issue between startups, not between Numinals and humans."

"Everyone knows your animosity with Miles Kirkpatrick." David Song's robes fluttered on phantom wind. "It's your word against his."

"We're protecting Myst this way," added Curtis.

Protecting Myst, my ass, he thought. More like, protecting your own. "Fine. We'll send a formal Request for Insight. Don't expect an answer right away."

"I'll make a call," said Simon. "Get it pushed to the top."

"To your *buddy* on the Council?" asked Rune. He knew Simon and the senator were friendly.

Simon flicked the ash off his cigar. "If you are going to accuse me of something, Christiansen, then do it."

"Enough!" cried Meredith. "Honestly, you bicker like children. Are we done here? I have dinner plans."

"Run off to your pool boy." Simon smirked.

Meredith scowled at him.

"Rune, you have a moment?" asked Curtis. "Stay on."

After the others left, Curtis leaned into the camera. "What the hell is going on here? First, these thefts, now you're attacking Miles Kirkpatrick?"

"I know."

"This isn't like you."

Rune clenched a fist and smiled tightly. "I appreciate the concern, but I have it handled."

Curtis leaned back and shook his head. "Simon has been floating the idea about calling for a vote of no confidence."

Rune swore under his breath. A vote of no confidence was not binding, but it was the first step they needed to take if they wanted to replace him.

"You know I won't support it," continued Curtis. "But you have missed critical KPIs."

"What the fuck does that have to do with anything?" Rune

snapped. "You know it's his own vendetta. He works for the Council. We all know that."

"A vote of no confidence would seriously jeopardize the future of Myst. We can't let that happen. I'll talk to Simon, see if I can get him to calm down. But nothing, you hear me? Nothing else can happen."

Rune ended the Zoom and sat back. It was clear to him now what was going on.

The Council was trying to get to him by going after Myst.

Nadia slouched down in her red velvet seat at the movie theater as she stuffed her mouth with popcorn. The Castro Theater was running a weeklong classic film festival, and Nadia had bought tickets for the Humphrey Bogart double feature: *Casablanca* and *To Have and Have Not.*

Rune had once told her that he liked classic movies. She had thought maybe they'd catch a movie there someday. Maybe their hands would brush in the popcorn bucket, or she'd lay her head on his shoulder. This was, of course, back before she had learned he was a demon and had lied to her for months about himself and his true nature. All dreams of watching a movie with him had been dashed, the tenuous strings holding the fantasy together snipped by his lying and deceit.

All around her, couples snuggled in together, friends sat and laughed, the flickering light of the screen illuminating their happy faces. Nadia felt so very, very alone.

Thomas popped into existence in the chair next to her. "Red Vine?" he asked, holding out the box.

Nadia grabbed one and bit down hard, ripping a piece away like a hungry carnivore.

On screen, Lauren Bacall opened a door and turned back, standing in the doorway.

"I love this part," said Thomas, gesturing to the screen. "'You know how to whistle, don't you, Steve'?" he mouthed. "'You just press your lips together and blow.'"

"Put," said Nadia. "It's supposed to be put."

"Hmm?"

"The line is 'You know how to whistle, don't you, Steve? You just put your lips together and blow.'" She was sure of it. She'd watched the movie dozens of times.

"Mandela Effect?" Thomas shrugged. Nadia rolled her head back against the seat in frustration. She did not have the time or energy to figure that one out. Thomas grinned at the screen, enjoying the show.

Nadia leaned over to him and whispered loudly, "How come you didn't tell me?"

"Tell you what?" he whispered back.

"That Rune was a *demon!*" she hissed.

Thomas threw back his head and laughed. A few audience members shushed him.

"What's so funny?" Nadia glared at his smug expression.

"I thought you knew! Are you really this naive? What did you think he was?"

Nadia's frustration threatened to choke her, and she viscerally shook. "I don't know! A powerful Fae or demi-god or some Numinal I've never heard of! He's been teaching me how to protect myself from demons. *How the fuck* would I know that the reason he's so good at it is because he is a demon himself?" More audience members shushed them.

Thomas turned around and zapped the humans with some demon magic. "You never suspected?" The couple fell asleep in their chairs, slumped over on each other.

Nadia tried to center herself and control her breathing. "I wasn't getting a demon read on him. Not like you, anyway."

A muscle twitched in Thomas's cheek, but he merely replied, "Rune Christiansen is a much older demon than I. He has had centuries to perfect his glamour to fool the world."

"I just wish someone had told me," Nadia grumbled.

"I'm sorry that he tricked you. How did you find out?"

"How do you think?" she snapped.

He shot her a worried look. "He fed from you?"

She nodded and grabbed another Red Vine. Maybe she could give herself a sugar coma and wake up in a different reality.

Thomas muttered something to himself. He looked like he wanted to punch something.

"What's this overprotective brother thing you're doing?" Nadia asked. "Why do you care?"

"Christiansen is a predator," Thomas muttered.

She wasn't sure if that was true. Nadia had definitely pursued him when she sent him topless photos. Had she been some Lolita nymphet, trying to seduce her boss? He hadn't wanted to kiss her. He'd tried to push her away. *Oh, gods!* What if he had been keeping her at arm's length, knowing he would feed from her, and she had just launched herself at his face? She had kissed him first, hadn't she?

Nadia didn't know if she had been the predator or the prey. She tried to scrunch down and melt into her seat, become as little as possible, and disappear from the world.

Chapter 29

"Pass me the shears, por favor," said Marina at the other end of the long wooden picnic table. Nadia floated them down to her, and Marina grabbed them out of the air. "Gracias."

They sat outside on Marina's back patio under a vine-and-twinkle-light-covered arbor. Dozens of gourds and pumpkins lay out on the table. For each, Nadia cut off the top with a large butcher's knife, scooped out the pulp, separated out the seeds to save for Marina, and then carved a face into it. As it turned out, stabbing things helped with Nadia's general disposition and overall mood.

Marina was at the other end of the table, an array of ingredients in little vials and pots and glass jars spread out before her: surplus Samhain stock for The Tambourine Lady's Shoppe, including potions, soaps, candles, sachet charms, and teas. She was currently mixing an all-purpose Samhain herb and spice mixture that could be drunk as a tea, used in cooking as a rub or seasoning, and even burned as incense or sprinkled in rolled joints.

Marina held up a dried leaf. "This is tobacco. I bet you've never seen it in this form, eh?"

Nadia shook her head.

"Tobacco is used for contacting the elders." Marina pinched off a piece of the leaf and added it to the bowl in front of her.

As Marina added pinches of this and that, she told Nadia

about Samhain and the magical uses of the herbs. Samhain was a time of ancestor work, honoring the dead, and banishing unwanted energies. Rosemary for protection and replacing bad vibes with good ones. Pumpkin seeds for prosperity. Roses for communication. Rue for banishing. Wormwood for summoning the dead. But be careful about having too much, or else you'd be seeing the green fairy. Marina's herb work centered on the seasons and how to best work within the wheel of the year, and all her October apothecary offerings were mindful of Samhain's influences.

Nadia finished carving another pumpkin and put it to the side. She picked up a wart-covered one and eyed it, turning it this way and that as she mentally designed a carving that would work with its strange lumps.

Marina glanced up. "That's a neat one." Nadia had just finished one of an art nouveau witch styled like a Mucha. After a long hiatus in college, Nadia was dipping a toe back into creating art, using the pumpkins as practice. "Did you carve a lot of pumpkins growing up?" Marina asked.

"We didn't really 'do' Halloween."

"What?" she exclaimed. "No hot apple cider? No drugstore costumes? No candy corn?"

"Mom didn't like Halloween. It was just another day in our house."

"That's a shame." Marina gave her a sad smile and continued working.

Nadia knew the unspoken truth about why her household never celebrated: her mother had turned away from her powers and heritage and didn't want anything to do with witches. Even though her mother had returned her powers to Mercurio and had no idea of Marina's involvement in the Blood Oath, she had never been the same. A fugue had settled over her life. She forgot the things that had once held meaning for her as she subconsciously avoided anything having to do with mysteries or the occult.

As a child, Nadia had been jealous of all the kids who had normal mothers: mothers who decorated their houses with cobwebs and pumpkins and hanging skeletons, mothers who made chocolate-dipped pretzels in the shape of fingers, ones who made homemade costumes and took their children trick-or-treating. Nadia had tried dressing up for a few years, but sitting at home by herself with a bowl of candy quickly became old, and she had mostly forgotten about the holiday until she had gotten her own car in high school and suddenly had the ability to go out. For the next several years and into college, Halloween had morphed into a party night: the ability to wear slutty costumes mixed with copious amounts of drinking.

But Nadia was enjoying delving into old traditions with her grandmother, getting to the roots of the holiday. Marina taught her about various customs, both Numinal and human, that she practiced each year. She was surprisingly sentimental, creating memory altars to her late husband Charles—Nadia's grandfather, who she never got to meet—and burning incense to their ancestor Maria—the first witch who had made the Blood Oath with Mercurio.

As she stabbed the next pumpkin—there really was a certain satisfaction about a sharp blade sinking into flesh—Nadia thought about the last time she had carved a pumpkin. It had been years. A dorm activity during her freshman year in college. She had carved a typical smiling jack-o'-lantern face with one triangle eye, one crescent eye, and a big ol' goofy grin with blocky teeth. Simple. Uncomplicated. Probably wouldn't get her put into a mental ward. The gourds and pumpkins she carved now were much different. Darker. More artistic. Some of them downright disturbing. It was the Season of the Witch, and all her creations reflected various iconic and archetypic imagery associated with them.

Marina wiped her hands on her apron. "Can I get you a refill when I go inside?"

"Yes, please."

Her grandmother grabbed her bowl and Nadia's cup and headed up the wooden staircase to the back patio. As she worked, Nadia was drinking sweetened mugwort tea. Without honey, the herb was quite bitter, with a distinct aniseed taste. She didn't particularly care for the taste, but mugwort was supposed to help with creating vivid dreams. While before she had run from Mercurio's constant barrage of sex dreams, she now welcomed the distraction.

She hadn't talked to Rune in days. Every time she walked into a room, he walked out, as if even being around her was unbearable. The whole thing stung. She might have been able to forgive Rune if he had explained himself. If he had talked to her. It's not like she had been completely truthful, herself. But it had been radio silence. She'd even broken down and tried to mind-speak with him after he ignored her increasingly desperate texts, but he refused to talk to her. She'd gotten zip. Nada. Nothing. Nadia was becoming resigned to her fate as Mercurio's Blood Muse. There was no other path forward.

But the one thing Nadia did have was her grandmother, and she latched onto that relationship. Marina had flown into caretaker mode over the last few days, mixing her herbal remedies to dull the heartache and energetically lobbing curses in Rune's general direction. She was in her element. Nadia almost thought her grandmother liked it when people were in crisis. She seemed to be the happiest when she was needed. But no matter what Marina's motivations were, it was nice to be building a relationship with her. After all this time, Nadia was finally getting to know and trust her.

Marina returned with a freshly brewed cup of tea for Nadia and set it in front of her. "At this rate, you're going to use up all my mugwort."

They worked for a while longer until Nadia was done for the day. She wiped her hands on a dish towel. "I think I'm all carved out. I'm going to go wash up before dinner." She took the tea and headed back inside.

Upstairs in her bedroom, Nadia stripped off her pumpkin-covered clothes, tossed them into a laundry basket in her closet, and tied her hair up in a bun. She wrapped a towel around her body and padded barefoot down the creaky wooden staircase to the second-floor hallway bathroom.

The bathroom light was on, steam coming from behind the closed door. Nadia knocked. "Avery? Let me know when you're done!"

The shower turned off, and there was a racket behind the door: the shower curtain pushed back quickly, a stumbling and sliding of feet, banging and rattling.

Nadia leaned her ear closer to the door. "Avery?" She knocked again. "Are you okay?"

There was a loud *bang*, and something crashed to the floor. Nadia rattled the locked doorknob. "What's going on?" she demanded. She thought about breaking down the door, but then remembered she had magic, and she quickly shot off an unlocking spell. The lock clicked open.

Nadia barged into the misty bathroom, half expecting to see Avery passed out on the floor. Instead, two large round eyes stared back at her from behind the shower curtain hanging askew from a downed rod.

She screamed. The creature—some sort of chicken lady with

a beak and bird feet—screamed back. Nadia tried to grab the curtain rod from it, wield it like a weapon, and fend it off, but the thing held on tight as they tug-o-warred over it. But then, Nadia saw that the thing was covered in Marina's aloe-drenched bandages and wraps that she made for The Tambourine Lady's Shoppe, the white strips of cloth stamped with the shop's logo.

Marina and Avery appeared in the bathroom doorway. "Everyone, stop!" Marina cried out. They froze, and Nadia finally got a good look at the creature. It was a kikimora, a Slavic house spirit that resembled a peasant woman with a long pointy chicken beak and gnarled chicken feet. Marina sighed deeply. "Babunya, this is my granddaughter, Nadia. Nadia, I see you have met our guest."

"I cannot believe you have been harboring fugitives in this house without telling me!" Nadia exclaimed. She sat at the kitchen table with Marina and Avery, sharing a bottle of limoncello as they tried to explain what exactly a kikimora was doing staying with them in a hidden bedroom—the very one that Marina had told her to stay out of when they had been trying to contain that flying infestation in the house.

Marina threw up her hands in a dramatic fashion and rolled her eyes at Avery, who nodded sympathetically. "This has been going on for years now!" said Marina. "I'm one of the NLA's safe houses. I only took a break for a few months when you first got here and were becoming acclimated."

"You still should have told me," Nadia countered. "I've been living in a home that turned out to be a Numinal halfway house. Who are these people? What if they're dangerous? What if Mercurio finds out?"

"These Numinals need our help," said Marina. "Mercurio takes advantage of the disenfranchised. Exploits them. Keeps them hooked on the very thing destroying them. They sell themselves, sell their parts. There are safe houses to get away from dark masters all over the country."

"I still can't believe you didn't tell me this before. Even after I told you what happened, how he tortured *me* to send a message to other witches, you didn't tell me that *you* were the one he was after! You didn't even stop what you are doing!"

"I am sorry that happened," said Marina. Her voice was even. Not a hint of remorse. "I truly am. But if you are to serve Mercurio, you're going to have to toughen up."

Nadia felt like screaming. "He's going to find out. What happens when Mercurio realizes that you are running an underground Numinal railroad and that's where all his supplies have been going?"

"He can't harm me, remember?" Marina shrugged. "He'd huff and puff, but ultimately, he can't make any strikes against me." She reached out and grabbed Nadia's hand, pulling it over and clasping it in her own. "Some things are worth fighting for."

And some aren't, thought Nadia.

Chapter 30

The whip cracked across Rune's back. He flinched, arms bound to the stone wall, muscles tensed. "Again."

Ananke, clad in black leather, wrapped the heavy metal chain tighter around her fist and hit him. The barbs cut into his skin, his flesh shredding. Blood ran in rivulets and pooled on the ground. With his Numinal magic, the wounds would heal quickly, but he wanted the scars. He wanted a reminder of his unworthiness.

"Again," he commanded.

Ananke hesitated. "I think that's enough."

"Again."

She sighed and hit him once more.

Rune gritted his teeth, refusing to cry out. The memory flashed again in his mind: the lust and desire in Nadia's eyes, the feeling of her soft lips against his, her tongue dipping in his mouth, her body pressed against him, begging for more. And then the look of horror and betrayal on her face when she pushed him away, a look that would forever be seared into his mind.

He hadn't meant to feed from her. He really hadn't. But he'd brushed up against that sweet Blood Muse energy, and something dark and hungry in him had surged forward and taken control. She hadn't screamed. That would have been easier. She just looked at him like she didn't know who he was anymore.

Demon. That's what he was. Monster.

Ananke hit him again, and a cry escaped his lips. White-hot pain ripped through his body, purifying him. He passed out, the darkness a comfort.

He came to, hanging by his outstretched arms, his weight heavy and pulling on the shackles. Ananke was behind him, dabbing his wounds with a cloth and rubbing a healing salve into his skin.

"She really did a number on you, didn't she?" asked Ananke softly.

"I don't want to talk about it."

"I've never seen you this worked up about a human." She hugged him from behind, resting her cheek against his shoulder carefully so she wouldn't hurt him further.

"I said, I don't want to talk about it. Not with you."

Rune could sense her anger.

"You want to feel something?" she whispered in his ear. "I'll make you feel something."

Claws ripped down his wounds on his back, and he screamed.

She left him in the small stone room, hanging by the chains that secured him to the wall. He went in and out of consciousness, his vision blurred, the room spinning, until someone unshackled him and carried him to the small bed in the corner.

When he woke, the establishment's madam, Odette, was sitting on the bed in a light blue silk robe. "Good morning. Coffee?" Her tone was chipper, but her ageless eyes projected worry.

Rune struggled to sit up, wincing at the pain of his flayed flesh. Someone had pulled his boxers back on.

As calm and composed as always, the older Numinal woman poured a cup of coffee for him from a small steaming pot on a bedside table and handed it to him. "You made quite the scene last night."

He took it from her, the cup rattling in its saucer from his unsteady hands.

Rune had rampaged through the city, ending up at Odette's. After he and the board had sent out a formal Request for Insight to the Council, he had cracked. Gone on a bender. Nadia had tried to mindspeak and text him a few times, but he couldn't—wouldn't—talk to her. How could he? He didn't know what to say. He had fed from her. Lost control. He was a monster. He didn't deserve to live.

The only way Rune knew how to regain control was through pain. It focused him. He should have been keeping himself in check this entire time, coming for regular sessions with Ananke, but with everything with Nadia and the launch ... he had slipped from his usual routine. And it had cost him dearly.

"I'll pay for any damage," said Rune gruffly. He coughed, pain ripping through his torso.

"I know you will," replied Odette. "You scared my girls. I don't think they've ever seen a demon prince out of control."

"Don't call me that," he snapped.

Anything but that.

Maya's DJ booth and music workstation—"the Nest," as Maya liked to call it—overlooked the main floor of Myst. Outfitted with an abundance of beige and cream feather pillows, Nadia had found that the space was a good spot to work. Nadia and Maya would chat about this and that and help each other brainstorm, and Nadia found she did some of her best thinking while listening to Maya compose.

Maya turned and twisted little dials over at her sound mixer, bopping slightly as she composed the music for the new Veil module. Nadia lay on the floor, her notebook open to a page covered in notes and scribbles. She had thought to do some automatic writing, clear her mind a little bit and let the Numinous take over, but when she read what she had written, it was all eights. Dozens of them, scribbled all over the page. Eights, eights, eights . . . she was either losing her mind, or she was about to unravel a giant life mystery. Most likely, she was losing her mind.

Nadia needed a lifeline. "What does the number eight mean to you?" she asked Maya.

Maya pulled down her headphones. "Like, numerology? Is this some witch stuff?"

Nadia shrugged. "There are patterns everywhere. Fractals. I'm just trying to figure out what they mean."

"Okay, what's going on? You've watched me make music, now you're talking about fractals. Something's up."

"It's my grandmother." She proceeded to tell Maya all about the incident of finding the Numinal in the bathroom.

Maya's jaw dropped. "She did what? She does know that Mercurio is the biggest gangster in San Francisco, right?" Nadia hadn't told her about their family ties to the vampire, choosing instead to make it seem like Marina was simply a vigilante who had decided to take a stand for justice.

"It's, like, enough already, crazy lady," said Nadia. "First, you bind my powers, and now you're wrapped up in some Numinal terrorist group."

"I mean, the NLA does have a point," said Maya. "They're trying to stop Numinals and humans alike from getting exploited by the illicit Numinal black market. People will sell anything if they're desperate enough, and there are a lot of desperate Numinals trying to figure out how to survive in a human's world. Numinal black markets flourish. Hell, they even help sustain life as we know it. Not many ways to get a hit of magic, otherwise. A lot of Numinals need that fix."

"I just wish my grandmother wouldn't get wrapped up in all of it." She grabbed another nearby pillow and stacked it behind her head.

"Did you tell Rune?"

"No."

Maya narrowed her eyes at her. "How's apprentice training going?"

Nadia flinched. "It's not."

"What happened?"

"Rune and I . . . got into a fight. It's complicated."

"You want to talk about it?"

"Nope."

"Fair enough." Maya went back to composing. "Eights . . . I wonder if . . ." She didn't finish her thought as she focused back on her work.

Nadia's cell phone vibrated. It was a text message from Avery. **Mercurio knows.**

Nadia rushed home in a Waymo. She fidgeted impatiently, yelling at traffic as she backseat drove. She was glad there was no judgment from the Waymo Driver. Nadia tried to open the door before the car had come to a complete stop and received a warning from the robot. When the car finally pulled over, she jumped out, ran full speed through the garden pathway, up the wooden staircase, and burst through the front door.

Marina was slumped on the living room couch, twitching slightly. Avery sat next to her, checking her pulse. Nadia rushed over. Her grandmother's eyes were rolled back to the whites; blood trickled from her right nostril.

"She can't hold out much longer," said Avery. "She wanted to speak with you before she goes."

"Why does she look like that?" cried Nadia. "Is she having a seizure?"

"The universe corrals her into obeying him," said Avery. "She's resisting right now."

Marina forcibly collected herself and focused on Nadia.

"He found out about the escaped Numinals I was hiding," Marina bit out. "My work with the NLA. He's retaliating against me."

"I thought he couldn't harm you!"

Marina lost control once more. Her head flew backward violently as she gasped for air.

"Marina!" Nadia cried, grabbing her upper arm to steady her.

Tears threatened to fall from Avery's eyes. "He normally gives her a nudge, lets her know he wants her. He's trying to hurt her."

That bastard. He would pay for this. She would make sure of it.

Marina brought herself under control once more. "If anything happens to me, I want you to know I am so, so sorry the way things turned out. If I had known that Helen giving her gifts back wouldn't stop the curse, I would have stopped her. I would have made sure that you had a mother. I would have had more time with Charlie."

"What are you talking about?" demanded Nadia. "What does my grandfather have to do with any of this?"

Marina started shaking uncontrollably. Avery helped her stand. "We can't hold out any longer."

Avery and Nadia helped Marina walk to the front door and down the porch steps toward Thomas, her steps shaky. It was like walking her to her execution. Nadia couldn't tell if she was more scared for Marina or of the fact that this would one day be her own fate: completely at Mercurio's mercy, unable to resist him without bodily pain and a possible brain aneurysm.

Thomas stood at the boundaries of the wards, checking the time. He looked mildly concerned about Marina's bloody nose and twitching.

"You'd better bring her back," she snapped at Thomas.

Thomas nodded solemnly as he took Marina by the arm. "I will do my best." And then there was a small *pop!*, and they were gone.

"How could you just let her go like that!" Nadia exploded the second she and Avery got back inside. She pointed a finger at him. "This is your fault!"

Avery raised an eyebrow at her, tucking a lock of his messy blond hair behind his ear. "I know you're angry. I'm angry too. We just need to stay calm, for Marina's sake."

"This is ridiculous! We can't just sit here, doing nothing!"

"What do you want me to do? We took a gamble and lost. Mercurio found out what we were doing. Marina knew the risks."

Nadia took a seat on an armchair. "What did she mean about my grandfather? What happened?"

Avery leveled her gaze. "Haven't you ever wondered how she bound your powers?"

Nadia's heart jumped into her throat. "What did she do? Tell me!"

"It's not my story to tell," said Avery. "Marina will tell you in due course."

Nadia glared at him. Their black cat, Monday, sat in the corner, emitting pitiful meows at Marina's absence.

She slumped down in the chair. "I just don't understand why she would risk everything for these Numinals she doesn't even know."

"You don't think a Numinal life is worth a human life, do you?" Avery's voice was full of reproach.

"I *didn't* say that."

"You didn't have to."

They sat in silence. The minutes ticked by on the grandfather clock standing against the wall. Avery magicked a book, some sort of Bible or other scripture written in High Fae, and paged through it, his lips moving as he read passages to himself.

Nadia looked about for something with which to distract herself. She scrolled mindlessly through social media, not really reading any of it. She picked up one of Marina's smutty romance novels with a shirtless man wearing a cowboy hat on the cover and opened it to a dog-eared chapter. She tried to lose herself in the story, but her mind kept churning. What was Mercurio doing to her grandmother? Was she okay? Would she come back in one piece?

"Marina and I have never told you how we met," said Avery, his voice breaking the silence. "I was one of the first Numinals she helped."

Nadia glanced up. Avery closed his book and magicked it away.

"I was in a bad place," he continued. His voice was flat. "I was living on the streets, hooked on *ousia*. I needed more. There was never enough. I heard that Mercurio paid handsomely for . . . parts." He hesitated before he added, "I sold my wings."

"What?" Nadia gasped.

Avery closed his eyes, a pained look on his face. "They sawed them off. It was . . . excruciating. I regretted it instantly. Nothing is worth that. Mercurio's guys threw me, naked, bloodied, and deformed, into the gutter outside his warehouse with a vial of *ousia*. I tried to snort it there in the mud puddle, but I dropped it. My hands were shaking too much." He smiled ruefully. "It was all for nothing. I wandered the streets in a daze. I didn't know if the pain or the withdrawals were worse. I eventually woke up from the fugue and was in Marina's kitchen. She had found me and took me in, wrapped the bloody stumps on my back. She healed me."

"Avery, I'm so sorry." Nadia wished she could give him a hug. "I had no idea."

"I wouldn't expect you to know. I try not to think about it."

Nadia glanced at his wings, tucked down behind him.

Avery flexed a translucent wing, extending it out. "These are prosthetic. Some sort of lab-grown replacement. The technology nowadays is so much more advanced than before. Before, Fae who lost their wings had few options. They're very difficult to re-attach once severed. I can't fly, but they respond to me like my own did, thank the Light."

Nadia didn't know that Avery couldn't fly. She'd seen him glide, but she hadn't thought much of it. She hadn't thought much about him at all, in fact, as preoccupied as she had been with her own drama and life. What else had she missed, wrapped in her own pain? She was ashamed that she hadn't bothered to get to know him better. She had told herself that she was fighting for something bigger, for freedom and justice, but she was living under the same roof as a man Mercurio had wounded and had failed to see it.

"Marina cares when a lot of people don't," said Avery. "She makes sacrifices for others. Helps people when she can. Gives what she can give, even if it's not much."

Nadia nodded, her throat tight. Marina had seen Avery's suffering and had chosen to help him. Nadia had seen nothing. Had chosen not to. Willful blindness had started out as a survival mechanism, but now it was beginning to feel like a hollow excuse.

"She's compassionate," Avery continued, "and even if her actions are sometimes misguided, she's trying to do her best by everyone. We need more people like her in the world."

Sometime well after midnight, Nadia roused from where she had fallen asleep in the armchair, waiting. She shook the fog from her head. There was the noise again, the scraping of the front door opening. She rushed to it, but Avery beat her there.

Avery had Marina in a giant bear hug, and she cringed from the contact like she was in pain. He pulled away and held her out, examining her for injuries. Dried blood peeked out from one of the sleeves on her wrist.

"I'm fine. I'm just tired," said Marina with a weak smile.

"What did he make you do?" Nadia could hear the fear in her own voice.

"I need to sleep," said Marina. "We'll talk later."

Avery pulled a shawl down from the coat rack, bundled Marina up in it, and led her slowly upstairs. Nadia's world wobbled with a sense of déjà vu. Was this a premonition of her life for the next fifty years or so? Was this her fate? Glassy-eyed and complacent, a slave to Mercurio?

Back in her room, Nadia tried to sleep, but she tossed and turned, her mind worrying over everything. Her grandmother, her mother, Avery, Rune, Mercurio. Her heart twisted. None of this should have ever happened. It was all too awful, too painful. Tragedies happened to other people. They weren't supposed to happen to her.

Nadia sometimes would think about what she would do in a crisis. A plane or car crash, a terrorist attack, a mass shooting. She would run through various scenarios, try to be mentally prepared in case it ever happened. It helped alleviate her anxiety . . . somewhat. But she didn't know she had to be worried about a different kind of crisis. A slow-burning crisis, one that had been building for years within her family, one she hadn't even been aware of until it had boiled over and scalded her.

Staring at the ceiling, her thoughts and emotions in turmoil, Nadia closed her eyes and tried to feel a connection to the Numinous or the Goddess. Anyone who might be listening. *Please help me.* A spark lit, a flame in a dark cave. An embrace enveloped her, drew her down, down, down into the ground, and she drifted off to sleep.

The next day, Nadia brought breakfast up to Marina.

"Knock, knock," said Nadia as she entered her grandmother's bedroom.

Marina was sitting up next to Avery, pillows behind her head, tucked under her floral comforter. Monday was draped over her lap like a lounging panther. Nadia placed the breakfast tray laden with pancakes and strawberries on the bedside table.

"Thank you, honey," Marina rasped out. Her face was gaunt, dark circles under her eyes. Her hair, normally peppered with gray, was now almost white.

Nadia took a seat on the edge of the bed. "We need to talk."

Marina nodded. "I know."

"First off, what happened with Mercurio?"

Marina glanced at Avery and took a deep breath. "They used me to practice some blood ritual." She held out her arms, covered in white gauze, and removed some of the dressing. Runic symbols crusted over with blood were carved into her skin. "Something they are doing on Samhain."

"Who is 'they'?"

"There was some woman there with Mercurio." Marina coughed. "I don't know who she is."

"So they cut you up, and then what?" Nadia tried to keep her voice calm and even.

"Thomas bandaged me up and brought me home," said Marina.

"What about—"

"I think that's enough interrogation for now," Avery interjected.

"It's fine," said Marina. She took Avery's hand and gave it a reassuring squeeze. "She needs to know what she is in for when the Oath passes to her."

Nadia fiddled with the edge of a blanket. "What did you mean about Charlie?"

"The spell to bind your powers called for a life . . . I . . . used your grandfather."

"You did *what*?"

Her grandmother appeared calm, resigned even. "I used his life. I used it to power the spell."

Nadia couldn't process what her grandmother was telling her. It was too gruesome, too unapologetic, too real. Her grandfather had lost his life because of . . . her. Her mind shot around, bouncing from implication to implication. Maybe she was misunderstanding. Maybe there was a perfectly reasonable and non-horrific explanation for it all.

"Was he willing?" Nadia asked. Maybe he had sacrificed himself. Known what he was getting into, trying to save his granddaughter.

"He didn't know what I planned to do."

"So, you murdered him. Great. You murdered my grandfather." The words were flat in her ears. Facts flattened themselves, wrung out the charged emotion, and assimilated into the family narrative.

Fact: her grandmother had murdered her grandfather.

"Charlie had just received a diagnosis," said Marina. "He had cancer. Stage four. We knew he didn't have long anyway." She smiled wistfully. "I honestly think if I had told him, he would have agreed to do it. He would have loved you if he had known you."

Nadia closed her eyes, taking a moment to breathe. This was too much. She didn't know whether to laugh or cry.

"Your grandmother did what she thought was best," said Avery. "Do not judge her for trying to save your life."

Nadia swept a hand around herself. "Well, look how it's all turned out! I'm still bound to Mercurio, all because of *you!*" Marina's eyes widened in shock at the outburst. Nadia continued, "You are the one who made me a Blood Muse. Oh, you didn't know, did you? You binding me made me a Blood Muse!"

Avery glanced sharply at Marina. "You turned her into a Blood Muse?"

Marina flinched. "I didn't know that would happen, okay? I'm sorry! All I can say is I'm sorry!"

Her words hung heavy in the air. Her grandmother took Nadia's hand, her knuckles more wrinkled than they had been before. "Listen, this is a blessing, you being a Blood Muse. He can't drain you. It won't be like this." She gestured to her body. "He can't use you up. Don't think of it as anything else except a blessing. Have I ever told you the story of Maria and how she made the deal with Mercurio in the first place?"

Marina proceeded to tell the story that had been passed down through the generations. Their ancestor had been a good woman. A hard worker, skilled in medicine and herbs. But she was beautiful, attracted a lot of attention, and other women hated her and their husbands' roving eyes. She had been pregnant out of wedlock when townsfolk cried "witch!" and came after her. Fleeing to the forest, she fell. She was having a miscarriage. The life of her daughter—she had known it was to be a girl—dripped out from between her legs. She was losing the child, and she would soon die herself.

Mercurio appeared, a shadow in the night. A dark, hairy creature, more monster than man. He told her that if she bound herself and her future daughters to him by making a Blood Oath to the Numinous, he could save her and the child. Maria made the Oath, drinking his blood and he hers, forever binding their lives and fates to each other. He gave her some of his magic, his Numinal powers, and they transformed her into a Septer. She healed herself and her unborn child, still in the womb.

Maria's blood changed Mercurio, as well. He transformed from monster to man, becoming who he is today. With Maria at his side as his partner and lover, he became unstoppable. With each generation, he received a new witch to serve him, one of Maria's female descendants, helping to cement his legacy and his power.

"Wait, so Mercurio was with Maria?" asked Nadia. "Like they were romantic with each other?"

"He supposedly loved her," said Marina. "I guess some of our ancestors got with Mercurio, and some didn't. He never seemed to force the issue. I never did it with him, but I'm pretty sure my mother slept with him at least once. She used to call him 'Alexi.'" She shrugged. "But the point of all this is that we owe our lives to Mercurio. Without that Blood Oath, Maria would have died and"—she snapped her fingers—"there goes the bloodline. We wouldn't exist."

"So that means he gets to own us? I didn't ask for this."

"The world is a mysterious place."

Nadia hid her face in her hands. Her grandmother was impossible. "Okay, fine. I get the point. But if we owe our lives to him, why are you working against him? Why do you fight him?"

Marina took Avery's hand in hers. "Because he hurts Numinals. That's not right. I don't care who he is; sometimes you just have to stand up and do the right thing. Listen, I've come to peace with what happened to me. I can take a punishment. But that doesn't mean that I wouldn't do it all over again."

Nadia held a vial up to the light. The liquid inside glowed a faint purple. Oil of wolfsbane infused with colloidal silver and a lock of Mercurio's hair. Marina had helped her create it, adding the ingredients into a pasta pot and boiling it on the stove. The tonic was a highly toxic poison to vampires, specially crafted to kill Mercurio.

They had come up with a plan: Nadia would text Thomas to get her an invite to see Mercurio. She knew that he had open sessions where he heard requests and petitions. She would make a deal that she would perform the Eights Ritual with him in exchange for their freedom. When they were alone and having a drink, she would drop the poison into it. He would die, and she could slip away—she and Marina and any future daughters finally free of him and the Oath.

Nadia was pretty sure she could do it. Not like one hundred percent sure, but a solid ninety-five, ninety-six. Poison was easy. No mess, no blood, nothing to clean up. Just the guilt and knowledge that she killed someone, and she could live with that if it meant her freedom.

Mercurio's cronies would know she did it, of course. They would have seen her at the petitioning session and know they had been off in some back room together. But with the Blood Oath gone, she'd be a free agent. She'd be able to skip merrily along with her life. And then she and Rune could be a thing, Mercurio out of the picture.

That is, if Rune ever talked to her again.

But she'd deal with that part later.

A strange sense of calm came over Nadia. She was taking the reins of her destiny. No more standing by the sidelines, watching it all play out. The ache of helplessness had drained out of her, replaced by a cold, clear certainty: no one was coming to save her. She would have to save herself. That truth had hurt. But instead of breaking her, it had hardened her. She turned to her window, drawn to the pale moonlight spilling across the floor like a path. Standing in its glow, she let the light wash over her, a faint smile on her lips.

Chapter 31

Samhain night. The air crackled with dark energy. Thomas met Nadia outside Mercurio's warehouse. The demon looked annoyingly dapper and relaxed as he leaned against the wall, wearing a gray three-piece suit with a daisy in the lapel.

"Why so glum, sugar plum?" he asked as Nadia walked up to him. "You should be dancing in the streets. You've figured out how to play the game. The world is your oyster, as far as I'm concerned." He took her hand and gave her a spin. "Lovely. Just lovely."

Nadia had planned her outfit. She wanted it to say she was a seductive force to be reckoned with. A Dark Goddess who devoured men in her path. She was wearing a black kimono-style dress, similar to the one Aiko had worn, and had paired it with red lipstick and a pair of black Louboutins with the red soles—a treat to herself for regaining control of her fate. She had tied back her glossy dark hair into a neat bun held together with chopsticks, and she wore Marina's cloak—the one imbued with warmth and protection spells. The vial of poison sat tucked in her bra.

Before she left, she had done a quick ritual to the Dark Goddess, filling herself with all the power and energy of the divine female spirit. She had channeled all the Blood Muses who had come before her and survived, clawing their way out of the pits of despair and toward their futures.

Thomas gestured toward the door. "After you."

Nadia hesitated, a pinprick of fear holding her in place.

"You don't have to do this if you don't want to," said Thomas gently. "You don't have to sell yourself like this."

A smile played on Nadia's lips. What would Thomas do with his freedom? Who would he become if Mercurio weren't around to control him? She vowed to herself that one day, when it was all over and done, she would tell Thomas how she poisoned Mercurio and freed them both. She would tell him how she had made the winning move and changed both their fates and destinies.

But she couldn't let him know she planned to poison their vampire master. "It's my body, my energy, my choice," said Nadia coolly. "Let's go."

Mercurio received business and took meetings in an echoey Gothic chamber with pointed arches and ribbed vaults. The space was ornately decorated, almost theatrically so, with rows of gargoyles on the top of columns and lit braziers that cast flickering shadows along the stone walls. The vampire sat on a throne at the end of a red carpet, surrounded by an audience. A small humanoid creature, an ogre perhaps, stood at the front.

"Lord Mercurio," started the man, "I humbly beseech you. A pack of demons has taken up residence in the alley next to my bakery in Russian Hill. They're scaring the customers and attacking them at night. Business is down. If you deem it . . . worthwhile to help me, I promise you . . . twenty-five percent of my profit."

A nymph in a black babydoll nightie handed Mercurio a bound stack of papers. He flipped through them. "Looks like your books are in order. Thirty percent, and you have a deal." The man nodded. Mercurio handed the stack of papers back to his assistant. "I'll send a team to clear out that alley. Welcome to the family."

The ogre creature seemed visibly relieved. "Thank you, sir. You won't regret this, sir."

Mercurio waved him away. "Next."

An elf walked to the front. She was young, sixteen perhaps. A runaway, if Nadia had to guess, by the oversized, dirty sweatshirt and Tory Burch flats she wore.

She jutted her chin out defiantly. "I heard that you pay for ears."

"How old are you?" asked Mercurio.

"Old enough."

He drummed his fingers on the chair arm. "Too young. Next."

Nadia glanced at Thomas, confused. Mercurio, showing temperance and mercy? Thomas shrugged, like *I told you he wasn't all bad, but nobody listens to me . . .*

Mercurio heard several other petitions. Some were Numinals who were selling parts of themselves, going to the back rooms if the vampire agreed to buy them. Others were small business owners who needed protection or had some issue with which Mercurio could help. The more that Nadia listened, the more confused she became. He didn't seem like a monster when he agreed to give out microloans to individuals to help start up their businesses or turned away at-risk Numinals who were trying to sell too much of themselves too quickly. He seemed like a Shark Tank businessman, with flashes of empathy and kindness.

Soon, it was Nadia and Thomas's turn. Mercurio sat up in his gold baroque throne as Nadia strutted up to the front. Thomas bowed, but Nadia declined to bend the knee.

"Thomas tells me that you're not quite the timid morsel that you used to be," said Mercurio. He leaned forward as he flicked his claws, his eyes flaring. "How delightful."

"I'm here to make a deal," said Nadia. "I know how you Numinals love your deals."

Mercurio chuckled. "My child, why would I make a deal with you? I hold all the cards."

"Because I'll give you something you want," said Nadia. "Something that you can't get any other way."

"And what, pray tell, is that?"

Nadia's voice threatened to quiver, but she said firmly, "I'll partake in the Blood Muse Eights Ritual with you."

An awful smile broke out over Mercurio's horrifyingly beautiful face. A murmur went through the crowd. "Now, that is an interesting proposition," he said, a hint of amusement in his voice. "What do you want in return?"

"I want my freedom. I want you to release me and my grandmother and any descendants from the Blood Oath that binds us to you."

The corner of his lip twitched, an almost smirk. "But you do understand that if we partake in the Eights Ritual, we will be bound to each other in a different way?" The rings on Mercurio's fingers caught the light as he rubbed the tip of his fang with his pinkie. "I will have been your first."

"I understand what it means."

Mercurio sat back and thought for a minute. A few Numinals drifted over and chatted briefly with him, trusted advisors weighing in on the situation. Nadia tried to keep her face impassive and neutral.

After a lengthy discussion with a Numinal woman in a toga, Mercurio called out, "My chief legal counsel has informed me that I am unable to release future descendants from the Blood Oath. I can only release you and your grandmother."

Nadia suspected as much. From all her research, she couldn't find a loophole around the fact that the Blood Oath had been made to the Numinous, not to Mercurio. He only had the power to release the current bonds that had manifested already, not future ones that existed in perpetuity.

"Then that will have to be enough," said Nadia. With Mercurio dead, she, Marina, *and* any future descendants would be free.

"We have a deal," Mercurio called out. "After we reach flow, I will release you and your grandmother from the Oath." He held out a hand to her. "Shall we?"

Nadia walked over to Mercurio and placed her palm in his. His flesh was icy cold. He stood, and they walked together to the back through a dim hallway lined with sconces. She had seen it before, in her dreams. Nadia's heartbeat thumped fast in her ears, and she was sure he could hear it. Mercurio stopped in front of a room and opened it with a brass key from a keyring on his belt. The carved wooden door swung open. Like the hallway, she had also seen this room before.

A monstrous four-poster bed—a Gothic nightmare with restraints and chains—was the centerpiece of the room, with a small sitting area in the corner next to a bar. Crushed velvet wallpaper lined the walls, emanating dark desires, Mercurio's sexual energy saturating every fiber. Giant mirrors circled the bed at all angles, the spectral images of the vampire and several others rising in Nadia's imagination.

"A drink first, perhaps?" Mercurio walked to the bar and poured an amber liquid from a crystal decanter.

Nadia took off her cloak and took a seat on the edge of a small settee. He handed her the drink and took a seat across from her.

"I am honored you would allow me to be your first," said Mercurio, his voice low and seductive. "This is an experience I have wanted for quite some time. I've never reached flow with a Blood Muse before. I hear it's akin to touching the Numinous."

Nadia took a large swig of her drink, her hands shaking slightly. She'd need liquid courage if she were to do this.

Mercurio chuckled at her nervousness. "Do you want to 'chat' first, or get down to it?"

Oh gods, was it time to do it already? "Maybe let's chat first."

The corner of his mouth turned up. "All right. What would you like to talk about?"

Nadia racked her brain for conversation. She needed to keep him occupied, keep him drinking, so she could slip the poison into his drink. "I guess . . . a toast?"

He raised his glass. "To us." They drank.

Mercurio manspread in the armchair. He fished his cell phone from his pocket, checked it, muttering something about "incompetent fucks," and then put it on silent. "So we won't be interrupted." He smiled, focusing his attention back on her, his fangs flashing in the low light.

Nadia was having a hard time reconciling the Mercurio in her mind with the man sitting in front of her. In her mind, he was a monster, terrifying and sensual, one who exploited and tortured people for his own personal gain. The man sitting in front of her, on the other hand, seemed like a tired businessman, slightly stressed by maintaining his empire.

"Can I ask you a question?" she asked finally.

"Ask away."

"Earlier . . . when you were helping all those Numinals . . . the ones who sold their parts to you . . ."

"Yes?" he asked, amused. "What about it?"

Nadia chewed on her lip, unsure of how to phrase this. Ah, to hell with it, she thought. "Do you torture people when they sell their parts to you?"

He gave her the strangest look. "No."

The words rushed out of her. "I know someone who sold parts. Wings. They said you hacked them off and it was super painful. And that whole thing with Fred. The supply chain guy . . ."

Mercurio laughed. "My dear, that was just a show."

Her heart leaped into her throat. "What?"

"I was priming your energy. You didn't even notice that I was harvesting it, the entire time?"

Nadia gawked at him. The whole thing had been an elaborate farce to get her to feel panic and terror? That glowing box he had made her stand on must have been some sort of harvester. "But what about that guy, Fred? You killed him . . ."

"Smoke and mirrors. I was testing out a new shrouding spell." He shrugged. "Now, I know your grandmother has launched some vendetta against me, the old hag. She's been a real pain in the ass, let me tell you. And it is true that some Numinals do feel pain, despite the analgesics we use. But usually that's because they're junkies and their pain receptors are shot to hell."

Well, fuck, she thought. She wasn't sure if he was telling the truth or not. Avery did say he had been a junkie. He very well could have hyperalgesia. Mercurio was throwing a serious wrench into her determination to kill him for being a sadist and a monster. *Eye on the prize, Winters.* Her freedom was *this close.* She just needed to poison him and be done with it. Monster or not, she was still going to be his slave if she didn't do anything about it.

"Another drink?" Nadia stood, took his glass from him, and went to the bar. Her hands shook as she uncorked the crystal decanter. Quickly, she must act quickly. She glanced over her shoulder, but he was fiddling with his cell phone again. Nadia pulled the vial out of her bra and tried to remove the top—

Mercurio grabbed her wrist in a crushing grip. She winced and dropped the vial onto the plush rug, whirling to face him.

He bent down and picked it up, holding the vial up to the light to inspect it. "You were going to poison me?" He didn't seem surprised.

Nadia was backed up against the bar. She looked for an escape, anywhere to run or hide, but she was trapped. Her breath came fast. She squeezed her eyes shut, readying herself for the impending attack, but he merely placed the vial on the bar, took the decanter, and topped off their drinks.

Warily, she followed him back to their seats.

"If you please," said Mercurio, gesturing for her to sit. He collapsed back into his chair. "I applaud your attempt. Feisty. I like it." He smiled lasciviously over the rim of his glass as he took a sip.

Nadia wasn't sure what to do now that she had failed. He had caught her. Her eyes flicked to the door. If she threw her glass at his head and then ran, then maybe she could reach it—

"Shall we continue?" he asked.

"W-what do you mean?"

"I'll honor my end of the bargain if you honor yours."

"You . . . you still want to do it?"

"I'm game if you are." The corner of his lip turned up slightly, his gaze intent on her, a devilish glint in his eye.

Nadia stared at Mercurio. This was her moment: her red-or-blue-pill choice. She could decline the offer, take the blue pill, and return to her regularly scheduled programming. It might not be so bad to accept her fate as Mercurio's slave and stay small. It was the path she'd been destined to follow all along. She'd admit defeat and take her lumps in life.

Or she could take the red pill—the one that meant venturing off the map and seizing control of her story. It wasn't a choice about diverging paths or a road less traveled. This was about destroying everything she thought she knew about herself and taking a leap of faith into the void. If she went through with the bargain, her descendants might not be saved, but she and Marina would be. And then she could truly start living her life for herself.

In the darkest hours of the night, as she was preparing Mercurio's poison, Nadia had let herself think about what it would be like if she had to fulfill the bargain and perform the Eights Ritual with him. Aiko had said sex wasn't strictly necessary, but from Mercurio's intense and sultry gaze, she was sure he expected it. And if the experience was anything like the sex dreams that he'd implanted into her mind, she was sure she'd enjoy it.

Nadia was tired of being the good girl and playing it safe. Good girls didn't survive; they were prey. And Nadia didn't want to be prey. She was a Blood Muse, and it was time she accepted it and used her new identity to her advantage. She wasn't being reckless, she told herself. She was being smart.

It should have been Rune. Nadia snuffed that thought out immediately. Now was neither the time nor the place for "shoulds." She cleared her voice. "I'll do it."

A cocky grin broke out on his face. "Smart girl." He downed his drink, stood, and held out a hand to her.

She took it without hesitation.

After, Nadia rose from Mercurio's bed and started to dress in front of one of the ornate floor mirrors that flanked the sides. Mercurio lounged naked, his head propped up by a silk pillow, smoking *ousia* and blowing concentric rings of smoke into the air.

"Take this tonic," he said, tossing her a little vial. For a second, Nadia thought it was the poison, but the color was different.

More of a shimmering orange. "This will mask your shift in energy. Christiansen will be sure to notice without it, and I want my star employee back in peak form."

"Thanks." Nadia uncorked the bottle and downed it in one gulp, bracing herself for a bitter medicine taste, but the elixir had a pleasant flavor, a little like effervescent mandarin.

Nadia stepped into her dress and reached around to zip it up. Mercurio had released her from the Blood Oath, and when Nadia felt the bonds disintegrate, she had nearly wept with relief and exhaustion from the knowledge that it was all over. Her life was a blank slate; she could do whatever or be whoever she wanted now. The power of the Dark Goddess had served her well.

Images and sensations of the previous hour whirled in Nadia's endorphin-filled mind: her and Mercurio's entwined bodies reflected in the ceiling mirrors, the sweet taste of *ousia* on his tongue, the low thrum of energy from the ritual enveloping them, his icy-cold skin warming under her fingertips as they reached flow and their energies became one. He hadn't been gentle. She hadn't expected him to be. But he had been reverent—something wholly unexpected from a man she had once considered a monster.

"Do you have any plans tonight?" asked Mercurio. "I know it's Samhain and you witches probably have something planned, but I'm going to an event if you'd like to join me."

Her eyes met his in the mirror. "No thanks."

He chuckled. "You do not need to run from me. I won't chase you. I thought we might enjoy each other's company, that's all."

"That's a generous offer then," she said, realizing he was being genuine, "but I think I'm going to spend the evening at home with my grandmother."

"Suit yourself." He took another hit of *ousia* and blew the smoke into a giant ring. "It's Impact tonight—Pact's user conference at Moscone? I've heard people are calling it 'Screamforce.' Supposed to be quite the spectacle. Pact's doing a mass harvesting, and I'm to oversee it. Make sure they don't muddy the energy or cause a big mess by killing everyone."

Nadia whirled on him. "Wait, what's going on?"

Mercurio shrugged. "Pact's been trying to do their own harvesting for months now, but of course, they couldn't handle it. They needed me back for tonight."

"You've been helping Pact?"

"It's not like it's a secret," said Mercurio, exasperated. "Everyone knows that they've been floating their cryptocurrency with the energy they harvest."

"What's happening at Impact tonight?" Nadia walked around to the other side of the bed near him.

He reached out an appreciative hand and caressed her thigh. "Diane Robbins, that beady old cunt, is trying to open a portal to the Other Realms. Thinks she's been hearing messages and instructions from some goddess. The woman's a complete loony. She's concocted some ritual, using the energy from the attendees. The ritual may or may not work . . . my money is on 'no.' But I need to make sure they don't kill everyone there. Balance the meters, so to speak. I thought you might like to see what I do." He held up a medallion. "Pact gave everyone these ridiculous things. Supposedly, they harvest energy from wearers and send it over the internet. I prefer energy to be harvested and stored locally, but they've been using something similar for their crypto, and it seems to work well enough."

Nadia's heart rate spiked. "Can I see that?" She took the medallion from him and opened the back to look at the battery configuration. Sure enough, it was nearly identical to Myst's— the ones that Dougie had sold to Miles.

Things suddenly became extremely quiet. Nadia clutched the commemorative medallion and knew two facts to be true: Pact had used Myst's faulty blueprints to design it, and everyone there was going to die.

Nadia shrugged on her cloak. "I'll have to take a rain check."

"Suit yourself." Mercurio took out his cell phone and fiddled with it, ignoring her now that he was done with her.

Nadia wove her way through the throngs of Numinals in the throne room, sneaking by Thomas, who was too busy flirting with a siren to notice her, and slipped out into the night to tell Rune what she had learned about Impact.

He might not want to talk to her, but he would if he thought his company was in danger.

Chapter 32

Rune sat in a black leather armchair in Vault Three, an open book splayed across his lap. A lamp hung over his head, illuminating the words of the antique tome. He tried to read, but the words swam on the page.

Nadia had tried to contact him a few times again, but he hadn't responded. He would . . . eventually. He just needed time. Time to process what he felt. Time to figure out what the hell to say. How to make it right.

He had to make things right with her.

Rune's cell phone vibrated. He glanced at the text. Another from Nadia.

It's been Diane Robbins this entire time. She's the one responsible for the demon attacks around SF. She's planning a mass harvesting at Impact tonight with the faulty blueprints to try to open a portal to the Other Realms.

Rune blinked. Of course this would be happening to him now. On top of everything. *Let the Dark take me . . .*

What about Miles? he mindspoke to her. *He was the one who was buying from the thief.*

I think she's been telling him what to buy. She's been running an energy harvesting scheme with Mercurio. The clickwrap agreement, the demon attacks, all of it, it's to artificially inflate Pact's crypto.

How do you know all this?

She paused. *I had a premonition.*

His heart hurt. He could sense she wasn't being completely honest. She didn't trust him now that she knew he was a demon. Their relationship, that closeness they had shared, their bonded magic, had devolved to this.

I'll call Kirkpatrick. He needs to know what's going on, thought Rune. *Meet me at the office.*

Rune grabbed his cell phone and scrolled through to Miles's number.

Miles answered on the third ring. "Christiansen. Called to apologize, have you?"

"No," said Rune smoothly. "But I have something you're going to want to hear."

Nadia rushed through Myst's headquarters on the way to Rune's office. The ground floor was abnormally empty for eight p.m., everyone out celebrating Samhain. Even Grudax and the pastry goblins were out. Their tiny wooden doors around the tree were all closed, gourds carved with faces guarding the entrances.

Nadia burst into Rune's office. He sat at his desk chair, looking way calmer than he should have been, all things considered. "Kirkpatrick's on his way. We're meeting him in the Firmament private dining suite. I have extra wards up around Myst for Samhain, and the Light knows he'll never find the front door."

She fell in step with Rune as they left his office. He glanced down and noticed she was all dressed up. Little black dress, Louboutins, mysterious cloak. She wondered if he could sense her shift in energy and prayed to the Goddess he couldn't. Rune started to say something but thought better of it. "Are we going to talk about what happened?" he asked finally.

Nadia kept her face impassive. She had thought about what

she would finally say to him face-to-face, practicing in the mirror to get the cadence and tone right. She wanted to say how important he was to her and that she forgave him. She wanted to tell him how she needed him in her life in some form or another. But now that the moment was here, the words she needed escaped her. "Water under the bridge," she said, flipping a hand nonchalantly.

He frowned, like he didn't believe her. "I should have told you. I should have—"

Nadia cut him off. "Talk later. We have far more important things to deal with right now."

Rune merely nodded and held the door open for her as they entered Firmament, Myst's in-house restaurant. Chihuly chandeliers hung down, tastefully illuminating small eating alcoves. They walked quickly through to a cathedral-like wooden door at the back of the room that led to the private dining suite.

Miles looked up from where he was sitting, slumped over in an overstuffed armchair. His head hung between his legs like a seasick sailor, his dress shirt rumpled, his blond hair in disarray. He held a crystal tumbler glass, a bottle of whiskey sitting on an accent table next to him.

"I hope you don't mind, but I took the liberty of pouring myself a drink." He tossed back a large gulp and inspected the glass. "Good stuff, if I do say so myself."

"Help yourself," said Rune graciously. He and Nadia seated themselves in two other armchairs, moon-shaped neutral seats loosely clustered around a live-edge table.

Nadia crossed her legs, making sure the bite mark Mercurio had given her on her inner thigh was hidden. Miles glanced at her legs, and Rune let out a low growl in warning. Miles averted his gaze and cleared his throat. "I can't believe Diane fucked me like this."

Rune sat stoically. "You need to take the system offline."

"I tried to ask her about that clause—I didn't authorize that, by the way—and she went ballistic on me and locked me out of the system!" Miles sat back, aghast. "I mean, I'm the CEO, for crying out loud! She's holding *my* company hostage!"

"You never had any indication she would turn on you?" asked Nadia.

"None!" exclaimed Miles. "I trusted her completely! She has access to everything—the tech, the finances, the Hacksilver." He sat back, shaking his head. "She played me. I ate up that tough love, mommy vibe. I thought she had it all handled, that she was just really, really good at her job, and instead she was using me the entire time!"

Nadia was fairly certain that Miles was just as complicit in his own undoing, with his reckless party boy nature and devotion to skating by with the least amount of responsibility, but she refrained from mentioning that opinion.

Rune stared Miles down. "We need to figure out how she plans on trying to open the Realm Gates. We know she is harvesting energy from attendees to power a spell, with help from a local crime boss who is adept at harvesting from humans. Pull up the specs for the event."

Miles scrolled through his cell phone. With the press of a tiny button hidden under a side table, Rune turned the domed walls into a single glowing screen, pulling in Miles's files through Bluetooth.

"These are the details about the evening," said Miles as he scattered notes and documents about the room. Concept images of giant monsters with tentacles, blueprints for Moscone Center, and various memos and project timelines populated the screen. "It's a Lovecraftian-themed interactive horror experience. We built a whole town inside Moscone—Arkham—and we are overlaying augmented reality and magic over real sets so that the attendees feel like they are transported to a different universe." Nadia glanced at Rune. It was almost the same concept that they used in Veil. Rune drummed his fingers impatiently.

Miles held up one of the commemorative medallions. "These are the medallions each user receives when they enter. Diane's been hounding me for months about the medallions—something that would harvest a little bit of the user's energy to power a glow-in-the-dark LED light and some Bluetooth capabilities. I, uh, borrowed your specs. I couldn't figure out how to make it work."

"You little shit," Rune growled, finally snapping. "You just take, take, take, don't you?"

"I'm sorry, I'm only human! I can't keep up with Numinal technology and advancement!" Miles covered his face with his hands.

The silence stretched, heavy and uncomfortable. Rune glowered at Miles. Nadia reached out and patted Miles's arm. He looked up at her, tears in his eyes.

"We need to focus," said Nadia. "The blueprints that you took were incomplete. The technology doesn't work. It's dangerous. It harvests at too fast a rate. We need to figure out what Diane is planning so we can figure out how to stop it. Can you help us with that?"

Miles sniffled and nodded. "The centerpiece of the evening is an occult ritual that Diane designed."

Rune shook his head, muttering, "Why are we just learning about this now?" He zoomed in on the screen and manipulated the image with magic so that the image expanded all around them like it had at Aiko's—an augmented reality 3D mock-up.

The ritual was set to unfold on a central stage, with the audience gathered in a circle around it. At the center stood a sacrificial table adorned for Samhain and crowned with a sculpture. A naked man lay bound upon it, symbols carved into his flesh. This had to be the blood ritual that Mercurio had been "practicing" with her grandmother.

"What's that?" asked Rune, pointing to the sculpture: a table with a tower sticking out of it. Nadia realized it was a 3D-printed miniature of the Hunters Point crane. She looked sharply at Rune.

She wouldn't . . . would she? asked Nadia.

She would.

"Whatever this is," said Miles, pointing back and forth between them, "can it please wait until after we've un-fucked my life?"

"She's planning on focusing the harvested energy through the crane," explained Rune. "It's an exact replica of the crane at Hunters Point—which was previously used for experiments trying to crowbar open the Realm Gates."

"That couldn't work, could it?" asked Nadia. "I mean, the scale . . . would it?" She sat back, thinking. In theory, it could work if there was enough energy amplification . . .

"There's a ley line that runs through Moscone," said Rune. "She could use that to power the spell. And I'm betting that it runs right through the ritual site."

"Okay," said Nadia. There was an obvious answer here. "Just . . . cancel the event."

"I can't cancel the event!" Miles cried out. "I have thousands of people attending. Not to mention the press and investors who are going to be there. I'd be ruined."

"Calm down," said Rune disdainfully. "Hysteria isn't going to help anyone right now. Thousands of people could die if we don't shut it down. Take the system offline."

Miles ran his hands through his hair in frustration. "I don't know how!"

"Rune," said Nadia. "If the system can't be taken offline, then anyone wearing the amulet will be harvested whether or not they are at Moscone."

"Fuck," Rune murmured. He shook his head, resigned. "I guess there's only one thing to do . . ."

They gathered around one of the war rooms—Rune, Nadia, Miles, Carson, Piero, Maya, and Sophie—staring at a 3D mock-up of Impact, twisted alleyways and city streets built to look like the town of Arkham.

Piero, dressed in a blue Virgin Mary nun's habit for Halloween, cocked his head. "It's a little derivative, isn't it?" Sophie, dressed as Madonna circa 1984, nodded.

Carson, wearing a red Mario hat and overalls, snorted. "More like extremely derivative." Carson and the others had been on the way to various Halloween parties when Rune had texted them to cancel their plans and meet at Myst.

Rune clicked on a red laser pointer and aimed it at the miniature of the Hunters Point crane. "This is the nexus site, where the energy from a laser beam running through a Hunters Point miniature intersects the energy of a ley line. At eleven forty-five p.m., Diane will lead a ritual that will culminate at the pinnacle of the eclipse at eleven fifty-three p.m., close enough to midnight when the veil is thinnest, to amplify the energy output from the ley line. With those energy sources all together, she will attempt to create a portal to the Other Realms and then use that to crowbar open the Realm Gates.

"To stop her," Rune continued, "we need to shut off the energy supply. I want to tackle this from all fronts. First, we need to decrease the energy output coming in through the laser beam until we can shut it off. The harvesting medallions work in a hive manner. The denser the crowd, the more they harvest. We need to keep the crowds at the ritual to a minimum."

Rune turned to Piero and Sophie. "That's where you two come in. Piero and Sophie will cause distractions to keep as many people as possible away from the ritual."

"On it," said Sophie. "I pulled a few strings, and guess who I got to help? Tommy Lightning!"

"Tommy will be playing here," added Piero, pointing to one of the far corners, "drawing the crowds away from the ritual, like the Pied Piper, with a modified whistler spell. Sophie and I will take the other side, here, and cause our own distraction."

Rune nodded. "Great. Now, Nadia and Maya, you two will take over the production office to shut down the energy beam. We need localized access to shut off the harvesting."

Nadia and Maya nodded. "Got it," said Maya.

"Carson and I will secure the nexus site and stop Diane and Mercurio from conducting the ritual," Rune continued. "Any questions?"

Miles raised his hand. "And what will I be doing?"

"Staying out of the way." Rune stared at him.

"It's my company, dammit!" Miles pounded his fist on the table. "I will be the one to take it back!"

Rune's expression was hard and uncaring. "No."

"Maybe I can reason with Diane," Miles started to protest.

"If you want to help," said Rune, "give us your credentials to Pact. We need to divert the energy to another source."

"Like I said, my credentials are blocked," protested Miles. "I tried hacking in the back entrance, but my firewall is too much, even for me."

"That won't be a problem," said Rune. "Carson?" Rune tipped his head in Carson's direction, and Carson sat back and kicked up his heels like Miles's firewalls were no challenge at all. He winked at Miles, baring his fangs.

Miles paled and nodded, grabbing a pen and a napkin. He jotted down his login information and slid the napkin over to Carson.

"I still can't believe we're helping Pact," Carson grumbled as his fingers flew over the keyboard. He projected his screen up so they all could see what he was doing, but Nadia couldn't really follow it. "I'm in."

Maya seemed impressed at how quickly Carson had gained access.

The wolf-shifter navigated through Pact's system. "I could make this so much more efficient," he murmured to himself.

"Can we please stop trying to improve Pact?" Rune growled.

"I'm a craftsman!" Carson protested. "I can't help it!"

Rune turned back to the group. "Are we all set?"

Chapter 33

The line to get into Impact at Moscone was wrapped around the block. Searchlights from the base of the boxy, glass-walled conference center lit up the night sky. Slutty Ninja Turtles and Marvel characters swarmed out front as the crowds tried to get into the event, ticketed as the biggest and most elite Halloween party in the city that year.

Dark energy saturated the cool night air. Lightning flashed. Thunder rolled through the sky. Forces were aligning, the veil between the worlds thinning, and no matter the outcome of the night, Nadia could sense in her bones that something monumental would pass.

Out front, Miles passed out VIP badges to everyone. "These will help us skip the line."

They moved to the entrance, and Miles waved his badge at a greeter dressed up as an evil doll with braided pigtails.

"Here are your commemorative medallions," said the evil doll, handing each of them a necklace. "These things are interactive. They open secret rooms, make stuff light up. Sort of like those Harry Potter wands at Universal Studios. Have fun!"

Rune took a deep breath. Nadia knew the unoriginality was killing him.

Once inside, they rallied next to a Victorian streetlamp. Rune held his medallion up, a marble-sized center orb spinning within a sphere. "I would recommend tossing these." He crushed it in his fist and threw it into the trash. All around them, the other attendees wore the light-up medallions.

"Yeah, no thanks," said Piero. He flung his into a receptacle. The others followed suit. A plague doctor strolled by, walking with a cane. He tipped his hat to them as he strolled by.

Nadia scoped the scene, getting the lay of the land. Impact was unlike anything she'd ever seen before. It was as if Disney had a baby with a Lovecraftian nightmare and had vomited out a Halloween extravaganza. Arkham was a Gothic town full of winding lanes and dark alleys, lamplit shops selling occult merchandise, and street vendors hawking wares. Nadia grabbed an event map from a nearby information booth and peered at it to orient herself. There were pubs and brothels, churches and graveyards, and even a haunted mansion that had once been a sanatorium, filled with interactive, immersive mazes, paid actors and VIP guests playing out various scenes and plotlines from The Call.

Rune called everyone to huddle up. "Set your watches."

"Countdown initiated," said Carson as he fiddled with his watch. "T-minus fifteen minutes."

"There's Tommy Lightning!" Sophie exclaimed as she spied the vampire rock star nearby, holding his guitar. He was decked out in tight black leather and sunglasses, and a crowd had formed around him, snapping pictures. Sophie and Piero broke off to grab him, and he started playing a sensual rock ballad when he saw Sophie. They whisked him away to a far corner. Attendees flocked after them like rats drawn to the music.

"The ritual site is in Hall C, that way." Rune nodded toward the back of the expo center.

"Follow me, then." Miles struck off first.

"Can we please ditch him?" asked Carson. "Seriously, he sucks."

"If I could, I would," Rune replied. "Let's go."

They disappeared into the crowd after Miles.

Maya turned to Nadia, the whites of her eyes glowing in the black light. "The control tower should be this way." She pointed toward Hall A.

"I'll follow you." Nadia moved through the crowd after Maya, holding on to the back of Maya's cape to stay with her.

They wove through cobblestone alleyways and past candlelit pubs and restaurants. Fire spinners threw flames into the air, while Punch-and-Judy-like puppets entertained on small stages. The atmosphere was festive and fun, the beginning of a night before everyone became sloppy and drunk.

"I don't want to be a total dick," said Maya, glancing back at Nadia, "but if we weren't saving the world right now, this would be a pretty epic party."

Nadia peered into the Jason and Chucky masks of attendees as they passed her. "I don't know . . . this crowd is a little . . . weird." An evil clown jumped in front of them and did a strange jig. Nadia zapped him away with a street smarts spell. They continued on. The amount of severed body parts and blood around them increased.

"There's a weird subsect of humans who are into murders and killings and true crime stories," said Maya. A Jack the Ripper bicycled past them. "Pact targeted them for this event."

"Of course they did."

The atmosphere changed as they got to Hall A: dilapidated docks on the outskirts of Arkham town. The hustle and bustle of the town center disappeared as the sound of waves crashing on the docks, seagulls, and the occasional terrified scream took over. Things became spookier and more ominous, long shadows and organ music seeping out of creaky wooden shacks. The few characters that scurried from shadow to shadow seemed more sinister and gruesome, psychopathic hags and possessed little

Catholic girls. Nadia couldn't tell who was an actor and who was an attendee. Everyone moved quickly from location to location, like they thought they were in actual danger. Nadia wasn't sure they weren't.

The production hub was perched in a creepy-looking tree house in the far corner. Nadia and Maya reached the back wall where a small locked door was marked "Staff Only." Nadia quickly cast an unlocking charm on the door, and it opened with a tiny click. They moved silently through the hallway and up a twisting staircase to the production room. Nadia hid on one side of the door, Maya on the other, and Nadia motioned to go on the count of three.

She kicked the door open with a battering ram charm. The door blasted open.

"Hey, what the—" a tech yelled, spinning in his chair at the intrusion.

Nadia cast a sleep charm, and he passed out, his head lolling to the side before he slid down to the floor.

Maya took out the other technician with some sort of Vulcan nerve pinch to the neck and gently laid him on the ground. She took his swivel chair and scooted up to the console.

"All right," said Maya, cracking her knuckles and neck. "Let's do this." Her fingers flew over the keyboard, and she started working on taking the system offline without overloading it.

Nadia peered out the door of the tiny room. The coast was clear. She turned back to inspect the room. Wires, electric circuit boards, and various panels with knobs and dials powered the electric, sound, and interactive augmented reality systems that projected throughout the event. Various screens showing a live televised feed hung over a large glass window that overlooked the festivities.

She rushed to the window and the screens. In the left corner, Tommy Lightning was putting on a show, a large crowd circled around him. In the right corner, Piero and Sophie were doing their act from the company talent show—half comedy routine, half magic demonstration—and had drawn away more of the crowd. But hundreds of people were still circled around the ritual site in Hall C, the main attraction of the night. Nadia scanned the area for Diane and didn't see her. But there were dozens of Mercurio's goons guarding the stage and preparing for the ritual. She didn't see the vampire.

They needed to get people out of Hall C.

"Can we cut the lights?" suggested Nadia. "Make people think there is a malfunction?"

"I'm working on it." Maya's eyes didn't leave the screen. "I'm not as fast as Carson."

"I saw the way you looked at him," said Nadia. "You going to forgive him, or what?"

Maya's eyes flicked up. "Sophie confessed that she and Carson never hooked up at Numinox."

"What?" demanded Nadia.

"She staged the entire thing," said Maya. "Piero's radical truth clown thing rubbed off on her. She felt guilty about tricking us and fessed up."

"That bitch."

Maya waved a dismissive hand and went back to work. "The fact that she took some responsibility for the situation shows me she's changed. She's annoying, but I'm not going to waste energy on her. She's clearly got her own issues if she feels the need to pull desperate crap like that."

"You're a more evolved being than I." Nadia was pretty sure she'd have pinned Sophie to the wall by the throat if she'd tried that with her.

Below, there was some sort of skirmish. A fight broke out between two guys, and they fell to the floor, wrestling and punching each other.

"People are being insane," commented Nadia as she peered out the window. "This is like a Juggalo meetup or something."

Before her, the night was devolving. Nadia couldn't tell if the medallions were warping people's minds, making them seem overly intoxicated and belligerent, or if something darker was stirring in the air, pushing them past the edge of normalcy.

Nadia went back to the video feeds of the different halls. In one for Hall C, Nadia searched for Rune and Carson in the crowds and finally spied them crouched down behind some speakers with Miles. Rune peered around the side, and then he and Carson made a move toward the center of the ritual site where the Hunters Point miniature sat, a laser beam of energy from the far side of the room hitting it.

Several Numinals rushed at Rune and Carson. There was some sort of scuffle, and Nadia lost sight of them in the throngs of people. They emerged again in a mass of bodies. A lynch mob of Mercurio's goons had attacked them and was carrying them forth to the nexus site.

"Rune!" Nadia cried out.

Maya glanced up at the screens. "Oh shit." She went back to the computer, fingers flying. "I've almost got the lights . . ."

The lights in Hall C went dark.

But the medallions around everyone's neck glowed, and several people held up lighters and lit torches. It appeared that the ritual was going to carry on. The crowd pressed up against the stage, pulsing in their need to be close to it.

"I don't know why the two of them thought they could take down an entire militia of Mercurio's men," said Maya. "Idiots."

Nadia rushed out of the room, down the staircase, and back to the event, sprinting across the haunted forest and back into the town of Arkham. She had to get to Rune. She had to help. She had to do something—

Rune's head whipped back as the ogre punched him in the jaw. He spat out blood, the cut on his lip already healing. "That was uncalled for."

"Shut up," grunted the ogre.

Mercurio's bodyguards hauled Rune, Carson, and Miles up to where the vampire sat, lounging on a throne to the side of the ritual site. Miles was limp, having passed out, and the ogre carrying him threw him off to the side. Carson snapped at his captors, and they took out a magical muzzle. It took three of them to wrestle it on. The guards then parked them both in front of Mercurio's throne, the ogres holding Carson's and Rune's hands behind their backs.

Mercurio, in a black embroidered vest and frilly blouse, seemed bored. He hung a leg over the armrest of his throne, his black leather pants pulling tight over his crotch in a blatant alpha male, cock-wagging move. "Christiansen. I should have known you'd interfere."

"The energy harvesters—the medallions—are faulty," said Rune. He shook the ogre off. "Everyone here is going to die."

"Well, that is inconvenient, isn't it?" Mercurio seemed annoyed and took out his cell.

Rune hoped he would see sense and call everything off.

Diane Robbins, dressed in a long black dress, strutted onto the stage like the star of the show. Two guards hauled a naked man after her and tied him to the table.

The ritual was starting.

*   *   *

Nadia erupted into the ritual site. A small Gothic cemetery and church were off to one side next to an elevated stage circled by lit braziers. The crowd packed in around her, the waves of people nearly crushing her as they tried to get closer to the spectacle. And a spectacle it was. On a long wooden table adorned with lit candles, pentagrams, and skulls, a naked guy lay, blindfolded, spread-eagle, and tied up.

Diane embodied the Dark Goddess. She wore black lace, a crescent crown set upon her blonde hair, an athame in her hand. Next to Diane was a huge leather-bound book propped up on the table. Behind the table hung a massive backdrop of stained glass covered with skulls and satanic imagery. And flowing through the middle of the scene was a golden river of Earth energy, a ley line that Diane had opened. A few of the San Francisco loa bubbled up to watch.

Diane read from a book. "I invoke thee, Yog-Sothoth!" she cried out.

She switched language into a magic one, guttural and flowing, and cut sigils in the air and on the man's body with her athame. The blood sacrifice cried out in rapture with each cut. The guests chanted Diane's words back to her, the magic returning threefold. Diane's eyes rolled back in her head, and she was overtaken with some sort of force, like a creature possessed. The energy from the ritual flowed toward the nexus, meeting with the other energies: the Hunters Point miniature energy beam and energy from the ley lines. Nadia checked the time. 11:50 p.m. She had only minutes until the eclipse.

The attendees around Nadia jostled her as she tried to reach the stage. The medallions around everyone's neck glowed brighter the denser the clusters of people—exponential hive harvesting. The attendees, all with glassy looks on their faces, held up their cell phones, joining in the ritual and following the instructions in The Call.

Nadia grabbed one of the attendees and shook him, trying to stop him from his monotonous chanting, but he shook her off and continued the ritual. She froze, unsure how to help, what to do. Her heart was a heavy drum in her ears. Rune and Carson were on their knees like prisoners of war, hands magically tied behind their backs, Mercurio's goons surrounding them. Miles lay in a heap on the floor, out cold. Mercurio reigned from his throne off to the side. And hundreds of attendees pushed toward the energy chalice like lemmings going off a cliff. The dark energy pulsed, the veil between the worlds thinning as the energy beam bore a hole into the Other Realms.

Nadia had to do something. She elbowed her way through the zombie-like crowd. The security guard at the bottom of the staircase to the stage tried to stop her, and she hit him with a stunning spell. She clambered up the steps and skidded to a stop in front of Mercurio. "You have to stop this!"

What are you doing? Rune mindspoke to her. *Get out of here!*

A leisurely smile crept up Mercurio's pale face. "Ah, my dear." He took her hand and kissed it before he spun her in a circle. He pulled her to him, trying to do a little tango with her, singing, "Ba-da-da-DUM. Ba-da-da-DUM," as he pressed her close, cheek to cheek. Nadia's eyes ripped from Mercurio to Rune, a look of confusion and doubt on Rune's face when he saw their easy familiarity.

"You need to stop the ritual," said Nadia, extracting herself from Mercurio's grasp. "People are going to die. The medallions—there's no off-switch—all these people will get over-harvested."

"Yes, yes, I've heard." Mercurio strode over to Diane, her

eyelids fluttering over the whites of her eyes as she muttered the incantation.

"Poor Diane here." He stood behind Diane and clasped her shoulders patronizingly with his sharp claws. "She thinks that she's hearing voices from some goddess. I don't care who she's been talking to, but I do know that whoever controls the Realm Gates controls the world. Imagine—all the riches from the Other Realms. The trade potential. And with only one access point . . . well, you see why I must let this go on. I didn't believe she had the power at first . . . our tests were inconclusive. But I've been assured of the future. A portal will be created. Tonight."

"If she succeeds, she will unleash hell," Rune yelled out. "She's invoking Yog-Sothoth. A portal of pure potential would manifest and bring forth all the energy that surrounds it. Look around, man! All of this would come to life!"

One of the ogre guards punched Rune in the stomach to keep him quiet.

"The risk is worth the reward," replied Mercurio. "And Diane has assured me that the portal she is opening will be to a safe place in the Other Realms." It seemed that Pact had found another use for that Pyli technology, after all.

Nadia had to do something. She rushed Diane and grabbed her wrist, trying to wrestle the athame away from her. Diane came out of her trance. "What are you doing?" she cried out. "The Goddess needs us!"

One of Mercurio's goons pulled Nadia off the Septer woman and pinned Nadia's arms behind her back. She twisted back and forth trying to get free, but it was no use.

Mercurio chuckled. "Oh, Nadia, I wish you had been this spirited in the Eights Ritual." An evil look of sinister pleasure calcified on Mercurio's face as he watched Rune's horrified expression. "Oh, you didn't know? How silly of me, of course you didn't. It's not like our dear Nadia is the most honest Blood Muse out there. Let me fill you in, Christiansen. Get you 'up to speed,' as she says. I had Nadia, as her first."

Rune's eyes went cold. Carson struggled against the bonds that held him and the muzzle around his face, but to no avail. Nadia tried to yell, but one of Mercurio's henchmen silenced her throat with magic, cutting off her voice. She gurgled and stuttered but could not speak.

Mercurio chuckled and turned back to Rune. His lips crept up into a dark smile as he gazed at Rune's stony expression. "But even before that, Nadia was planted at Myst to be my spy. She's been betraying you the entire time, stealing secrets, and reporting back to Drake."

Thomas stepped from the shadows in a casual manner, a look of hatred on his face. "Hello, Rune."

Rune fought against the chains that bound him. "Thomas Drake. I thought you were dead."

"Not dead," he replied jovially. "Just demonic. Like you. Oh, you didn't know I knew, did you?" Thomas turned bright red, his fists balling up at his sides. "I suspected as much, but I knew when I saw you hunched over Emily. I saw your eyes, and I knew what you had done, how you'd killed her!"

Nadia finally wrested her arm away from the ogre's crushing grasp and unbound her voice. She felt like she was in a bad soap opera. She had misjudged the entire situation. She had been a pawn in a game that had started many, many years ago, one between men. Her eyes flicked back and forth between Rune, Mercurio, and Thomas, uncertainty rooting her to the spot.

Mercurio laughed. "Drake, your little attempt at vindictive revenge is so . . . boring." He feigned a yawn. "But the hour approaches, and we have a Realm Gate to open." He signaled with two fingers, flicking them in the air. "Carry on."

Diane launched into the ritual again, chanting, performing a series of wild hand gestures, creating sigils in the air, and carving them into the now unconscious man before her. *What kind of psychopath uses human life as a catalyst like this?* All these people, her grandmother included, were insane.

Nadia had hoped Maya would be able to stop the energy laser, but the beam of energy stayed strong, aimed at the miniature of Hunters Point. The ley line of energy intensified.

"Diane, please!" Nadia cried out. "The Goddess wouldn't want all these people to die!"

The woman's head snapped up. "*You* have no idea what the Goddess wants. She wants to be free, for the Realm Gates to be open once more."

"This isn't the way!"

"You little bitch," Diane spat out. "I paved the road so you could dance on it."

"Diane," warned Mercurio. "The hour approaches."

Nadia glanced at her Psionic. The time switched to 11:53 p.m. The pinnacle of the eclipse. Diane raised the athame into the air, holding the hilt with both hands like she was about to stab down.

No time to think. With a primal scream, Nadia rushed at Diane again and body checked her, sending her flying to the ground. She leaped on top of her and tried to wrestle the blade out of the woman's hand, but it sliced Nadia's palm, blood dripping and flying. She shrieked in pain, holding on fast, but Diane managed to cut downward in the air at the nexus of energy. A small cut appeared in the air—a slice into another reality.

"It's working!" Mercurio yelled.

The energy laser powered off at last, but the damage had been done. The small cut remained, a tiny black hole portal, its edges collapsing inward like a doughnut.

Diane scrambled to her feet. "I have heard your cries, Goddess, and I come to release you from your prison!" She grabbed the Hunters Point miniature and used it like a crowbar, prying open reality. Her eyes glowed with dark psychic power, her hair swirling around in the electromagnetic field she had created. Nadia looked on in horror as the cut grew to a large gash.

Diane, her eyes wild, banged and hacked at the hole with the model crane. The portal opened to the size of a manhole. A black bird, a crow, hopped out of nothingness. It flew at Diane's face, black wings pumping, and plucked out her eyeballs, one and then the other. The woman screamed as blood spurted in a crimson arc. She fell to the floor, writhing in pain and rapture.

Another bird emerged. And then another. And then a bat. And then something inky and creeping. And then a maelstrom of demons and dark creatures burst forth from the portal like an erupting geyser and filled the auditorium, blurs of black wings and scales. Nadia screamed. Something with claws and wings attacked. She ducked, holding her hands over her head, and dove to a corner, curling up tight in a ball. *Make it all go away.*

Someone hauled Nadia to her feet. Mercurio. He had her by the arm and dragged her over to the ritual site. "Close it, now!" he snarled.

"I don't know how!"

"Figure it out!" He threw her next to Diane's body, twitching in her own pool of blood.

Nadia, the ley line! thought Rune to her.

She opened her eyes and looked down at her feet. Energy radiated forth from the ground, undulating slightly like heat waves on pavement. At the ritual site, the golden river of Earth energy that Diane had accessed was still open.

I don't know how to stop it! she thought back.

Don't stop it. Use it.

Nadia didn't have time to think, let alone weigh her options. She ran over to the ley line and tried to pull energy from it into her outstretched palms. Nothing happened. The loa, the tiny globular creatures that bubbled up from the ground, still did not accept her, and she needed their blessing. Nadia rifled through her pockets for anything she could give to them.

"What do you need?" Mercurio demanded as he watched her frantic searching.

"I need something the San Francisco loa want!" Nadia cried.

Mercurio's nostrils flared. He grabbed Diane's athame and sliced across his wrist. Black blood pooled up.

"Give them this," he bit out. Drops of his blood fell to the ground like black tears. Nadia slit her own wrist—red blossoming up—and she held her wrist to his, letting the blood mingle. Black and red fell to the earth. Nadia held Mercurio's gaze, and something softened in his cold stare. Flashes of earlier erupted into her memory like fireworks. The feeling of flow, his body pressed to hers, the two of them engulfing each other, swallowing each other. The memory mixed with the blood and dropped to the ground. After a few seconds, the loa bubbled up, pink-tinged from eating their essence, and bowed to them.

Accepted by the loa, Nadia sank to her knees in front of the golden, shimmering river of Earth energy. All around her, Halloween horrors had come to life: bats swirling, monsters snarling, people screaming as they were picked up by flying creatures and dropped onto the crowd. Mercurio backed away. Diane lay lifeless. Rune—Nadia couldn't see him. She scanned the crowd, but all she could see were masks and jagged teeth, swirls of darkness and monsters. Black-winged creatures and scaly shadows swooped through panicked attendees who fled for their lives. Survival instincts from all the imaginary disasters kicked in. She could do this. She had to.

Nadia closed her eyes and reached for the golden river of energy in front of her. The words she needed—a spell from the Numinous she hadn't known before—rose in her mind, and she chanted them, the words pouring out of her as the energy poured in. She blocked all else. The screeching and cawing faded to a faint roar. She felt the urge to move and swayed back and forth, rolling her shoulders, and then she got to her feet. The spell was a full-body one, and waves of energy rolled through her, moving her limbs. She made growling noises like she was a dragon, a low rumble from deep in her chest. The movements turned into a strange mix of martial arts and dance: leaps, kicks, belly dancing hip rolls, Bollywood arm movements. She felt self-conscious. *What am I even doing right now?* She looked like an idiot, prancing around on stage, the pulsing, hypnotized crowd egging on the show. Fear and doubt ravaged her mind. Her eyes met Rune's, and his face said it all: she was a total fucking disaster. Self-doubt took over. The darkness inside her bubbled up, thick and rotting, a black fungus blooming inside her chest. There was no slipstream here up to the clouds and to the Light. No guidance. No mercy. If she wanted to cast, she would have to face the Dark. She'd have to meet it. She'd have to become it.

Time slowed. The world fell away, soundless. It was just Nadia and the blackness. It enveloped her, pressed against her eyes, her ears, her skin, her face. Her lungs filled with thick mud, the tar suffocating her, pulling her down. Her limbs were heavy. She wanted to sleep forever. Every instinct told her to fight, to claw her way back to the Light, to resist.

But she didn't.

With one deep breath, black tar filling her lungs, she let go.

She surrendered.

She fell down, down, down, past thought and fear and self. She sank into the darkness, into shadow, let it consume her, take her over, dissolve her until she was it. There was no difference between Nadia and the darkness that held her. It was her.

I am the Dark.

The spell burst forth from her body in a giant rolling wave and hit the portal. It wobbled and fluxed and flipped inside out. Nadia braced herself. The monsters, the swirling chaos and winged devils, were sucked back into the portal, entropy reversing, matter screeching and smearing into the void as it disappeared. The black hole shrank into nothingness. A musical note rang out, reverberating through Nadia's entire body. Fireworks exploded in her mind. She was Light. She was Dark. She was One with the Numinous.

Her spark hit the ley line. It was like a bomb detonated: a loud *boom* and a mushroom cloud of energy. The impact threw Nadia backward, a rag doll in the wind. Rune's arm circled around her as they folded away.

CHAPTER 34

Nadia opened her eyes to vines and leaves and fireflies dancing. They were in the middle of Myst's gardens, in the center of the labyrinth. Nadia clung tightly to Rune, and he set her down on her feet, probably a little rougher than he could have.

Rune folded back out, and Nadia was left alone in the gardens.

Nadia examined herself for damage. Her dress was torn, her lacy black bra showing through the tattered rags. A few scrapes and cuts, some blood . . . she needed stitches, but she'd live. Nadia took a seat on one of the benches, tracing the labyrinth with her eyes, trembling slightly from shock. After some time, Rune reappeared, popping into existence in the center of the labyrinth.

"Everyone's safe," he said gruffly. "The portal is closed. But we need to talk."

Rune's shirt was torn as well, revealing his muscular frame covered in blood. He was breathing heavily, his chest rising and falling. Nadia stared at him. This Numinal, this demon. Even after everything, he still held his glamour, his face cruelly beautiful. She clutched her arms around her midriff—for warmth or protection, she couldn't say. Even though he was just in front of her, the chasm between them threatened to swallow her whole.

"You can fold?" she asked finally, to break the ice. "Why have we been taking your car or motorcycle this entire time?"

His eyes snapped to hers, cold and hard. "I prefer to live as close to human as I can. Plus, folding, especially with another person, takes a substantial amount of energy, and believe it or not, I try not to feed on humans." He swayed for a second but regained his balance.

"Do you need to feed now or something?"

He looked up with a sardonic expression on his face. "You offering?"

"No."

He gave her a faint smile. "Didn't think so."

"What happened back there—"

"You used our training well," said Rune sadly. "You heard the spell the Numinous gave you to close the portal. The spell you needed right then. Congratulations. You passed the final test and are now in the Order."

Nadia held out her wrist. The triangle tattoo flashed, permanently inked in by the Numinous. Rune gazed at his own finished tattoo and idly rubbed it.

She rose slowly and walked to him, her body thrumming, their magic bonded permanently. "I can explain everything. The women in my family have been bound to Mercurio through a generational Blood Oath since the seventeenth century. I told you that my grandmother had bound my powers. Well, that was only part of the story. She tried to hide me from him so I wouldn't have to serve. It destroyed our family."

"And he planted you at Myst to spy on me?" asked Rune. Nadia nodded. His mouth was a grim line. "I see."

The words came out in a rush. "I never gave him any information. Okay, maybe little bits here and there. But I never wanted to hurt you. Or Myst. Thomas tricked me into stealing the Wolf and the Ram spell. I didn't want to do any of it. But I had no choice—"

He cut her off, suddenly very close. "There is always a choice! It might not be the one you want to make, it might not be the easy way, but there is always a choice. You could have told me. You could have talked to me."

Nadia took a step back away from his menacing figure. "And told you what? That my ancestor made a Blood Oath with a vampire that I am forced to fulfill? And hey, look! His first task was to plant me as a spy to get close to you and the company. Whoopie!" She scoffed. "Yeah, I'm sure that would have gone over real well."

Rune's dark eyes bore into hers. "We could have figured it out together."

"It's not like you've been exactly forthcoming about everything, either. You lied about being a demon."

Rune ran his hands through his dark hair. "I never lied to you."

"A lie by omission."

Rune looked up at the stars on the ceiling of the conservatory. "Look, I saw how scared you were of demons, how you flinched at the thought, especially after you were attacked. I knew what you would think. I'm not ashamed of what I am, but I wanted to get to know you, have you get to know me, before I told you. And I'm sorry about feeding from you. I lost control. I would never try to harm you."

"Do others know?" Nadia turned away, the pained expression on his face too unbearable to see.

"Some do. Carson, Imogen, Vega. I don't broadcast it. Demons don't have a great reputation, as you know. Most Numinals assume I'm some sort of Fae."

Rune led them over to the bench, and they sat down. Nadia stared at him, unsure what to say.

"Start at the beginning," Rune said. "Tell me everything."

Nadia took a deep breath. She told him about her twenty-third birthday, how she had broken the bindings that her grandmother had used to try to hide and protect her from Mercurio. How Thomas had appeared and told her she was a witch. How he had demon lackeys feed from her and scare her into submission. How Mercurio had planted her at Myst. How they had tricked her into obedience. How she had stolen the Wolf and the Ram spell and tried to undo the mess she had caused when she found Thomas trying to break into Rune's computer and steal information.

"I wondered what happened to my laptop," said Rune. "Continue."

She told him about her plan to break the Blood Oath: to apprentice with him to grow her powers and cast her Soulwish to save her family. How Aiko had told her about the Eights Ritual, and how she knew that was the one card she could play to finally stop the curse. How she planned to poison Mercurio, but he caught her attempt. She glossed over the Eights Ritual—no need to torture the poor guy with explicit details. She talked a lot about her grandmother's scheming, about her lonely childhood, how she would take her mother's pulse to make sure she was still alive after too many mimosas and painkillers. She told him about her grandmother and the NLA, and how Marina had come back all used up from Mercurio's punishment. How scared and helpless she felt seeing what was going to be her fate.

Rune hung his head in his hands. "But don't you see what you've done?"

"Apparently not."

"You lied, and cheated, and stole. I can't trust you."

Nadia sucked in a breath. "I may have lied and stolen, but I never cheated."

"You cheated on *me*." Rune's voice was rough.

"News flash!" Nadia leaned back in exasperation. "We aren't together! Boss, employee"—she gestured in a sweeping motion between them—"master, apprentice. Nowhere in there have we ever discussed anything more."

His eyes flared. "Some things don't need discussion. Sometimes they just *are*."

"You're mad that I slept with him?" she demanded.

"I don't care about that! Fuck whoever you want!"

"Then why are you so upset?"

"You know you are bound to him in a different way now?" His voice was angry now. "You reached a state of flow with him. Your energy mingled. You carry a piece of him and he of you."

"I knew that going into it."

"And you still chose to do it . . ." He shook his head. "I was so wrong about you. So very, very wrong."

"You took me to Aiko's because *you* wanted to be my first." Nadia hurled the charge at him. Thomas had said he was a predator. He was just as bad as Mercurio, grooming her from the start.

He didn't deny the accusation. Nadia stood to leave. She was done with this conversation.

Rune grabbed her hand, a frenzied look in his eyes. "Don't leave me. You're supposed to be mine."

Nadia yanked her hand back and gaped at him. She was pretty sure she was having some sort of neurological event. "What are you talking about?"

He pulled her back down to sit next to him. "Listen, I've never told you about my Soulwish. How all of this started." He took a deep breath and launched into the story: "I met Thomas Drake in London, in 1754. We were both members of the

Hellfire Club. Yes, that one," he added, when he saw the question forming on Nadia's lips. "I was the younger son of a Lord Christiansen from a vague Nordic region. It's easier to pass if people don't think you are going to inherit. You're often overlooked. I had been sent abroad to receive an education, I told people. I met Thomas at one of the meetings. He was an idiot . . . bumbling around, spilling sacred oil. I magicked it back in. He knew I had magic, but not more. Not about . . . me. We became fast friends. Whoring, scheming, spending other people's money. We never wanted for anything.

"Thomas had a sister named Emily." Rune smiled slightly as if he were remembering her face. "She was lovely. A vision in pure white. I was obsessed with her, couldn't stop thinking about her. I had to have her. I discovered later she was a witch . . . she had cast a spell upon me. Even though I knew she had twisted fate to bring us together, I was enchanted. We were married near the water, under a full moon. I gave her everything. An estate, horses, jewels." It sounded like he had thought about this story many, many times. Like he had tried to figure out where it went wrong. "But nothing was ever good enough. She was young and frivolous, and I was in love. I locked her up and wouldn't let her out. I didn't want any other man to look at her, to take what was mine."

That's where it went wrong, thought Nadia. No woman wants to be in a cage.

"She missed society," Rune continued. "She missed the parties and the gossip. The conversation. Being seen. She was vain and knew she was beautiful, and she needed attention. She grew to resent my touch. She began to see the estate as a prison. She begged to be released, but I wouldn't let her go. We fought often—great, emotion-drenched fights full of screaming and broken furniture. And we made up just as passionately."

Nadia sat back, crossing her arms. Rune pressed on. "When we made love, I fed from her. Never too much. Just a little. I didn't want to hurt her. She never knew. Even though she was a witch, I never showed her my true self.

"One night, after a fantastic fight, I lost control." Rune closed his eyes, pain marring his features. "I couldn't stop myself. Her body . . . lifeless . . . Thomas found me, hunched over her as I tried to do something . . . anything to bring her back. I fled into the night. I had no idea Thomas was still alive, that he's been harboring resentment toward me this entire time. I'm sorry that I did this to him."

Thomas must have turned into a demon because of his obsession with Rune and the death of this woman. How sad, thought Nadia. He hadn't been able to help himself, the years of festering emotion taking over his life.

Rune stared in front of himself. "I fell into a deep darkness. I had killed the one thing in my life that had been good. Snuffed it out. I swore I would never love again and threw myself into work. But I knew deep down, I had a longing. I cast my Soulwish. I wished for a Soulmate, a partner, someone to travel this crazy life with . . . And then the universe sent me you."

Nadia blinked. The words he had just said rattled around in her brain and then punched her in the gut. "Are you saying . . . are you saying I'm your *Soulmate*?"

He nodded. "I didn't believe it at first. I couldn't believe that the Numinous would be that giving to me . . . a demon. I had lost hope, and then you came along. At first, I fought it. Fought my feelings. I didn't want to use my position of authority to manipulate or coerce you. I thought if I kept my distance, kept it strictly professional, my feelings would fade. But they didn't."

He told her about the seer who said that a raven-haired woman would ensnare him with fire. "'When the great dragon rises, you shall know it is she who you have been seeking,'" he repeated. "You. You're the dragon."

"No, no, no, no, no." Nadia stood up. "This can't be happening." She paced back and forth, working things out. She had just freed herself from the shackles of Mercurio. And now Rune was telling her that fate had a different plan, and she was bound to . . . *him*? She didn't want to be bound to anyone! She wanted free will! And if there was a Soulwish involved, Nadia would never know if it was the magic making them fall for each other, or if it was real.

"You don't seem to be taking this well," said Rune, his voice flat.

"How am I supposed to take it?" Nadia demanded. She stopped pacing and turned to face him. He stood up, grabbed her, and gave her a possessive, crushing kiss. Nadia shoved him off.

Rune sucked in a sharp breath. "You can't push me away now. Not after everything."

His eyes searched hers, like he was looking for some sort of sign or answer. Nadia felt herself lured in. He was using his demon magic on her, trying to seduce her. Nadia fought it off and backed away.

"Stop that," she bit out. She put up mental shields, blocking him out.

"I can't do this anymore." Rune shook his head. "You drive me crazy. I can't sleep. I can't concentrate. You act like you want to be together, but then you break my heart, my trust, lie, cheat, and steal. And I'm ready to forgive all that, and you still push me away. Nadia, what do you want? I thought you wanted this."

Unbelievable. He still didn't get it. "I want it to be my choice! You can't come in here and drop something like 'Soulmate' and just expect that I will be happy about that! I just told you I removed the Blood Oath, and now you are binding me all over again!"

Rune let out a long breath and closed his eyes, his pain and suffering manifesting as Algea spirits around them—tiny sadness creatures that reminded Nadia of dark *kodamas*.

"You're right," he said after a bit. "This would have never worked. We belong in two different worlds. I thought if we gave it time . . ." His voice was drenched in remorse. "I don't think you should work at Myst anymore."

Nadia whirled on him. "You're *firing* me? Because what? I won't date you?"

"You know that's not what this is," he said with disgust. "I'm letting you go. Go, be free. Defy the Numinous." He swept his hand to the sky. "Prove that you have free will and can make your own choices. You're in the Order now. That should open some doors for you." He turned away.

The gravity of the situation finally hit Nadia. Everything that she had been working toward all these months—finding her place in San Francisco, settling into a new life—was gone. Up in flames. Vanished in smoke. All she had was a pile of ash.

But Nadia wouldn't let him have the final word. She had to flip the script or die trying. "I know what you're doing right now. You're pushing *me* away. *You're* scared."

Rune stilled, breathing heavily, and turned to her. Nadia stepped closer to him, chest to chest. He leaned down, his lips close to hers.

"I would have been the best thing that ever happened to you," she breathed. She stood up on her tiptoes, her lips brushing his. He groaned, fighting it. And then he captured her mouth in a kiss, deepening it with each lap of his tongue. His hands cupped her face. It was a sad kiss, full of mourning and loss for what could have been, but never even had the chance to start.

Breaking the kiss, Rune leaned his forehead against hers. "I'm sorry," he said gruffly. "I can't do this."

He turned to leave. Nadia grabbed his hand, stopping him. Rune let himself be pulled back, and they kissed again, losing themselves in that moment.

Rune pushed her away, his breath catching in his throat. "I have to go." He disappeared behind glass doors back into Myst.

Nadia sat for a while in the garden, watching the fireflies dance on the fragrant flowers and bushes. The lights inside Myst went out, and Nadia was plunged into darkness. She sat there for a while, a tornado of emotions swirling inside her, before she got up to leave and face the world.

It was almost two a.m. by the time Nadia left Myst and walked through the dimly lit streets toward home. The Halloween revelry had mostly died down, but a few drunken stragglers were still out and about. Normally, Nadia wouldn't have wanted to risk a demon attack or a mugging by walking alone at night, but her world had been burned to the ground. She dared someone to come at her. She would have welcomed a fight.

In the Mission, she bummed a cigarette from a chick in an Elmo onesie and lit it with a quick-fire charm from her Psionic. Leaning against a building, she texted Maya. Rune fired me.

Maya texted back right away. What???

She didn't feel like explaining it all now. Long story. I'll call u tmrw.

Everything had gone to shit. She had been trying to be the perfect witch, the perfect granddaughter, the perfect employee, the perfect apprentice, and all she had done was manage to fail. She had been given a second chance at Myst, and all she had done was squander it. She had thought if she could stay on the straight and narrow and hide her past transgressions, she could move past everything. But she had fallen into the same patterns and had managed to fuck it up even more. And Rune ... she had thought she wanted him, but the second she had him, she pushed him away. *What is wrong with you?* If there was a rock bottom for Nadia, surely this was it. She heard her mother's voice in her head: *You're nothing but damaged goods now.*

When Nadia got home, Marina was waiting for her on the couch. "I felt the Blood Oath bonds release. Is he dead?"

Nadia shook her head. "But it's over. We aren't bound to him anymore."

Marina rushed forward and enveloped her in a big hug. "How did you ever do it?"

"We'll talk about it later." Nadia didn't have the mental energy to explain everything that had happened. She carefully extracted herself from her grandmother's grasp.

Marina's eyes were wide in relief. "Well, however you did it, I hope the cost wasn't too high."

Me either, she thought.

Marina touched the fabric of Nadia's ripped dress. "Are you okay? Avery felt the portal open. Every Numinal and Septer out there did."

Nadia sank into the couch, exhaustion starting to settle in. "We stopped it."

Marina took a seat on the armchair. "I assumed so, or else we'd probably all be dead."

A smile tugged on Nadia's lips at Marina's dry sarcasm. "Where's Avery?"

"Some sort of Fae business," said Marina. "Everyone has been called back to their brethren to figure out what it means that the Realm Gates can be opened."

Nadia threw her head back. "I don't want to think about it." She stared at the ceiling, patterns in the texture popping out at her as her mind tried to find meaning in the nonsense. "Rune fired me."

"Oh, honey. I'm sorry to hear that. I know how much you liked working there." Marina slapped her thighs with her palms and stood up. "I think we need a toast." She went and poured them each a whiskey. She held her glass up. "Happy Samhain." *Clink.* "We each have a tabula rasa," Marina added, the gratitude glowing from her face.

Nadia slammed back her drink. The burn felt good.

A black candle burned in front of Nadia as she sat cross-legged on the floor in her bedroom, a blood-red pomegranate and an antique brass key illuminated by the flame. The key had been Maria's. It felt fitting that it now be used to call upon the goddess Hecate, the goddess of crossroads, portals, and new beginnings.

Nadia centered herself and activated her Zisurrû to meditate. She emptied herself of everything—all the bullshit, the anxiety and dread she'd been experiencing. The regret and panic and sense of doom. Everything that had happened with Rune, the lies and the secrets and the fear. She let go of it all, wiped the slate clean, until it was no more. She was an empty vessel, ready to be filled. Nadia invoked the energy of the Goddess, the energy of the Dark Goddess, the energy of Hecate, and allowed it to fill her, the sweet smoke seeping in through the cracks of her psyche until all she could breathe was Her air. It consumed her, lit her on fire, burned everything away, so all that was left was the core of Nadia, forged in the Goddess's image.

The moonlight poured in through her window, a pale splash

of silver across the floor. The words to cast her Soulwish entered Nadia's mind—placed there by the Numinous. The words formed on her tongue, rising in her mind as she spoke them, safe vessels on a changing tide. Everything was unsure. Nothing was certain. Except for her deepest desire.

Nadia stared at the flame of the black candle as she cast her Soulwish, sending it out from her heart to fly through the night.

Epilogue

Rune lay back on his couch and flipped through the channels. Infomercials, late-night movies, and reruns filled the flat screen in quick succession, but Rune couldn't focus and pick anything. A plastic carryout container from a late-night chicken joint in the Mission rested on his stomach. He took a bite of a half-eaten wing, barely tasting it, and threw the bone to the side. He took a swig of beer. Empty. He magicked a new one from the mini fridge, twisted off the cap, and threw it to the floor. He normally wasn't this disgusting, but right then, nothing mattered.

His heart was raw and battered. Rune had thought Nadia was the One—the answer to his Soulwish and his deepest heart's desire to find a mate. But she had turned out to be nothing more than a duplicitous little girl. He knew that Nadia had secrets—everyone did—but he *never* could have imagined the depth of her deceit. All that time . . . all the careful training and mentoring and hoping that she would someday be an equal partner . . . wasted. He could never trust her. They were doomed before they even could start. *If only she had talked to me . . .* Rune shook his head. It was pointless to think about it. What was done was done.

His cell phone vibrated. He glanced at the caller ID. Rocky.

"Yo, my man," said Rune as he answered the phone.

"Your pawn leveled up."

Rune sat up, chicken container sliding to the ground. "What do you mean?"

"I'm picking up major seismic activity over in Noe. Originating from her house. I don't know what your girl did, but that's some *strong* queen energy. Major spikes."

Rune's heartbeat quickened. "But the Counter-Prophecy—"

"Is real," Rocky finished. "Who knew?"

"But the conjunct—"

"Hey man, a portal opened. Maybe it was a conjunction in a different realm. I don't know. I don't have any answers right now."

Rune was silent. Rocky continued, "But get this—now everyone is going back through all the linked prophecies and trying to see if they're real too. Trying to figure out what the hell is going on. The hot one right now is one of Celextina's . . . 'When the great dragon rises . . .' People are going *nuts* trying to figure out if it's the same 'she.'"

"What did you say?" Rune snapped.

"People are going nuts?"

"No, about the dragon."

"The line goes, 'When the great dragon rises, you will know it is she who you have been seeking.' Rumor is circulating that HBO paid her to promote, but she denies it. Says it's real."

Rune was silent. That seer . . . the one who had told him about the raven-haired woman who would ensnare him in fire . . . the making of his true Soulwish . . . she had also told him about the great dragon rising. He had assumed it was a one-off prophecy. But now . . . was it all linked? Nadia couldn't be the queen . . . could she?

As if reading his mind, Rocky continued, "And get this. Your girl, she could be it. The Prophecy Queen. I plugged in her birth date as the date to calculate the Eighth House, and . . . *ehhh* . . . let's just say, I wouldn't rule it out."

"We tried her birth date," Rune countered.

"Energy poured in from the Other Realms. Dark matter. There's a whole new algorithm now, a whole new set of factors."

"How much time do we have?"

Rocky made a noncommittal noise. "Couple of years, tops. Once the queen comes into play—assuming it's her—it's only a matter of time."

"Thanks. I'll be in touch." Rune hung up the phone.

He lay back, running the implications of what Rocky had told him through his mind as he tried to calm his heart. The Council would be after her, that was for sure.

Rune wanted to write her off. He wanted to move on with his life. But he kept thinking about her face, her eyes, her mouth. *Weak.* He was so weak. He closed his eyes, pained with the knowledge that no matter what, he would try to protect her.

Acknowledgments

It takes a village to bring a book into the world, and this one has been a journey in every sense of the word. Writing is a solitary act, but publishing is not. I am deeply grateful to the people who supported, challenged, encouraged, and believed in me every step of the way.

To my beta readers Chrissy Casey, Katherine Carter, Michelle Schaefer, and Gabrielle Manchester: thank you for your thoughtful feedback, sharp eyes, and heartfelt encouragement. You each helped shape this story into something stronger and truer. Your notes not only improved the book but reminded me that there are readers out there who *get it*, and that is everything.

To Seth Harwood and the workshop crew: thank you for creating space where craft, honesty, and community meet. Your feedback and camaraderie have kept me going, and I'm grateful for every insight and every push to dig deeper.

To my amazing editors, designers, and publishing team Jaye Manus, Augusto Silva, Laurissa Kesling, Sandra Ogle, and Fiona McLaren: thank you for your guidance, care, and insight as you helped me turn my manuscript into a finished book. Your ability to spot what I couldn't see helped keep me on track and get to the heart of the story, and I am fortunate to have worked with you.

To my husband, Sam: thank you for putting up with me during the chaotic, self-doubt-ridden storm that is my writing process. Your unwavering belief in me and my abilities is the only thing that kept me going. Every time I found myself in the pit of writing despair, you pulled me out and reminded me why I wanted to tell stories in the first place. Thank you for reading shitty drafts and listening to me talk about fictional people's problems as if they were real. I couldn't have done this without you.

Elizabeth Coleman lives in San Francisco with her husband, daughter, and two extremely spoiled cats. She writes across genres and mediums, but her stories all delve into what it means to be human, and because life is better with a little bit of magic, they usually contain elements of the fantastic.

Connect with her at www.thelizcoleman.com and @thelizcoleman.